D0207111
Secrets
Satisfy your desire for more.

Caged Wolf by Cynthia Eden

Alerac La Morte has been drugged, kidnapped, and taken to some hole in the wall far from civilization. To make matters worse, Alerac realizes his captor, Madison Langley, is actually his destined mate. Madison hates his kind—she blames Weres for the death of her father and wants vengeance. But when captor is turned captive, will Alerac be able to convince her he's not the monster she thinks, and when they mate… it's forever?

Wet Dreams by Larissa Ione

Injured and on the run, DHS agent Brent Logan needs a miracle. What he gets is *Wet Dream*, a sport-fishing boat owned by Marina Summers. Pursued by killers, ravaged by a fierce storm, and plagued by engine troubles, they can do little but spend their final hours immersed in sensual pleasure. But soon they discover that the danger they face on the high seas is nothing compared to the danger to their hearts.

Good Vibrations by Kate St. James

Can one wild weekend really make up for two years of planned celibacy? Lexi O'Brien vows to swear off sex while she attends grad school, so when her favorite out-of-town customer asks her out as she's about to give notice at her job, she decides to indulge in an erotic fling guaranteed to super-charge her fantasies throughout academia. Little does she realize Gage Templeton is moving home, to her city, and has no intention of settling for a short-term affair.

Virgin of the Amazon by Mia Varano

Virgin librarian, Anna Winter, gets lost on her Amazon vacation and stumbles upon a tribe whose shaman just happens to be looking for a pale-skinned virgin to deflower. Coop Daventry, a British adventurer and the tribe's self-styled chief, has a plan to save Anna from the shaman's bed, but which man poses a greater threat to Anna's virginity—the shaman or Coop himself?

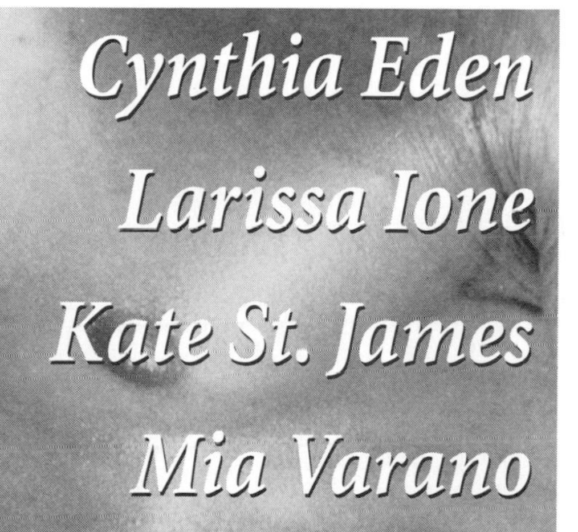

Volume 21

Secrets

Satisfy your desire for more.

SECRETS Volume 21
This is an original publication of Red Sage Publishing and each individual story herein has never before appeared in print. These stories are a collection of fiction and any similarity to actual persons or events is purely coincidental.

Red Sage Publishing, Inc.
P.O. Box 4844
Seminole, FL 33775
727-391-3847
www.redsagepub.com

SECRETS Volume 21
A Red Sage Publishing book

ISBN: 1-60310-001-6 / ISBN 13: 978-1-60310-001-4

Published by arrangement with the authors and copyright holders of the individual works as follows:

Photographs:
Cover © 2007 by Tara Kearney; www.tarakearney.com
Cover Models: Reby Sky and Jimmy Thomas
Setback cover © 2000 by Greg P. Willis; GgnYbr@aol.com

Printed in the U.S.A.

Book typesetting by:

Quill & Mouse Studios, Inc.
www.quillandmouse.com

Contents

Caged Wolf

by Cynthia Eden

To My Reader:

In the 1760s, a strange, wolf-like beast prowled the French countryside. According to some accounts, this creature killed dozens of people… and many of the locals began to think that a werewolf was hunting at night. History now calls this creature the *Beast of Gevaudan.*

I've always been interested in the *Gevaudan* story. So when I decided to try my own hand at writing werewolf stories, I created heroes (*Weres)* who hailed from France, the birthplace of the legendary beast.

Of course, my *Weres* aren't blood-thirsty monsters. They're strong, loyal, brave men… who just happen to be able to transform into wolves.

I hope you enjoy *Caged Wolf (*my third *Were* story for Red Sage). (Previous titles: *Bite of the Wolf* in ***Secrets, Volume 15****,* and *The Wolf's Mate* in ***Secrets, Volume 18****.)* Please feel free to visit my website at www.cynthiaeden.com or you may email me at info@cynthiaeden.com.

Prologue

He could smell his mate. Her scent, light, feminine, beckoned to him across the smoke filled bar.

Alerac La Mort felt every muscle in his body tighten. Anticipation, need, *hunger* burned through him. She was there. He knew it with utter certainty.

He stood from the table in one swift move, his chair crashing to the floor behind him. He was focused now on one goal, only one goal... finding his mate.

Mon Dieu, but he'd almost given up on her. He'd watched his cousins find their mates, felt despair tighten his heart, but now, *now*, he'd found his woman.

Or, rather, he was about to find her.

Shoving aside dancers and drunken idiots, he marched to the back of the bar. Her scent teased him, aroused him, lured him ever forward.

His cock was hard and hungry. His muscles tight. What would she look like, this mate of his? What would she feel like, when she was spread beneath him, taking him deep into her core?

He couldn't wait to find out.

Once before, Alerac had thought that he'd caught his mate's scent. Though he'd searched for her, he'd been unable to find her.

And he'd been left with only his dreams.

Dreams of her. Always of her. Dreams of a slender woman cloaked in shadows. A woman who teased him, who stirred the beast within him.

This time, it wasn't a dream. This time, he *knew* she was there. He *would* find her.

A door waited in front of him. A plain wooden door, scuffed by time. Behind it, he was sure he would find her.

His mate. His.

Finally.

Alerac shoved open the door.

A young blond woman whirled, her pale blue eyes widening. He paused a moment, staring at her. He… knew her. He'd seen her before—

A slow smile curved her full lips. "I hoped I'd see you tonight, La Mort."

The hair on his nape rose. Something was wrong. Very, very wrong. He could sense it, could sense—

She raised her hand. Her fingers were curled around the butt of a gun.

Horror filled him. No, this couldn't be happening. She was his mate, all of his senses told him she was the one woman destined to be his for all time. She couldn't do this, couldn't—

She pulled the trigger. A white-hot lance of pain burned through his chest. He fell to the floor, and a thick, drugging heaviness swept over him.

Was this death?

The woman walked toward him, her high heels clicking softly on the concrete floor. "Don't worry, wolf. I don't plan to kill you… yet."

Wolf. She knew, he realized, as the room began to dim, she knew what he was. He struggled to keep his eyes open, struggled see her, to speak. "Y-you're going t-to pay for th-this, *cherie.*" Mate or no, he would see her punished.

Her lips curved into a cold, hard smile. "No, wolf, it will be you who pays."

He tried to reach for her, but he couldn't move. Darkness swept over him, and he saw no more.

Madison Langley stared down at the prone man on the floor. Her heart was racing, her palms soaked with sweat.

She'd done it. *She'd actually done it.*

Fumbling, she managed to jerk her cell phone out of her back pocket. Her fingers trembled as she punched in the number.

A man answered on the second ring. "Did you get him?"

Her gaze was still on Alerac. Still on the strong, unmoving figure. "Yeah, I got him."

"Good." A pause, then, "Two of my men are waiting behind the bar. They'll help you move La Mort. When he's secured, call me back."

"Right." She ended the call and crouched beside Alerac. Her hand lifted, hesitated over his body.

A strange desire to touch him filled her. To touch that blond mane of hair. To feel his strong flesh beneath her fingers.

Her hand fisted.

What in the hell was wrong with her? *He was a monster.*

Her teeth clenched and she jerked away from him.

Alerac La Mort was a murdering bastard. And soon, very soon, he would get exactly what he deserved.

Chapter 1

Sonofabitch. Alerac opened his eyes slowly, every muscle in his body aching. Where was he? What in the hell had happened to him? Why was—

"Ah, wolf, good, I see you're awake."

The drawling voice of the woman had his lips curling into a snarl. His fangs burned, and his memory blasted back to him.

The witch had shot him with something. She'd actually shot him!

She stepped toward him, her pale blond hair shining, her lips twisted into a mocking smile. "I was beginning to think I'd dosed you with too much tranq. I wasn't sure of the measurements, you see. So, I just gave you enough to down an elephant."

He lunged for her.

And was immediately jerked back against a cold stone wall.

The light, musical sound of her laughter filled the room. "Ooooh… someone sure seems angry."

He turned his head slowly, staring in disbelief at the thick chains that bound his hands and feet. Silver—the damn bonds were made of silver. He wouldn't be able to fully change into his wolf form with silver bonds imprisoning him.

His back teeth clenched. "Let. Me. Go." The words were a growl. His hands tightened into fists. The beast within him began to roar, its rage building.

The blond shook her head. "No can do." She stared down at him, her eyes narrowing. "It took me too long to get you here."

His nails lengthened, changed into razor sharp claws. The wolf couldn't stand confinement, couldn't stand being held prisoner—and the man didn't like it one damn bit, either.

He stared at her, stared at the woman who was his mate, and his kidnapper. She was a small woman, too thin for his normal taste, and a little below average in height. Pretty though, with fair skin and large, pale blue eyes. A sprinkling of freckles dotted across her straight little nose, and a tiny mole rested at the corner of her full lips.

His gaze dropped down her body, fell to study the curve of her breasts. Yes, she was slender, but she still had very nice—

"Stop it," she gritted, her hands rising as if to shield her body.

He raised a brow.

His captor took a deep breath and lowered her hands. "I don't want you looking at me… like that."

Her scent rose around him. It was the scent of roses. Of woman. And of fear. *Fear*. He straightened, feeling the cold metal bite into his skin. She was afraid of him. Good. She should be. Because when he got loose—

A feral smile curved his lips. He would make her beg for mercy.

She stiffened at the sight of his smile and backed up two steps. "Wh-why are you smiling?"

Ah, his little captor didn't sound so confident now.

"You shouldn't have brought me here, *cherie*." He pulled against the chains, testing their strength. Hmm. They were solid, thick, but they wouldn't be a match for him, not when the full moon rose.

Not even silver would be able to hold him when the moon rose. He still wouldn't be able to change into the wolf, but his strength would be enhanced enough to allow him to break free of his bonds.

Luckily for him, the moon would be full tomorrow night. He looked back at her, imaging all that he would do to her.

"I know what you are," she whispered, licking her lips.

Alerac stared at her, cocking one brow. "*Oui*, I figured that out." He pulled against the chains. "These aren't really necessary, you know."

She nodded her head almost frantically. "Yes, they are." Her breasts lifted as she drew in a deep gulp of air. "You're going to stay there un-til—"

"Isn't kidnapping against the law, *Officer* Langley?" He threw the title out deliberately, a hard smile on his lips as he waited for her response.

Madison jerked. *Hell.* A sick, heavy feeling of dread lodged in her stomach. *He knew who she was.*

Alerac kept smiling at her, and she could see just the faintest hint of fang. "I remember you," he said softly, his French accent making the words sound strangely seductive. His golden eyes locked on her. "You were at the Compound that night, when that bastard Lou Stalls came and tried to kill my cousin's mate."

She nodded. There was no point in denying it. That night, the night her unit had been called to the mansion just outside of Atlanta to arrest Stalls, she'd learned the truth about Alerac.

Lou Stalls had been on the run from the Chicago police. Wanted for several murders, he'd evaded the cops for months. Stalls had decided it would be fun to hunt down and torture the woman who'd testified against him, Kat Hardy.

What Lou hadn't counted on was that Kat had apparently gotten herself involved with a very powerful werewolf. A werewolf who hadn't taken kindly to Lou's threats.

When Madison had arrived on the scene, the once fierce killer had been a crying, shaking, utterly white mess. He'd kept shouting about werewolves. About men changing into beasts before his eyes.

Of course, the other cops had thought he was just another nut job. But she knew differently. She knew werewolves were real.

She'd seen them before.

She'd known, just from looking at Alerac, that he was one of them.

One of the monsters.

"You've been staring at me for several minutes, Officer," he said, tilting his head to the side. "Do you like what you see?"

She flushed.

He smiled again. Flashed a dimple.

Damn. Her heart rate seemed to double. All right, she could admit, to herself anyway, that Alerac La Mort was a fine looking man… er… werewolf. He was tall, sleekly muscled, with a dark golden tan. He had blond hair, a thick heavy blond mane that fell to his shoulders. His cheekbones were high, perfectly cut. The man had a strong, hard jaw, a straight, sharp blade of a nose, and firm, full lips that—

"Ah…" He nodded once, looking satisfied. "I guess you do like what you see." He licked his lips, his gaze falling to her breasts. "And I certainly like what I see."

She stiffened. "What I see…" she gritted, "is a monster."

His eyes narrowed. "Be very careful, *cherie.*" He pulled against the chains, and the metal screeched a protest. "I won't forget your words."

Madison lifted her chin. "I'm not the one who needs to be careful." Not anymore, anyway. She held the power now. She stepped toward him, close, but not close enough for him to reach.

His nostrils flared.

"I'm not the one chained up," she told him quietly.

"No." That golden gaze skated down her body, drifted down to stare at the juncture of her thighs. "But the idea has definite possibilities." He licked his lips.

And, unbelievably, a hot tide of desire rocked through her.

"Umm..." He leaned his head back against the wall. His gaze lifted to her face. "Like that idea, do you, *ma petite belle?*"

She shook her head. "Don't be ridiculous." She couldn't want him. He was a monster, a murdering bastard who—

"I can smell your arousal."

Her jaw dropped.

"You're wet for me," he continued, his pupils flaring. "You want me right now."

"N-no." Even as the denial sprang to her lips, she knew she was lying. She could feel a dampness on her panties. Her sex clenched, tightening in hunger.

Madison realized she could smell him, could smell his warm, strong masculine scent. The scent teased her, wrapped around her, and urged her forward, forward...

She caught herself just in time. Madison gazed down at Alerac in horror. She'd been about to go to him. To put herself within the beast's grasp.

What in the hell was wrong with her?

"We'll be good together," he promised her, his accent even more pronounced. "When you spread your legs and let me into your body, when we mate—"

When they mated? Horror filled her. "I'm not mating with some kind of—of—animal!"

A low growl rumbled in his throat.

And she realized it was time for her to get away from the wolf. *Playtime was definitely over.* She spun on her heel and headed for the stairs.

"Officer Langley!"

She tensed. Glanced back at him. "I'm not a police officer anymore." No, not anymore. When she'd agreed to take this assignment, she'd turned in her badge. She couldn't have two loyalties. So she'd had to choose, and she'd chosen to step down from the force. Chosen to step outside the law, to fight the darkness.

His eyes narrowed.

Madison straightened her shoulders, turned back toward the stairs.

"Madison..."

This time, she didn't stop. Didn't glance back at the soft, seductive call.

He would be safe enough chained in the basement. She'd go up to her room, call Brennon and update him on the mission's status.

Brennon would be glad to know she'd secured the wolf. Soon, he would come to take Alerac to Scions Laboratory.

Then there would be one less monster on the streets. One less killer preying on the weak.

"Madison!" Alerac's shout seemed to shake the foundations of the house.

She stilled, and glanced back over her shoulder once again. His hands were clenched into fists, his face a mask of rage.

Even though he was chained, the sight of him caused a shiver of fear to trickle through her. "You'll be fine here," she muttered. "There's food beside you, and a bucket for... you know." The chains were long enough that he'd be able to reach the supplies, and take care of his more nature-oriented needs.

"Don't leave me." An order.

She met his stare without flinching, a feat that required serious effort. "Why, wolf, scared to be alone?" Who would have thought that the big, bad wolf would be scared of anything?

His golden eyes seemed to shine. "*Don't. Leave. Me.*" His eyes glowed even brighter. "*Come back to my side.*"

A dull headache pounded behind her eyes. Her legs began to tremble, and it took all of her strength not to move.

"Come back to my side."

The bastard was trying to use a compulsion on her. She knew it, knew that his kind possessed the psychic power to influence others.

But she'd been trained, carefully trained by Brennon to resist powers like his. So, she turned, slowly and carefully, and even though the movement seemed to rip at her soul, she walked away from him.

"Dammit! Don't go!" His shout followed her up the stairs. "*Mon Dieu*, witch, you wait until I get my hands on you—"

She was almost to the top of the stairs now. The door waited in front of her. So close.

"You'll beg me for mercy. Beg me!"

Her hand reached for the doorknob.

"Don't leave me!"

She pushed open the door, realizing that her entire body trembled.

"Don't you dare—"

Madison slammed the door behind her, shutting out his furious cries. Then she collapsed onto the floor, tears leaking from her eyes.

Oh, God, she'd done it. She'd actually done it. She'd captured a werewolf.

A real, live, freaking werewolf.

Just like the one that had killed her parents.

She knew, with utter certainty, if Alerac ever got free, if he broke those chains, he'd kill her.

"That's what monsters do." She could almost hear Brennon's voice. *"They kill."*

Alerac would kill her, if he got free. His rage was so strong, so overwhelming—

Her eyes closed and she shuddered.

She had to make sure the bastard never got free. Never.

Madison took a deep breath and reached for the phone. She had to check in with Brennon to arrange the pick-up.

He answered her call immediately. "Madison?" A worried edge filled his voice and gave her pause.

"Ah, yeah, it's me." Her hands tightened around the cordless phone. "La Mort's chained in the basement. He'll be fine until some of your guys can transport him tomorrow."

Brennon didn't respond.

A knot of dread formed in her stomach. "Bren? Bren, what's wrong?" Brennon was like an older brother to her. He'd been one of the first people on the scene that horrible night ten years ago.

She'd run straight to Mrs. Sue's house, banged on the door, screamed, begged for help. The police had arrived moments later, and when the swirl of blue lights lit the small lane, her neighbors had all crept from their homes.

She'd been sixteen. Scared, half-out of her mind.

He'd been twenty-eight. He'd been living in the neighborhood for less than three months. He'd brought her a blanket. Held her hand when her parents' bodies were brought out.

He'd taken care of her that night. Taken care of her over the years.

And he'd taught her about werewolves.

"The transport has to be delayed."

Oh, hell, no!

"His pack is already looking for him."

Shit. She'd hoped they'd have more time. Alerac had only been missing a few hours.

"I'll get him out of there as soon as I can, but…" He sighed, the frustration in the sound carrying easily over the phone. "It's gonna be a few days."

Madison tensed. "How many days?"

"I don't know yet."

Great. Just great.

"Keep up your guard, Maddie. Alerac's smart and he's damn dangerous."

Yeah, she knew that. *And he was chained up in her basement!*

"I'll contact you soon," Brennon promised. "Stay on guard with him, at all times."

Madison hung up the phone and fought the urge to throw the handset across the room.

Damn. Looked like she and the wolf were going to be roomies for a while.

A shiver skated down her spine.

Chapter 2

The house was pitch black.

Madison crept up the porch steps, her fingers clenching around the keys in her hand.

Why was the house dark? Mom and Dad always waited up for her. Always.

It was barely ten o'clock. They shouldn't have gone to bed yet.

She touched the old, wooden front door and with a soft creak, the door swung open.

Her heart began to race. The door should have been locked, it should have—

A low, furious growl sounded from the bowels of the house, and Madison froze as raw terror swept through her.

She became aware of the smell then. Aware of the thick, coppery scent that hung heavily in the air.

She wanted to run. Wanted to turn and run back to her car. Drive back to Susan's.

But she couldn't. Her parents—they were in that dark house. She knew they were.

Madison inched forward.

The coppery scent flooded her nostrils, thicker, stronger now.

"M-mom?" She slipped, sliding in some kind of liquid that had spilled on the floor. Madison fell, hard, landing on her side with a grunt.

Something wet and sticky coated her arm. Her hand. Her legs.

Pushing up, she winced and crawled forward. There was an end table nearby, with a lamp on it. Her grandmother's Tiffany lamp. If she could just turn on the light...

Her fingers touched the hard edge of the table. Fumbled, slipped up and found the base of the lamp.

She heard the growl again. The menacing, angry growl of a dog.

But they didn't have a dog. Her parents had never let her have a pet, even though she'd begged them so many times and—

Her fingers snapped on the light. A soft, white glow illuminated the room.

Madison realized that her fingers were red. Blood red.

"Oh, God..." Her gaze fell to the floor. Locked on the pool of blood that coated the hardwood. The pool that led straight back to the body.

Her mother's body.

Madison screamed, a raw, desperate sound.

Her mother's green eyes stared sightlessly back at her, and her mouth was open in a silent shriek of agony.

"M-mom?" No, please, God, no...

She lunged toward her mother, needing to touch her, to—

A large, black wolf jumped in front of Madison, its lips twisted in a snarl, its thick fur matted with blood. A wolf, not a dog. A huge, horrifying wolf.

Madison stumbled back, and her legs hit the end table. The lamp slammed into the floor with a crash, and the room plunged back into darkness.

The furious snarls of the beast grew louder, closer.

The wolf's eyes, its shining blue eyes stared out of the darkness. Stared straight at her.

Madison screamed, and the hot breath of the wolf blasted across her skin as she ran for the door...

Madison jerked upright, her heart slamming against her chest. Sweat coated her skin, tears trickled down her cheeks. .

Dammit. She'd had the nightmare again. *Would it ever stop?*

She jumped out of bed and stalked to the window.

Madison knew why she'd had the dream, of course. Because of him. *Alerac.*

He was just like the wolf that had killed her parents. Just. Like. Him. A murdering monster.

Brennon had told her all about werewolves. Told her how they became mindless killing machines when the change was upon them. The *Weres* would destroy anything, *anyone*, in their paths when the bloodlust rose within them.

He'd trained her how to fight them. Taught her to use a silver dagger to go for a wolf's heart. Silver, that was the werewolf's weakness.

Alerac's chains were forged of silver. He'd never be able to break free of them.

Brennon had captured other werewolves before. He'd taken them to Scions Laboratory and studied them. In his experiments, he'd learned of their silver weakness. At first, he'd just thought that was an old myth. Like vampires and garlic. It turned out that werewolves really couldn't stand the touch of the precious metal. Sometimes, if the silver was pure enough, it even burned their flesh.

She'd been at the lab once when a *Were* had gone through the change. His bones had broken. Stretched. His body contorted and thick black fur had covered his body. In less than a minute, he'd gone from being human… to a growling monster who tried to destroy the observation room. He'd shattered furniture, attacked two scientists, nearly ripping one's chest open with his razor-sharp claws.

It had taken four guards, armed with the powerful tranqs, to subdue him. If she tried, she could still hear his howls.

Those loud, wrenching howls…

A tear slipped from the corner of her eye.

His captor walked slowly down the stairs, an expression of acute distaste on her lovely face.

Alerac didn't move from his position on the floor. He'd tested the chains earlier, and he knew that he could stand up, walk five feet. But he didn't move. Just stayed on the stone floor, his back pressed against the wall, his hands on his updrawn knees.

Her fingers clenched around the edge of a plate. He could smell the meat she carried. His stomach rumbled.

Madison's fine brows drew together as she glanced at the tray she'd left him earlier. "You didn't eat."

Yeah, like he'd be fool enough to trust anything she brought him. "Couldn't take the risk." The witch would probably try to poison him.

Her full lips thinned. "The food is perfectly safe." She held up her latest offering. Scrambled eggs. Bacon.

He wanted to drool. He managed, barely, to keep his face expressionless. "You'll forgive me if I don't trust you." He lifted his hands and jerked against the chains. "So far, you haven't exactly shown me the warmest hospitality."

She'd left him. Left him alone in the damn basement for six hours. Dawn was approaching, and even though there was no outside light in the basement, he knew the sun was rising. He'd been counting every minute of his captivity, and he *knew* it was time for the sun.

Just as later, it would be time for his moon.

"Suit yourself." She dropped the plate onto the stone floor with a clang. One piece of bacon fell onto the cracked slab.

He realized that his little captor was pale. Too pale. And her blue eyes were wide, almost bruised-looking.

His body tensed. "What's wrong?" Something had happened, He shouldn't give a damn. This was the woman who'd drugged him, chained him.

She was also his mate, and the thought of someone hurting her, causing her any pain… it roused the beast within him.

A growl rumbled in his throat.

Madison's gaze lifted and she stared at him, as if transfixed.

He felt his cock tighten, swell. Her sweet, warm scent filled his nostrils.

"Come here." The order slipped past his lips.

She shook her head.

He dropped his gaze to the floor, staring at the faint scratch marks he'd carved into the stone to mark his cage. Five feet. That was all he had.

If he could just get her closer to him. Just get her to cross into his reach…

"Y-you're gonna be here for a long time," Madison muttered, lifting her hand to rub the back of her neck. "If you don't want to eat, that's your bus—"

"How long." Not a question.

She dropped her hand. Squared her thin shoulders. "As long as it takes."

To do what? What was his little mate planning to do? "Why did you bring me here?"

She took a step toward him, bringing her a few precious inches closer to the etched lines on the floor. "Because I can't stand the idea of a monster like you on the streets."

His eyes narrowed. "Careful, *ma cherie.* You really don't want to make me angry."

She laughed, *laughed* at his words, and her hands gestured toward the chains. "Why, wolf? What are you gonna do? Growl at me?"

Oh, he knew what he'd like to do. He'd like to grab her, strip her. Pin her too-thin body beneath his and drive his cock into her so deep and so hard that she shuddered, that she begged him to stop. And then begged him to keep fucking her.

And she would beg. It was only a matter of time.

Her sneakered foot nudged the plate toward him. The tempting aroma of the eggs and bacon filled the air. His stomach growled. If only he'd eaten before he'd left the Compound, then he wouldn't be so damn hungry now.

Weres had a different metabolism than humans. They had to eat more often, their bodies demanded greater protein and nutrients to keep up their superior strength.

Her lips curved into a smile. "So you *are* hungry."

He nodded once, a curt move of his head. "I can't reach the damn food." A lie, of course, but…

A frown drew her brows together. She looked down at the tray, then back at him. She used her foot to push the plate a few inches closer.

Oh, yes, just a little more.

He let his head fall forward, carefully lowering his eyes so she wouldn't see the triumph he knew would be in his gaze.

"There," she muttered, tapping her foot. "It's close enough now."

But she wasn't. "Closer…"

"Dammit!" Madison snatched up the tray, stomped forward and—

He lunged for her, grabbing her arms and sending the food flying to the floor.

Oh, shit. Madison stared up into Alerac's blazing gaze as fear ripped through her.

She hadn't realized how fast he could move. He'd leapt on her, jumping in a blur and locking those hard, strong hands around her.

She could feel the edge of his claws, feel them biting into her arms.

"Well, well…" His warm breath feathered across her face. "Look what I caught."

Her back teeth clenched. "Let. Me. Go."

Alerac shook his blond head. "I do not think so, *ma cherie*. Not when I've been waiting so long to… catch you." Then he stepped back, moving closer to the stone wall, and pulling her with him.

His nostrils flared, as if he inhaled her scent, and he wrenched her against him. Right up against his body. His hard, muscled, *aroused* body.

Oh, God. He was turned on. She could feel his cock, feel the thick, pulsing length of his erection pressing against her.

His hand lifted and his claws—*dammit, when had he grown claws from his fingertips?*—drifted across her cheek.

Then he lowered his head, and kissed her.

She bit him.

"*Salope*!"

She didn't know what the hell he'd just said, but she figured it wasn't good. She lifted her leg and then, as hard as she could, Madison rammed her knee into his groin.

Alerac jerked back right before she made contact, growling low in his throat. He spun around and shoved her against the wall. He caught her wrists in one hand, lifted her arms high over her head, and pinned them against the wall. His legs pushed between hers, spreading her wide and leaving her helplessly trapped as he stared down at her.

She realized that he looked… different. His golden eyes seemed to glow, to shine. His face was sharper, more defined. Almost like an animal's. And his teeth… they'd changed. The sharp hint of fangs glinted behind his parted lips.

"So you like to bite, do you?" he whispered, and even his voice was different. Rougher. "So do I…"

He lowered his head toward her throat, and his teeth pressed against her flesh, the sharp fangs biting lightly into her neck.

"No…" The word slipped past her lips as she struggled against him. But there was nowhere for her to go. He was too strong. She couldn't break free of him.

Dammit, why had she stepped closer to him? Why had she lowered her guard for even a moment? *Why*?

She should have just let the bastard starve. Yet for a moment, she'd stared down at him, at his slumped shoulders, his lowered head, and she'd felt… pity.

Someone give her the damn crown for stupidity. Why in the hell would she pity a monster?

Now, because of her idiotic sympathy, he was probably going to rip her apart.

"I-if you kill me, you'll never get free." She didn't have the key to the chains on her. Thank God, she'd had enough sense to leave the key upstairs.

His tongue rasped over her skin, and she gasped as a strange current of heat rocked through her.

"I'm not going to kill you, love." He didn't lift his head. His breath blew over her. His teeth scored her flesh. His cock pushed against her. "I'm going to fuck you."

Chapter 3

"The hell you—"

His mouth captured hers. She expected him to be rough, expected his lips to force hers apart as the hard stab of his tongue plunged into her mouth.

Instead of taking, of forcing, Alerac seduced.

His mouth touched hers, feather-light. The whisper of his breath blew against lips, then his tongue rubbed softly against her mouth.

Oh, God, his tongue…

He released her wrists, and his hands slipped down her body, touching her, stroking her, sending waves of heat, of hunger coursing through her.

He was a monster, a *werewolf*, a killer.

But he felt so damn good against her, *so right.*

Her arms lowered, then locked around him.

His head lifted, a bare inch. "I've waited for you." His eyes were bright with desire, with desperate need.

What? Madison shook her head, trying to make sense of his words, of the riot of feelings bursting through her. Her body felt strangely tight, too hot. Her skin seemed to prickle, and the hands that held him shook.

His index finger, and that frighteningly sharp claw, stroked down her cheek. She struggled to hold onto her sanity, fighting against the desire filling her. "L-let me go."

Alerac shook his head, and kissed her again.

This time, there was no gentle exploration. This time, he took.

His tongue thrust into her mouth, deep and hard, and he tasted her, as if he had the right, as if he'd been starving for her.

The hot ridge of his cock pressed against her stomach. She tried to step back, tried to pull away, but the wall was against her back. There was nowhere to go, nowhere—

His hands shot to her waist and his fingers dug into her flesh, forcing her closer to him. His fingers tightened against her, but his claws—his claws never so much as pierced her skin.

His body was hard, tight with muscles and lust. And that hunger inside of her, that fiery need, it burned hotter, hotter—

His tongue swirled over hers. His hand slid up, cupped the curve of her breast.

A moan rose to her lips, and Madison realized she wasn't repulsed by his touch, wasn't furious that he dared to put his hands, his mouth, on her.

No, she was… aroused.

Her sex creamed.

His teeth pressed lightly into her lower lip. Then his tongue stroked over the soft bite.

The ball of heat inside her exploded. Madison growled low in her throat, and her tongue met his.

Her fingers clenched against the strong muscles of his arms, her nails dug into his skin. A dark hunger flooded through her. In that moment, all she cared about was him. Alerac.

I'm going to fuck you.

Oh, hell, yes.

Madison's body pressed against his. The thick, rich scent of her arousal filled his nostrils.

He jerked up her shirt, shoved her bra out of the way, and stroked her breasts. Her soft, sweetly rounded breasts.

Alerac tore his mouth from hers and stared down at her exposed flesh. His mate was thin, but her breasts, they were perfect. The nipples were tight with need, flushed a dark pink. His fingers caught her nipples, holding them lightly, plucking, teasing.

Madison moaned, and the husky sound sent a shaft of pure lust straight through him.

He didn't feel the faint burn of the silver manacles on his flesh any longer. He only felt Madison. Her smooth skin. The seductive warmth of her body.

His head lowered, and he caught her nipple between his teeth. Her fingers fisted in his hair. But she didn't try to push him away. She forced him closer.

His mouth widened over her breast, and he sucked the nipple, drawing it deeply into his mouth. His teeth scored her flesh, a light, gentle bite.

Later, he'd give her a wolf's bite. *Later...*

Alerac's hand snaked down her body, moving lightly over her flat stomach, down to the front of her jeans. He grabbed the top of the rough fabric, jerking the button free, wanting to shove his hand inside, *needing* to touch the core of her sex, to feel her, creamy, hot, ready—

The soft hiss of her zipper filled the air.

Still, she didn't fight. He pulled back, gazing at her, at her red cheeks, her lush lips. Her eyes were tightly closed, her breath panted out.

Her breasts thrust toward him, nipples tight. Her jeans were undone, showing just the faintest hint of white lace.

She was the sexiest thing he'd ever seen.

And she was his. *His.*

His fingers slipped between the open edges of her zipper. Her soft hands pressed against him, her nails scored his flesh.

He took a deep breath, and smelled her. Her arousal. The heady scent of her cream. His cock was rock-hard, shoving against the front of his jeans.

His knuckles pressed against the edge of her panties.

Her breath choked out. Her eyes flashed open, and the faint sky blue was gone. Her eyes glowed, bright and brilliant. *They glowed.*

What in the hell?

Then those eyes widened in apparent horror and she screamed. Her nails raked him, slashing deep into his arms.

She shoved him, thrust him back with such strength that he slammed onto the floor.

Madison ran past him, yanking down her shirt. She didn't look back, just ran straight ahead. Her sneakered feet thudded against the old wooden stairs as she fled upstairs, and then the door slammed above him.

Alerac sat up, and he gazed down at the deep marks on his arms. They were long, angry, glistening with blood.

He didn't understand how he'd gotten the wounds. Because Madison didn't have long nails. She didn't have the sharpened manicure that some women fancied. Her nails were short, carefully trimmed.

The marks he bore, they looked like—like claw marks—marks one of his kind would make in the heat of anger, or passion.

But Madison wasn't like him. She was a human. Not a *Were.*

Yet... *Her eyes had glowed.* For the briefest of moments, her blue eyes had shimmered, taking on a bright, unearthly light.

He rose to his feet, aware of the hard lust that still filled his body and tightened his cock. The scent of her arousal hung in the air, surrounding him, maddening him. In his mind's eye, he could see her, see her perfect breasts, tight and hungry for him. See the lace of her panties, the thin lace that guarded her sex.

He fought to hold back a howl of rage. He wanted to go after her, to chase her down.

To claim her.

His hands clenched into fists. The burning silver scored his flesh. Slowly, using all his strength, he pushed back the hunger of the beast.

Madison. He wanted her, and he would have her.

Soon. When the moon rose, he'd have his freedom. Then he would hunt his mate. Claim her.

And learn all her secrets. Because he was sure, damn sure, that Madison Langley had secrets.

Her eyes had glowed.

They'd glowed like a werewolf's, right before the change.

Oh, hell, oh, hell, oh, hell. Madison splashed water onto her face for the fifth time and then glanced up at her sodden reflection.

What had she done? What in the hell had she done? She'd let that man, that monster, touch her, kiss her, practically strip her. And she enjoyed it. Reveled in it. Like some kind of damn dog in heat.

She'd moaned for him, rubbed her body against his, kissed him. Almost screwed him. *Him.* The freaking werewolf.

Why?

She jerked the faucet, turning off the flood of cold water with a quick snap of her wrist. The splashing wasn't enough. She needed a shower. A very, very cold shower. Because her body, it was still hungry. Still tight with lust. For a monster.

Her head slumped forward. What was wrong with her? She'd lost her control, and she'd become… his. His for the taking. She'd wanted him so badly, wanted to crawl over him, to stroke his cock, to feel the thick shaft between her legs.

She'd been seconds away from completely surrendering to him. Seconds. If she hadn't stopped, hadn't opened her eyes and seen that strange golden glow in his gaze, the glow that reminded her of exactly what he was, she would have been lost.

But she'd looked into his eyes, and she'd seen the beast within him. The beast she knew could kill her as easily as the man could seduce her.

So she'd fought him and then fled.

She'd have to face him again, she knew she couldn't hide forever. But she wouldn't get close to him, wouldn't be so stupid as to stumble within his grasp. No, she'd never make that mistake again.

Madison stomped toward the shower. Jerked on the cold water. Then she stripped, dropping her clothes onto the floor in a heap. She shivered, remembering the feel of his mouth on her breast. The feel of his hands on her body.

Raising her foot, she stepped into the shower. She closed her eyes and let the spray hit her face, let the cold water slide over her body and wash away his touch.

Yes, she'd wash away his touch, but she wouldn't be able to forget the look she'd seen in his eyes, the hunger—the burning hunger in his glowing eyes.

Hours later, the door above him squeaked softly. Alerac didn't look up. He sensed Madison stood there, knew instinctively it was her before she even took a soft, tentative step down the stairs.

The faint sound of her breathing reached him, a sound no human would hear, but a sound that reached his sensitive ears all too easily.

She was breathing hard. Quick, rasping breaths.

A slow smiled curved his lips. Little Madison was afraid. Good. She should be.

His nostrils flared as he inhaled the sweet aroma of food. Ah, so she'd brought him something else to eat.

He'd finally eaten the bacon and eggs she'd brought him. He figured if the woman truly wanted to drug him, all she had to do was shoot him with her damn tranq gun.

Madison didn't speak to him as she crept down the stairs and then walked across the room. Her lips were pressed into a tight little line, and her blue gaze was narrowed.

"This is the last thing you're getting today," she muttered, dropping the tray and then crossing her hands over her chest. "I'll come back in the morning, and—"

"You didn't bring me lunch." He'd waited for her, wanting to see her, to smell her.

Her shoulders stiffened. "You're lucky I brought this to you. After what you did—"

He rose from the floor, stretching his muscles and carefully inching toward her. "What I did? Hmmm, I seem to recall you doing a few things, too."

She swallowed. "Just eat your damn food, okay?" Turning on her heel, she started to march away.

"Madison!"

She froze, but didn't glance back.

Darkness approached. He sensed the coming night, felt the the call of the moon, the call of his power. *Soon.* "This is your last chance, *cherie.* Let me go."

Madison turned her head, glanced back over her shoulder. "My last chance?"

He would give her no other warning. "Let me go," he repeated.

Her lips trembled. "I-I can't. I have to stop you, I have to stop you from killing, from slaughtering innocent people."

"What?" What was she talking about? He'd never killed an innocent. No one in his pack would dare—

"You're all alike," she whispered, and he could have sworn he saw a flash of pain in her eyes. "Murderers. Animals."

The silver bit into his wrists and ankles as he jerked forward.

"I-I'm not letting you go." Her gaze was clear now. Determined. "Brennon will come for you soon. He'll take you to Scions Lab, and you'll never hurt anyone else again." She drew a deep breath and turned her head away. Stalked away from him, her back ramrod-straight.

Alerac didn't know who this Brennon bastard was, but he sure as hell wasn't going to let the guy take him to Scions or any other damn place.

Madison had nearly reached the stairs now. Her steps were slow, measured. The woman was leaving him, again.

Merde. "You wanted me. You wanted me to touch you, to take you."

Her hand reached for the railing. Trembled.

"Didn't you, Madison?" He pressed, needing her to say the words, to admit that she wanted him just as much as he wanted her.

She glanced at him. "I learned long ago that you don't always get what you want."

Her gaze held his for a moment. Then she looked away. Moved up the steps.

He watched her, watched every slow glide of her body. His gaze stayed on her until she disappeared. Until the door clicked softly shut behind her.

Then he smiled.

Because he wanted her, more than he'd ever desired anything or anyone in his life. And, unlike Madison, he always got what he wanted.

When the moon rose, she'd be his.

Chapter 4

Madison stared up at the thick, round moon that hung in the sky, a faint swirl of gray fog creeping briefly across its face.

She couldn't sleep. Every time she closed her eyes, she saw… him.

Alerac.

Damn if she didn't still feel his touch on her skin. Didn't still smell him, taste him.

Her hand lifted, touched her lips. The press of his mouth against hers had been hard, hot. His hands, when they'd slid over her flesh, when they'd cupped her breasts, had felt so strong. So good.

A faint moan rumbled in her throat and she slowly slid her hand down the front of her tee-shirt, pausing just a moment over the curve of her breast.

She could still feel him.

Her panties were wet. Her sex tightened with need. Her skin burned, ached. She needed Alerac so much, the hunger flooding through Madison made her feel like screaming. Like throwing her head back and screaming at the moon.

Her hand hovered over her breast, dropped just a bit, and her fingers skimmed against the tip of her nipple. He'd taken that nipple into his mouth. Licked it, bit—

Madison shuddered.

She knew what he was. Knew all the things he'd done. She understood what he could become… *but she still wanted him.*

Dear God, she wanted him.

The full moon was up. Alerac could feel its power filling the night, feel the power pouring into him.

He stretched slowly, rising from his position on the cold stone floor.

He pulled against the chains, and the faint groan of the metal echoed in the room.

The strength of the wolf swept through him. His nails lengthened, turning into deadly claws. His incisors burned, the canines growing, sharpening.

His muscles bulged as the power of the beast shook his body. Power, strength, *the force of the wolf.* Alerac lifted his arms, raising them high into the air and then he ripped the chains straight from the wall.

Almost too easy.

He jerked open the manacles, nearly crushing the metal in his fist. He freed his legs, shoving aside the cursed chains, and threw them against the wall.

Red burn lines circled his wrists and ankles, but he knew those lines would fade soon. His kind healed quickly, and now that he was free of the imprisoning silver, his flesh would repair itself in mere moments.

A slow smile curved his lips as he glanced toward the stairs.

His mate was nearby. *Madison.*

It was time she learned not to play with a hungry wolf.

Making no sound, he stalked toward the stairs. He'd watched Madison closely. He knew which steps creaked, knew exactly where to step. He wouldn't make the mistake of alerting her. He wanted to catch her completely unprepared.

Just as she'd caught him.

Once he was at the top of the stairs, he followed her scent, tracking her easily through the quiet house.

He stopped before a plain, white door. *Her* door. His fingers curled over the knob and very carefully, he opened the door and crept inside.

The room was cloaked in shadows. Madison stood in front of a large picture window, her head tilted back as she gazed up at the full moon. A faint moan slipped past her lips, and her body shuddered.

The scent of her desire filled the room. It surrounded him, tempted him.

Then she shifted, turning slightly, and he saw that her hand was on her breast, her fingers stroking against her nipple.

The beast within him was already aroused. As her hand dropped, as her fingers slid down the curve of her stomach to the apex of her thighs, the man lost control.

In a heartbeat, he'd crossed the room, grabbed her, spun her around to fully face him, and pulled her against his body.

Madison blinked, staring up at Alerac in dawning horror. "How did you get fr—"

Alerac's mouth crashed down on hers, hard, hungry. His tongue pushed into her mouth, stroked hers, claimed. Demanded her response.

Her body, already so ready for him, so eager, responded instantly. Her breasts tightened. Her sex creamed. And her tongue met his as she kissed him back just as hard.

Madison knew she should fight him. Knew she should shove him away from her. But she couldn't. Her skin felt too tight, her mind was spinning, and the hunger she felt for him was overwhelming her.

His hands snaked down her body, curled around the top of her jogging shorts and shoved the material down her legs. Then his fingers, those long, strong fingers, slid under the edge of her panties and stroked her sex. Rubbed her clit.

She nearly fell to the floor.

"You want to be touched," he growled against her lips, "then you let *me* touch you."

Her breath caught on a moan. "Alerac—"

"That's right." His voice was a rumbling growl in the dark room. "*Alerac.*" His head lowered toward her neck, and his breath blew across her flesh.

Her hips arched against him, a helpless, desperate movement. She wanted him to touch her more, harder. She *needed* more. "Ah… give me—"

His fingers pressed against her clit. "You're so wet for me." He licked her throat. One long, slow lick of his tongue, then the edge of his teeth pressed against her neck. "You're going to come for me, aren't you, sweet Madison?"

Oh, God, she was already close. So close. Her breasts ached, the nipples tight. She wanted to feel his mouth on them, needed him to suck her nipples, to lick them. And she wanted to feel his cock, to feel the thick length thrusting inside of her core. She wanted—

Alerac picked her up, and tossed her onto the bed. Madison lay among the tangled bed sheets, her legs spread, her aroused nipples shoving against the front of her tee shirt.

He stared down at her, and his eyes had the glow of the beast.

Madison swallowed. She knew she should be afraid of him. The monster inside of him could rip her apart. She *knew* she should be afraid, but she wasn't.

"Do you accept me?" His voice was low, gravelly, barely human.

She nodded. There was no other response for her. At that moment, *she had to have him, had to feel him inside of her.*

He yanked off his shirt, threw it onto the floor. "Say the words. *Say them!"*

"I-I accept you."

He leaned over the bed, caging her by placing his arms on both sides of her body. "There will be no going back."

The hunger rose even higher inside her, and her heartbeat pounded desperately, the sound filling her ears.

"You'll be mine. *Toujours*." Alerac lowered his head and he sucked her nipple through the thin cotton. "It's the way of the wolf."

She arched toward him, choking back a moan. She could barely hear his words. Didn't understand what he meant—

His head lifted, his eyes gleaming with ferocious hunger. He jerked open his jeans, shoved down the zipper and her hands joined his to push the denim away. Then she took his cock into her hands. The long, thick length filled her grasp. He was so warm. So hard and strong. Madison squeezed him, then swept her fingers over the broad head, finding a light drop of moisture on the tip.

She wanted to taste him, wanted to bring that drop to her lips and taste him. She lifted her hand and Alerac froze above her. Staring into his eyes, she brought her fingers to her lips and licked away his essence. Then she smiled at him and whispered, "I want more."

His control broke. She actually saw it shatter right before her. It was in the flare of his eyes, the sudden tremble of his hands as he grabbed her arms and pinned them to the mattress. He held her wrists with one hand, and the other slipped down her body, and ripped aside her panties.

"I'll give you more, love, I'll give you more." His cock pressed against her folds. His jaw clenched. "Damn, but you feel good."

So did he. Never, never had she wanted someone so much. If he didn't thrust inside her soon—

His cock pushed just inside her body. Alerac shuddered. "You're so tight… and wet." He swallowed. "And you're mine!"

And he was big and thick and—

Alerac thrust into her, driving his cock deep into her pussy. Madison cried out in pleasure. Finally, *finally,* he was inside and he felt so good. *So good.*

Then he was moving, pulling his cock out, then thrusting back, hard, again and again. Her legs wrapped around his hips, and she arched toward him, meeting him, urging him on. Her sex clenched around him, her head thrashed against the pillow.

Her pussy felt stretched, too full. But, oh, God, the way he moved, the way his cock pressed inside her…

Pleasure lashed through her.

Then his fingers were on her. Rubbing against her clit. Pushing. Stroking. And he kept thrusting, kept driving that thick cock into her body.

He freed her hands. Shoved up her shirt, and took her breast into his mouth.

Madison felt the sting of teeth, then he sucked her nipple, drawing her breast deep into his mouth.

"Alerac!" She couldn't take much more. Her muscles locked tight as she shuddered, as she bucked beneath him, as she—

Her orgasm rocked through her, wringing a desperate cry from her as she came, shuddering on a powerful climax.

Still he kept thrusting. Driving into her, over and over again. Deeper. Harder.

His cock swelled even more within her. "A-Aler—" His glowing eyes locked on her. His cheeks appeared hollowed, sharper. His fangs glinted.

The beast was close. She could see him. Feel him. But still, she wasn't afraid.

His mouth moved to her throat. Kissed the pulse that beat so frantically. His tongue laved her skin, and the edge of his incisors scraped across her flesh.

When he bit her, a second climax shook her body. A hard, fast, wrenching climax that had her crying his name and holding onto him with all her strength. Her nails dug into his hips, pulling him closer.

His cock pumped into her and then he stiffened. His semen flowed into her in a hot, heavy tide.

And she realized she'd just had the best sex of her life… with a werewolf who hated her.

Brennon Donalds watched the television screen. Watched as Madison writhed beneath the werewolf, as Alerac bit her neck. Watched as she climaxed beneath him, screaming in pleasure.

The bitch. He'd thought he was wrong about her. Believed he could trust her. But at the first chance she'd had, she'd whored herself to a monster.

"Sir?"

Brennon didn't look up from the screen. The bastard was still on the bed with her. Stroking her damn hair. Kissing her brow.

All these years, he'd waited. Waited for Madison. He'd been hoping, *hoping* she would be different.

Hoping she could be his.

But now, her true nature had shown itself.

"Ah… sir?"

Brennon looked over the top of the screen, meeting the eyes of his newest recruit. No one else had seen Maddie's… performance. Just him.

The bitch. The fucking bitch.

His eyes narrowed. Throwing Maddie into the wolf's path had been a risk, but he'd had to do it. For so long, he'd watched her, and she'd seemed so… normal. He'd had to test her, so he'd let the wolf catch her scent.

Now, he knew what he had to do. "Get the tranqs ready."

His. Alerac licked Madison's neck, growling softly with pleasure.

He'd taken his mate, given her the bite of the wolf. The bite was the first step in a wolf's claiming. Once he took her again, in the way of his kind, she'd be bound to him. Forever.

He stretched languidly. Madison was curiously still beneath him, and he wondered what his little mate was thinking.

His head lifted and he gazed down at her. The glowing of her eyes had faded back to a light, sky blue. When she'd come beneath him, her eyes had shined so bright. *So bright… just like a Were's.*

Madison stared up at him, barely seeming to breathe.

His fingers trailed down her cheek. "You're keeping secrets from me, *cherie.*" Mates weren't allowed secrets. There had to be complete honesty between bonded couples. It was the law of the pack.

Her brow furrowed. "No, I—"

The faint squeak of a door reached his sensitive ears, and Alerac tensed. "Get dressed."

He sprang from the bed. Pulled on his jeans. The shoes he didn't even remember kicking off.

She yanked down her shirt. "What are you—"

"*Get dressed! Now!*" His eyes scanned the room. He needed a weapon.

Madison glared at him. "Dammit, don't yell at me!"

He growled back at her. He could hear the soft tread of footfalls, the faint moan of the old hardwood floor. There wasn't much time.

Still glaring, Madison climbed from the bed. She grabbed her shorts, jerked them on, not bothering with underwear. Then she tugged on a pair of tennis shoes, hopping slightly as she pulled them on her feet. "Look, this—this was a-a mistake—"

The hell it was.

"Y-you were angry, and I was—"

He grabbed her arms, pulling her against him. "I wasn't angry."

Her lips parted. "But you—"

"I was so fucking hungry for you I would have gone crazy if I hadn't gotten you beneath me." And, already, he wanted her again. Longed to feel the tight, wet clasp of her pussy around his cock as she came.

She shook her head and her blond mane flew around her face. "No, you wanted to punish me! You said—"

Screw what he'd said. When he'd seen her, all he'd wanted to do was get her naked beneath him.

Damn, they didn't have time for this conversation. Not now.

He could smell the other men coming. They were too close.

Keeping his hand locked around her wrist, he pulled her over to the window. They were only one floor up, the jump would be nothing to him. They could—

The bedroom door flew open, slamming against the wall.

"You bitch! You betrayed us!"

Madison gasped at the furious shout, whirling around. "B-Brennon!"

Alerac snarled and spun toward the threat, his claws out, his fangs barred.

Two men stood in the doorway. One blond and young, looking like he'd just gotten out of high school. The other guy was tall, dark, and held a gun.

"Brennon, it's not what you think!" Madison stepped forward as if she were going to cross to his side.

Oh, the hell she was. Alerac jerked her back. "Don't even think about it." She'd go to that bastard over his cold, dead body.

"Save it." The gun never wavered from its position. It was pointed straight at Madison.

"Yeah." A high-pitched giggle came from the kid. "We all knew you'd turn. Knew you'd wanna fuck the wolf—"

What in the hell was going on?

Alerac glanced back at Madison. Her face was chalk-white and she was staring at the men in horror.

"What? You knew I'd—"

The dark guy, had to be Brennon, smiled at her. "Blood always tells, Maddie. It *always* tells." His fingers tightened around the gun.

Oh, hell, no. "Who the fuck are you?" Alerac growled as he stepped in front of his mate. The red haze of the *fureur de la mort* pulled at him. *The death rage.* These men, they'd been behind his capture. They were threatening Madison.

Two damn good reasons for them to die.

His muscles tightened as he prepared to attack.

"Who are we?" Brennon's green eyes narrowed. "We're the ones who are going to destroy your race, *Were*."

Alerac lifted one brow. "You can try, human. You can try." Then he pointed toward Brennon with one claw. "But I think you're going to find I'm hard to destroy." He smiled, deliberately flashing his fangs.

Brennon stared back at him, his face tense. "I've killed your kind before, and I'll be damn happy to do it again."

He'd killed his kind before? This bastard had murdered *Weres*?

Brennon looked over Alerac's shoulder. "Maddie, come here."

"Don't fucking move, Madison," Alerac snarled. The beast roared inside him, and it took all of his strength to maintain his human form.

"Alerac..." Her voice was strained, but she didn't move.

"*Screw this shit*!" The kid screamed, and pulled a small, black gun from the back of his jeans. "Let's take 'em both down!" Then he aimed his gun at Alerac and fired.

Chapter 5

Alerac lunged across the room so fast Madison barely saw him move. He knocked the gun aside, and the tranq shot into the wall. He attacked the other man, his claws raking down the guy's chest.

The man, she remembered his name was Philip something, fell to the floor with an ear-piercing scream.

She stood there, frozen, unable to tear her gaze away as Alerac attacked him.

The sounds Alerac made—the growls, the snarls, they weren't human. But then, *he* wasn't human.

Philip was whimpering now, curled up on the floor, and he held his arms to his chest as the blood trickled over his hands.

A loud crack of static cut across his cries. Brennon's voice rumbled as he barked an order for back-up into his radio, and Madison realized that all hell was about to break loose in her house.

She ran across the room, just as Brennon lifted his tranq gun toward Alerac. "Brennon, no!"

It was too late. With a roar, the gun fired. Alerac staggered back at the impact, and his eyes widened in pain and confusion before he fell to the ground, blood flowing from his shoulder.

Blood flowing from his shoulder...

Oh, God. Brennon hadn't fired a tranq. He'd shot Alerac, with real bullets, probably silver so Alerac wouldn't be able to heal immediately and—

"Your turn, bitch!" Brennon lifted the gun and aimed it right at the middle of her chest.

No, no this couldn't be happening. Brennon was her friend, her family. He wouldn't turn on her, he wouldn't—

A smile twisted his face. A cold, deadly smile of intent. And, her heart sinking, she realized that he was, indeed, going to shoot her. "Brennon..."

"You could have been mine," he whispered, a flash of agony hardening his eyes. *"Mine!"* Then he pulled the trigger.

Madison screamed.

Just as the gun fired, a giant white wolf shot through the air and slammed its body into Brennon.

The shot went wide. Madison felt a fiery pain burn across her left arm.

Brennon had shot her. Her right hand lifted, touched her arm, came away stained with red. *He'd actually shot her.*

She looked back at him, a cold, sweeping numbness filling her. The white wolf was on top of him. Snarling. Fangs lowered dangerously close to his throat. The wolf was going for the kill.

The wolf—no, *Alerac*—was going to kill Brennon. Going to rip out his throat.

"They're monsters." Brennon had said that to her, told her about the bloodlust that could consume a *Were.* He'd told her about them the day after her parents were murdered. *"When the bloodlust rides them, they'll kill anything, anyone in their path."*

"No," her voice was a hoarse whisper. Her world had suddenly gone out of control. The man she'd trusted, the man she'd loved like a brother, had just shot her.

And Alerac—Alerac had transformed into a mindless beast right before her eyes.

"Damn animal!" Philip's scream. He'd managed to get to his feet. Grabbed Brennon's gun.

Madison ran across the room. She couldn't let Philip shoot Alerac. She couldn't. She jumped in front of him, wrestling for the gun. He screamed again, a high, shrill scream, and punched her with his fist.

The wolf snarled.

The beast leapt off Brennon and jumped toward them.

Philip whimpered. His eyes rolled back in his head, and he slumped onto the floor in a dead faint. Madison grabbed the gun, the cold metal nearly slipped from her sweaty, blood-soaked fingers. But she clung to it, and when the wolf's hot breath pressed against her body, when he looked up at her with his glowing gold eyes, a tremor swept over her.

"They'll kill anything, anyone in their path." Oh, shit. Madison licked her lips. Wished that her arm would stop throbbing. Wished Alerac wasn't a giant wolf who looked like he was seconds away from gobbling her up. "N-nice, wolf. N-nice, b-big wolf."

He inched closer to her.

Behind him, Brennon stumbled to his feet and ran from the room.

At any moment, Madison expected to feel the wolf's long, sharp teeth on her throat. Her fingers tightened around the gun.

She didn't want to hurt him, didn't want to have to use the weapon, but if he attacked—

His front legs pressed against her, shoving her onto the floor. Then he was on her, before she could struggle, before she could fight, he was on top of her. His mouth was over her neck, His fangs poised to rip and tear.

This is it. She squeezed her eyes shut. *Her worst nightmare was about to come true.* She would die, killed by a wolf, just like her parents. She would—

A warm, wet tongue rasped over her neck.

Her eyes shot open.

The wolf crouched above her. Eyes bright and focused. But he didn't attack. He just stared at her.

Slowly, not wanting to do anything that might set him off, Madison lifted her hand toward him. The wolf lowered his head, and her fingers sank into the thick, luxurious fur.

The wolf made a rough, rumbling sound, almost like a, well, whatever the wolf equivalent of a purr would be.

"A-Alerac?" Was he still in there? Did he still have control?

The wolf stared back at her, and in the beast's eyes, she saw the man.

How was that possible? Werewolves were overwhelmed with bloodlust when the moon rose, they—

The wolf stiffened above her, his mouth twisted back into a snarl.

Then she heard the sound of thundering footsteps. Brennon had called for backup, and his team had arrived. Oh, damn, even with Alerac in his uber wolf form, they'd never be able to fight off an entire team of operatives. They were screwed, they were—

The wolf slipped off her, padded across the room. Pressed his nose against her window.

Madison rose to her feet. "Wh-what are you doing?" Automatically, she checked the gun. At least she had a weapon. She could use the gun to defend herself against the men who were supposed to be on the same damn team that she was on.

Alerac looked at her, then pushed his muzzle against the window once again.

She started to get a bad feeling. "Uh, look, we're on the second floor here, and—"

He paced away from the window.

"Oh, good, so you're not—"

A low howl filled the room. Then he ran straight into the window, bursting through the glass and flying into the night.

Oh, hell. Madison ran to the shattered window.

The moonlight spilled onto the yard below. Glittering shards of glass covered the ground. The wolf shook his body, then jerked his head toward her and howled, howled as if—as if he were calling to her.

Madison shook her head. No way. No way was she following him.

He was the enemy. She had to remember that. So she'd given into a case of temporary insanity and she'd had sex with him. But running off into the night with him… that was a whole other matter.

Besides, she'd probably break a leg if she jumped out of the window. And she sure as hell wouldn't be able to run anywhere with a broken leg.

No, she couldn't follow him, she couldn't—

"There she is!"

Madison jerked at the shout and glanced back over her shoulder. Brennon ran into the room, followed closely by four other guys, all dressed in black, all sporting tranq guns. Or at least, she really, *really* hoped they were loaded with tranqs.

Brennon smiled at her. "Looks like the wolf left you."

"Brennon…" The situation was way out of hand. They were supposed to be on the same side, supposed to be partners. "Give me a chance to explain." Her arm throbbed painfully and a trickle of blood slid down her elbow.

His smile twisted into a sneer. "You don't need to explain, Maddie. I always knew you'd turn on me."

What? She frowned. What was he talking about? She'd been loyal to him. *Before Alerac.* "No, no, I didn't turn. It wasn't like that. I—" What? What had she done? Had sex with the enemy?

He shook his head. "Blood tells, it always tells." He motioned to the man on his right. "Tranq her. We'll put her in the lab with the others."

She lifted her weapon, pointed it at him. "No one's tranqing me."

Brennon took a step toward her. "What are you going to do, Maddie? Shoot me?"

The bastard had shot her. Hell, yeah, she'd shoot him.

"You going to shoot all of us?" He jerked his head toward the men who surrounded him. "You think you can do it before we take you down?"

No, she knew she wasn't that good. But she wasn't about to let him see her fear.

"Madison!" Alerac's voice.

She inched back, and glanced down through the broken window. Alerac stood just below her, his arms outstretched, human again, and completely naked.

"Jump to me!"

She licked her lips, measured the distance down to him. It was a long fall. If he didn't catch her…

"Don't do it," Brennon snapped. "Don't go to that bastard!"

Her gaze darted between Alerac and Brennon. Dammit. There wasn't a choice. Not anymore.

She dropped her gun and lunged through the window.

Brennon screamed behind her. A hot blast of pain hit her back.

Then she was falling, falling fast toward the ground, toward Alerac.

His arms were open, waiting for her. *Waiting for her.*

She fell into his arms, and he didn't even flinch as he caught her weight. His arms tightened around her, and he pulled her close, held her against his hard, bare chest.

His eyes burned with gold fire as he stared at her. She tried to lift her hand, wanting to touch him, but her hand… it felt so heavy. And everything was getting dark. The glow of the moon was fading. Fading…

"Al—" Her tongue felt thick, her mouth too dry. She tried to swallow, tried to speak again, but she could only manage a faint moan.

"Madison?"

She couldn't answer him. Shouts echoed above them. Brennon would be coming after her. After them. Her lips moved, and she fought again to speak, even as the consuming darkness swept over her. And, this time, she managed to say one last word before the darkness swept her away. Softly, she whispered, "Run."

Chapter 6

Alerac crouched by a stream and carefully lowered Madison onto the ground. Her face was pale in the waning moonlight, far too pale. He caught a small pool of water in his hand, then dripped the liquid over her face.

She flinched, but her eyes didn't open.

"Madison… Come on, love, wake up." He'd been running with her through the woods for at least two hours. He thought he'd lost Brennon and his gang of assholes. He didn't hear the thudding of their footsteps anymore, didn't smell their stench on the wind.

Now, if Madison would just wake up.

He stroked her brow. Smoothed his fingertips over the delicate skin. "Wake up. *Ouvrez vos yeux, ma cherie.* Open your eyes." But she didn't.

Dammit. How much of the tranq had those idiots given her? He knew they'd shot her. He'd heard the soft thud of the tranq hitting her skin just as she'd jumped through the window to him. He'd caught her, held her tight, and then she'd passed out.

Madison moaned softly, and her lashes fluttered.

Every muscle in his body tightened. "Madison?"

Her eyes opened. "Al-Alerac?"

Relief swept through him. Finally. "*Oui,* love, it's me." He wanted to pull her tight against his chest, to hold her, to—

"Y-You're naked!" Her recently opened eyes widened.

Yeah, and running through the forest as a naked male had been a real bitch, but if he'd been in his wolf form, he would never have been able to transport her.

Madison tried to push herself up. She groaned, then muttered, "What the hell did you do to me?"

His hands were gentle on her shoulders as he braced her against his chest. "I didn't do this." A slow curl of anger began to grow in his stomach. He'd saved her. Taken her to safety and she—

"Shit." Madison grimaced. "Brennon hit me with the tranq. I-I can't believe he hurt me."

"Believe it." He'd seen the rage, the hate in the other man's eyes. "I hate to break it to you, love, but it looks like your monster squad has gone bad." He needed to get back to the Compound, needed to tell his pack leader Gareth about Brennon and his men, about Scions Laboratory and the *Weres* who were being held there.

Her gaze dropped to her wounded arm and her lips twisted. "Well, at least my arm's stopped bleeding."

Her arm. Alerac swallowed back the bile of rage that rose in his throat. She'd taken the bullet meant for him. Jumped in front of him. Protected him.

Those bastards had hurt her. Made her bleed. Tried to kill her. Once Alerac had taken Madison to safety, he'd go after them. He would hunt those bastards and make them all beg for death—

"Uh, Alerac?" Madison pushed against his chest. "You-your eyes are doing that glowy thing again, and I, uh, don't think I'm really up to another wolf encounter tonight, okay?"

His arms dropped to his sides, and she rose, somewhat unsteadily, to her feet. Her gaze swept over the lake and the dark woods. Her sneakered feet moved carefully over the small rocks at the edge of the stream.

"Brennon." She paused, licked her lips. "What happened to him?"

So she was worried about the asshole. Alerac rose. "Did I kill him, is that what you mean?"

A jerky nod.

"No, I haven't killed him." *Yet.* "I lost him in the woods." He'd discovered Madison's home was located in the middle of absolutely nowhere. When he'd fled her house, he'd had two choices: follow the old dirt road or go straight into the thick, waiting woods. He'd known Brennon would track him instantly on the road, so he'd chosen the woods.

They were safe for the moment, but they couldn't risk staying too long in the open. Brennon was still out there, hunting them.

A soft sigh—*of relief?*—slipped past her lips, and, suddenly, the furious tension within Alerac snapped. He grabbed Madison's arms, pulled her against him. "What is this Brennon to you? A lover?" Oh, he damn well better not be.

Her jaw clenched and her chin shot into the air. "Let me go."

Never. She didn't realize it yet, but when she'd given herself to him, when she'd made love to him and accepted his claim, well, they'd joined in the equivalent of a *Were* engagement.

Once he completed the claiming ritual, they would be bound forever.

"What is he to you?" He snarled the question again. Hot, thick anger churned through his veins.

She twisted against him, struggling to break free of his grasp, and when she stiffened, when her eyes widened, he knew she'd felt his arousal.

"Alerac?"

He was stark naked, it wasn't like he could hide his condition. Hell, he damn well didn't want to hide it. Madison was his. *His.* He wanted to take her they stood, with the moon shining down on them.

And, dammit, he'd do it. His hands dropped to her hips, and he pulled her closer against him, flush against the hard, thick length of his cock.

"Alerac—"

His mouth slammed down over hers. His tongue stabbed deep, and the beast inside him roared with pleasure.

He needed her naked. Needed to see her spread her pale thighs and take him deep into her body. He hungered to feel the tight, wet clasp of her pussy around his cock.

It wasn't the right time. Brennon could find them at any moment.

But he had to take her.

His hands edged around her body, clasped the curve of her ass. Damn, but she fit his hands perfectly.

Her nipples stabbed against his chest. Hard, tight buds that he wanted in his mouth. The rich, heady scent of her arousal, of her cream, filled his nostrils.

He had to taste her. Had to feel her cream on his tongue, her clit against his mouth.

His fingers clenched in the fabric of her shorts. He jerked them down. Heard her gasp.

He forced himself to stop. He lifted his head. His control hung by a thread, but he had to stop. Had to give her a choice.

Madison stared up at him, her eyes wide, her mouth slightly swollen.

"If you don't want me, then you'd better say so now." Because he was less than five seconds away from pushing her onto the ground, shoving apart those pale, slender legs, and burying his face between her thighs.

Her lips trembled, and he saw the struggle on her face. Saw the hunger, the same raw lust he felt. But he also saw… fear.

Mon Dieu, but he didn't want her to fear him. He wanted her desire, her passion, her love, but not her fear. Never her fear.

"Why do I feel this way?" she whispered, her voice a husky tremble of sound that slid along his nerve endings and had his body tightening even more. "Why do I want you so much?"

Because she was his mate. Because they were linked, chained since birth. Her body knew it, responded to him as a mate should, even though her mind didn't understand what was happening.

His jaw locked and he stepped back.

"No." She reached for him. Her small palm skimmed over his chest and Alerac felt the heat of that touch all the way to his soul. "God, it's wrong I know, but—but I want you."

That was all he needed to hear.

Besides, her five seconds were up.

Her eyes widened when he lowered her to the ground. He peeled her shorts over her tennis shoes. Madison hadn't been able to put on underwear before Brennon and his men had burst into the bedroom, so without the shorts, her sex was completely exposed to him. He pushed her thighs apart, spread her wide so the fading moonlight shone down on her light nest of curls. His fingers stroked over her clit, one long, slow stroke. Madison bit her lip and her hips arched toward him.

His fingers probed deeper, found her wet, creamy center. His index finger dipped inside of her, pushed deep.

"Alerac!"

He worked a second finger inside of her. Pushing. Thrusting deep. A hard, steady pressure.

Damn. He could already taste her in his mouth.

With a growl, he lowered his head, pulled his fingers out and drove his tongue into her sex. She tasted just as he'd known. Rich. Sweet. Perfect.

His.

He pulled back, laving his tongue over her clit. The sound of her moans filled his ears. She writhed beneath him, her fingers buried in his hair, her thighs completely open to him.

His finger slid back in her wet channel. She was so tight. So wonderfully tight and creamy. He licked her clit, moved his finger to the entrance of her sex, drove his tongue deep—

And felt the orgasm that ripped through her.

Madison's body shook, spasmed against him. But it wasn't enough for him. Not. Enough.

Alerac grabbed his cock in one hand, pushed the head against her quivering sex, then thrust hard and deep into her.

Her pussy squeezed him, the strong contractions of her orgasm rippled against him. His hips pressed against her, his body pinned her to the ground, and he thrust into her, over and over, harder, deeper…

Madison moaned, her legs wrapped around his hips, her ankles digging into his buttocks, urging him on, urging him to fuck her harder.

Her gaze met his. The blue shone, too bright, and he knew his own stare would mirror that same burning glow.

His balls tightened, his spine prickled, and he came, spilling his seed inside of her, then, incredibly, her sex tightened around his cock as she climaxed again.

Pleasure filled her face. Her lips parted on a soft sigh. Her mouth curved into a smile of satisfaction, and tiny white fangs pressed lightly against her lips.

Wow. Madison's heart thundered against her ribs. Her sex still throbbed with delicious aftershocks, trembling lightly around his cock.

They were in danger, being hunted by Brennon and his men, but she didn't care. She'd just had sex with her wolf again. Wild, passionate sex. She felt so—

Alerac stiffened against her, and the hands that had been holding her so gently, now shackled her wrists to the ground as he glared down at her. "Why didn't you tell me?" he snapped.

Some of her nice post-sex glow began to fade. "Tell you what?" Oh, damn, but was that husky, croaking voice really hers?

His right hand rose to her mouth, slipped past her lips, and tapped her tooth.

Tapped her tooth?

"These, love." His fingers spread over her mouth, pressing lightly against both of her cuspids.

She knocked his hand away. "What the hell are you talking about?" Madison wished they weren't having this insane conversation *while he was still buried balls deep inside of her.* She shivered and knew he felt the telling movement when his cock hardened inside of her.

"You've got fangs, love."

What?

Her tongue snaked out, tapped against her right canine, and felt the long, sharp point of a fang. *OhmyGod.* Her palms rammed into his chest as she shoved him off her, and *dammit*—had she just ripped open that wound again?

Blood started to trickle down her arm as she jumped to her feet and grabbed her shorts. The rocks had bit into her legs, her ass, but she ignored the sting, just as she ignored her throbbing arm. There was something far more important for her to deal with at that moment—

She had fangs! She pulled on her shorts and glared at Alerac as he rose to his feet. "What the hell did you do to me?" she snarled.

One brow rose. "Well, I thought I fucked you."

Her hands clenched and a blast of heat filled to her cheeks. "You… turned me." He'd bitten her before, back at the house. She remembered the feel of his teeth, nibbling on her neck. He'd bitten her, and now she had fangs and—

"Sorry, love, it doesn't work that way." A pause. "I think you know that."

This could not be happening. Could. Not. Be. First, she'd gone hormonally crazy for the jerk, and now, now he'd infected her with his wolf bite and she would become like— "Oh, *hell, no*." No way would she transform into some wolf that howled at the moon. She'd seen men change before. The change was damn painful.

"Your eyes are glowing," he told her softly.

Madison blinked. Alerac's eyes glowed. The gold was bright, seeming to burn with light. *The glow of the beast.* The wolf within.

"*Your eyes are glowing.*" She squeezed her eyes shut. Counted to ten. Prayed that she was having some kind of really, really bad dream.

"What have you done to me?" she whispered, but didn't open her eyes. Because she was afraid.

Madison Langley, ex-officer of the law, was scared to death.

She was terrified that she was becoming her worst nightmare.

The touch of his hand against her cheek made her flinch.

His fingers curled around her chin. Tilted her face up. "Look at me." An order.

Her eyes snapped open and she glared at him.

He glared right back. "People don't become werewolves because they get bitten."

"I am *not* a werewolf," she gritted. Something else was happening to her. Something that he'd done.

He kept talking, as if he hadn't heard her words. "Werewolves, my kind, we're born this way."

No. Hell, no. She jerked away from him, stumbling back, her shoes sliding into the stream. Her fangs pressed against her lips. *Fangs.* Her hands lifted to her mouth. She needed to touch them, to feel—

Her eyes widened as she stared at her hands. Her nails were gone. No, not gone. Changed. Her short, pale fingernails were longer, darker. Oh, God, they were *claws.*

His glowing stare pinned her. Hunger, need looked back at her from the depths of his golden eyes.

She gulped. Damn. He was so tall, so strong and sexy. Her sex tightened as her gaze drank in his gloriously nude body.

What was wrong with her?

She was turning into a monster and she couldn't stop lusting after Alerac. She'd just had him, had that thick cock in her body, just come so hard her sex still quivered.

Yet she wanted him again.

"You did something to me." Her arms wrapped around her body and she began to rock back and forth. Maybe he'd put her under some kind of compulsion. Maybe she'd been more susceptible than she'd thought.

Sure, she'd trained to fight mind control. Brennon had spent months teaching her to build mental shields. But perhaps her safeguards weren't strong enough.

Alerac was a powerful *Were.* He could have broken through her barriers, planted the suggestions, twisted reality.

Yes, that was it. Madison exhaled heavily. She'd been placed under a compulsion. He'd made her want him, made her think that her body was changing, transforming.

But it wasn't. She didn't really have fangs. She wasn't really becoming a were—

"Passion stirs the beast," he told her softly. "When we're together, when we mate, the beast comes to the surface."

When we mate.

For one terrifying moment, she actually felt her heart stop. "We-we're not mated." She knew about werewolf mating. The *Weres* mated for life, just like real wolves. It was said that a *Were's* mate was picked at birth, and werewolves could only have children with their destined partners. When *Weres* bonded, the union lasted forever.

Alerac just stared back at her.

"No." She couldn't, *could not,* be mated with him. It was just another of his tricks, another compulsion. "You're just trying to plant ideas in my head. Trying to make me believe—"

He grabbed her arms, jerked her against him. Water splashed against his bare legs. "Believe this," he snarled. "You're mine. *My mate*. I've been searching for you my entire life, and now that I've found you, I'll never let you go."

Madison shook her head. Tried to jerk free but found his hold unbreakable. "Y-you're putting ideas in my mind, making me think I'm turning, making me think I want you—"

The growl that rumbled in his throat had the hair on the nape of her neck rising.

"I didn't *make* you want me." His glowing eyes narrowed. "Your body responds to me because it recognizes its mate."

And her body was responding. Her nipples were tight. Her sex eager. She had no control with him. None. "You've put a compulsion—"

"I tried, the damn things don't work on you!" His fingers tightened around her arms, and she felt the faint sting of his claws. "Probably because you're a *Were*."

A loud ringing filled her ears. Her skin felt hot, fiery hot, then icy cold. "I. Am. Not. A. Werewolf."

"Oui, cherie, you are."

"No, no I can't be! I'm not a monster, a murderer—"

"Careful, *cherie*."

But she didn't want to be careful. She was trapped in a nightmare, a horrible nightmare. She wanted to scream, to snarl at him. Because… this couldn't be happening. She couldn't be one of those creatures! "*Weres* are m-monsters," Madison barely managed to choke out the words. "Killers." They slaughtered innocents, ripped out their throats, clawed—

Alerac whistled softly. "That bastard sure did a number on you."

Brennon hadn't been the one who'd made her fear the *Weres*. She *knew* what they were like. Her parents' torn and bloody bodies had told her all about the nature of the werewolves. She lifted her chin, stared up at Alerac. "Werewolves are killers." And she was not a killer.

"Not always."

Yeah, that wasn't exactly reassuring. "Let me go," she whispered.

He gazed down at her, held her tightly. One minute. Two. Then his hands fell away, but he didn't step back.

She lifted her arms, looked at her hands. Her breath rushed out of her in a relieved rush when she saw that her nails were back to normal. *Oh, thank God!* Her tongue slipped over teeth, checking for the sharp points of her fangs—*they weren't there!*

"The change will come again," he told her softly. "The wolf is in you."

"The hell it is!" Madison didn't understand what had just happened, but she knew one thing for damn certain—she wasn't a *Were*. She turned away from him, began to stomp across the stream.

"Why do you hate us so much?"

His voice stopped her cold.

"Why, Madison?"

She looked back at him, glancing over her shoulder for the briefest of moments. "Because *Weres* killed my family."

His eyes widened. "I-I didn't know. I'm sorry, *cherie*."

He sounded so sincere. So damn sincere. Suddenly, she had to know. Needed to know… if Alerac was like the others. Or if maybe, just maybe, he was different. "Have you… ever killed, Alerac?"

Alerac's jaw clenched.

And she knew his answer before he even spoke.

Her knees started to shake. She'd thought, *hoped,* that maybe she was wrong. He hadn't attacked her when he'd become a wolf back at the house, he'd stayed in control then, he'd—

"I did what I had to do." His quiet words cut through her swirling thoughts.

"What you had to do?" She repeated. "Just what the hell does that mean?"

"You were a cop, Madison. Don't tell me you never had to pull the trigger."

She hadn't. Once, she'd come close. When she'd stumbled onto a robbery, seen a guy holding a knife on a grandmother who'd been so scared her entire body shook. The perp, a kid in his teens whose eyes had been bloodshot and whose body smelled of cheap liquor and cigarettes, had refused her order to drop the weapon. Instead, he'd run toward her, lifting his knife, screaming at the top of his lungs.

She'd managed to take him down, to knock the knife out of his hands and pin him to the ground. But in the split second when he'd first charged her, her finger had trembled on the trigger.

"Cops do that, correct? They kill… in order to protect."

Her arms were chilled. "Is that what you did? You killed someone because you were protecting yourself? Protecting someone else?"

His lips tightened.

The night seemed quiet. Too quiet. The only sound she heard was the faint ripple of the stream. After a moment, she turned to fully face him. "Why'd you do it, Alerac? Why?" *Why'd you kill a man? Was it because of the wolf? Because you can't control the monster inside of you?*

He opened his mouth to reply, but then stopped. He jerked his head to the side, staring into the darkened woods.

She actually felt the tension that swept though him. "What is it?"

Alerac's gazed stayed locked on the woods. "We're about to have company." His lips twisted. "They're persistent bastards, I'll give them that." Then he grabbed her, scooping her off her feet and tossing her over his shoulder.

"*Alerac!* Put me down right—"

His hand swatted her ass. "*Quiet.*" He ran across the stream and her body bounced against his strong shoulder as she squirmed against him.

He carried her into the thick brush. Lowered her onto the ground. Madison scrambled to her knees as Alerac crouched beside her and peered through the bushes. "What are you—"

He grabbed her hands, held them tight in one of his, and slapped his other hand over her mouth.

"*Mrrph*!" Oh, he would pay for that.

Then she heard the voices. The shouts. Her eyes widened as she stared across the stream at Brennon and his men.

Alerac's mouth was right next to her ear. "Do you want to go back to them?" he whispered, and his breath brushed across her, sending a shiver over her body. "Or do you want to stay here with me?"

Stay with him? He was a killer. He'd just admitted it to her.

Her gaze swept over Brennon's team. They were all armed. She couldn't tell if those were tranq guns or the real, I'll-kill-you-now variety.

Damn. Her life had changed so fast on her. Her best friend had tried to kill her. But Alerac... Alerac had gotten her out of there. Carried her for miles.

He'd had the chance to hurt her, she realized. He could have killed her, if that had been what he wanted. But he hadn't. He'd never hurt her. Hell, the guy had even been taking special care not to jar her wounded arm.

He was supposed to be a mindless killing machine. A beast without a conscience.

"What's your choice?" he whispered, lowering his hand from her mouth.

Madison swallowed. "You." She might have just made the worst mistake of her life, but she was staying with Alerac.

And she would find out exactly what in the hell was happening to her. Because if he'd spoken the truth, if he hadn't put her under a compulsion, and she'd really started to transform—

Then she could be the thing she'd always feared most. *A Were.*

Chapter 7

The glow of the headlights fell on Madison's body, highlighting her gorgeous legs and the bare expanse of her arms. Alerac stayed crouched in the bushes as the approaching pick-up slowed. His muscles were tense, tight. Damn. He didn't like using Madison as bait. Every instinct he possessed screamed against having her out there, exposed on the road. And if that truck driver showed any signs of—

"Would you stop growling?" Madison snapped, never taking her eyes off the truck. "We don't want this guy to hear you."

His teeth clamped together. They'd stumbled upon the road ten minutes ago. Then Madison had gotten the brilliant idea of flagging down a car.

"I'm a woman. Alone. Trust me, folks will stop for me. They'll want to help." Her words rang in his head. She'd slanted a speculative glance down his body. *"I don't think they'll stop for a naked man."*

He'd agreed to go along with her plan, mostly because he hadn't actually expected anyone to be driving on the deserted road. When the faint shine of the headlights had appeared, Madison had let out a squeal of delight and then shoved him in the bushes.

His eyes narrowed as the truck pulled to a stop and the driver's door opened with a squeak. Oh, this was definitely not his idea of a good plan.

The driver sauntered around the pick-up and whistled softly. "What you doin' out here all alone, honey?"

Alerac glared at the guy. His night vision showed the fellow clearly. A young man, tall, lean, a guy probably in his early twenties, with beady eyes, a nose that had been broken more than once, and a scraggly black beard.

"My car broke down." Madison shrugged, and the guy's squinty eyes dropped to her chest.

He'd better not even think of—

"I could sure use a ride back to town," Madison continued, her voice just the faintest bit husky.

Alerac's hands balled into fists.

The jerk stepped closer to her. “Oh, honey, then I guess this is your lucky night.” He licked his lips. “Or maybe it’s mine.”

Alerac lunged from the bushes. He grabbed the asshole’s collar and shoved him back against the truck. “No, it’s not.”

“Wh-what—Man, you’re naked!”

Oh, he was an observant ass. Deliberately, Alerac smiled, flashing his fangs. The guy’s beady eyes got pretty wide.

“Ha!” Madison stepped to his side. “Told you it would work.”

He lifted his head, glared at her.

She smiled back. “It worked.”

“Get in the truck,” he snapped. The idiot human looked at her again, his gaze on her legs. Alerac felt the man’s lust. The lust for *his* mate.

“Get in the—” The guy’s mouth opened and closed like a fish. “Hey! That’s *my* truck!” His furious stare shot back to Alerac.

“*Oui*, but you’re going to let us borrow it, aren’t you?” Alerac called on the power of the wolf, pressing a compulsion into the other man’s consciousness. He knew his eyes were glowing with power when he said, “You’re giving us the truck for the night, and you’re going to stay here until I send a car back for you.” Once he got to the Compound, he’d send a guard to retrieve this… good Samaritan.

The human’s Adam’s apple bobbed as he swallowed. “I’m gonna stay here,” he muttered. “You’re takin’ my truck.”

“Right.” Alerac glanced down at the man’s body, his eyes narrowing. “And I think I’m also going to take your clothes.”

Madison wasn’t talking to him. Alerac slanted a quick look at her as he sped down the highway. She was staring out the window, her gaze on the endless stretch of pine trees that guarded the road.

She’d watched him with the human. Seen him control the fellow’s mind. And then she’d looked up at him, stared him in the eyes and said, “You’re one scary guy, Alerac.”

Then she’d turned around and walked to the truck, her shoulders stiff.

She’d been giving him the silent treatment ever since.

Damn, but what he wouldn’t give to know what was going on in his mate’s mind right then. *Scary.* Hmm. That wasn’t exactly the way he wanted her to think of him. Strong. Sexy. Those were good descriptions.

But scary—scary wasn't the sort of word a woman would use to describe her lover.

"Turn here," Madison said, the husky sound of her voice causing his hands to jerk on the wheel. "We can take this exit and be in downtown Atlanta in twenty minutes."

He didn't slow down. Made no move to turn.

"Alerac?" From the corner of his eye, he saw her finally glance at him. "Didn't you hear me? We need to turn—"

"That's not the road we need to take," he told her softly. He looked at her, a quick, hard perusal. Her eyes, her big, blue eyes, looked tired, almost bruised. He wanted to take her into his arms and hold her close, protect her from the world.

She looked so fragile just then. So delicate. She'd been through hell in the last few hours, and he wanted to get her to safety. But, well, he had a feeling she wasn't going to like his safe house.

Madison swallowed. "Just what road do we need then?" She paused a beat then demanded, "Where, exactly, are you taking me?"

The next exit loomed up ahead. That was the exit he needed. "I'm taking you home."

Her thumb jerked behind her. "My home's that way."

Not anymore. "The Compound is about twenty miles north of here."

Her head shook in a definite "No" manner. "Forget it, wolf. There's no way I'm goin' there. That place is *Were* central."

Which was exactly why they needed to get there, fast. He needed to tell his pack leader, Gareth, about Brennon and his men. About Scions Laboratory and the *Weres* who were being held there. He needed to discover if Gareth could find out any information about Madison's parents.

Weres killed my family. He didn't doubt her claim. Like humans, *Weres* could be good… or they could be complete bastards. The only difference between them was that *Weres* had a fierce strength, an undeniable power that made them perfect killing machines. If a *Were* went rogue, then he could easily leave a trail of terror in his wake.

His own sister Lisa had been murdered by a rogue werewolf when she'd been just a girl. He'd been the one to find her body, her bloody, broken little body, in the woods.

Her eyes had been wide open, her mouth frozen in a scream. And she'd just been… thrown into the bushes. Tossed away by her killer.

Lisa. His little Lisa.

But he'd gotten vengeance for her, he'd made Rafe—

"Who's Lisa?"

"What?" His head snapped toward her. She was staring at him, her blond brows drawn low. "What did you say?"

Her lips thinned. "Lisa," she repeated. "You just said her name."

His gaze turned back to the road. They'd be at the Compound soon. Madison would be safe and—

Her hand touched his arm. He flinched.

"Alerac? Who's Lisa?"

"*Mon seour.*"

"Your sister?" Her hand still pressed against his arm. Her fingers felt so warm against his skin. "I didn't know you had a sister."

"Lisa... Lisa's dead. She died many years ago." She'd been the last female *Were* born to their pack. Females were rare, very rare. Every female birth was celebrated among his kind. The packs exchanged news of females instantly—to birth a female was a cause of immense pride.

That was why he didn't understand Madison's existence. The woman had to be *Were*. Had to be. All of the signs were there. Hell, he could even smell the wolf on her. He should have known about her. Gareth should have known. A female couldn't have escaped notice by the packs.

Her breath exhaled heavily. "Oh, Alerac. I'm sorry."

So was he. He moved his arm, captured her hand, held it tight against his own. "You would have liked her. Everyone liked her. Lisa was so sweet and funny. I swear, I think she was always laughing." Until the end, when she'd screamed and screamed, when she'd screamed so loudly he'd felt the psychic echo of her agony.

There were at the entrance to the Compound now. Two guards stood near the entrance, patrolling, but when they saw Alerac, they waved him inside, instantly opening the heavy metal gates.

Madison unsnapped her seat belt and moved to his side. Her head pressed against his shoulder. "It's hard, isn't it? Losing the ones you love. No matter how much time passes, that emptiness, that ache—it's still there."

She would know. Her parents' deaths—they were so similar to Lisa's. Yes, Madison would know how she felt. She would understand exactly. He parked the truck. Turned off the engine. Took her into his arms and kissed her. Kissed her with all the hunger and need he had. Because he did need her. So desperately. *Madison.* After years of emptiness, she was his hope for a future. For a true family once again.

He would do everything in his power to keep her by his side. To make her happy. To make her love—

The driver's side door was wrenched open. "Well, damn, Alerac," a disgruntled male voice rumbled right next to his ear, "we thought you were in trouble, not out with some—"

Alerac's head turned toward the voice. "Careful, Michael." The words were a warning.

His cousin merely smiled. Then Michael Morlet's gaze dropped to Madison. "Who is she?"

My mate. He had to bite back the words. "Where's Gareth?" He needed to talk to him first. "We've got problems." *Big problems.*

He climbed out of the truck and pulled Madison behind him. She struggled against him, so he had to give her a sharp tug as she muttered, "Look, Alerac, I don't think I should—"

"You are… familiar to me." Michael's blue eyes narrowed on Madison. "Where have we met?"

She rubbed the bridge of her freckled nose. "You guys do catch everything, don't you?"

Alerac kept her pinned to his side. "Officer Langley has been here before." He didn't like the glint in Michael's eyes as he studied her.

"Officer Langley?"

A snort of laughter came from behind them. Alerac turned to see Michael's *petite* mate, Kat, sauntering toward them. "So you've been in jail, huh, Al?" She tossed her red hair over her shoulder and smirked at him. "No wonder the pack couldn't find you—you were in the slammer."

He slanted a quick look at Madison. "I was locked up, but I wasn't exactly in jail."

Madison's face flushed.

"Your scent…" Michael stepped closer and stared intently at Madison. "I could swear that—"

Kat elbowed him in the ribs. "How many times do I have to tell you to stop sniffing other women?"

He grabbed her hand and kissed her palm, but he never took his gaze off Madison.

Alerac stepped in front of her. "I need to take Madison inside."

"Madison, huh?" Kat smiled. "I thought she was Officer Langley."

Madison stiffened her shoulders and stepped around him. "Look, there's something you all need to know." She glanced at Michael, bit her lip, then looked at Kat. "I, ah, kidnapped him."

Michael burst out laughing.

Kat's smile widened. "Huh. With these guys, it usually works the other way."

Madison frowned at her. "No, really, I kidnapped him."

Michael's laughter slowly faded away. His head cocked to the right as he studied her.

Alerac captured Madison's wrist and pulled her toward the house. "We need to get inside." He sent Michael a hard glance over his shoulder. "Company's following us."

Michael nodded, a nearly imperceptible move. "I'll alert the guards."

"Do it. And tell Gareth that I need to see him right away." His jaw clenched as he remembered Brennon and his armed men. "Someone's hunting the pack."

Chapter 8

Oh, shit, she was in werewolf central. Madison paced the confines of her room, her palms damp with sweat, her heart racing.

She should have tried to run from Alerac. Tried to jump out of the pickup.

She should *not* have gone meekly with him to packland.

Dammit. Her hands tightened into fists. Alerac had been gone for over three hours. Talking to Gareth Morlet, the pack leader, telling him about Brennon, about Scions.

About her.

Madison didn't exactly understand the packs, didn't understand all the nuances of how they worked, but there was one thing she knew: anyone who attacked a pack member was punished. Severely punished.

At the bar, she'd been the one to shoot Alerac. She'd drugged him and kept him in silver chains.

She was so screwed.

A knock sounded at her door. She spun around just as Alerac walked in. Alerac, and a tall, too-handsome-to-be real man with midnight black hair and dark, molten gold eyes, eyes a shade darker than Alerac's.

Her throat was suddenly very, very dry because she knew, she *knew* that she was staring at the pack leader. Gareth Morlet.

"*Bonjour, mademoiselle.*" He inclined his head toward her.

"Uh, hi." *Shit.* Was this the part where he ordered her killed? Imprisoned?

Alerac smiled at her and crossed to her side. "Gareth has a few questions for you."

Great.

"This… Brennon… who is after *Weres.*" A pause. "You know him well?"

"Well enough," she responded somewhat hesitantly.

"He is your lover?"

Her what? Madison's jaw dropped.

"No," Alerac snarled before she could answer. "The bastard's damn well not."

"H-he's a friend." Her lips thinned. "Just a friend." Or he had been, until he'd tried to kill her.

"So, the two of you were hunting werewolves, is that it?"

Oh, yeah, he was definitely getting ready to kill her. "Something like that," she muttered.

"Why?"

Beside her, Alerac stiffened. "I told you about her parents."

"Ah, *oui*." Gareth's golden eyes were calculating and very, very cold. "Vengeance. A lust you both share."

Now what the hell did that mean?

Alerac growled softly. Gareth's upper lip curled in the slightest of responses.

The tension in the room was suddenly, suffocatingly thick. Madison stepped between the men. "Look, I helped Brennon, okay? I was on his team. I've been with him since I was sixteen. Since the day I walked into my house and found a werewolf crouched over my mother's body." She could still smell the blood. Still see the two covered bodies that had been brought out of the house. "I thought *Weres* were killers, mindless monsters, that they deserved to be captured. That they *had* to be captured so that society would be safe." Safe from the wolves who stalked the night, safe from the wolves who killed, ripped, tore—

"What made you change your mind about us?" Gareth asked softly.

"Ah…"

He stepped closer to her and his nostrils flared slightly. "What made you decide that we aren't monsters?" His hand lifted toward her cheek, his nails were razor-sharp claws.

Instinctively, she brought her own hands up, ready to attack him, ready to fight, ready to—

Her nails were claws again. Madison yelped and stumbled back. As she stared at her fingers, the claws slowly receded. "Oh, God…"

"So it's true," Gareth murmured, nodding his head. "You are one of us."

Blood tells, it always tells. Brennon's words echoed through her mind.

Madison shook her head. But she didn't know what she was denying. Gareth's words. Brennon's. Or the truth right in front of her.

"You have a choice, now, *mademoiselle.* You can join our pack, help us to free the *Weres* at Scions, or…"

"Or what?" She lifted her chin, stared into his glowing eyes. She didn't like ultimatums, not one damn bit.

His cheeks hollowed. His fangs lengthened. "Or you can be our enemy."

Alerac growled and put his hand in the middle of Gareth's chest. He shoved the other *Were* back, hard. "Don't fucking threaten her, Gareth."

The pack leader's eyes widened. "You challenge me?"

"For her? Damn straight." Alerac's claws were out. "She's mine. *Mine.* And no one, *no one*, is going to touch her but me."

"Fine." The word was barely human, more the growl of a beast. "Then I suggest you claim her now. Bring her into the pack. Make her one of us." Then he smiled, a chilling sight. "Or else I *will* consider her an enemy." He turned on his heel and stalked from the room. The door slammed behind him.

Alerac exhaled heavily.

Madison stared at the vibrating door, not sure what had just happened. Had Alerac just challenged his pack leader, *for her?* "Uh, Alerac…"

He turned to her, and his golden eyes glowed, just like Gareth's. He walked toward her with slow, measured steps. The steps of a hunter who knows his prey cannot escape. His hand lifted, stroked her cheek. "There's no choice any longer."

Her fingers trembled. She knew what he meant. *The bonding.* The werewolf bonding. Unless she wanted to find herself considered enemy number one to Gareth and his Weres, she had to accept Alerac and his claim on her. Had to become part of the pack.

Not even in her worst nightmares had she imagined this. Joining a pack. Become mated to a *Were.* But Alerac—he wasn't like the others, she knew that. He'd had so many chances to hurt her, to kill her, but he hadn't. Even when he'd become the beast, he'd never attacked her. *He'd protected her, even as a wolf.*

The mindless killing rage she'd seen in other *Weres* hadn't appeared. He'd stayed in control.

He was so different from the others.

God, she was actually starting to trust him. With her life, and maybe, just maybe, with her heart.

"Join with me," Alerac whispered, his stare heavy upon her own. "I swear to you, Madison, I will care for you as no other could, I will protect you, shield you from any danger that threatens." His fingers pushed back an errant strand of her hair. "And I will give you all that you desire in this world."

She realized the thing she desired most was… him. Alerac. Tall, golden Alerac. With the muscles of steel and the touch of a lover. Her lover. Taking a deep breath, Madison accepted the fate, the man, who waited for her, and she said good-bye to her old life. "I'll do it, Alerac. I-I'll bond with you." But not because Gareth ordered it. Because she wanted him.

Alerac.

Her *Were.*

"What are you doing, Gareth?"

Gareth Morlet turned away from the wooden door, a satisfied smile on his face.

Trinity Morlet's gaze narrowed as she eyed her mate. "That's the room you assigned to Madison." She knew, she'd taken the quiet blond there earlier.

"Um." Gareth sauntered toward her, bending to press a hot kiss to her neck.

"What were you doing in her room?" A small lick of jealousy shot through her. Damn. This whole mating thing was still new to her, and finding her mate/husband coming out of another woman's room with a satisfied smirk on his face was not the kind of thing that made her happy. Definitely not.

Trinity pushed Gareth away from her neck. The man wasn't going to distract her when she was working herself up to a fine state of extreme pissiness.

"Relax, *ma belle*. I was just helping Alerac." He tried to lower his head toward her throat again.

With an effort, she managed to hold him back. "Helping him? How?"

A faint Gaelic shrug. "His need for the bonding is great. So I merely… sped things up for him, and for his Madison." He caught her hands in his, and his mouth found the soft curve of her neck. When his tongue pressed against her pulse point, her knees turned to jelly.

"Ah… okay… but… don't let me catch you in her… room… oh, that feels good… again." Cause she'd hate to have to hurt the blond.

Gareth laughed softly. His breath fanned over her skin. "My love, you know there is no other for me."

Yeah, and he'd better not forget it.

He licked his way down her neck as he lifted her into his arms. "And now," he murmured softly, "there will be no other for Alerac."

Alerac watched as Madison paced toward the bed. His hands clenched as he fought the urge to just go to her, to strip her clothes, to toss her on the bed and claim her. To give her his bite. To bond them.

Take it slow. Slow. He had to take it slow. He didn't want to frighten her, and he'd heard from others that the bonding could be overwhelming.

They'd both changed clothes when they'd arrived at the Compound. Trinity had donated a shirt and a pair of jeans for Madison.

She faced him, and her fingers lifted to the buttons of her blouse, opening the material and exposing her flesh to his hungry gaze.

"Will the bonding hurt?" she asked, and there was curiosity in her gaze, but not real fear.

He hoped not, but he wasn't going to lie to her. "I don't know."

The blouse dropped to the floor. She wore a thin scrap of black lace across her breasts. The mounds of her breasts spilled over the edges of the bra, and he could just make out the tight press of her nipples. He licked his lips, already tasting that sweet flesh on his tongue.

"Trinity gave it to me," she muttered, and he saw her gaze drop down to the bra. "It's a little small for me but..."

But it looked damn good on her. It pushed her breasts up, lifted the plump mounds and, through the black lace, showed a tantalizing glimpse of her nipples.

Oh, *oui,* it looked damn good on her. His cock was already fully erect, the length pressing against the fabric of his pants.

Her hands dropped to the top of her jeans. Her fingers trembled.

"Madison?"

She didn't look at him, but kicked off her borrowed sandals, and pushed off her jeans. "Wh-where... um... should I just lie on the bed?"

A tiny pair of black panties matched her bra. His mouth went dry.

Alerac crossed to her. He took her chin in his hand, forced her to lift her gaze, forced her to look at him.

Fear lurked in the depths of her eyes now.

Damn. He didn't want her afraid. He wanted her hungry, desperate, so aroused that she begged for release. "Do you trust me, Madison?"

She swallowed, then nodded. "Yes."

Relief swept through him. "Good." His hands skimmed down the smooth skin of her shoulders. Her trust was a very precious gift, and he'd make damn sure she never regretted putting her faith in him.

She would belong to him, and he would treasure her for the rest of his life.

But first… first he would take her. The beast would claim his mate.

He kissed her, pressed his mouth against her faintly trembling lips, pushed his tongue deep inside and tasted her. His hands squeezed her slender hips, pulled her against the thrust of his cock. Alerac wanted her to feel his hunger, wanted her to know how much he lusted for her.

His mouth fed on hers. Hunger, voracious need, bloomed within him. His fingers slipped under the edge of her lace panties, eased down to the thatch of hair between her thighs. The scent of her growing arousal filled his nostrils, and he knew, even before he touched her sex, that he would find her wet, hot.

Her cream coated his fingers. He pushed into her heated core, buried two fingers knuckle-deep into her pussy while he worked her clit with his thumb. She moaned, and her breath caught on a choked sound of pleasure.

"Alerac… oh, yes… deeper." Her hips squirmed against his cock, and she jerked open his shirt, sending buttons flying to the floor.

Oh, he would give her deeper…

Alerac pushed her back onto the bed. Staring into her eyes, he lifted his hand and licked her cream from his fingers. Her pupils dilated as she watched him. Her skin flushed.

Her legs were spread for him. Her breasts pushed against the top of her bra, the nipples just peeking out at him, tempting him.

He wanted those nipples in his mouth.

Alerac stripped, tossing his clothes onto the floor. Madison's eyes followed his every move, and when his pants fell, her gaze dropped to his cock. And she licked her lips.

He froze. Every muscle in his body became rigid.

Those lips… that little pink tongue… he wanted to feel her mouth *on him*. Alerac stepped to the edge of the bed.

Madison pushed herself up.

He stroked the length of his cock, wanting her mouth on him more than he wanted his next breath.

Her hands reached out, wrapped around his thick length, and stroked. Pumped. From base to tip, over and over, smooth sure glides that had his cock tightening even more.

Her eyes were bright. Her breath panted out in excited gasps. Her sex was wet for him. And he'd never wanted her more.

When she slid off the edge of the bed, and fell to her knees before him, his control nearly shattered.

Her soft hands still cradled his cock, stroking him. Madison leaned forward and her breath blew over the head of his erection. "I think it's my turn… to taste," she whispered, glancing up at him from beneath her lashes.

His muscles were locked tight. He was so damned ready for her that—

Her index finger moved in a slow circle over the tip of his cock. When she lifted her finger, it glistened with moisture. Madison brought the finger to her lips and sucked it slowly.

A growl rumbled in the back of Alerac's throat. He didn't want her to suck her damn finger. He wanted her to suck him, wanted her to take his cock deep into her mouth and work him with her pink tongue until he came.

His fingers tangled in her hair, urged her forward. She'd started this, and he would make sure she finished it.

Her breath fanned over his erection, a soft, slow exhalation of air that just teased him, made him nearly mad for her.

She didn't take him into her mouth. Didn't close the one last inch that separated them. "Madison…" Her name was a groan, a hungry, desperate groan. He needed her mouth.

She smiled up at him, hesitated a second longer, then took him into her mouth.

"*Ah, Mon Dieu, that's good.*" Her mouth was so warm and wet around his cock. So fucking perfect. Her tongue swirled around him, her cheeks hollowed as she drew him in deeper, deeper…

His spine tingled. His balls tightened, and it took every ounce of his self control not to come right then.

But he had to claim her, had to bond her to him. Had to take her in the way of his kind.

Slowly, and damn regretfully, he loosened his hold on her hair and pushed her away.

Madison blinked up at him, her lips red, her eyes slightly dazed and languorous with desire. “Wh-why did you stop me?” For a moment, uncertainty clouded her features. “Didn’t you like—”

He stroked her cheek. “*Cherie,* I liked it too much.” *Far too much.* Alerac lifted Madison to her feet. “This time, I must take you my way.”

A pleased smile curved her lips. “I liked it, too,” she whispered. “I like the way you taste.”

Did the woman want him to beg? He clenched his hands. It was either clench them, or grab her and shove her onto the bed. And he was trying, very hard, not to break down and become a beast with her.

But the woman sure wasn’t making things easy on him. “Madison…” Her name was a hoarse cry. His control held by a thread.

Her smile widened. Her hands lifted, unhooked her bra and eased the straps off her shoulders. The bra fell to the floor. Still staring at him, still smiling her seductive, inviting smile, she lifted her hands, cupping her breasts, offering them to him.

His control shattered.

Chapter 9

Alerac's eyes began to glow, and when he lifted his hands toward her, his nails shifted into claws.

The beast had come out to play.

A strange, hot bolt of excitement shot through her, and she knew this was what she'd wanted. She'd wanted to push him, to drive him past control, to force his *Were* nature to the surface.

She wanted him, all of him, man, *Were*. Everything.

And she was sure as hell going to take him.

Madison reached for him, wanting to touch his cheek, but he snagged her hand, his fingers locking around her wrist in a tight, unbreakable grip.

"You've roused the wolf," he growled, and his voice sounded different. Deeper. Rougher. A shiver skated down her spine. "Are you ready for him?"

An answering hunger swelled within her. A dark, consuming hunger.

His gaze dropped to her bared breasts. Then his head lowered toward her. Her nipples were already so tight, aching with arousal, that when his mouth touched her, she couldn't control the pleasure-filled gasp that sprang to her lips.

His mouth locked on her nipple, the faintest edge of his teeth pressed against her flesh. Not hurting her, no, oh, no. His bite felt too good to ever be termed pain.

His tongue licked her nipple. His mouth sucked her. Her sex tightened, creamed.

She wanted him buried balls deep inside of her and thrusting, thrusting hard and fast in her until she came. Until he came, until the terrible, burning hunger inside of her was quenched.

Her skin felt too tight. Too hot. She moaned, rubbing her body against his. She needed him, craved more—

Alerac spun her around.

"What are you—"

He pressed her face-down upon the bed. Shoved her legs apart.

The soft mattress rubbed against her breasts. Tickled her belly. Madison lifted up onto her elbows, not certain of what Alerac had planned. She glanced back over her shoulder, her heart racing. "Why did you—"

His cock rose from the thatch of hair at his thighs. Thick. Long. Fully aroused.

God, she couldn't wait to feel him inside her.

She tried to roll over, ready to jerk off her panties and feel that cock driving into her.

Alerac's hands flashed down, caught her hips and pinned her to the bed. "*My way*, Madison."

She gulped.

His fingers moved to caress her buttocks. Slid between her cheeks. Again, she tried to roll back toward him, but his left hand held her hips trapped against the bedding.

His fingers teased her, stroked lightly, oh, so lightly, then he pushed his hand between her thighs. A gentle scrape of his claws against the tender flesh of her legs. Just the barest of touches.

Fabric ripped. Was torn apart.

Cool air swirled over her sex. The bed creaked as Alerac moved. He pushed her thighs farther apart. One inch, two. Then she felt his mouth on her. Felt the warm, wet press of his tongue against her clit.

Madison buried her face against the bedspread and shuddered.

Alerac was relentless. His tongue rasped over her clit, again and again, teasing the sensitive flesh, then he stabbed deep into her pussy, wringing a desperate, muffled cry from her.

His tongue, God, his tongue…

She tried to jerk away from him, but there was no escape. None.

Her hands clutched the soft bedspread. She shoved up onto her arms. Her climax came closer, closer…

And still he worked her with his mouth. Licking. Sucking. Stroking her clit. Filling her with his tongue.

"Al-Alerac!" Her climax burst over her in a blazing wave of pleasure. Her knees dug into the mattress and she bucked beneath him.

His tongue licked her once more. A long, swirling lick that made her shudder.

His hands lifted her hips. His cock pressed against her sex, the thick tip just entering her pussy. "You'll be mine, now," he growled.

She already was. Madison knew it. Just as he was hers. This wolf, this *Were*, was *hers*. She pushed back against him, trying to force him inside.

But he held back. Just teased her with the head of his erection. Just pressed lightly against her hyper-sensitive clit.

His head lowered. His fingers caught her breasts, fondled the nipples, squeezed her, plucked. His breath blew against her ear. "Ask for my bite, *cherie*. Ask for it."

Oh, damn, she was nearly ready to beg for it. His fingers teased her breasts, stroking her tight nipples, sending currents of desire shooting through her body.

She was so wet for him. Her sex was spread completely open, ready, so ready, for that first, deep thrust. "Give… give me your bite."

He licked her neck. She shuddered.

The faint prick of his fangs scored her flesh. Madison tensed—

His cock drove into her, deep, hard. Filling her completely, filling every inch of her sex. So full, so thick. So hot.

So damn good.

Madison moaned. Squeezed her eyes shut. Her hips slammed back against his. Harder. Faster. *Faster.*

She braced herself on her hands and knees. Alerac surrounded her, and the faint thud of flesh against flesh filled the air.

His teeth, oh God, his teeth… they were on her neck. A light, tender bite.

While he fucked her, hard and deep.

A second orgasm was building. Her body tightened. Shoved back against his. "Alerac—more!"

He growled and thrust.

Madison came with a half-scream, her body bow-tight. His teeth bit into her flesh, the fangs piercing her skin.

Her breath caught. In that instant, in that one, shattering instant, a tide of feelings, memories, swamped her. She felt hunger. Lust. Need. Love. Fear. Rage. She saw flashes of Alerac. Saw him with a young girl, running through the woods. Saw the same young, blond girl—oh, God, she was covered in blood, her lips parted in a scream of silent agony. And then she saw Alerac again, standing over the body of a white wolf. The white fur was matted with blood. The wolf shifted, became a man, a man with a stream of red pouring from his chest.

The images ended in a swirl of darkness. A thick, consuming darkness. Madison felt Alerac's body against hers, felt the reassuring strength of his touch. She tried to call out to him, to ask about the images. The feelings—

But the darkness was too strong. It pulled her down, down…

Madison's eyes were closed, her breathing faint but steady. Alerac stared down at her, smoothing back a strand of her pale, blond hair.

They'd mated. Bonded. Their souls would be linked forever. He'd finally found the one woman who could complete him. Who would make his life whole. Who could give him children.

A *Were* couldn't have a child with just anyone. Their bodies had to match, their genetic codes be compatible.

There was no one more compatible for a *Were* than his destined mate.

He pressed a kiss to her brow, tasting her skin. When they'd bonded, in that instant when their spirits had linked, he'd had a flash of Madison's emotions. He'd felt her passion. Her lust for him. Her growing trust.

He'd also felt her fear. Fear of what Brennon would do. Fear… of herself. Of the truth she suspected about her own nature.

Alerac had felt her pain, felt the grief that still haunted her, and he'd seen an image, a brief, bloody image of a woman's body and of a wolf's glowing eyes.

The woman had been her mother, he knew it. He'd seen the blond hair, the pale mane an exact match to Madison's. Her nose, her mouth, just like Madison's.

But the wolf… the wolf who'd stalked toward him in the vision. Who had that—

"Alerac?" Madison blinked up at him.

His arms tightened around her. *His mate.*

She licked her lips. "That was… pretty intense."

Damn intense, and damn good. Being in Madison's body, feeling the tight clutch of her sex, the warm cream of her pussy, felt better than anything he'd ever experienced in his life.

His knuckles stroked against the curve of her breast. When she inhaled sharply, he smiled. His cock was already hard again.

Alerac lowered his head toward her breast, wanting to taste that sweet nipple once more.

"Alerac…" Her fingers touched his chest. "I-I saw what you did."

He stilled.

Madison shook her head. "I don't really understand what happened, but I *saw*. I saw the wolf. Saw you shoot it—him. Then—then I saw him change into a man."

Alerac didn't speak. He wasn't sure what to say. He'd heard before about the visions that appeared during the change. An elder had once told him that he'd see images from his mate's life, images of her greatest joy, or her greatest sorrow. The bonding stirred emotions, shared them, and if a bond was powerful enough, couples could exchange memories, just for a moment.

He'd seen the event that had shaped his mate. Seen the event that had shattered her as a teen, and made her hungry for vengeance as an adult.

Madison had seen into him, as well. She'd seen him murder Rafe with cold calculation.

"It's not what you think," he told her. Yes, he'd long planned to kill Rafe. At first, he'd thought to attack the rogue as a wolf. He'd longed to feel Rafe's neck in his jaws. Alerac had imagined ripping him apart with fangs and claws. He'd wanted the other *Were* to suffer, to howl in agony.

Just as his sister had.

Yet when the time came, he'd made a clean kill. A quick, clean kill.

An execution.

He'd been protecting his pack leader, protecting the pack, and stopping a murderer.

Would Madison understand? She'd been a cop. She realized there was evil in the world. She knew that some killers couldn't be rehabilitated. Knew that if you didn't stop them, they'd just keep killing, keep slaughtering the innocent.

"Tell me what happened." Her hand rested on his chest. A warm, soft weight against his heart.

"Rafe was rogue."

Her brows drew together. "Rogue? What's that?"

Alerac sighed. "Rogue is a term for a wolf that's gone bad." And Rafe had sure as hell gone bad. Very bad. "Rafe had gotten overwhelmed with the hunger for blood. Gotten a true taste for the kill, and that bloodlust drove him to slaughter—humans *Weres*, anyone who came in his path. He killed for the pleasure it gave him. For the thrill." The pack had hunted Rafe for years, dogging his heels as he fled across the world.

The pack had originally established the Compound just outside of Atlanta so they'd have a base of operations in the U.S. for tracking Rafe and the other rogues who hunted in America. Over the years, the other rogues had been caught, but Rafe... Rafe had been a tricky bastard.

Then the hunted had turned hunter, and Rafe had gone after Gareth and his mate, Trinity.

"Who was the girl I saw?" Madison's lips pressed together and a sudden knowledge filled her gaze. "It was your sister, wasn't it? The one you said died!"

His head moved in a slow nod.

"He attacked her, didn't he?"

"Yes." And so many others. Sometimes, he felt like he could still hear their screams.

Her brow furrowed. "You killed him while you were a man, not a wolf." She stared at him in confusion. "I-I thought *Weres* always killed in wolf form. Brennon said—"

"*Brennon* doesn't know everything about us," he snarled. He didn't like talking about this. Hated reliving the memories, reliving the horror of losing Lisa.

"I'm sorry." Her hand fell away from him, and he immediately missed the warmth of her touch.

No, he didn't enjoy talking about his past, but he wanted Madison to understand what he'd done, why he'd done it. "I stayed as a man because I didn't want to be overwhelmed by the *fureur de la mort*." No, killing Rafe hadn't been about rage. It had been about peace for the pack. Justice for Lisa.

"What's the... *fureur de la mort*?"

"The death rage."

Madison's eyes widened. "*What?*"

"A *Were* loses control during the *fureur de la mort*. Loses all reason. The only instinct is to kill." The beast ruled then. Ruled with savage hunger.

Madison looked a little pale. "Just how often do you guys suffer from these rages, huh?"

Great. Now he'd scared her. He stroked her arm, trying to soothe her. "Only in extreme instances. If our lives are threatened, if our mates or families are in danger. Then the strength, the rage of the wolf, can become overwhelming. The instinct is to fight, to protect, by any means necessary."

By any means necessary. His words echoed in her mind.

She remembered the *Were* she'd seen at Scions, the one Brennon had demanded she observe as part of her training.

The wolf had been out of control. Slashing. Biting. Destroying everyone and everything in his path. Until the guards had tranqed him.

"I told you, they're monsters." Brennon had glared at the Were as the guards hauled his prone body to a cell. "They kill without thought, without remorse. They're butchers. Butchers. We have to stop them."

"That's why he attacked the scientists," she whispered softly.

"What?"

Madison shook her head, realizing she'd gotten lost in the past. "There was a werewolf, at Scions. Brennon wanted me to see him, wanted to show me what *Weres* were like." Her gaze held his. "He attacked two scientists, nearly killed them before the guards were able to tranq him."

Now she understood. She understood why the *Were* had fought so hard, why he'd seemed so out of control.

Oh, God, what had she done? Why had she believed Brennon? Why had she helped him?

"Yes." Alerac inhaled softly. "And I think that's why your father… threatened you."

"*What?*" What in the hell was he talking about? "My father never threatened me! He loved me, he never hurt me, he—"

"I saw, Madison."

She pushed away from him, climbed from the bed and jerked on her clothes. "I don't know what you *think* you saw—"

He followed her, stalking her across the bedroom, but not bothering to dress. "I *think* I saw your mother's death. In a dark house. Your house. And I saw a wolf snarling at you, preparing to attack." A pause. "That wolf—its eyes were blue, the same blue as yours."

Oh, my God. No, no, that couldn't be true. That wolf hadn't been her father. Had. Not. Been. "My father died that night, Alerac. Just like my mother. Someone else was there, someone else killed them. *My father did not do it.*"

His lips thinned. "I can't say what really happened that night. But that wolf, its eyes—those *were* your eyes."

Sweat coated her palms. Her heart raced in a frantic rhythm.

"*Weres* are born with the gift of the wolf," Alerac continued in that same, implacable voice. "That means one of your parents, or both of them, had *Were* blood.

"You have the wolf inside you, *cherie.* I've seen it. Seen it staring out at me. When we bonded tonight, I felt the beast's power, felt it in your passion."

When she tried to shove past him and run to the door, he grabbed her arms, pulling her against him. "I saw into you tonight, felt your emotions, touched your memories. I *know* the wolf is there, and so do you."

"Why haven't I changed?" If she were truly a *Were*, she would have transformed by now. *Weres* changed when they hit puberty and—

"You were probably about to go through your first moon cycle… then you found your mother's body."

So much blood. Madison swallowed against the sudden dryness in her throat.

She'd started to fear that night. Begun to fear the creatures that hid in the darkness. And she'd started to hate. When the police arrived with their swirling blue lights that flashed across her yard and when the MEs rolled out her parents' covered bodies, she'd started to hate.

"That night, I think it changed you." His hands were still around her arms, but his hold didn't hurt her. "You locked the wolf deep in yourself, deep inside, and since then, you've been fighting your true nature."

Because she didn't want to be a monster.

"You can't keep fighting yourself. You have to let go of your control. Have to face the beast."

No. She wasn't ready to face the beast. Not yet.

"If you don't, if you kept struggling to leash the wolf, then one day, the beast *will* break free. Then you will truly lose control."

Madison didn't want to lose control. Because losing control, well, that was a bad thing in her book. Very, very bad. Especially if that loss of control caused her to have one of those damn death rages. *Death rages.* Not. Good.

Dammit. She had to get out of this place. Had to think. She sure as hell couldn't think with Alerac in front of her, gazing down at her with concern etched on his face and looking so damn gorgeous he scrambled her brain.

The man confused the hell out of her, and if she was going to make sense of the madness surrounding her, then she had to get away. If only for a little while.

His hands rubbed down her arms. "I've got Michael researching your family now. Your father had to be Lone, it's the only thing that makes sense."

Very damn little made sense to her then. "Lone?"

"Oui. He must have left his pack, otherwise, they would have come for you when your parents died." His eyes narrowed. "Perhaps he left for your mother, if she wasn't a *Were*, then—"

Enough. Madison jerked away from him. "I-I can't take anymore of this right now." *Lone wolves. Bonding. Rogues.* It was just too much.

A dull drumming filled her ears. Her hands shook. And, damn, but it was getting hot in there. So fucking hot.

One trembling hand rubbed against her forehead, wiped away the sweat on her brow. Alerac waited silently, watching her. Standing strong, still naked and sexy as hell. And gazing at her with those golden eyes of his. Eyes that saw too much. *Too much.*

One of your parents, or both of them, had Were blood. His words kept playing in her head, over and over.

If what he said was true, then her life, everything she'd always believed… it had been a lie.

Oh, God. She had to get away. Had to think, had to—

Madison jerked away from him, ran, and yanked open the bedroom door, sending it flying back against the wall.

Then she fled down the hall, not looking back.

The wolf within Madison was rising closer to the surface. Alerac studied the broken bedroom door.

The beast's strength already flowed through her body.

Soon, very soon, the change would come.

It was almost time for the wolf to play.

And he could hardly wait to play with Madison.

But first—first he had to take care of that bastard Brennon and his laboratory.

Because no one, *no one*, fucked with *Weres* on his watch.

Chapter 10

"What do you mean I can't leave the grounds?" Madison snarled.

The guard, who'd identified himself as Marcus moments ago, maintained his polite smile. "Sorry, ma'am, but I've got orders that you aren't allowed to leave the Compound."

Oh, hell, no. "And just who," she gritted, "gave these orders?"

"I did."

Alerac. Madison spun around. "What? Who the hell do you think you are? You can't keep me prisoner here—"

"Why not?" His lips curved in a half-smile and his dimple flashed. "That's what you did to me."

Her jaw locked. He was the right, the bastard, but that had been before. Before she'd understood about *Weres*. Before she'd made love with him. Before she'd started to have all these damn confusing feelings. "Look, I just want to get out for a while, okay? Clear my head." Think about her parents. About him.

His smile faded. "You can do that here." He motioned to the guard. "Go back to the gate, Marcus."

"Yes, sir."

Glancing over her shoulder, she saw the guard turn on his heel and return to his post. Right at the gate, blocking her exit. After scoping the area, she'd learned that a fifteen foot stone wall completely surrounded the Compound. There was no way she'd be able to scale that thing. Her only escape route would be through the gate—the gate currently blocked by Marcus and three other goons.

"It's not safe out there for you, not until Brennon is taken care of." Gravel crunched beneath Alerac's shoes as he stepped toward her.

Madison glanced back at him. "Taken care of? What does that mean, exactly?"

"He's a threat to the pack. He's got to be neutralized."

Neutralized. Killed.

"I'm taking a team and going to Scions tonight."

Her breath caught. "You're going to free the *Weres.*"

He nodded.

And she knew what she had to do. Finally, she understood how she could fight the guilt churning in her gut, how to make things right. "I'm coming with you."

"What?"

"You heard me." She lifted her chin. "I'm coming with you."

"The hell you are."

Oh, yes, she most definitely was. Her index finger jabbed against his chest. "I'm going. Look, I was on Brennon's team. I listened to him, believed that crap he fed me. Now I have to help those men, I have to get them out." Or she'd never be able to sleep at night. She'd keep picturing them, imagining them in their cells, hearing their howls.

For an instant, his hard face seemed to soften. "I'll get the men out. I give you my word. No *Were* will be left at Scions."

That wasn't good enough. "I'm going."

Alerac shook his head. "It's too dangerous. I won't risk you—"

"I *have* to go." A low growl rumbled in her throat, and a dark, swirling anger began to churn within her. She'd been a fool, listening to Brennon all those years. Trusting him. Now it was her turn to set things right. "I'm not asking you, Alerac. I'm telling you. I'm going to Scions."

It was time for her nightmare to end.

A muscle flexed along his jaw. He opened his mouth—

"You heard the lady." Gareth stepped out from the guard station. "Looks like she'll be going to Scions with you."

When the pack leader gave an order, you didn't ignore it. Unless, of course, you wanted to find yourself dead.

But when Gareth had told him to take Madison to Scions, Alerac had come close, very close, to fighting his friend.

He'd only held back because of Madison. He'd sensed her desperate need, seen the determination in her glittering eyes.

He'd felt her guilt, knew the heavy weight she carried on her shoulders. His mate wanted to atone for the things she'd done. For the things she thought she'd done.

So he'd agreed to take her. Not because he'd been ordered, but because he couldn't bear to see the pain in Madison's eyes.

It was time for her to face her past, and he intended to make damn sure he was with her every step of the way.

The lead SUV pulled to a stop in front of Scions. Michael had gathered Intel on the lab, and his team was ready to break in and destroy all the evidence of a *Were* population.

Two other black SUVs braked behind them. His team was back there, getting ready to storm the lab. Just a few more minutes...

Alerac grabbed Madison's wrist before she could open her door. This was the last chance he'd have to talk to her before they went inside, and he wanted to make damn sure she understood the situation. "You stay with me, *comprenez-vous* ? Every single moment. You stay with me."

Madison glared at him. "I was a cop, remember? I do know how to handle myself."

Fuck that. "You stay with me," he repeated. "You move when I say move. If I tell you to get out of there, then you damn well better obey me." He jerked her across the seat toward him.

"Alerac—"

His mouth crashed down on hers. His tongue thrust past her lips. Her breasts pressed against his chest. Her nipples were tight, hard. He wanted to strip her out of her black turtle neck, to jerk off her slacks. His cock was iron-hard with the need to thrust into her. *Mon Dieu,* but he wanted to bury himself in her as deep as he could. Right there.

Dammit, he didn't have time. Not now. But he had to touch her. His hand slipped between their bodies, dropped between her legs. Rubbed against her sex.

"You're... not... ah... playing fair."

His fingers strummed against her core. "Oh, love, I'm not playing."

Her hips twisted against him and a low moan built in her throat.

"We go in, you obey me, obey *every* order I give, and when we get out," he lowered his head, licked her neck, tasted her skin, "when we get out, I'm going to thrust so hard and deep into that silky pussy of yours that you'll *know* you're mine."

Madison's fingers tangled in his hair. "I already know that," she whispered. "I've known it since the first time you touched me."

His head snapped up. His cock was fully aroused, ready to thrust into his mate's sex. "What?"

Her tongue snaked out, licked her bottom lip. "I think you heard me."

He wanted her to say it again. He jerked open her slacks, shoved them down her hips. Pushed his fingers under the edge her panties. "Say it again."

"Ah… God, Alerac!"

He rubbed her clit. Felt her cream on his fingers. Good, his mate was ready for him. Already aroused. That would make it so much easier… He pushed his fingers into her pussy, felt the tight, wet clasp of her heat around him. So fucking tight…

His body shook with hunger, but he couldn't take her. Not with his men right outside. Not with them so close.

No, he couldn't make love to her, but he could have a taste of her. A taste to hold him until later.

His head lowered over her throat. His fingers plunged deep.

Her body jerked against his, and he realized her climax was close. Madison was just seconds away from coming, but not yet—no, not just yet…

"Tell me again," he whispered, his breath blowing over her skin, his fingers pulling out of her sex. Teasing her clit. "Tell me again that you're mine."

"*Aler—*"

"Shh… love, not so loud. The others are just outside." He kissed her, drove his tongue deep into her mouth just as he buried his fingers in her pussy.

His fingers thrust into her, again and again. He rubbed, stroked, thrust.

And felt the tell-tale tightening of her climax.

His head lifted, his fangs burned. "Tell me!"

Her eyes, burning blue, met his. "I-I'm yours!" She came, shuddering, shaking against him.

He kept his fingers inside her, waited until the last tremor left her body. Then he withdrew. Brought his hand to his lips and finally got his taste.

Madison watched him, her breath ragged. He smiled at her. "When the mission's done, I'll have you."

Her hand moved in a flash, stroked the thick length of his cock. "And I'll have you, wolf."

A soft knock sounded against the tinted driver's window. Alerac stared down into Madison's shining eyes. The beast was hungry for her, so fucking hungry.

He would have her. Soon.

His hand clamped over her wrist. Lifted her fingers away. Kissed her palm.

Then, before his self-control broke, Alerac pulled away from her, shoved open his door, and gave the order to start the attack.

Alerac didn't let her out of his sight. He stayed two steps in front of her for every move they made in Scions. He'd given her a gun, a Beretta that fit perfectly in her hand. Madison followed behind him, helping to free prisoners and guarding his back.

Her entrance code had still worked at the main door. She would have thought Brennon had changed it, but she guessed he hadn't counted on her returning to Scions so soon.

Lucky for them, but bad, very bad for that bastard.

Alerac's team was comprised of six *Weres*. They easily subdued the skeleton staff of guards and began to systematically destroy all the data stored at the lab.

It was almost too easy, really. Brennon obviously hadn't been expecting the attack, not so soon. Or else he would have had more guards on duty, would have changed some of the system's passwords.

Though they searched the facility for him, there was no sign of Brennon. Madison figured he was still out in the wilderness, searching for her and Alerac.

She only wished she could see the expression on his face when he returned to find his lab in ruins.

They freed over a dozen *Weres* from their cells, and when they burst from their prisons, Alerac made damn sure he was between her and any threat that might come.

The last cell waited, less than five feet away. Madison recognized the cell. It was *his* cell. The *Were* who had attacked the scientists. The one who'd changed before her.

She typed in her security code. Heard the soft swish of the locks disengaging.

"Step back, *cherie,*" Alerac's voice was a harsh whisper. "This one's different from the others. His rage… I can *feel* it."

Her jaw clenched but she obeyed his order. Alerac stepped forward, pulled open the door.

There was no light in the cell. Just darkness. Darkness—

And glowing silver eyes.

A fierce growl sounded from the back of the cell.

"Don't move," Alerac whispered.

The hair on her nape stood. Sudden, desperate tension surrounded them.

"We're not here to hurt you, *mon ami,"* Alerac held up his hands as he entered the cell. "We want to help you."

The silver eyes didn't so much as blink.

"Relax, *mon ami*, we're not—"

The wolf launched through the air with a snarl, heading straight for Alerac. Madison screamed as the beast rammed into him. The wolf drove Alerac to the floor and the creature's mouth—his glistening flangs—shot toward Alerac's throat.

Alerac's claws flashed up, and he caught the wolf before those deadly fangs could rip into his throat. "Not really the way you should greet your rescuer, *ami,*" he gritted, then threw the wolf across the room.

Madison switched on the lights. A gray wolf was slumped in the corner, and faint, rumbling growls came from his throat. The wolf climbed to its feet, shook his head, and began to stalk toward them.

"We aren't here to hurt you," Alerac told him, rising quickly.

The wolf kept advancing.

Oh, this wasn't good. "Alerac..."

The wolf froze.

Slowly, oh, so slowly, the wolf's head turned. His silver eyes locked on her. His mouth pulled back into a snarl.

Shit.

The wolf lunged for her.

Madison threw up her hands, ready to claw him, to fight—

Alerac grabbed the wolf before he could touch her. He wrestled the creature to the ground and Alerac was growling... *changing* before her eyes.

Clothes ripped. Bones snapped. Fur rippled across his skin. A horrible howl filled the air. And as she watched, Alerac stopped being a man, and he became a wolf. A big, furious, white wolf. A wolf with bright golden eyes. With long, razor sharp claws and bared fangs.

He attacked the other wolf. Biting. Clawing. But the gray wolf fought back with desperation.

Howls of rage, of pain, echoed in the cell. Blood dripped onto the floor. The wolves crashed around the small room, fighting with furious intensity.

And she could only watch as Alerac battled the other *Were.*

The other wolf—he was a bit smaller than Alerac. Thinner. But the beast attacked viciously. His teeth slashed across Alerac's back. His claws raked Alerac's side. More blood spilled onto the floor. Their paws slipped in it—

"No!" Madison ran toward them. "Stop it! Stop it!" She tried to step between them, but Alerac shoved her back with his body.

The other wolf dug his claws into him.

Alerac snarled, the sound a terrible combination of rage and pain.

Then he turned on the gray wolf. He moved so fast, his body actually seemed to blur before her. His jaw snapped, his fangs ripped, and in seconds, he had the other wolf pinned beneath him, the beast's throat between his teeth.

Madison licked her lips. Alerac gazed down at the other *Were*, his huge body tight, his claws buried deep into the creature's side. And unless she was very wrong, he was moments away from killing the gray wolf.

The wolf they'd come to save.

"Alerac..." Her voice sounded weak, *too* weak. Dammit. She tried again, "Alerac."

He didn't look at her. Just stared down at his prey.

Madison crept toward him. Her shoes made no sound on the concrete floor. Her hand lifted toward him. Her fingernails had lengthened into claws. Hmm. She was almost getting used to that now.

Crouching down beside him, she reached out, touched the thick white fur, stroked him, tried to soothe him. "He's not fighting anymore, Alerac. You can let him go now." She didn't know if the wolf *could* fight anymore. His breathing was shallow, his body covered in blood.

The white wolf's jaw relaxed. His fangs released their hold on the *Were's* throat. Then Alerac looked back at her.

His fangs were stained red. His eyes glowed with a bright, hungry light. His hot breath blew across her face.

Madison froze, and she waited, *waited...*

He bumped his nose into her shoulder, pushing her back. Madison scrambled to her feet. Alerac kept pushing her. Another step. Another. He kept pushing until she was across the room. Then he changed. She heard the sickening crunch of bones, saw the fur melt from his body. Saw his skin stretch. His front paws shifted back to human hands, his back paws turned into feet.

In less than a minute, she was no longer staring at a wolf. She stared at Alerac. Her Alerac.

And he looked seriously pissed off.

"What the fuck were you thinking?" he snapped.

Uh, oh.

He grabbed her arms, shoved her back against the cold stone wall. "Don't you know better than to get between two wolves? We could have torn you apart!"

Yeah, she'd thought about that. Thought about that damn *fureur de la mort.* But when it came right down to it, well… "I couldn't let you kill him," she told him simply, meeting his gaze directly.

"And there was no damn way I was going to let him kill you," he growled. Then he kissed her. His tongue licked her lips before driving deep into her mouth.

She kissed him back. With every ounce of passion in her, she kissed him back.

A faint groan reached her ears.

Alerac pulled back, swearing. They looked down at the fallen wolf. But he wasn't a wolf anymore. He was a man. A man with dark hair. With a handsome, but haggard face. He rose carefully to his feet.

There was no sign of injury on his nude body. His muscles rippled as he stood. He bowed his head toward Alerac.

Alerac's jaw clenched.

Madison pushed his hands aside and stepped forward. The guy didn't look like he was in the mood for a fight, but she could still feel the tension rolling off Alerac. "Ah, look, we really aren't here to hurt you."

His head lifted and his eyes, no longer glowing, but now a faint, gun-metal silver, met hers. "I know you."

She nodded.

"I've seen you, with those bastards."

Alerac tensed.

"Yes." She'd been with them. But no longer.

The man looked between her and Alerac and sudden comprehension filled his gaze. "You're… his mate."

She was still getting used to that one, but… "Yes." Madison drew in a deep breath. "I know this probably isn't going to mean anything to you now but, I'm sorry, okay? Sorry for the hell you've been through. Sorry I didn't help you sooner. Sorry you've been locked up in this cell for—"

He lifted his hand, and his fingers trembled. "Little sister, you didn't put me here."

Little sister. "But I didn't get you out…"

He glanced toward the open door. "Looks to me like that's what you're doing now."

Yeah, but as the saying went, it was *too little, too late*. The man had suffered, the other *Weres* had suffered.

"What's your name?" Alerac asked.

"Fallon. Fallon Drake."

"Your pack?"

Fallon shook his head. "I'm Lone."

"We have cars waiting outside," Alerac told him. "Our pack has a place near here. You can recover with us."

Fallon nodded. "I'd appreciate that." His gaze met Alerac's. "I… didn't mean to attack. I-I haven't been myself in quite a while. When I saw the woman, when I smelled her, I thought the guards were coming again." His lips twisted. "And I was so fucking tired of them."

"Go." Alerac pointed to the door. "You've been here long enough."

A faint smile curved his lips. "Damn straight."

Fallon turned and left the room. Naked, proud. He never glanced back at his cell.

Madison sighed, heady relief filling her. It was over. The *Weres* were all free. Alerac's team should be finished destroying the files. Brennon wouldn't have his precious data.

It was over.

Alerac's head jerked to the side.

"Alerac?"

His eyes were on the door. "I thought I heard…" He broke off, shaking his head.

She reached for his hand, looked up at him. At his strong, handsome face. He'd fought to protect her, used all of his strength to keep her safe.

Her Alerac. Her wolf. In that moment, as she stared into his golden eyes, she knew, *she knew*, that she'd found more than just a lover. She'd found her future. A future with her *Were*.

Her breath blew out in a nervous rush. "God, Alerac, I swear, I think I love—"

A gunshot rang out, and as she watched in growing horror, a circle of red bloomed on Alerac's chest.

Then he fell to the floor.

"No!"

Chapter 11

Brennon stood in the doorway, a small, black gun in his hand.

"You fucking bastard!" Madison fell to her knees beside Alerac. Blood. So much blood. She touched his chest, tried to staunch the wound. Her fingers were instantly soaked in this blood.

"Don't waste your time," Brennon told her, and she looked up to find him smiling down at her. "I aimed for his heart. Oh, and Maddie, the bullet was silver."

Oh, God.

"Your wolf will be dead in minutes."

No, hell, no. Not when she'd just found him, when she'd just realized she loved the gorgeous, arrogant as hell *Were*. No, no, he couldn't leave her.

"Get up." Brennon pointed the gun at her.

She didn't move.

He cocked the hammer of his gun. "I said get up."

Alerac barely seemed to be breathing. His eyes were wide open, staring at the ceiling.

Alerac.

"It's a pity, I had such plans for you." Brennon sighed. "Then you went out and started fucking the animals."

"Alerac isn't an animal!" She snapped, jumping to her feet. Anger churned within her. A hot, boiling anger that filled her belly, that rose, building higher, higher…

Her skin began to sting. Hot, then icy cold prickles crawled across her flesh.

Her teeth burned. Her vision sharpened, narrowed on him. Brennon.

He'd shot Alerac. He'd shot her mate. *Her mate.*

She growled, a hard, furious tremble of sound.

Brennon's eyes narrowed. "What are you—"

A lancing pain knifed through her stomach and Madison doubled over, gasping. The pain ripped through her, snaking down to her legs, then to her arms, her head.

Brennon whistled. "Sonofabitch. I always wondered about you. Wondered if you'd be like your mother or your father."

Her hands began to jerk. Her body to spasm. She looked back up at Brennon, saw him staring down at her in fascination.

He licked his lips, lowered the gun. "I kept waiting, hoping… Never had a female *Were* before…"

Madison cried out as the pain burst over her. Vaguely, she heard the crack of bones. The world seemed to explode into a ball of light. A bright, shining ball of light.

Then… it was over. She blinked. The pain was gone. She felt different. Stronger. Every muscle in her body felt alive, and so damn strong. Her vision was sharper. She could see the sweat sliding down Brennon's cheek. Could hear the fast thud of his heartbeat.

The bastard had a smug smile on his face now. He'd lowered his gun, and he *was smiling* at her.

"You can change me," he said, desperate elation in his voice. "You can change me. A female can transform a male, I'm sure of it. You can bite me, then I'll be like you. Your father, he said he couldn't change me. Said I couldn't transform. But you—you can do it. A female can change me, I know it!"

She stalked toward him, her feet moving softly on the floor. She had to tilt her head back to better see him.

"I tried to get him to change me, you know. I tried everything. When he wouldn't—I got him back. I got him!"

Brennon's words came hard and fast, and he stared at her with wide, excited eyes.

"I killed his bitch. Left her body for him. Then I took care of him. Shot him so many times even his *Were* blood couldn't save him!"

Madison stumbled to a halt as his words registered in her mind. He'd killed her parents. A rogue *Were* hadn't killed them. *Brennon.* Brennon had killed them. All these years… he'd lied to her. Betrayed her.

Suddenly, she understood. The wolf she'd seen that night—it hadn't been trying to attack her. It had been *protecting* her. The wolf hadn't tried to bite her, it had guided her back to the door, to safety.

And the wolf had stayed inside, stayed to face Brennon.

"Come here." He motioned with the gun. "I need a bite from you, just one bite. Then I'll change. *I'll change!*"

Oh, she'd give the bastard a bite all right.

"M-Madison…"

Alerac's voice. Weak. So very weak. She glanced at him. Saw that his eyes were on her now, and they were filled with wonder, a soft, loving wonder.

"Y-you're b-beautiful, *cherie*."

"*No!*" Brennon's shriek.

Her head jerked back toward him. He aimed his gun at Alerac. "You're gonna die, you hear me? You won't have her! She's mine! *Mine!* She'll change me, she'll—" His finger tightened around the trigger.

Madison lunged for him. Jumped through the air. Her claws were outstretched, her fangs barred. She slammed into his chest. Brennon screamed, stumbling back and ramming into the stone wall behind him. He hit it hard, then he fell to the floor.

Madison stood over him, panting.

His heart slowed. The thud was faint, weak. Her gaze lifted to his neck. It was broken. Brennon, her friend, the man who'd killed her parents, was dying.

A tear slipped from her eye.

And his heart stopped.

Madison paced outside of Alerac's room. Two days. Two damn days.

They'd kept Alerac in wolf form to aid the healing. Kept him as a wolf, kept him tied to tubes, monitors.

Two long days. The *Were* doctors had only let her in for the briefest of visits.

The silver bullet had tunneled into his chest, missed his heart by less than two inches. Thank God.

So much for never missing…

Lucky for her, and Alerac, Brennon had been an over-confident asshole.

She turned at the end of the corridor, started walking back. Yes, the bullet had missed his heart, but the silver had gotten in his blood. Made him so damn weak.

Her hands balled into fists. She needed to be inside with him. Needed to see him, to touch him—

His door opened. A thin, bespeckled man stepped outside.

It took all of her self-control not to grab the doctor and shake him.

He sighed when he saw her. Then motioned toward the door.

Madison stopped pacing. "Can I—see him?" Oh, he'd better say yes, he'd damn well better say—

"Yes."

She shoved past him. Ran into the room, and found Alerac, the man, not the wolf, in bed. Sitting up, looking as sexy as always, and smiling at her.

Madison jumped on the bed, grabbed him, and kissed him.

He kissed her back, and his arms rose, wrapped around her, and pulled her tightly against his bare chest.

Oh, God, but he felt good. She could hear the sound of his heart. Hear the strong, steady rhythm. Madison pulled back, gazed at his face, and snapped, "Don't you ever do a thing like that to me again!"

His brows lifted.

She swallowed. "I mean it, Alerac. I-I thought you were going to die on me."

He pressed a kiss to her brow. "*Cherie,* trust me, it will take more than a bullet to take me away from you." His fingers trailed down the vee of her blouse, teased the skin between her breasts.

Her nipples immediately tightened.

"You know," he told her softly, "you make a damn gorgeous wolf."

Her lips trembled.

"All that beautiful white fur," he continued. "Truly, the most beautiful wolf I've ever seen." His gaze held hers. "The wolf is no longer on a leash, *oui?"*

Her eyes wanted to tear, but she blinked, refusing to let the drops fall. "Yeah, she's free now." It felt so good to be free.

For the first time in her life, she felt whole. Complete. Her spirit seemed to soar. And her heart was full. Full of love for her mate.

The mate who was currently naked beneath her in bed. "Are you all right now, Alerac?" She knew that *Weres* healed fast, and he looked perfect to her. His chest wasn't marred by so much as a scratch. Thank God for that wonderful *Were* blood.

A knowing smile curved his lips. "Oh, yes, love, I'm quite 'all right.'" He stroked her hair. "I do know what can make me feel even better…"

And so did she. Her hands slipped under the sheets. Found his cock hard and ready. Her fingers tightened around him. "I seem to remember making you a promise." Before everything had gone to hell.

I'll have you, wolf.

His smile stretched. His dimple flashed. "Ah, I was hoping you'd remember that." His hands curved around her thighs, rubbed lightly against the soft fabric of her pants.

Then his fingers rose, pressed against her sex.

Desire lashed through her.

Her nipples pebbled against his chest. His hands lifted, and his fingers curled around those hungry peaks.

Oh, God, yes…

Madison had worried she'd never know Alerac's touch again. He'd been so frighteningly still when the *Weres* carried him out of Scions. But he was whole again. Whole. Strong. So wonderfully alive.

And hers. *All hers.*

Her fingers teased his cock. She could see the desire on his face, in his eyes. Damn, but she wanted this man. Couldn't wait to feel the hard drive of his cock inside her once again.

She squirmed against him, desperate to feel more of him. To feel—

"Ah, love, you're wearing far, far too many clothes…"

Yes, but she wouldn't have that problem long, not with her hungry *Were* already starting to work on the buttons of her blouse.

Alerac gazed into her eyes. "I've waited for you my whole life, *cherie.*"

Her fingers smoothed over the edge of his erection. "And I've been waiting for you." She'd been waiting, and hadn't even known. Hadn't even realized—not until they'd mated that first time and he'd touched her heart, her soul.

His hand lifted, stroked her cheek. "*Je t'aime.*"

Oh, Lord, she'd never been more grateful for her high school French class. "I love you, too, wolf."

And she would keep loving him.

Her wolf. Her man.

Her mate.

No more monsters. No more fears.

Just a lifetime of loving her *Were.* A lifetime of loving that was most definitely going to start *now.*

Madison scrambled from the bed. Kicked off her shoes. Shoved down her pants and panties.

Then Alerac grabbed her, tumbled her back onto the bed and pinned her beneath him.

The broad tip of his cock pressed against her sex. "Alerac…" It had been too long, she needed to feel the hot slide of his flesh to reassure herself that he was real. That he was whole. Alive and safe.

He drove into her. So deep that she shuddered. So thick that her whole body felt stretched.

So good.

He kissed her, pushing his tongue deep, and his cock thrust into her, again and again.

Her legs wrapped around him, pulled him closer. Closer…

His fingers strummed against her clit, and she came, her orgasm rocking through her. She grabbed him, pressed her lips against his throat, against his warm, golden skin, and she bit him.

His hips bucked against her, and he climaxed, his semen filling her in a long, hot rush.

Then his head lifted. His lips curled into a sexy smile. "Love, did you just bite me?"

Madison knew her eyes were glowing. She could feel the wolf within her, feel the beast's hunger… and its delight. "Oh, yeah. Want me to do it again?"

His own eyes were alight with an inner fire. He smiled at her, lowered his head, and whispered, "*Oui, cherie, oui.*"

Moonlight fell through the window, spilled across the bed. Madison realized that maybe, just maybe, being a *Were* wasn't so bad.

If fact, as Alerac began to thrust once more, she realized that being a *Were,* and being mated to one, well, it was pretty damn fabulous.

About the Author:

Give me ghosts, give me monsters—vampires, werewolves—all of those creatures that people fear, and secretly love.

Caged Wolf *is the third werewolf tale that I've written for Red Sage. My first werewolf story,* Bite of the Wolf, *appeared in* ***Secrets, Volume 15****, and my second Were story,* The Wolf's Mate, *was published in* ***Secrets, Volume 18****.*

I've had such a wonderful time writing about my werewolves, and I certainly hope you enjoy the tales, too.

I would love to hear from my readers. Please visit my website at www.cynthiaeden.com *or you may send an email to* info@cynthiaeden.com.

Wet Dreams

by Larissa Ione

To My Reader:

I've always loved stories involving strangers who find themselves alone, in danger, and mired in a situation where they must learn to trust each other in order to survive. Extreme stress strips people down to their essences, and through elements such as teamwork, honesty, vulnerability, and sacrifice, they develop intense bonds in short periods of time. I'm fascinated by this dynamic, whether the bonds form between lovers or friends, and I don't know anyone who hasn't gone through something similar. In *Wet Dreams*, Marina Summers and Brent Logan experience this dynamic firsthand when they must conquer dangerous men, rough seas, and their own fears in order to get out of a bad situation alive. Please, come aboard and share their story.

Chapter 1

Brent Logan had always wondered what being shot felt like. He'd expected pain. He'd expected blood. What he hadn't expected was the burning impact of the bullet, or the way it knocked him off his feet and sent him sprawling.

He hit the dock on his left hip and rolled into a ball, clutching his calf. "Fuck," he gritted out. "*Sonofabitch.*"

Sweat beaded on his forehead as he sucked panting breaths through his clenched teeth. Warm, sticky blood oozed between his fingers. Shit. He didn't have time for pain. Not when nearly a dozen arms-dealing scumbags chased him like a pack of starving wolves after a wounded deer.

Stifling a groan, he pushed to his feet and prayed his leg wouldn't buckle. The injury and sudden pain-induced nausea made standing difficult enough, but now the roll and pitch of the floating dock threatened to knock him on his ass again.

Wiping his hands on his jeans, he limped along the vast network of boat slips. He ducked between sailboats, catamarans and fishing boats, keeping low as he peered into the night at the outbuildings lining the shore. Lamps bathed sections of the marina in light, but elsewhere, he could make out the shadowy outlines of six men moving rapidly toward him, guns drawn.

Cursing the fact that he'd handed over his own pistol at the arms trade, he slipped between two massive yachts. A shot rang out, and a bullet punched a hole in the side of one of the boats, close enough that its wake blew a hot breeze across Brent's ear. Double shit. Dying wasn't on his to-do list tonight. Ignoring the stinging pain in his leg, he picked up his pace, weighing his escape options.

Here in the southern California marina, he had few.

He could stop, face off with the men chasing him, and get a bullet through the brain. If he was lucky.

He could jump in the water and drown.

Or he could hide on any of the hundred moored boats and hope the local cops showed up before the bad guys found him.

Not much of a choice, after all. He crouched low alongside a sailboat, his injured calf muscle twitching in agonizing protest. Ahead, a boat with the words "Wet Dream" painted on its stern bobbed in the choppy water, partially hidden by what was probably an expensive-ass yacht, but open enough on one side to allow for a good view of the scumbags.

Right now he needed a miracle, but a wet dream would have to do.

Marina Summers' body tingled. Her breath came in gasps. Her blood thudded through her veins as she raced toward an orgasm that had started in her dreams and followed her to her current state of semi-awareness.

Ephemeral, erotic images floated through her mind as the rocking of the boat lured her back toward slumber, but her body's need and the very real feel of her sweaty sheets kept her hanging on the precipice of consciousness. She had no idea if she'd had a partner in the sensual dream, but she knew she didn't have one in her bed.

With a sigh she wasn't sure reflected disappointment or relief, she slipped her hands under her T-shirt and slid them over abdominal muscles that were rigid and hard from years of heavy lifting but not a single sit-up. She caressed upward, until the flat of her palms skimmed her pebbled nipples, and her soft moan joined the slap of waves hitting her hull. Cupping her breasts, she stroked her thumbs over the rounded swells, sending a swirl of warmth curling through her veins. The heat felt good, and she sought more, dragging her hands lower, over her belly, beneath the waistband of her sweat shorts, and between her legs, where her silky moisture told her how ready she was for release.

How long had it been? Too long, if her body sought relief in her sleep.

She worked a finger back and forth between her dewy folds, and then circled her entrance before dipping two fingers into her core. Her slick walls pulsed around her knuckles as she drew her fingers in and out, but it wasn't enough. In her mind she conjured a man, a dark-haired, dangerous man to replace her fingers with his tongue. A whimper escaped her as his hot mouth opened against her, teasing, probing, licking.

She was close, so close. Tossing her head and arching her hips, she pressed her thumb against her throbbing clit, not sure if she wanted to delay or expedite the sweet conclusion. The sounds of her panting breaths competed with the pounding of her pulse for dominance in her ears, and the gunshot tried to intrude, but…

Gunshot?

No, no, no. She put the sound out of her mind and went back to her dream man. The one who plunged his tongue deep into her pussy to stroke her from the inside out, making her writhe and moan. The one who sucked her clit between his lips as his fingers—

Another shot. Closer. What the hell? Who would fire a weapon inside a marina, especially at this time of night? Not that it hadn't happened before. There had been the time party-goers on a yacht decided to shoot skeet at two A.M. Then there was the dumbass who got his jollies by shooting seagulls the night his wife left him…

Damn it! She was going to kill whatever idiot had interrupted *her* jollies. Cursing, she swung her legs over the side of the bed. Her bare feet hit the deck with a thump, and for a split second she considered putting on slippers, and maybe a robe over her shorts and cropped T-shirt, but the sound of a thud followed by the sudden violent rocking of her boat changed her mind. If some drunken fool had smacked her boat, she'd make chum of him.

She hurried out of her aft stateroom into the small salon living area and stubbed her big toe on the base of the dining table. "Ow! Shit." Hopping on her uninjured foot while holding the other, she glanced out of the windows, but all nearby vessels were moored. So what had struck her boat?

She grabbed her cell phone off the table, then dropped her foot and half-limped, half-hopped to the exit to the welldeck. A cool, rain-scented breeze washed over her face when she cracked open the door. Heart pounding with both uneasiness and unspent sexual energy, she swung the door wider and stepped cautiously over the threshold. She peered into the cloudy night, refusing to jump at the shadows splayed across the fiberglass deck she'd just installed.

At first glance, everything seemed normal. Silence hung over the marina. Her boat creaked as it rocked in its slip. Her new fighting chair and bait tank glinted beneath the dock's lights.

A strange man crouched in the shadows next to the door.

Holy shit. Her heart shot to her throat, trapping her scream.

He lunged. His hand clamped down on her mouth, and his other hand grasped her around the shoulders to drag her roughly into a kneel beside him.

"Be quiet," he whispered in a faint European accent she couldn't identify, his lips moving against her cheek. "It's all right."

All right? How was anything about this situation be *all right?* She wished she could turn just enough to see his face, wished she could peer into his eyes and get a good look at what she was up against, but so far the only thing she knew about this Eurotrash was that his size dwarfed her, his strength humbled her, and his stubbly jaw scraped like sandpaper against her skin.

Oh, and he smelled good, like spice and leather, with a hint of something not so good, something familiar but elusive. So he wasn't a fisherman, a strung-out junkie, or a drunk on a binge.

Who the hell was he, and what was he doing on her boat?

Not that it mattered, because the guy had picked the wrong woman to screw with. The greater part of twenty-six years spent in wharf-side pubs and on commercial fishing boats in the company of rough, macho fishermen had landed her in worse situations than this, and she'd always come out on top.

She fingered her phone and forced her muscles to relax, waited for him to think she wouldn't resist. For a long moment he held her tight, his own body rigid as though he were listening for something. The pulse in his palm bounded against her mouth, and then it slowed, and he loosened his grip. She breathed deeply, relaxed more.

"Good girl," he murmured, drawing back slightly.

Seizing the opportunity, she twisted, drove her shoulder into his ribs, knocking him flat on the deck. His low curse ended on a grunt when she kneed his leg as she scrambled past. She dove for the side of the boat tied to the dock. She had to get away from this nut.

The nut had other ideas.

As she reached for the rail, he tackled her, slamming her onto her belly so hard that the breath whooshed from her lungs. He clapped his hand over her mouth, and his heavy body pinned her so she couldn't move. Beneath her hip, her fingers twisted around broken bits of plastic. Her phone. Damn him.

"Look, lady," he panted into her ear, "I'm a federal agent. You need to be really, really quiet, okay?"

Did he expect her to take him at his word? He could be a serial killer for all she knew.

"Fuck you," she mumbled against his hand.

"Babe, any other day I might take you up on that offer, but now's not the time."

Funny guy. She could be funnier. Wrenching her neck upward for leverage, she sank her teeth into his hand. His harsh intake of breath told her she'd hurt him, but he didn't flinch.

"Let go."

If her lips hadn't been mashed into his palm, she'd have smiled. Instead, she bit down harder into the flesh she'd pinched between her teeth.

He hissed in pain, and then suddenly she was the one sucking air when he jammed a finger into the pressure point behind her jaw. She released his hand, and he let up on the pressure point. The pain melted away, replaced by a wicked throbbing sensation.

"Thank you," he said, as if she'd passed him the salt and pepper at the dining table. "There's a gang of heavily armed men searching the marina. Men dying to shoot me and feed me to the sharks." He paused. "Are there sharks?"

"Jump in and find out, asshole."

"That's not a very nice way to talk to a law enforcement official."

"How—" She tossed her head until he loosened his grip on her mouth so she could speak properly. "How do I know *they* aren't the cops and *you* aren't the bad guy?"

"Because if I was a bad guy, I'd have already killed you to shut you up."

Oh, yeah. He was a riot. A really *heavy* riot. She wriggled beneath him, trying to shake off some of his weight, and maybe the elbow he'd jammed into her ribs.

The nut who might or might not be a federal agent finally took the hint and eased off of her. With one arm around her waist, he pulled her up to her hands and knees. She breathed a sigh as her lungs fully inflated with air again, and then she groaned when she looked down at the broken remnants of her phone.

"Did I hurt you?" He kept a hand on the small of her back as he sat on his heels beside her. No doubt he wanted to be ready to slam her to the deck again if she tried to run.

"Your concern is touching," she snapped, keeping her voice low like he had. If he was being truthful, she'd rather not attract the attention of gun-wielding criminals.

She brushed her hair out of her eyes and turned to him. Oh. Oh, my. This wasn't your average thug. From his tight jeans to his white silk shirt and black leather jacket, he was all class. And from the neck up, he was all hunk. In fact, he might have been the very man she'd conjured into her fantasy.

His face, though mostly shadowed, appeared bronzed, the sharp angles and hard planes glistening with perspiration. His eyes… she thought they might be brown, but definitely dark, same as his hair he'd slicked back into a ponytail at the base of his muscular neck. A small gold hoop glinted on the lobe of one perfectly shaped ear. Normally she didn't go for men with long hair and earrings, but the contrast of foreign accent mixed with American speech, and rebel bad boy with classy rich dude fascinated her too much to dislike.

Not that she'd go for him in any circumstance. He was either a criminal, a federal agent, or Eurotrash, maybe all three, and none of those appealed to her. No way.

"Come here," he whispered, inching through patchy light and shadow toward the side of the boat, where he peeked over the rail. "Take a look."

Reluctantly, she crawled beside him. Her stomach bottomed out at the inky outlines of men using dark recesses to creep along the docks and sneak aboard moored boats. Funny how she couldn't see their faces, but the guns in their hands stood out like neon signs.

Oh, God, she didn't need this. Not now, not when so much was at stake—a new life, a new business. A new business which was scheduled to open tomorrow with her first set of customers.

"Get off my boat," she whispered.

"I can't. They'll see me."

"Then get into the water. You can hide under the docks."

He shook his head. "Not an option."

"It's your best option."

His jaw clenched, and his lips pressed into a thin, hard line. For the first time, she noticed the strained lines bracketing his mouth. He was either in pain or seriously stressed. Of course, if he hadn't been stressed in this situation, she'd have had to wonder about him.

"I can't swim," he ground out.

"Nice try."

"I'm serious. I can't even dogpaddle. Just being on this rustbucket is making me nervous."

Rustbucket? "I'll have you know, I've had this boat completely restored and overhauled. She's hardly a rustbucket. And if you don't like her, get off. Oh, wait. Wasn't that what I just told you to do?"

"Look, lady—"

"Marina."

He gave her a double-take, and she waited for the inevitable jokes, but he just shook his head. "Look, *Marina,* I need your help." He cast a quick glance over the rail, and she sensed more than saw his body go rigid. "Shit."

"What?"

"It's what's about to hit the fan."

Chapter 2

A woman screamed. Angry shouts tangled with the horrifying sound of her wail. Marina peered over the port rail and swallowed hard as two thugs dragged Dale and Helen Cavenaugh from the cabin of their yacht several slips away. The creeps forced the couple to their knees and held them at gunpoint while more thugs searched the boat.

"Damn." Agent Dude, if that's what he really was, rubbed a dark-stained hand over his face, and then dropped it to his thighs…

Thighs covered by jeans streaked with something that looked suspiciously like blood. He must have wiped his bloody hands on them. Oh, God, it was blood she'd smelled earlier, but more importantly, whose?

"I've got to draw them off or those people are going to be shark bait."

He started to stand, but in a move that surprised even her, she reached up under his jacket, grabbed the pocket of his jeans and yanked him back down beside her. It didn't escape her notice that the denim pocket lay tight on a very firm ass.

"Are you crazy?"

He frowned at her. "You just told me to go."

"Because I thought you were lying."

"And now you don't?"

"If you were a bad guy, you wouldn't care about those people." She grasped his hand and tugged. "C'mon. We'll sneak into the cabin. You can hide, and we can brainstorm a distraction."

He shook his head, which made his hair whisper against his jacket. "They'll see the blood. They'll know I was here."

She didn't understand until he gestured at the dark smears and droplets spattered on the deck. How had she missed them before? Then she noticed the wet stain surrounding a hole in his jeans.

"They shot you?" He nodded. Great. She didn't know the severity of the injury, but it would no doubt hinder him if he took flight. "I'm going to get my med kit."

He snared her arm. "We don't have time."

The voices on the yacht grew louder. One of the goons punched Helen in the face, and she dropped to the deck. Marina slid a glance at Agent Dude, whose mask of barely-controlled rage mirrored what she felt.

She held her breath. Remained absolutely still. Utter helplessness sank like a sour glob in the pit of her belly as she watched Dale throw a punch in an attempt to defend his wife. A bad guy brought the butt of his rifle down on Dale's head, sending him sprawling.

"Bastards," Agent Dude snarled. "I have to get them away from those people."

"No! I have an idea."

The rain she'd smelled earlier began to pelt the deck as she slipped into the cabin and snatched her keys off the table. Her hand shook, and she nearly dropped the keychain. She paused, allowing fear to consume her for the count of two, and then she took a deep, calming breath. She'd been in hairier situations than this, both at sea and on land when she'd been a paramedic.

Burying her terror as deeply as she could, she crouched so low her thighs hurt as she hurried back to the welldeck. A gust of windblown rain stung her cheeks as she unlocked a cupboard and removed her serrated dive knife. She unsheathed the blade, then crawled to each of the mooring lines and sliced through them, not wanting to spare the time to untie the knots.

Someone shouted. Running toward them at full speed, a man zigzagged across the maze of docks, gun drawn. The fear she'd buried a moment ago bubbled up, clogging her throat.

Agent Dude cursed. "Our secret's out. Give me the knife."

Marina went into overdrive. She slapped the knife into his palm and dashed through the cabin doors to the cockpit forward of the salon. Once again, her hand shook, and this time she dropped the keychain. Cursing, she scooped it up and jammed the key into the ignition. The engine coughed, sputtered.

"Come on," she coaxed. "Come on, sweetheart. C'mon, baby."

She didn't spare a glance back, too afraid of what she'd see beneath the marina lights. Instead, she pleaded once more with her boat, and finally, lights flicked on as the motor rumbled to life and settled into the most beautiful purring sound she'd ever heard.

"*Yes,*" she breathed, giving the helm a fond pat. "Thank you, little lady."

A shot rang out, and a bullet broke out the side window, showering her with glass. She yelped and gunned the engine. Slowly, too slowly, the forty-foot boat eased away from the dock.

She allowed herself a glance back now, and instantly wished she hadn't. Four men sprinted along the dock, closing fast.

"Get down!" Agent Dude shouted from his crouching position on the lit deck.

Rapid gunfire shattered the air. She sank down, peeking up over the helm just enough to steer. Thuds and cracks vibrated the boat. Damn them! She'd just paid a fortune—her life savings—in renovations, and those scumbags were shooting up her baby. Her dream.

She craned her neck around to see one of the goons reach the end of the pier and leap across the water at her rear deck. He hit the stern, half in, half out of the boat. His lip curled into a snarl that exposed ugly, big teeth as he struggled to climb inside, still holding a pistol.

Agent Dude lunged at the guy, and they wrestled for possession of the gun. Marina's chest ached with the breath she held as she alternately steered the boat out of the harbor and watched the two men struggle. Back at the dock, three men fired at them. Bullets crashed into the hull. One punched a hole in her cabin door—and punched fear straight into her wildly beating heart. She'd always wanted to die out on the ocean, but not like this. Not from a bullet.

The bad guy somehow held onto his weapon and the side of the boat—until Agent Dude smashed his fist into the guy's face. Once. Twice. On the third strike, blood exploded from the thug's nose, and he flew backward into the boat's wake, taking the gun with him.

Gunfire still thundered across the distance, but the bullets fell short, erupting in tiny splashes as they plunged into the water. Thank God.

"Go faster!"

Faster? She already had the craft at full throttle. Frowning, she turned. In the distance, through the veil of rain, she could barely make out the men as they sprinted back to the Cavenaugh's yacht. Oh, no. *No.* They were going to steal the boat and give chase. Why was her passenger so important to them?

On cue, her handsome stowaway limped to the bridge, either his injury or lack of sea-legs causing him to careen off bulkheads and furniture. "Did you hear me? Faster."

"We're going as fast as we can."

"You're kidding." He gripped the back of her chair to steady himself, and once again she caught a whiff of his scent, a masculine, clean smell that would leave a wonderful lingering impression on her sheets. And wasn't she insane for thinking such a thing at a moment like this? Then again, he *had* interrupted the finest sexual moment she'd had in months.

"That boat they're hijacking… is it slower than this one?"

She snorted. "Wet Dream's top speed is seventeen knots." She jerked her thumb at the ultra-luxurious Beneteau Antares. "That pretty lady? She can pull thirty. They can catch us without even trying."

"We can call the Coast Guard." His gaze flickered over the equipment in the cockpit. "Where's the radio?"

"Probably sitting in some guy's warehouse."

His head snapped up, and his dark eyes bored into her, even through the darkness. "What?"

"I've been renovating the boat so I can take my first sport fishing group out tomorrow afternoon. All that's left is for the new radio to be installed in the morning."

At least, that's all that had been left. Now she had bullet holes to patch, glass to replace, and water damage to repair if the bullets caused any leaks.

"No radio," he muttered in a voice thick with irritation. "That's fucking great."

"It wasn't like I expected to get underway while being chased by criminals tonight." She shot him a glare. "And if it weren't for you throwing me to the deck and breaking my phone, we'd be able to call for help."

He stared at her for a moment, his gaze intense, his lips set in a grim line that she suddenly wanted to see softened. A heartbeat later, he ran his hand over his slicked-back hair and heaved a sigh.

"I'm sorry I got you into this. It didn't occur to me that people might live on these things."

He spoke as though "these things" were a particularly nasty disease. But then, she should have expected as much after he called Wet Dream a rustbucket.

She gazed out into the darkness, where only the whitecaps of the rolling seas were visible. The slap-slap of the windshield wipers blended with the purr of the engine and the rhythmic wash of the waves on the hull. Too bad her rattled nerves prevented her from enjoying the comforting melody only those who loved the ocean could appreciate.

"What—" she cleared her throat of the sudden squeakiness in her voice. "—What happens if they catch us?"

She turned, looked into the dark depths of his eyes. She knew before he answered. But knowing didn't change how chills shivered down her spine when he said bluntly, "We'll die."

Swallowing the sudden lump in her throat, she swiveled around to face the stormy weather ahead. After all, the storm front before them scared her a lot less than the evil that pursued them from behind.

Chapter 3

Brent braced his hip against the back of a loveseat in the living room—he didn't know its nautical name; his boat lingo was limited to bow and stern. His position put him a couple feet from the woman he'd involved in a situation no civilian should have to be in. Her hands gripped the steering wheel with white knuckled tenacity as she guided the boat out of the bay and into open water, and bigger waves. Recessed lights in the ceiling revealed the terror apparent in her wide-set green eyes and the hard set of her jaw.

The moment they crossed the bar, she flipped a switch, and the lights snuffed out, leaving the cabin illuminated only by the eerie green glow of the radar. "I shut off the running lights." She cast a glance toward the rear of the boat. "I'm hoping they won't be able to see us out in the open."

"Do they have radar, too?"

She nodded, and her shaggy, dark bangs brushed across tan skin. Skin that had been cool and fresh against his lips when he'd held her down on the deck.

"I'm sure they do. But the goons might not know how to operate it, and even if they do, we won't make much of a blip. Not once we get into the squall."

"Squall?" He hoped his voice hadn't sounded as candy-assed to her as it did to him.

"Yep. Hold on." She spun the wheel to the right, and even with the warning, the craft's sharp turn knocked him off balance. The sudden weight on his injured leg sent searing pain streaking from his calf to his thigh. Damn. He'd almost forgotten he'd been shot.

She cast a sideways glance at him. "You okay?"

Only if agony was okay. "I could use an aspirin."

"Aspirin thins the blood. It'll make you bleed more."

"Thank you, Dr. Marina."

She shrugged, the motion lifting her cropped T-shirt and giving him a momentary but tantalizing view of the plump underside of her left breast. Of course, with the way her wet shirt clung to her breasts like shrink wrap, he didn't need to see bare skin. Every slope, every curve, and both hard nipples were perfectly outlined.

"I'm a paramedic. Well, I *was*. This is my job now."

"You gave all that up to live and work on a boat, huh?"

"I've done both my entire life."

He suppressed a shudder. He couldn't think of anything worse. Not even being shot. "Give me a dry, sturdy, high-rise apartment any day."

"Wow. Marriage would be a bitch for us."

A wave tossed the boat, and he gripped the love seat as firmly as he could without looking like a pussy. "Dating would be a bitch for us. Once I'm off this thing, I'm never stepping foot on another boat. Nothing good ever happens on boats."

He didn't know her from Columbo, but he already knew her sly grin spelled trouble. "Sex is good, and much better than on dry land," she said, and his body chose that moment to realize she had a low, sultry voice. "What with all the rolling and rocking."

Add to that sultry voice a body which would make a saint drool.

Oh, yeah. Bronzed, toned legs that disappeared beneath baggy pink sweat shorts, a flat belly and slim waist he could span with his hands, and a rack that begged a man to stare. He suspected her hot little bod could almost make him forget he'd been trapped on a boat. Almost.

"Yeah, well, I'll never find out about boat sex, because like I said, this is it for me."

"You get sick?"

He shook his head. "I hate the water."

She looked at him like he'd told her he hated daisies and kittens. Then she shrugged again, revealing even more breast, and went back to steering the boat through increasing rain and fog. How she knew where she was going, he had no idea.

Well, other than the radar and GPS. *Dolt.*

Rain pelted the windshield, and when the bow dropped into the trough of a wave, Brent's stomach went with it. No psycho criminal he'd ever faced had been as pitiless as the churning, white-capped ocean surrounding them. Give him Charles Manson, the Green River Killer, hell, Jack the freakin' Ripper, any day.

The boat took a rough swing upward, and his feet went one way, his body the other. His hip struck the sink to his left, and then he wheeled to right. He grabbed at the nearest object to steady himself. The object just happened to be Marina.

How he managed to not fall on his ass was a miracle. How he managed to end up with a beautiful woman in his arms was a godsend.

"Are you okay?" she asked, turning into him and standing there in the rocking heap of junk without so much as swaying. Even her steady, sultry voice didn't waver.

"You keep asking that."

"You keep falling," she pointed out, rather unnecessarily.

The boat pitched forward, giving him a perfect excuse to tighten his grip on her muscular shoulders. She looked up at him, which put her lips mere inches from his. How would those delectable lips feel beneath his? Would they be soft and pliant, or firm and demanding?

Un-freaking-believable. He was in one of the most fucked-up predicaments of his life, his leg screamed with pain, and yet, he wanted to kiss this woman.

Later, he'd do exactly that. But now wasn't the time or the place.

She arched a dark eyebrow. "You're staring at me. Why?"

"No reason." He took an awkward step back, but she moved with him.

"It's okay, you know. Kissing me, I mean."

Jesus. The woman's insanity matched his. He liked that. Liked it so much he completely ignored the clanging alarm in his head telling him something didn't jibe here, and he lowered head and touched his lips to hers. A spark of fire shot from his mouth to his gut, where it spread out like a net of warmth over his entire body. Whoa.

She put up with the polite kiss for less time than it took to load a gun magazine, and then she cupped the back of his head and held him while she flicked her tongue along the seam of his lips.

His fingers flexed on her shoulders, sinking into the firm muscles that spoke of frequent physical activity. No, nothing about this woman could be described as delicate, at least, not that he could feel, and man, did he want to feel.

He wanted to feel her skin on his. He wanted to feel her full breasts against his chest. He wanted to feel… wanted.

Yeah, asshole, because women so often wanted men they'd just met who had plunged them into danger.

Then again, she'd offered up the opportunity, was even now encouraging him to open up to her with a low moan and the firm thrust of her tongue.

Hungrily, he complied, swept his tongue passionately through her mouth. She tasted like toothpaste and sin, and Jesus, could she kiss. She wrapped her arms around his waist and moved more firmly against him so that her soft parts met his hard parts—some of which were growing harder than others.

Her scent, natural, subdued, like sun-warmed skin, made him long to taste more of her, to see if she tasted as good as she smelled. Earthy, womanly… he wanted to get down and dirty, to lick every sweet inch.

Smoothing his hand down her back, he cupped her ass, pressed her against his swollen cock. This was stupid, so stupid, but when she groaned and ground her belly against him, he didn't care. At this point, most of his thoughts originated from below the belt.

The boat rocked, and he braced himself against the wall next to the steering wheel. *The steering wheel.*

He tore his mouth away. "Uh, don't you need to drive?"

"Probably." She smiled, and damn if his breath didn't get sucked right out of his lungs. "But can I get your name first? I'm not exactly in the habit of kissing strange men."

"Brent Logan."

"Nice to meet you, Brent Logan." She stepped back, and suddenly the warm smile became a cold glare, and in her hand, she held a gun. A flare gun. A flare gun pointed at his chest. "Now, why don't you tell me who you really are, and why you no longer have an accent?"

Shit. Next time, when the clanging alarm rang in his head, his dick would have to ride shotgun instead of sitting in the driver's seat.

Marina kept an eye on the guy who had just swabbed her deck with the best kiss of her life, and wondered why she always hooked up with the freaks. She'd really thought this one might be a decent guy. But no, he'd been playing her with that phony accent, and had probably been faking his concern over the fate of the Cavenaughs. Like an idiot, she'd fallen for it, had managed to get herself stuck out in the middle of the ocean, alone with a man who could be a serial killer.

Making things more interesting, fate had thrown in a cloudy night and a storm. Son of a bitch. She'd been cast into a damned horror movie.

Brent—if that really was his name—held up his hands in a placating gesture. "Everything's cool. Why don't you put down the weapon?"

"Not a chance, bud." She shifted the gun to her right. Over his heart. "Now, who are you, and why are those men after you?"

"Look," he said, in a calm, composed voice, "my leg hurts and—"

"It didn't hurt so much that you couldn't kiss me, so I imagine you can take the pain for a few more minutes."

He quirked an eyebrow, not nearly terrified enough of her and her gun. "I could be bleeding to death."

"You aren't." She pointedly glanced at the fly of his jeans. "If you were, you wouldn't have enough blood for that boner."

"And here I thought there was nothing delicate about you."

"What?"

"Nothing. He crossed his arms over his broad chest. "You must have been a great paramedic. 'Don't worry ma'am. Sure, your guts are hanging out, but they've been that way for an hour, so what's a few more minutes while I drink my coffee?'"

Oh, she wanted to shoot him. Not kill him, though, because she'd love to kiss him again. Preferring to not examine the motivation behind that too closely, she motioned with the gun.

"C'mon," she urged. "Spill."

He scrubbed a hand over his face. She wondered if his stubble felt as rough on his palm as it had on her chin. Oh, but it had been a good rough.

"I told you," he sighed. "My name is Brent Logan. I work for a small, secret agency within the Department of Homeland Security."

"Got I.D.?"

"Sure. Right here in my pocket, next to the mega-phone I use to announce who I am."

"So, that would be a no."

The smartass gave a humorless snort. "It's not wise to carry a badge with you undercover."

"The accent was for the undercover work, then."

He nodded. "Once I told you who I was, I stopped playing undercover guy. Guess it took a while for the accent to wear off. Usually does, after a long gig."

"How long?"

"Five months."

"Who are you supposed to be?"

"A Basque middleman."

Which explained the clothes, the hair, the general look she found oddly appealing. Very odd, since she usually went for what she was most comfortable with. Gruff, unrefined, fisherman types.

"Middleman for what?"

He said nothing, merely watched her as though searching for a way into her brain. The sensation of being stripped bare, not of her clothes, but of her barriers, swept over her. No man had ever done that to her, had ever tried to figure her out, and it threw her off balance like the rocking boat never could.

"Middleman for what?" she repeated, a little less steadily, and she hoped he didn't notice.

His eyes narrowed, and he took a minute step closer, filling her vision with his broad shoulders. The cabin, which she'd always found to be spacious, closed in. "You aren't going to shoot me," he murmured, like he knew her better than she did.

"Oh yeah, Mr. Confident? I know exactly where to fire to maximize the pain but not kill you. You really wanna tell me I won't shoot?"

An arrogant jerk of his head, like he still didn't believe her, made his earring glint in the light from the radar. "I can't tell you everything, but what I can tell you is that the men chasing me are financiers for a terrorist organization. They're attempting to procure an experimental new weapon built for the U.S. Army to use against our own troops overseas. My cover was blown tonight during a meeting in one of the marina outbuildings, and I have information that will put a lot of people in jail. Good enough?"

Reaching out slowly, he wrapped both hands around hers that held the flare gun. For a moment she hesitated to let go, but her gut told her he'd been truthful, and she'd learned a long time ago to trust her instincts. Finally she released the weapon, and he placed it in the helm chair seat, his left hand still holding hers.

His strong, firm grip pulled her closer, so close that she had to tilt her head to look into his gorgeous eyes. "Thanks for not shooting me."

Did he have to say it like he knew all along she wouldn't? "The night's still young."

Squeezing her hand, he gave a theatrical groan. "I have a feeling this is going to be a long night."

She didn't voice her thoughts, that she hoped it *would* be a long night, because that would mean the bad guys hadn't found them and dumped their bodies into the ocean. Instead, she concentrated on the long, soothing strokes of his thumb over the sensitive skin of her wrist.

Though she'd never been the type of woman to need a man for anything, his touch sent a hot, pleasant stab of awareness through her body. She wondered if he could feel her pulse hammering, wondered if he knew what his caress did to her, if only innocently.

Then again, she had a sneaky suspicion there was nothing innocent about Brent Logan.

A sudden sputtering sound brought her out of her sensual trance. Dropping Brent's hand, she spun to the helm. The sputtering melded into a choking noise, followed by a tortured hiccup. Then, finally, silence. She checked the gauges, tried to restart the engine. The grinding whirr made her wince. Her poor, poor baby.

Brent watched, his lips pursed. "Well?"

"Well," she sighed, "the night is going to be longer than you thought. We're out of gas."

Chapter 4

"Out of gas? You've got to be kidding!"

Marina swore like a sailor. Which he supposed she was, in a way. He couldn't help but be impressed by the extent of her vocabulary.

"I thought I had a full tank. Damn it!"

He borrowed a few of her choicer words as frustration ripped through him. Had they been on dry land, he'd know what to do. Being stuck here in the middle of nowhere and stranded on a boat left him feeling useless and vulnerable and nervous as hell, three things he hated the most.

"What do we do now?"

She blew out a breath. "We deploy a sea anchor and drogue, pray the storm doesn't get any worse, and we patch you up before you bleed all over my new carpet."

He looked down and winced. "Too late."

"You're a real fun guy to have around, you know?" She fished a flashlight out of a drawer in the tiny kitchen and used it to point at the loveseat. "Sit. I'm going to anchor us and get my jump kit."

She passed him the flashlight and disappeared. He washed the dried blood off his hands and then eased down into the seat she'd indicated. For the first time since the shooting, he checked out his calf. Blood no longer ran in a trickle down his boots, but it still oozed through the hole in his jeans.

Marina emerged, soaking wet, from off the rear deck. "Take off your boots. You don't need them anyway." She dropped an orange medic kit on the floor, and crouched in front of him, already gloved up.

He held the flashlight in one hand and unlaced the boot on his uninjured foot with the other while she worked on the other, bloody boot. "So, uh, what happens if the storm gets worse?"

She tugged off his boot and sock, and he gritted his teeth against the pain, which wasn't as excruciating as he'd expected. "The anchor and drogue will stabilize us, but extremely rough conditions can turn us, put us in a position to be pooped or broadsided by a wave."

"And that's bad?"

"Ever seen The Perfect Storm?" She shrugged as though sinking to the bottom of the fucking ocean was a regular part of her day. "If it makes you feel any better, I checked the radar, and it looks like we've already passed through the worst of it." He hoped she didn't notice his sigh of relief as she removed a pair of shears from her bag. "I have to cut your pant leg away from the wound. Looks like the denim is stuck to the dried blood, so this may hurt a little." She shrugged a shoulder again. "Or more than a little."

"You really know how to put a patient at ease—ow!"

"Sorry." She gave him an innocent smile as she peeled fabric from his skin. Sorry, his ass. She enjoyed his pain. The sadist.

"You don't have AIDS or anything, do you?"

"Tact isn't one of your strong suits, is it?"

Not looking up at him, she worked quickly and efficiently, cutting a strip of denim away from the wound. "I bit your bloody hand. I need to know if I should get tested."

"I'm clean." Her single nod made her chunky layered hair swing over her cheek, concealing her expression. "How bad is it?"

She shook her head. "I'm going to clean it and see. There's an exit hole in your pants, so it could be bad." She leaned closer to his leg and frowned.

"What? What are you staring at? Is it bad?"

"I think you'll live." She reached for a gauze pad. "The bullet grazed you. It's just a scratch."

A scratch? All that pain for *a scratch?* "Bullshit."

"See for yourself."

"Damn straight I will." He bent forward to see a bloody gash, the edges wiped clean by Marina's steady hand. Fuck a duck. He'd been sprayed with shrapnel, knifed, and nearly strangled over the course of his military and DHS career, but it figured that the first time he got shot he wouldn't even get to keep the bullet as a souvenir.

When he looked up again, she was watching him with a told-you-so expression. Had he ever met a cockier woman? He didn't think so. Was it a huge turn-on? Hell, yes.

"You gonna patch it up or gloat?" he asked, and she laughed.

"Maybe a little of both." She pressed a sterile pad over the scratch and then taped it in place. "This will work temporarily, but once we get back to land, you need to see a doctor. You don't want to risk infection." Her fingers, warm through the latex, pressed against the top of his foot.

"What are you doing?"

"Checking pedal pulses. Making sure blood flow hasn't been compromised by the wound."

"I thought it was just a scratch?"

She smiled up at him, a smile that hit him hard, right in the dick. Damn, she was beautiful. Full lips, strong, square jaw, a nose that might have been a little too big for her face but only added to her commanding presence.

"I'm very thorough," she said.

She could be thorough all she wanted. Her hand on his foot ignited his desire, and her warm breath, blowing in soft caresses over his shin, only intensified it. Her touch was in no way sexual, but he hadn't been with a woman since he started the undercover gig, and even her innocent medical touch had made his heart beat faster.

Which she knew. She looked up at him, an eyebrow raised, her fingers still pressed to his pulse. "You're tachy. Your pulse is racing. Why is that?"

"You tell me, doc."

"Paramedics aren't allowed to diagnose. Only treat."

"You aren't a paramedic anymore, remember?"

"Good thing," she murmured in a deep, dusky voice, "because paramedics get into big trouble when they kiss their patients."

"You kissed me to distract me."

One corner of her mouth tipped up in a wicked smile. "Doesn't mean I didn't like it."

A hot sizzle spread through his muscles. "Does that mean you're planning to kiss me again?" Please, please, let her answer be yes.

"Do you want me to?"

Every part of his body answered instantly, hardening, aching. What was it about this woman who made him forget that sex should be the last thing on his mind, given his situation?

The boat rolled hard to the right, and he nearly slid off his seat. So much for the sex on the brain. Survival had taken over.

"That was bad. Was that bad?"

Marina shook her head. "I've been in much worse." She peeled off her gloves and tossed them, along with her used supplies and wrappers, in the kitchen trash can. When she was done, she sat on the floor in front of him, cross-legged.

"Why'd you never learn to swim?"

If that wasn't a loaded question. The answer pretty much defined his entire life, from childhood to the present. Funny how one event could encompass everything. Hell, the first question he'd asked his Army recruiter had been, "Will I be required to swim?"

"Brent?"

He realized Marina's hand rested on his knee, squeezing gently. For the first time, he saw the compassionate side of the paramedic who'd been only coolly efficient. Not to mention sexy as hell.

"Yeah?"

"What happened?"

The boat took a deep dip to the left—port?—and he gripped the table so hard he thought he might leave indentations. "God, I hate boats," he muttered.

At her curious look, he blew out a breath. "I grew up in a shithole town in Oregon, and my dad sometimes took me and my brother out on the lake to fish. It was hell."

He almost laughed, because "hell" didn't even begin to describe the fishing trips. He'd been nine, and his brother, Barry, had been a year older. Their mom worked her ass off in a school cafeteria during the day and at a convenience store at night so their dad could sit on his lazy butt and drink cheap whiskey all day.

The old man's idea of "bonding with the boys," had been to take them out on the lake in a borrowed boat and then pass out while Brent and Barry baked in the sun. If dear old Dad came to in a good mood, he'd take them back to shore, leave them on the dock, and spend a few hours in the local pub. If he woke up in a bad mood, he'd do the same, but he'd knock them around the boat first, because they didn't catch enough fish.

"He took you out on the lake and never taught you to swim?"

He laughed, a bitter sound that scratched his throat. "He tried." He covered her hand with his and marveled at how soft they were despite the calluses that spoke of a lot of work in her life.

"But?"

The way she said it, like his drill instructor from so many lifetimes ago, had him wanting to tell her his life story. Not that opening up was a big deal; he almost enjoyed telling people what an asshole his old man had been. But the fact that he couldn't swim had always been a sore spot.

"You really want to know?"

She gave a sharp nod that was demanding and bold. This gal didn't expect anyone to turn her down, and damn if he was going to dash her expectations.

"See, my old man was of the mindset that the way to teach someone to swim is to toss them in the water. If they sink, you can always make another kid, right?"

"Oh my God. Seriously?"

"Yeah."

Her fingers closed around his hand and squeezed. "Obviously you didn't sink."

"Yeah, I did. I drowned." A suffocating sensation tightened around his chest like a steel band, and red flashes burst behind his eyes, just like it had happened that day in the lake. He remembered everything; the terror, his brother's screams, the pressure, the pain. Whoever said drowning didn't hurt was full of crap.

"Who saved you?"

"My dad was too shit-faced to swim. He thought I was faking. My brother jumped in, but he couldn't swim, either. Some passing boater saw Barry floundering and yanked him out of the water before he drowned, and then they pulled me out and brought me back with CPR."

Marina's jaw clenched. "And your dad?"

"The cops took him to jail. My mom left his sorry ass, and we never saw him again." Didn't matter, though, because the memories had been burned into Brent's brain.

"Good. What a bastard."

"Yeah. Do we have to talk about this?"

"What would you rather talk about?"

Around them, rain pounded on the glass, reminding him of their precarious situation. "You could tell me we won't die out here if this deathtrap sinks."

She pushed up to her knees and placed both hands on his thighs. Her warmth burned right through the fabric of his jeans. "Since I know your background now, I won't take offense to the fact that you called my dream a deathtrap." Her voice dropped to a low, velvety drawl. "And maybe, just maybe, I can change your mind."

The blood rushing through his veins began to steam. "I doubt it."

She pushed his legs apart and slid between them. Her saturated clothing dampened his jeans, but the cool wetness helped ease the burn that had settled over his skin. "Don't be so sure. I love a challenge."

"And the challenge here is to convert me to your cause? To lure me to the dark side?"

Leaning in, so close he could smell the coconut scent of her shampoo in her hair, she said, "To make you appreciate boats."

He didn't have the heart to tell her it would never happen, and besides, it wasn't like her method of conversion involved torture. Far from it. Her hands massaged their way up his thighs, and her mouth met his urgently, like she needed the contact as much as he did.

It wasn't enough. He dropped his hands to her waist and pulled her closer, so close she couldn't miss his rock-hard erection against her pelvis. His heart hammered, his skin tingled. God, how long had it been since he'd been with a woman like this? And when had it gotten so hot in here?

Arching his back, he quickly shed the Italian leather jacket the agency had paid for. In one smooth motion, he tossed the coat to the table and returned his hands to her bare waist. Damn, but she felt good, all silken skin and toned muscle beneath.

She tore her mouth away from his and kissed a trail along his cheekbone. "I'm not usually this forward," she murmured against the shell of his ear, "but you owe me an orgasm."

"No need to apologize. Forward works for me." He moaned as she sucked his lobe into her mouth, and then he pulled back. "I owe you an orgasm? Did I miss something?"

"Just touch me."

"Yes, ma'am."

He pushed his hands under her T-shirt, smoothed his palms over her ribs until his thumbs brushed the fleshy swells of her breasts. She purred, honest-to-God purred as he stroked upward and flicked the tips of her nipples.

Beneath him, the boat tossed, but he barely noticed… at least, not until the biggest wave yet nearly knocked them both onto the floor.

"Whoa." His muscles froze up, clenched so hard he could barely breathe. Terror he hadn't felt since that day in the lake washed over him like a tidal wave.

"No." Marina framed his face in her hands, her touch tender. "No. Stay with me." Her steady gaze slammed into his, holding him in the present when all he wanted to do was sink into his past.

"Marina—"

"Shh. Trust me."

She had no way of knowing his capacity to trust had drowned with him that day, but, unlike his body, his trust hadn't been revived. She slanted her mouth over his and climbed into his lap, straddling his thighs. The soft juncture between her legs cradled his cock, and she rocked against it, jump-starting his heart.

"Touch me," she repeated, *demanded*, and nipped his bottom lip before soothing it with a stroke of her tongue.

His hands still clutched fistfuls of bench padding. Spreading his legs to brace his feet more soundly on the floor, he released his death-grip on the bench and grasped her hips. Firm flesh yielded to the pressure of his fingers as he thrust against her, letting her ride the ridge behind the seam of his jeans until she whimpered.

Closing his eyes, he slipped a hand beneath the leg opening of her shorts, and his thoughts scattered when he discovered her tantalizing lack of panties. She was enthusiastic, uninhibited, and he wondered how far he could go and how many times she'd let him.

"So beautiful," he whispered against her lips. "So damned sexy."

"God, the sound of your voice makes me hot."

Smiling because no one had ever told him that, he doubled his efforts, stroked the sensitive skin in the crease of her leg until her breathing came in ragged gasps. She went wild, tore at the buttons on his shirt, and when she finally touched the bare skin of his chest, need nearly overwhelmed him. He wanted to tear off their clothes and take her on the floor that bucked beneath them.

He tunneled his hand deeper into her shorts until his thumb found her hot slit. With a groan, she threw her head back and lifted her hips, granting him better access. The way she writhed, moved with his hand, made his head swim with the need to take her in every one of a dozen ways. He lifted her shirt to bare her breasts, to taste them even as he stroked his thumb deep between her legs.

"Yes," she moaned, "there, oh, God, there..."

He pushed a finger inside her slippery core and she cried out, pumped her hips against him. Heart pounding, sweat beading on his forehead, he swirled his tongue around a plump nipple and then took as much of her breast into his mouth as he could. Such soft, supple skin, he could caress it with his tongue for hours. She moaned again, sending heat curling through his body.

"Tell me what you want, Marina."

"I want it all," she whispered, her tangy, aroused scent rising up around them until he was mindless with lust.

All that mattered was finding that sweet place with his tongue and licking her until she screamed.

He lifted her to her feet so one foot rested against each of his outer thighs. Roughly, he pulled down her shorts and tossed them to the floor. His breath caught at the beautiful sight of her pussy, lightly dusted with dark, trimmed curls. He looked up at her, at how she watched him with heat and curiosity in her eyes, and then, holding her gaze, he closed his mouth over her.

"Brent." The sound of his name, uttered low and rough, shot through him, made his balls throb.

She braced her forearms on the wall in front of her and made sexy little noises as he spread her with his thumbs and dragged his tongue through her slick valley.

"That's so good, oh, so good." Bending her knees, she pressed down on his mouth, letting him know exactly what she wanted.

Happy to oblige, he sucked her clit between his lips, then released it, only to catch the swollen nub with the tip of his tongue and tease her with alternating light and firm pressure. She whimpered, begged him to lick her harder, faster, to give her more.

His own sex aching, he dropped one hand to the fly of his jeans and released his cock to stroke it as he thrust his tongue inside her. The boat tossed, but he used the motion to push deeper, to swirl his tongue around her creamy walls that had begun to clench.

She tasted like warm salt water and ripe fruit, and he wanted to drink her in forever, but she came with a scream that drowned out the wind and rain. He brought her down with several gentle laps through her glistening folds, each one making her shudder. Panting, she dropped to her knees to straddle him once more, wiggling so his cock nestled along the length of her hot slit. He arched against her, the contact making him burn.

Fire erupted over his entire body, and as she took his mouth in a deep, sensual kiss, all he could think about was how he'd gladly take another bullet if it meant he could make Marina come over and over.

"You more than made up for owing me." She reached between them to stroke the head of his cock, and he nearly lost it right then and there.

"Shit," he said, his voice sounding raw, "I don't have any condoms."

"Not standard issue for undercover agents?"

"If they were, they'd probably break."

Laughing, she pulled back and gave him a wink. "I'll be right back." She scrambled off him and tugged her shorts back on.

Her ass swung in the most enticing rhythm as she sashayed away and disappeared down into a dark entryway. After a moment, a light came on, and through the door frame he could see the foot of a bed and the edges of a dresser.

"Brent!" Get down here!"

He stood, already planning what he would do to her in that bed.

"We're taking on water!"

More effective than a cold shower, her words sent all thoughts of bed out the gunshot-shattered window. He hurried to the bedroom, hoping Marina had a few tricks up her sleeve, because he was completely out.

Chapter 5

Marina invented some creative new curse words as she scrambled to the head through ankle-deep water. Her heart still pounded from the mind-blowing orgasm of moments ago, but now the water gushing through a bullet hole in her stateroom had her heart racing so fast it threatened to seize like her boat's engine.

Brent appeared in the doorway, his five o'clock shadow standing out starkly against the unnatural pale color of his face. "What can I do?"

She grabbed a hand towel off a shelf and shoved it into his hands. "Plug the hole. I'm going to mix up some epoxy to patch it from the outside." She started up the ladder. "The towel should be enough, but I'd rather be safe than sorry."

"Yeah. Ditto."

She hurried to the welldeck, where, to her relief, the rain had decreased in intensity. Wet Dream still tossed like a toy in thirteen to fifteen-foot seas, but weather conditions were much improved. Of course, improved meant the bad guys would have an easier time locating them with radar. Hopefully, they were too stupid to use it.

She grabbed a tub of epoxy mix and hurried into the kitchen, where she mixed up a gooey glob to the consistency of chewed bubblegum. Brent emerged from her stateroom, his jeans unbuttoned, his shirt still open, revealing a fine line of dark hair and a muscular chest her fingers had mapped. The man was a menace to women everywhere.

"I'm going to need your help." She nodded at the bench that ran along the salon's starboard bulkhead. "Beneath the seat are life vests. Grab two and a line."

"Line?"

"Rope."

"I don't like the sound of this," he muttered, but he dug the items from the storage space and tossed her one of the vests.

"It'll be a cakewalk." She ignored his dubious snort and donned her vest, checked his for proper fit, and then grabbed the line. "Come on."

She flipped the switch for the outside lights and led him out to the welldeck, where rain and cold ocean spray stung her skin. She tied one end of the line around her waist, and secured the other end to a cleat. "The rope is just in case."

"In case what?"

"In case you drop me." She moved to the starboard side of the boat and peered over the rail at the shadowed area where a bullet had pierced the hull just above the water line. "I think I can reach the hole, but you'll need to hold me so I don't go over."

"No way. Let me do it."

"I can't hold you. We have to do it this way. Besides, I've done it before."

He wiped rain out of his eyes and looked out over the churning ocean. "That's not very reassuring."

She leaned over the rail, shivering when the icy metal bit into bare skin where her stretch had exposed her belly between the vest and her low-slung shorts. "Just come here and hold tight."

Curses blistered her ear as his thighs pressed against the back of her legs, his pelvis pressed into her butt. Damn it, they could have been in this position for entirely different reasons and having a helluva lot of fun doing it.

When his hands grasped her life vest, she bent forward, stretching to the puncture in the hull. Though the anchor and drogue helped stabilize the craft, waves still threatened. Each one struck with violent force that rolled the hole into the water and nearly sent her overboard. Her head and torso slammed under water, and her chest crunched into the hull. If not for Brent's strong grip, she'd be swimming for her life and hoping the safety line didn't break.

"This is crazy!" Brent shouted. "I'm not—"

Her head went under, drowning out his voice. The boat righted itself, and she gasped for a breath made difficult because her upper body had tightened in reaction to the cold.

"—pull you up?"

She ignored him, having missed most of whatever he'd said, anyway. Stretching until her muscles screamed, she cursed when her fingers fell short of the hole by mere millimeters.

"I need more reach!"

"No!"

"Do it!" Her head dunked into the black water again, and she came up sputtering when the boat rolled back upright. Brent swore, but he dropped her a couple more inches. She slapped the putty over the hole with fingers that were stiff with the cold. Almost… almost…

The boat rolled again, and she snapped her mouth shut, held her breath between clenched teeth. Her trembling fingers mashed the putty into place, and when she came back up, the hole was patched.

"Marina, fuck! I'm losing my grip!"

"Pull me up!"

Though he lifted her easily and with incredible strength, her thighs scraped the railing as he drew her upward. The boat tossed, and his grip slipped, making her hips and pelvis strike the rail with bruising force. Before she could cry out, a large wave caught the bow and they nearly both went over. Somehow, Brent held tight, and when Wet Dream righted, he yanked her onto the welldeck and they both went down like a couple of flopping swordfish.

Brent immediately crawled to her as she lay on her side, shivering and sucking in huge gulps of oxygen. "Are you okay? Jesus, did I hurt you?" He untied the line from her waist and then laid a hand on her shoulder, squeezing gently, his expression tight, concerned.

"I'm fine," she said, pushing to her knees. "You didn't hurt me."

Relief flooded his expression. "Don't do that again. Jesus. That was scary shit."

"Trust me. I've been in worse situations on a boat. Many times."

"Lady, you're insane."

"Says the man who hangs out with criminals for his job."

"At least criminals are predictable. You're like this damned ocean!"

She knew he hadn't meant it as a compliment, but she smiled as much as her trembling lips allowed. "Aww. I'm beautiful and deep and full of life."

Several heartbeats passed as he looked at her like he wasn't sure if he should strangle her or hug her. Then, shaking his head, he drew her into the warmth of his arms. "Those things, too, I guess."

She snuggled closer, seeking his heat. It felt good to lean on someone. Better than anything had since her father died two years ago.

"Let's get you inside before you freeze to death."

Hypothermia was the last thing she worried about. Being found by violent, homicidal men placed much higher up on the list. And if said criminals were going to find them, then no way in hell would she allow them to ruin what might be her last few hours on earth.

Brent had already demonstrated his lovemaking skills, and she couldn't think of a better way to pass the time, especially now that her adrenaline pumped hotly through her veins.

"Marina? Did you hear me? I think we need to warm you up."

"I have an idea about that," she said, burrowing her face into his neck.

Dipping her tongue into the curve there between his collar and throat, she traced the pulse alongside the straining tendon. Mmm, salty and male and all kinds of delicious. The scent of him, powerful and musky, mixed with that of the rain and the ocean, making for a powerful aphrodisiac.

"Marina…"

He pulled back, and gazed down at her so intently she could feel longing radiate from him. He cupped her cheek in his hand, brushed away the rain with his thumb. His gentle strokes warmed her like no heater could.

The boat's bow pitched, sending them both sliding forward. Brent threw out his arm and slammed his hand against the bait tank, preventing her spine from taking the brunt of the impact. His chest crushed hers, his hip dug into her pelvis.

"You okay?"

The uneasiness in his voice tore at her. "I'm good."

Heart breaking for what he'd gone through as a child, she wished she knew how to fix his pain and chase away his anxiety. He was so strong and confident… the helplessness of this situation must be a blow to his ego and a return to a time of terror.

He wasn't a coward; when he'd talked about the men who wanted him dead, and there had been no fear. Instead, there'd been an intense, almost excited quality about him. Yet when the boat rocked, when he'd spoken of his past, he'd been afraid. How strange that she suffered from the opposite problem. This weather, the boat being dead in the water… none of it fazed her, but the thought of being hunted like a shark after a seal filled her with bone-numbing terror.

Right now they were both scared, but for different reasons, and they both needed a distraction.

"Let's go inside," he said, water dripping from his lips and chin.

"Uh-uh." Bracing her hands on his chest, she leaned in and captured the drops on her tongue. She let her lips linger on his jaw, and she thought he shuddered, but it could have been the motion of the boat.

"This is crazy," he muttered, even as he brought his mouth down hard on hers and pulled her tight against him.

She shivered again, but not because of the cold. Pleasure sent chills sweeping through her body as Brent's tongue curled around hers and one hand dropped low to her hip. She twisted and wriggled until she was beneath him, cradling his weight on the deck.

Raindrops tapped lightly on her arm and face, adding pinpricks of sensation across skin that was already super-sensitized. He rolled his pelvis against her, and his wet jeans rubbed the insides of her tender thighs in a strangely erotic friction. When his hand dropped to mid-thigh and smoothed upward, she cried out.

Sex had for too long been a solitary sport, and with every touch, something inside her shifted. No one had ever held her like this, as though she was a lifeline. For the first time, she grasped at someone else in the same way.

Brent dragged his mouth away from hers and kissed a slow, sweeping trail along her jaw and down her throat. She arched up against him, cursing the life vests that prevented her chest from touching his.

"You're so pretty, sweetheart," he said against her throat. "Crazy, but pretty."

"Mmm, you say the nicest things."

"Yeah, I'm a charmer."

She'd have laughed if his hand hadn't dipped below the waistband of her shorts to cup her butt and press her upward into his very noticeable hard-on. Instead of laughing, she moaned. Oh, God, she was so ready for this.

He thrust against her, and pleasure became pain when the small of her back scraped the rough deck. "Wait," she said. "Stand up."

She tightened her arms around his broad shoulders as he stood, lifting her from the deck. "Are we going inside?"

He sounded so hopeful that she almost felt sorry for him. But not enough to say yes. Oh, no. Her adrenaline surged, her heart raced, and as she stood in the rain and the wind, she felt alive, truly alive for the first time in years.

He set her down, his eyes narrowing as he grasped her face in his hands. "Marina... what are you plotting? Something bad, I suspect."

She smiled. "Bad? You have no idea."

Mr. I-Hate-The-Ocean was about to get a crash course in what the guys her dad used to work with called "semenship."

Chapter 6

Marina studied the fine lines bracketing Brent's talented mouth as he gazed at the cabin doors.

"Uh-uh," she said, shaking her head. "No fun."

"Oh, we could make it fun." His voice, rough and husky, left no doubt as to how they could entertain themselves inside where it was warm and dry. This wasn't about being comfortable, though. He sought the relative safety of the cabin, and while she understood, she wouldn't allow him to give in to his fear.

Planting her palms on the bait tank behind her, she hopped up to sit on it, and then wrapped her legs around his waist. "I'd rather be bad."

The intensity in his gaze burned through her, setting fire to her blood, liquefying her bones. His hands settled on the bare skin of her waist, their progress upward impeded by the life vest.

She clicked through the buckles along the front of the jacket, but he grabbed her hand to stop her. "No. It's too dangerous."

"I've—"

"I know. You've been in worse. I don't give a shit. I want you safe. Not dead."

"But—"

"But nothing."

His fingers deftly clicked all the fasteners back into place. Once finished, he scattered kisses along her neck, across her jaw, and then finally, her mouth. She nipped his lower lip and moaned, because as much as she wanted Brent to touch every inch of her, there was something erotic about the way the life vests squeaked as they rubbed together. Not that she'd admit such a thing to anyone.

"I want to touch all of you," he said, as though reading her mind, and nipping her right back, "but we can do that later, when this is over."

Later. Oh, God, would there be a later? Even if they survived the bad guys, would there—*could* there really be a later? She wasn't the kind of woman men liked to keep around. What had her most recent ex said when he broke up with her after her longest relationship ever—which amounted to three months? *You're a lot of fun, but you aren't the kind of girl a guy wants to take home to Mom.*

Right. Because who wanted mom to know your girlfriend preferred fishing over gardening, hanging out in wharf-side dives instead of country clubs, and slamming boilermakers over sipping champagne?

No, Marina was what her mother would have been, had she not trapped her father into marriage by getting knocked up. She was the fun, hang-out and do crazy things with kind. Not the marrying kind.

Which was fine, because married people gave up on the dreams they had before marriage. They made boring love in beds. They didn't have wild, wet, on-the-welldeck sex.

He wedged himself between her thighs, and his tongue pushed more deeply into her mouth. Tingles shivered through her as he rocked against her, the movement of the boat creating an uneven rhythm that kept her senses deliciously off balance. *Yes, there, oh no, not there, but yes, there is nice, and oh, God, yes, there...*

She wrapped her arms around his neck and his pony tail brushed her arm, tickling her wet skin. More. She wanted his hair loose and touching more of her. Her half-frozen fingers found the rubber band binding his pony tail, and she worked it loose until his hair spilled over his shoulders in a wet blanket.

"Have you always had long hair?" She tilted her head to allow him access as he dragged his mouth down her chin to her throat.

"I grew it out for an undercover gig a year ago." His hands slid into her shorts and cupped her ass, kneading lightly. "Kept it for this job. Why? Do you hate it?"

His fingers slid lower, spreading her cheeks, teasing and probing, and she gasped, arching against him. "No, I don't hate it," she breathed, wishing it wasn't true. She'd always detested long hair on men, but on this man, she loved it when she shouldn't love anything about him.

Slowly, she trailed her palms down his arms, over the hard muscles that leapt at her touch. She traced the bulging veins, circled his elbows, and then dropped her hands to his waist. She used a thumb to stroke down the hard length of him through his jeans, and he hissed air between his clenched teeth. His reaction filled her with anticipation. How would he breathe as orgasm approached? Would he hold his breath when he entered her? Would he moan, call out her name at climax?

Suddenly, the need to know the answers became too much to bear. She fumbled with his fly, her trembling fingers too clumsy to work the buttons. Growling, she gave a violent yank and ripped open his jeans.

Her fingers found what they sought. His hissing intake of air barely registered over the roar of the ocean and the gusting of the wind, but it echoed through her ears like the most welcome music. She'd given pleasure before, but never to someone who needed it, and never when she'd needed it just as much.

She closed her hand around the thick length of his cock and sent several firm strokes from the velvety head down the shaft. He stiffened, threw his head back so his wet hair whipped around his face and the straining, corded muscles in his neck. He was beautiful, a creature of the land fighting the nature of the sea… and winning.

He no longer struggled for firm footing on the rocking boat, but instead, he rode the waves with the easy grace of a seasoned sailor. Or a pirate. She circled his cock with a forefinger and thumb and squeezed, and he bared his teeth. Oh, yeah. Pirate.

Returning his heated gaze to hers, he tugged her shorts down past her hips until they caught on her spread legs. "I need to be inside you."

She slid her hand down to cup his heavy balls. "You read my mind."

Slinging her a cocky grin, he unhooked her legs from around his waist and took a half-step back so he could pull off her shorts. When he had them around her ankles, she stopped him.

"Hold on." She dug around in the left pocket and pulled out a condom. "I put it there before I discovered the hull hole in my stateroom."

"You are full of surprises," he said, removing her shorts and dropping them to the deck. She kept hold of the condom while he pushed his own jeans down and returned to the intimate position between her legs. Warmth surrounded her as he leaned into her, his thick length resting along her moist crease.

The boat rocked, creating a delicious friction between them, and she whimpered, wanting so much more than this, and wanting it now. Patience had never been one of her virtues.

His fingers wrapped around her thighs, pulling her close, holding her steady as he thrust against her, his erection sliding from her opening to her clit, coating her in her juices. Every stroke was like a jolt of electricity burning her from the inside out. She reached down, touched the pad of one finger to the weeping tip of his cock, and spread the silky moisture around as he continued to rock against her.

His angular face was an intense mask as he looked down between their bodies. The way he admired her, took her in, felt like a sizzling caress. Slowly, seductively, she reached behind her and laid both palms flat on the rear of the bait tank. Then she leaned back and spread her legs, giving him a view of their mating. His nostrils flared and his jaw tightened, and when his gaze slammed into hers, the smoky heat in his eyes took away her breath.

"That condom would be a good idea right about now," he said, his voice a rough, masculine rumble.

She handed it to him and then returned to her exposed position while he tore open the packet, his eyes never once moving from hers. It was so sexy, the way he watched her for her reactions, the way he wasn't afraid to try and get into her head.

Sexy, but scary. She wasn't ready to have a man in her head or in her heart, and she didn't know if she'd ever be ready.

She averted her gaze, needing to shut him out of her mind. Instead, she watched as his large hand smoothed the condom over hard flesh, and the other braced him against the bait tank. Her heart pounded, and her vagina pulsed as though flexing and stretching in preparation for him.

She couldn't tear her eyes away as he unrolled the condom, and then, when he was done, his hand stilled at the base of his cock.

She held her breath, her head spinning at the sight of his hand there. A heartbeat later, he slid his fist up slowly. He circled the head with his palm and then drove his hand down again. Up. Down. Oh, God, she wanted to touch, too, but it was far too fascinating to watch him pleasure himself.

Which, no doubt, was exactly what he wanted. She felt his gaze on her, knew he watched the change in her breathing, her throat working on suddenly difficult swallows, the more clinical signs of arousal like pupil dilation… if he could see her breasts he'd note the way her nipples had tightened painfully. The bastard tormented her.

She liked it.

He knew it.

She hooked her ankles behind his thighs and drew him in, at the same time lifting her hips, exposing herself like she'd never done before. This was the man of her dreams, the one she'd conjured in her head while in bed, and she wasn't about to let the fantasy be anything but perfect.

"Well? What are you waiting for?"

She'd offered herself up like dessert on a platter, and from the looks of things, he was as hungry as she.

Chapter 7

What was he waiting for? No idea. Maybe he hoped to see a look on her face that spoke of fierce need. Maybe he wanted to see an invitation in her eyes that was more than an open door into her body but into her mind as well.

Maybe he was a sappy fucking idiot.

His cock, straining painfully upward, agreed.

Catching her tongue between her teeth, she wiggled impatiently, and he surrendered to the desire he'd felt almost since the moment he laid eyes on her. With one hand on her thigh, he used the other to guide himself near. He circled the rim of her opening with the head of his cock and then slid it up between her silky folds. God, he wanted to rip open her life vest and caress the skin of her belly, the plump flesh of her breasts.

Instead, he used his thumb to stroke the crease at the top of her inner thigh as used his dick to lightly caress her erect, swollen clit. She bit her lower lip, clamping down on a moan he wished she'd let loose. The expression on her face, highlighted by the glow of the moon that peeked through the breaks in the cloud deck, told him as much as the moan would have, though, and his ego ballooned.

"You're still waiting," she said, giving him a narrow-eyed glare.

"You're an impatient little thing, aren't you?"

She sat up slightly and grasped his penis in a vice grip that gave him goosebumps. Good goosebumps. "I know what I want, and I don't like to wait."

"I guess I shouldn't keep a lady waiting, then."

"Damn straight."

She released him to settle back on her elbows, sprawling before him like a feast. She watched him as he breached her tight warmth. Her legs quivered as he eased each inch slowly inside. When he slammed home in a fit of impatience, she cried out, the sound of her passion mingling with the slap of the waves on the side of the boat. Waves that now added to the excitement of the moment rather than the fear.

Not wanting to analyze the fact that terror was the last thing on his mind right now, he leaned over Marina and took her mouth in a deep kiss. She wrapped her arms around his neck, clinging as he drove into her. Slowly at first, increasing speed as her cries grew louder. Her butt slid on the wet metal thing, the motion enhancing his powerful thrusts.

"Brent," she gasped, throwing her head back, exposing her throat to his hungry mouth. "Mmm, yes. Like that. Just like that."

His skin burned, his blood boiled, his mouth dried up at the exquisite sensation of her inner muscles clenching him, massaging him. Sweet Jesus, every part of his body felt too tight, like he was being squeezed in a giant fist. This woman was incredible, magic.

Her ankles dug into his buttocks, and her fingernails sank into his biceps. There'd be marks tomorrow, and yeah, he'd wear them with pride. Right alongside his bullet wound that no longer hurt, that no longer mattered, especially when she dropped her arms from around his shoulders and grasped his ass. He pumped; she ground, and oh, man, he was done for.

Bursts of light flashed behind his eyelids. He heard a shout, a curse—he wasn't sure which, but he did know the sound had been ripped from somewhere deep inside him. He also knew he'd always been silent in his lovemaking, but Marina had released something he'd always kept caged, civil.

Panting, knees weak and his cock still pulsing, he looked down at her exquisite beauty as she bucked against him, hovering on the pinnacle of her own release. Screw civility. She was his woman now, whether or not she knew it.

He rammed into her, bringing her over the edge to a place where she screamed out his name and clenched her inner muscles, milking every last drop of cum until he felt it in the tight, dry squeeze of his testicles. She convulsed, and he braced his legs against the power of her orgasm and the power of the sea.

Planting his palms on either side of her thighs, he shuddered as her grip on his butt relaxed and her thighs around his waist eased their hold. He sucked great gulps of air too rapidly, and man, he didn't think his breathing would ever get back to normal.

"Wow," she said, leaning forward to prop her forehead on his shoulder.

"Wow about covers it."

She looked up at him, her kiss-swollen lips turned into a sultry smile. "See how great sex can be on a boat?"

"The boat didn't make the sex great. You did."

Her laughter rippled through him, all the way to his heart. "You're smooth, I'll give you that."

"Yeah, well, I can't admit the wow factor had anything to do with the boat after all my bitching, can I?"

Still smiling, she rolled her eyes. "Men."

"Ya gotta love us."

She cocked an eyebrow at him. "That, Agent Dude, is debatable."

Maybe. Not up for debate was how lovable he found her. Tough, sexy, sensitive, and she didn't fall apart when faced with danger. She was a fighter. Oh, yeah. Lovable.

"So, you've never been in love?"

Something flashed in her eyes, and he wished the deck lights weren't behind her so he could have identified whatever the emotion had been. "I'm freezing. Let's get inside."

She twisted away, and an instant loss swept over him as he withdrew from her body. She swung her legs onto the deck, bent to grab her shorts—giving him a scrumptious view of her behind—and then disappeared into the cabin. He jerked his icy-wet jeans up around his waist and buttoned his fly.

The boat tossed on a wave, and he instinctively reached out to brace himself. Before his hand touched the rail, however, he pulled back, steadied his legs and winced at the sting in his injured calf. A ribbon of anxiety rippled through him, but it was a far cry from the bone-numbing terror he'd experienced when he first jumped onto the boat.

"Huh."

He inhaled deeply, taking in the damp salt air, the cool, crisp breeze. The sky had begun to go gray to the east, signaling the approach of morning. More than five hours had passed in a blink, something that yesterday he'd not have believed could happen on a boat. Five hours should have felt like five years.

But now that the dawn topped the horizon, the bad guys would soon be able to see Wet Dream, and he might be measuring his remaining time in minutes instead of hours.

Marina quickly changed into dry jeans and a sweatshirt, and then rummaged through her closet until she found an old flannel shirt that had belonged to her father. It had been his "Sunday shirt," the one he wore while watching football on weekends when he wasn't at sea. Bringing the soft, worn garment to her nose, she could almost smell him in the fabric, reminding her of the very reasons she hadn't been able to throw it away. Maybe Brent could get some use out of it until his own shirt dried out. The guy had to be freezing.

Then again, his skin had burned into hers, his touch hot, his words steamy. There was nothing cold about that man.

Her heart pounded, her skin pulled tight in response to her thoughts about him and what they'd done on the welldeck. She'd always been uninhibited in her sexuality, had always enjoyed sex. But with Brent, sex had been more intense than any she'd experienced, more emotional.

Emotional? Emotions played no part in what she'd done with him. At least, not heartfelt emotions. The intensity could be explained by the danger they faced, and the rest… same thing. Danger.

"Marina?"

Startled out of her thoughts, she turned off her stateroom lamp. "Coming."

She grabbed her largest pair of sweat pants from the drawers beneath her bed and then sloshed through the cold seawater in the carpet, stepped up the ladder, and found Brent rubbing his arms vigorously as he looked out the bridge window. "I brought you some clothes. The fit might not be great, but it's better than the wet stuff you have on now."

She expected him to refuse, to play the manly part of *I-might-be-freezing-to-death-but-I-have-to-pretend-I'm-okay.* Instead, he thanked her and took the clothes.

"Wow," she said. "Not afraid of the girl pants and ratty shirt?"

He looked up from unbuckling his life jacket. "Turning down dry clothes would be stupid. We could wind up in a shitload of trouble soon, and being weak from the cold wouldn't help."

"Thanks for the reminder," she muttered. Still, his lack of ego impressed her.

"I'm sorry," he said, and in the dawning morning light, she could see the genuine emotion in his deep brown eyes. "I didn't mean to get you into this. If I'd known—"

She pressed a finger to his mouth. "Shh. I know."

He reached up, took her hand in his, and kissed her finger tenderly. Warmth oozed through her, heating parts that had no business heating up again so soon. Her heart warmed too, and the traitorous organ had even less business doing such a thing than the rest of her parts.

"You'd better stop that, or you won't need to get dressed."

"That'd be a shame, huh?"

He smiled, but released her hand and peeled off his soaked shirt. The muscles of his chest and arms flexed and rippled, the definition beneath his skin making her drool as he shrugged into her father's shirt. He was perfectly capable of working the buttons, but she needed to touch him, even if it was only in innocence.

She pushed his hands aside and buttoned the shirt, allowing her fingers to brush his stomach and chest, and each time she did, his flesh leapt, his breathing hitched.

She ran her finger over a shiny crescent beneath his left pec. "Nasty scar," she murmured, and then dragged her hand down to where two larger, more ragged scars zigzagged across his stomach.

"Shrapnel."

Although she'd patched his bullet wound, she hadn't given much thought to the fact that he might have a violent past. The idea that shards of metal could have taken his life… it infuriated her. Someone had tried to take him from her before she even met him. Of course, she had no idea why she cared, because although he'd talked about things like, *later,* men always talked about later only until they got what they wanted.

Not that she hadn't also gotten what she wanted, which happened to be the best orgasms of her life.

When she'd buttoned all but the last two at the neck, she dropped her hands to his waist and unbuttoned his jeans.

"I'm capable of undressing myself."

She grinned. "I'm more capable."

He held up his hands in surrender and watched her tug his jeans down. She bent to push them to his knees, putting her at eye level with his impressive cock. Even semi-erect, it was perfect… thick, textured with pulsing veins, the head smooth and plum-ripe. A new surge of desire winged through her, and she tamped it down before he decided she wasn't anything more than a cat in heat. Then again, she didn't care what he thought of her.

Keep telling yourself that, and maybe you'll believe it.

Careful not to catch his pant's leg on his bandage, she pulled the denim over his feet and then helped him into the extra-large black sweats in which she lounged around the boat. They were too tight and too short, the cuffs falling to mid-calf, but the drawstring waist fit.

"Thanks. Feels good to be out of the wet stuff."

"No problem. I'm going to check the radar, make sure we're in the clear." She brushed past him. "Want some coffee? It's instant."

"That'll work."

The radar was clear, so while he planted himself at the table, she zapped some water in the microwave and mixed up two cups of instant coffee. "Black?"

"Yup."

"Thought so. You don't strike me as the cream and sugar type."

"Neither do you."

She slipped into the seat across from him and handed him a cup, only half-full since he wasn't accustomed to drinking in rough seas. "Are you saying I'm not sweet?"

He slanted her a cocky look. "You're a lot of things, Marina, but sweet? Nah."

She blew steam off the surface of her coffee. "You think you know me, huh?"

"Not as well as I'd like to."

"Is that so?"

He shrugged. "Do we have anything better to do?"

"While we wait for the bad guys to show up, you mean?"

"Or the good guys."

She cocked her head and watched him for a moment. "So, how did you end up with a job as a good guy?"

A blast of wind rattled the windows, and he looked out at the ocean before turning back to her. "I joined the Army when I was eighteen, worked for their investigative unit for my last four, and I got out right after the September 11 attacks when DHS offered me a position." He ran a hand through his wet hair, pushing it back from his face. "It gives me a lot of freedom. Cool assignments."

"If, by cool you mean being chased and shot at by thugs, you have issues."

He chuckled. "Not the first time I've heard that." Then he cursed when a wave tossed the boat and coffee sloshed out of his cup.

She hid a grin in her own cup. "You said earlier your cover was blown. What happened?"

A chill ran up her spin at the dark shadow that fell over his expression. "I'd gone to a meeting with the arms-dealers in a warehouse near the marina. I had to give up my gun, go through a search for wiretaps, *et cetera*. We were in the middle of the meeting when one of the scumbags' gofers came in. I'd busted him in the past, and he blew my cover." Brent shook his head. "Someone fucked up the intel, and they're gonna go down for it." He braced his forearms on the table and leaned forward. "Now, you've heard enough about me. Your turn."

"What do you want to know? My life's an open book."

"You said you've always lived on a boat. Here?"

"Massachusetts. I've lived on a boat since I was eight and my mom took off with another man. Left me with my dad."

"I'm sorry."

She sipped her coffee. "It's okay. I don't remember much about her. Really, the only thing I know is that she got pregnant to trap my dad, and she worked a lot at a twenty-four hour diner. My dad lost the house when he couldn't make payments by himself, so we moved onto his cousin's fishing boat, where he worked."

Life on the boat had been hard, and she didn't think she'd ever forgive her mother for that. Her father had hoped to own his own sport fishing company, but because he'd been forced into marriage and family, his dream had died a long, miserable death.

Never once, though, did Marina feel unwanted or unloved. He'd always said he would have made the same choices because she'd been worth all the hardships.

"You grew up on a commercial fishing vessel?"

She bristled. "So?"

"Just seems like a tough way to grow up." His curious, non-judgmental tone lowered her hackles. "How did you go to school? Did you go out fishing with the crew?"

"Dad home-schooled me until I was eleven, and then I stayed with his girlfriend when he fished during the school year. By that time, he'd bought his own boat, and when I wasn't in school, I went out on the boat with the crew."

She kept to herself the part where, when she hadn't been on the boat, she'd been inside her dad's girlfriend's tavern, where she helped out with dishes, cleaning, and serving food. As a very young girl, she'd played with her Barbies on the wooden floor under tables.

"Dangerous, wasn't it?"

"Sometimes."

A lot of the time. She'd seen men fall overboard, get impaled with hooks, bitten by sharks, mangled by machinery… the list went on. The helplessness she'd felt at times like that had been the reason she'd become a paramedic. Her skills had saved lives on board her father's boat more than once.

They hadn't, however, saved her father.

"So, how did you end up in California?"

Drawing her legs up under her, she sighed. "Aren't you bored yet?"

"Not even close."

His interest stirred up a longing in her, one she'd never experienced. No one had ever asked about her life, and she suddenly realized she wanted to share the bits of her past with someone. No, not anyone.

Just Brent.

Both disconcerted and excited, she braced her forearms on the table to tell him the rest.

"When I was twenty-two, my dad decided he was tired of commercial fishing, and he always had this dream of being a fishing guide somewhere warm, so he sold everything and moved out here. I'd been working at an ambulance company and on my dad's boat, so I didn't have anything to tie me to the East Coast. I came with him to help start up his fishing guide business."

Brent made a broad gesture that encompassed the boat. "And this is it?"

"Sort of. Dad bought Wet Dream, but she was a junker. He couldn't afford much, so he started taking people out for cheap fishing trips. I got a job at a private ambulance company and helped him out when I could." She sighed. "He lost a lot of money, and before things could pick up, he suffered a heart attack."

He'd crumpled to the dock in front of her. She hadn't been able to bring him back. Her father had taught her that she could do anything—*anything*—if she wanted to, and though her life had been one aggressive move after another, nothing she'd done had made a difference in his case. He'd died en route to the hospital.

The next day, she quit the ambulance company.

"You took over the business? Fixed up the boat?"

She nodded. "I took out a bunch of loans, got myself into a ton of debt, and now I'm getting ready to make something of this baby."

He leaned back in the seat and carefully downed his coffee. "For you? Or for your dad?"

"That's an odd question."

Shrugging, he used the back of his hand to wipe a drip of coffee from his chin. "Just seems like if you love chartering so much, you would have gone into business with your dad in the first place."

"Maybe I had to spread my wings a little. Do something different."

"Then why aren't you still doing it?"

"Paramedicine?" At his nod, she cast her gaze into her cup. "It's not for me."

"Because you couldn't save your dad?" he asked softly.

If he'd sliced her with a scalpel he couldn't have opened the wound wider.

"Doesn't matter. This is my life now." She pushed away from the table and dumped her cup in the sink. Figured she's be stuck in the middle of the ocean with Curiosity-Boy.

He stood, moved behind her and wrapped his arms around her waist. She stiffened, but his soothing voice against the top of her head kept her from wheeling away. "I didn't mean to bring up bad memories. I just want to get to know you better."

She relaxed against him, soaking up his warmth, reveling in his embrace. When was the last time a man had held her like he cared? She couldn't remember any man doing that. No one except her father.

"Why do you want to get to know me?" Damn it, did her voice have to shake like that?

"Because I've never met anyone like you, and you fascinate me."

"Why?"

"You say what you think. You aren't afraid to take risks. You don't pretend to be anything you're not. And under all that is a woman who forgot to fill her gas tank."

She snorted. "I told you—"

"I know. You didn't expect to have to peel out of the marina while being chased by bullets."

"Exactly." She frowned. "It's just… it doesn't make sense. I know I filled it." Maybe she was losing her mind. Unless… "Bullets."

"What?"

She broke free of his embrace and ignored the empty feeling. "Bullets. I know I filled the tank. One of the bullets must have hit the fuel line or something."

"Could it be fixed?"

"Yes, but it wouldn't do us any good if the fuel drained out." She gnashed her teeth. It felt better to know she wasn't a ditz who forgot to fill the tank, but helplessness still ate at her.

"Would it hurt to try the engine again?"

She shrugged. "Guess not." Uttering a silent prayer, she stepped up to the helm and turned the key. A grinding noise made her wince, and then a chugging noise, and then…

The engine turned over.

"Oh my God," she whispered. "Maybe gas settled back into the tank from the lines. It won't last, not if the line has a hole."

"What do we do?"

"I've got to patch the line." She reached to shut down the engine, but Brent's voice stopped her.

"Is there supposed to be smoke?"

"What?" She whirled around. Black smoke billowed up from the engine compartment in thick, greasy rolls. "Shit!"

She cut the engine, grabbed the fire extinguisher, and rushed out to the welldeck. Brent followed, but he took the extinguisher from her when they reached the engine compartment hatch.

"I've got it," he said before she could argue. "Tell me when."

She nodded, and on the count of three, she opened the hatch. Flames burst from the opening. Heat singed her eyebrows. Brent aimed several bursts of spray into the fire, and clouds of retardant and smoke engulfed the welldeck, making them both cough and choke.

Eyes watering, she waited for the smoke to clear, and then she peered down into the mass of charred metal and melted fiberglass and rubber. Water half-filled the compartment, probably leaking in from a bullet hole beneath the water line. She swore a string of foul oaths that kept her from crying, but no amount of swearing made her feel any better. Her baby was now nothing more than the heap of junk Brent thought it was.

"Marina?"

"What?"

"Is that what I think it is?"

She looked up from the horror that was the engine compartment and followed Brent's gaze. Her stomach took a dive. "Yeah, it is. It's a boat."

Chapter 8

The tiny speck of white on the dark water grew larger. Marina prayed it wasn't the bad guys. Binoculars. She needed her binoculars. She ran inside the cabin, Brent on her heels.

"Got any weapons besides the flare gun?" he asked, reaching for said gun.

She nodded as she grabbed the binoculars from the drawer near the helm. "Hold on."

Nausea churned in her stomach when she focused the lenses on the approaching boat. The Cavenaughs' Beneteau Antares. Her hand shook. She dropped the binoculars.

Even if the bad guys couldn't work the radar, they wouldn't miss the column of smoke.

She wrapped her arms around her middle and resisted the urge to rock back and forth like a mental patient. "What's likely to happen?"

"They won't shoot before boarding. They want me alive. My guess is that they'll tie up to us and take us that way."

He sounded so matter-of-fact about it. So calm. Like he faced death every day. Maybe he did. Oh, God.

"Why do they want you so badly?"

"They want to find out if I told anyone what I know." He shot her a sideways glance. "And I have a million dollars of their money stashed away. They'd like it back."

"Nice." This kept getting worse and worse. She pointed to the helm chair. "There's a compartment under the seat. You'll find more flares."

Precious seconds ticked away as she hurried out to the welldeck and retrieved her spear gun. A staple on dives, she never thought she might be forced to use it on a person. Could she do it?

She'd been trained to save lives, not take them. Then again, her life was at stake. Her life and the life of the man she'd made love to only minutes ago. Could she impale a bad guy on the end of a spear?

Hefting the weapon in her hand, she looked out at the growing dot on the horizon. Yeah, she'd nail those bastards to the side of that yacht if she had to.

Inside the cabin, she found Brent tucking flares into the waistband of his sweats, his movements brisk, military-precise.

"I want you to hide." He looked out the window at the Cavenaugh's boat, not a hint of fear that threatened to paralyze her in his expression. "I'm going to give myself up to them if they agree to leave you alone."

"That's crazy. I won't let you do that."

"There's no other choice."

"We can fight. Make a stand. You're not giving yourself up."

"I'm not risking your life, either. I've already put you in enough danger."

"They'll kill you."

He shrugged. "I might be able—"

"Don't bullshit me. I'm not an idiot. They're going to kill you, probably after a lot of torture."

Images of Brent bleeding, broken, in pain flashed through her head, and her heart missed a beat.

"That's my problem. Not yours."

She shook off her morbid thoughts and rolled her eyes. "Stop being so macho."

"I'm not. I got you into this."

"And you're getting me out of it," she assured him. "But not by sacrificing yourself."

Cursing, he pinched the bridge of his nose between his thumb and forefinger. "We can't just sit here."

"They're going to kill us. We might as well take out as many of them as we can first."

"Doing that is a ticket to getting dead. You have a chance if I surrender."

"God, you are the most stubborn man I've ever met. I said, no."

He swung around, took two predatory strides and backed her up against the salon's port bulkhead. "Now's the time where *I* get to say I've been in worse situations. We're entering my turf now. We deal with this my way." He crowded her, used his height and build to intimidate her. "Don't make me have to tie you up."

"Don't make me have to call your bluff." She lifted her chin and stared him down.

"You think I'm bluffing?"

She shook her head. "Oh, you're capable of tying me up—", and in any other circumstance, the idea would be fun to entertain "—but you aren't going to risk them not taking your deal and coming after me, and then finding me unable to defend myself."

He glared. She'd have smiled if not for the fact that a boatload of bad guys was on their way to slaughter them, and what she should be doing was crying.

"So," she said, giving him a firm push backward, "since we can't leave the boat, and you aren't giving yourself up, I guess we should dig in for a fight."

He made a noise that sounded suspiciously like a growl and looked around the cabin. His eyes locked on the life jacket he'd tossed to the sofa.

"What is it?"

"I have an idea," he said, "but I hate it."

Uh-oh. "I'm going to hate it, too, aren't I?"

Slinging her a sideways glance, he grabbed the life jacket. "It's pretty crazy."

She smiled. "Well then, I'm in."

She just hoped by "crazy" he didn't mean Butch Cassidy and the Sundance Kid crazy. Because for the first time in the last few hours, she couldn't say that she'd been in a situation worse than this.

Brent shrugged into his life vest and buckled it up as Marina did the same. His stomach churned, but at least he hadn't told her his idea yet. She'd come uncorked.

"Okay." She picked up the lethal-looking spear gun. "What's the plan?"

She looked so eager, so ready to take on the world, he had to smile. He loved strong, capable woman, and he could see himself falling for this one.

If they didn't die in a hail of bullets.

Pulling in a long breath, he laced his fingers in hers, which earned him another dazzling smile. "We're going to set your boat on fire."

Her smile fell off her face. Slid to her not-so-delicate toes. "Are you insane? Burn my boat up? What kind of idiotic plan is that?"

"Someone might see the fire. And if not, we have plan B."

"Perhaps you could let me in on plan B? Because plan A sucks."

"The smoke will also cover our escape off the boat. We jump into the water—I can't believe I'm saying this—and hide against the side of the boat. When they board, we climb into their boat and steal it."

"Is there a plan C?"

"Not unless you have one."

"No, but burning my boat isn't an option."

He glanced at the yacht that grew larger on the horizon with each passing second. His sense of distance was skewed on the water with no landmarks, but he guessed they had only a few minutes to make a decision.

"We don't have a choice, Marina. If they have binoculars, they'll see us get into the water. We need smoke for cover. We need a chance for someone to see the smoke and come for a rescue.

"No."

"Marina—"

"I said, no. This is my dream. I won't watch it go up in smoke. Literally."

"Is it?"

"Is it what?"

"Your dream." He gave her a hard stare. "Or is it your father's? Are you living your life, or do you feel so guilty for being born that you're living his?"

Fury turned her green eyes as stormy as the sea. "How dare you? You have no idea what kind of life he had. How he had to give up everything he wanted because he loved my mom who didn't deserve it. How he gave up everything because he loved me even though he didn't have to. He needs to know he was more than a cold-water fisherman with no future."

Damn, she was beautiful and dangerous, full of life and passion. The way she'd loved her father, so wholly and unconditionally, fascinated him, made him wonder what it felt like. He'd hated his own old man, his brother had died in a car accident ten years ago, and Brent and his mom weren't close. Love of life, of the job, had kept his heart beating. Until now. Until Marina had crept into his soul and filled something he hadn't known was empty.

"Marina, he knows. Look at you. Look at how you turned out. That's proof that he was more than just a fisherman. He was a great dad. I promise you, Wet Dream is nothing compared to you. He wouldn't want you to die to save it."

Tears welled in her eyes, and she turned away. Reaching out, he hooked her chin with his finger, pulled her face around. She swallowed hard, and a tear rolled down her cheek. "Please, sweetheart. Let's do this. Trust me when I tell you it's our only chance."

She stared for a moment and then nodded, just barely. "I hate you," she whispered, but her lips quivered, and her eyes told him something completely different.

Even though they had not a moment to spare, he dipped his head and steadied her trembling lips with his own. She wrapped her arms around him, clung to him like he was all that was left in her collapsing world. She opened her mouth to his, kissed him hard.

Two breathless heartbeats later, she pushed back, gazed up at him with determined eyes. "Let's blow up my boat."

A flash of pain ripped through him at her words, because although he hadn't believed her when she'd said she hated him, he knew that later, when they were safe and no longer being hunted, she would hate him for what they were about to do.

He may have found something special today, but he had a very real feeling that no matter how this turned out, he would lose it today as well.

Chapter 9

Marina's stomach churned as she poured kerosene from her emergency lamps into the charred engine compartment. As much as it sucked, Brent was right; they had no other choice.

When she finished, she grabbed the flare gun next to where Brent had placed her dive knife and spear gun on the deck.

"Ready?" He pulled a flare from his waistband.

"Not even a little."

"Okay then."

He struck a match, and she moved to the starboard side of the boat. Gripping the railing, she squeezed her eyes shut tight. She knew what had to be done, but she couldn't do it herself. Nor could she watch.

The throbbing hum of her pulse pounded in her ears, but it didn't block out the whoosh of flames as the engine compartment caught fire.

Oh, God.

Brent's arms closed around her. Right now she didn't want to be comforted, but neither did she want to be alone, so she buried her face in his chest and buried her nails in her palms.

The fire roared and hissed, and soon breathing became a struggle. She opened her eyes, squinted through the thick, black smoke that obscured anything beyond the length of her arm.

"I think I hear an engine." Brent lifted his head, listening. "Maybe it's the Coast Guard."

The drone of a motor grew louder, and her stomach knotted. "Too expensive. It's the Cavenaugh's boat."

He coughed. "Damn." Hugging her close, he kissed the top of her head. "We'd better jump."

Pulling away, she peered up at him through the smoke. The blood had drained from his face, and his eyes, though dark and determined, were bloodshot. From the smoke or the fear of jumping into choppy water, she didn't know.

"I'll take care of you," she promised.

His gaze snapped downward, so full of trust it stole her breath. "I know."

She went over first, quickly, before she lost control of her emotions and he lost his nerve. The icy ocean water struck her like a blow, stopping her heart and breathing. Brent splashed into the water beside her, and as soon as she could suck in a breath of smoky air, she reached for him. Panting, he clung to the side of the boat with one hand, his other clutching the spear gun.

"Y-you okay?" Intense shivering garbled her words.

"We should have considered a plan C."

The roar of an engine overlapped his voice, and then she heard shouts. A thud and a sharp jolt against Wet Dream's hull knocked them both violently into the side, and she knew the yacht had pulled up to port.

Brent motioned her toward the stern, and they quickly worked their way around, Brent clinging to the side, and Marina keeping one hand on his shoulder as she swam behind him. As they ducked under the drogue line, Wet Dream rocked. At least two men had boarded the small vessel.

"Put out the fire!" one man shouted, and seconds later, the sound of extinguishers mixed with the roar of the flames. "Logan! I know you're here. Come out now, and the girl won't suffer."

She felt, more than saw, Brent tense. The man on the boat swore.

"Danno, find the bastard. Both of them. I want them alive."

The boat rocked as another man hopped aboard.

"Now," Brent mouthed, but he didn't move. His hand gripped the rear ladder and wouldn't let go.

"Trust me," she whispered. "I won't let you drown."

He watched her, doubt flashing in his dark eyes, but only for a moment. After a deep, audible breath, he released his grip. The panic evident in his furrowed brow and tight jaw lessened as he bobbed in the water, and after a few seconds, he gave her a thumbs-up.

"They aren't here!"

Brent swore. "Hurry. They'll look in the water now."

Fear urged them into a hasty paddle to the other boat's ladder. Brent went up first, knife blade between his teeth, took the ladder with the silent grace of a hunting predator. The man might not be comfortable in the water, but once out, he moved with a deadly, concentrated purpose that made her glad he was on her side.

As soon as he went over the side and onto the boat's deck, she did the same.

A shout rang out. The situation became a blur as Brent shoved her to the deck and swung the spear gun in a graceful arc toward Wet Dream's welldeck. He fired. A man's scream tore through her, and then gunfire erupted.

Brent hit the deck beside her, and she handed the flare gun to him. A man burst through the yacht's aft doors. In one smooth motion, Brent hurled the dive knife, catching the man in the neck. He went down, and Brent rolled up on one knee, fired the flare gun at someone on Wet Dream.

"Get the knife and give me his gun!" he shouted, and she pushed to her knees.

She crawled to the man, whose hands were wrapped around his throat, blood gurgling up around the blade. Hands shaking from terror or adrenaline or a combination, she seized the pistol he'd dropped and slid it to Brent. When she turned back, the man had gone rigid, his eyes glazed over.

"Better you than me," she breathed, and wrenched the knife from his body.

Gunfire punched holes in the boat all around her as she crawled to the side of the boat where they'd tied up to Wet Dream. With one quick slice of the bloody blade, they were free.

Brent ducked low, shot her a glance. "I'll cover you. See if you can get us out of here." He peeked up over the edge. "Go... now!"

He fired, and she sprinted. A bullet shattered the sliding glass door as she clambered over the body of the dead guy. A shard bit into her shoulder. She yelped and dove inside the cabin.

Scrambling to her feet, she nearly tripped over the Cavenaughs, who were tied up together on the floor of the salon.

"Are there more of them?" she asked on her way past, and Dale shook his head. "I'll untie you after we get out of here."

She bolted by them, launching herself into the cockpit. She punched the start button, and the engine roared to life. A trickle of blood ran down her arm as she slammed the boat into drive. As the craft lurched forward, she radioed for help.

The sound of gunfire continued. It was a nightmare that wouldn't end, a repeat of last night. Glass shattered, and bullets thudded into the fiberglass and wood.

Heavy footsteps pounded behind her. Icy fear gripped her heart. She spun, struck out. Her fist slammed into Brent's palm as he deflected the blow.

"Easy, sweetheart. It's me."

"Oh, thank God." She threw herself into his arms, but he barely gave her a squeeze before setting her aside.

"I'm going to clear the boat and untie the Cavenaughs."

"They said there's no one else on board."

"Gotta make sure. Did you call for help?"

She nodded. "Coast Guard should be here any moment. They saw the smoke."

"Good—" he broke off with a curse and grasped her injured arm. "What happened?"

"It's just a cut. It'll be fine."

"Puddle Pirates better bring a medic," he growled, and considering how Brent looked pissed enough to inflict a lot of pain, the bad guys were probably lucky to be dead.

"I told them we needed one for the Cavenaughs."

"They'll check you out, too."

Before she could argue, he slipped away, gun in hand to hunt any remaining bad guys.

She sank into the captain's chair, her adrenaline rush easing off and leaving behind a serious case of mushy muscles and shakes. In the distance, the beautiful white, orange, and blue of the Coast Guard cutter topped the horizon, and she never thought she'd been happier to see those guys. Usually, their boardings were a pain in the ass. Now, she wanted to throw them a party and invite them to hang out.

It didn't take long for them to pull to port and send an inflatable to hook up with the Beneteau Antares. While Brent contacted whoever he needed to reach on the yacht's radio, she helped the Coastie medic tend to the Cavenaughs while she answered a young lieutenant's investigative questions.

After a little prodding, he told her the police had arrived at the marina moments after Wet Dream pulled away from the pier, and the ensuing shootout had resulted in one officer injury and the deaths of three suspects. Before Lt. Thompson could tell her more, the radio on his belt squawked.

The garbled voice on the other end informed them that Wet Dream had gone down. One bad guy had been pulled, shot but alive, from the water. The other two had gone down with the boat.

Her knees buckled. Strong hands caught her before she hit the floor, and she knew without looking that the hands belonged to Brent. It didn't matter. Her mind had gone numb, her vision blurred. She'd known what would happen when they set fire to her baby, but to hear it...

"Marina?" Brent held her steady against his side until she regained her composure. She wouldn't cry. She. Would. Not.

"Mr. Logan, the pilot's ready."

Pilot? She blinked her watery eyes, the ones that threatened to overflow with tears despite her tough girl thoughts, and glanced out the port window at chopper on the cutter's helipad.

She turned to Brent. "You're leaving?"

"I have to. Gotta take down the rest of the arms dealers."

Anger and pain and a million other emotions she couldn't identify swirled through her. Her chest and throat constricted. She'd just lost her boat, her home, her dream, all that was left of her father, and now, Brent.

Who had been the reason she lost everything else in the first place.

His mouth drew into a grim line. "I'm sorry about Wet Dream."

She jerked away from him. "Don't. I don't need to hear your lies on top of everything else. You hated that boat." Not caring that the Cavenaughs and the four Coast Guard guys hovered nearby, she clenched her fists at her sides and let loose as exhaustion, emotion, and years of feelings of abandonment surfaced in one explosive bubble. "You enjoyed striking that match, didn't you?" Did Wet Dream sink fast enough for you? You sure there was no plan C?"

He stepped close again, rubbed the back of his neck where his wet hair plastered to his tan skin. "Marina—"

"Go. Just go."

Hurt glittered in his cocoa eyes, and she suddenly wanted to take it all back, every word, but nothing would change. He'd still leave.

"The Coast Guard will arrange for your return," he said in a voice rougher that it had been a moment ago.

He hesitated, his lips set in a hard line as though he wanted to say something else, or like he wanted her to say something, but when she didn't, he turned on his bare heel and left with one of the Coast Guard guys.

She hadn't cried since her father died, but now, as she watched Brent ride away in the inflatable, the tears flowed like never before.

Epilogue

Dismantling a terrorist organization had never been so satisfying as the one Brent had taken apart over the course of the last four months. Technically, none of the bastards had been directly responsible for the loss of Marina's boat and livelihood, but they'd all paid for it.

He glanced around his empty high-rise Florida apartment one last time, and handed the keys to David Gray, his best friend and fellow DHS agent. "It's all yours."

David shook his head. "I can't believe you're doing this. You had it made. Promotions. People kissing your ass. What you did was major."

Major put it mildly. The second he'd been debriefed on the situation as it stood following the arms trade clusterfuck, he'd gone on the offensive. He and his team had pressed the little rat who'd blown his cover until he gave up the info they'd needed, and then they'd cleaned house.

There were still some assholes on the run, but DHS had crippled the organization and saved a lot of soldiers' lives by making sure the top secret weapon the bad guys would have procured couldn't be used against them.

Now, Brent had one thing left to do. He had to move to California and convince Marina that they were meant to be together.

Brent hefted his garment bag onto his shoulder and picked up his suitcase. "What I'm about to do now is pretty major, too."

"You're crazy, man," David said. "You knew her all of what—a day? And during that time you nearly got her killed, sank her boat, and ruined her life? There's a match made in Heaven."

The tiny scar on Brent's calf itched like it did every time he thought of Marina. Yeah, he was crazy. Insanity was a trait he and Marina shared, and he had no doubt if his match existed anywhere in the world, she was it.

Now, with his transfer approved and his belongings en route to California, it was time to go. Time to see just how crazy he was.

Because despite her angry parting words, he believed they had a shot of finding something special together.

"I'm done prepping Dream Two, boss lady."

Marina took the check-out clipboard from Mike Rawlings, her second-shift EMT. "Thanks. Have a nice night."

"Will do." He headed down the dock to the marina parking lot and his beat-up old Volkswagen. He'd be back in a few minutes; Mike always forgot something, either inside the tiny medic hut or in one of the two ambu-boats.

She opened the hut door and prepared to lock up. Her boats ran during daylight hours and overnight on weekends, and her company had been credited for saving several lives over the last four months. In fact, her idea had been so successful that several more resort areas were taking her idea and running with it.

Someone cracked the door. She looked up and smiled. "Hey, Sean."

Sean had been one of the Coasties who'd come to the rescue the day Wet Dream went down. He owned a small catamaran in the marina. "Your boats look great. Can't believe how fast this came together."

Neither could she. She'd planned to use Wet Dream's insurance settlement to buy another fishing boat, but Brent's question kept running through her head, bouncing around in her skull until her head ached.

"Your dream, or your father's?"

As much as she hated to admit it, her father's dream had taken over her life, had done exactly what she'd sworn would never happen. She'd traded her dream of saving lives for that of making her father's wishes come true. Love had forced her to abandon a dream… except it was her love for her father and not for some random guy.

Instead of buying another fishing boat, she'd compromised and started up a water ambulance business. She'd seen far too many people die out on the water because medical treatment had been delayed.

Sean's keys jangled as he pulled them from his jacket pocket. "Want to grab a cup of coffee or something?"

"I'll take a rain check."

He gave her an exaggerated pout at having been turned down again. "I'll wear you down eventually," he promised, and took off down the pier.

She liked the guy, but she couldn't date him. Not when she was still mooning over Brent.

A familiar ache twisted her gut when she thought about the hurt in his eyes as he'd turned away from her. She'd tried to contact him, but DHS wouldn't release any information. She only wished she hadn't been such a jerk. He hadn't wanted to involve her in the dangerous situation, but once they couldn't turn back, he'd been willing to sacrifice his life for hers.

In the end, he'd saved both their lives, and he hadn't deserved the way she'd taken out her entire life's frustrations on him.

Sighing, she placed the clipboard Mike had given her in its drawer, and then turned out the medic hut's lights and stepped outside to lock the door. The sound of footsteps behind her made her chuckle.

"What did you forget tonight, Mikey?"

"Do I need to kick this Mikey guy's ass?"

Marina whirled. "Brent." Her mouth opened and closed like a fish sucking air. "How's your leg?" She couldn't have sounded dumber. Not without trying, anyway.

"It was just a scratch," he drawled. "Some hot paramedic patched it up so well it hardly left a scar."

"Oh, good."

Damn, he looked fine. As muscular and tall as she remembered, and still inhumanly sexy in jeans and a black sweater. He'd cut his dark hair, but a five o'clock shadow roughened his jaw, and the hoop earring had been replaced by a smaller stud. She wanted to jump on him, but for all she knew, he'd come to get another statement about the crap that had happened months before.

She bit her lip and searched for something else dumb to say. "I, uh, what are you doing here?"

His intent gaze slid down to her breasts that tightened under her heavy sweatshirt, to her stomach, and her denim-covered legs. Heat followed in its wake. "I'm here because I need to finish the job I started."

"Oh." Disappointment sank like a fishing lure in her gut. "Bad guys still running around, huh?"

He took a step closer, and the ocean breeze brought his scent to her, the one she'd known would make a lasting impression on her sheets, and her heart squeezed.

"I meant you."

She sucked in a stunned breath as he moved even closer, his bold, possessive gaze holding her in place. "I know we didn't meet under the best of circumstances..."

"They couldn't have been much worse," she agreed in a hoarse whisper.

His hand came up to cup her cheek, and she nearly shuddered at the feel of his touch on her skin again. "I want something good to have come out of it."

"Something did." She pressed her palm to the back of his hand and leaned into his caress. "You were right. I was living my dad's dream, not mine. But I am now."

"I know." She blinked, and he arched an eyebrow. "I've been checking up on you."

Anger took a big bite out of her sappy feelings. Not anger that he'd checked up on her, but that she'd tried to do the same and couldn't. "The DHS jerks wouldn't tell me anything about you."

He grinned, a flash of white teeth against the deep tan of his skin. "So you did check up on me."

"Well, you don't have to sound so… gloaty." So what if gloaty wasn't a word? It fit.

"That's what I like about you—you always say what's on your mind."

Her pulse skittered in her veins. "You actually like my big mouth? After the horrible things I said to you?"

He took her hand, brought it to his chest, where his heart beat erratically enough to make her glad she'd just bought a new defibrillator for the medic hut.

"Yeah, I do. I like all of you. It would be so easy to fall for you, Marina." His voice broke, and she realized how hard it must have been for him to say those words. "More than that, I trust you. You saved my life when you didn't have to."

She stood there, shaken and tongue-tied in a way that rarely happened. How could he think that she, or anyone, would have left him to die on the docks that night? Then she remembered what his father had done. If a parent, who should love you more than anyone in the world, could stand by and allow his own child to drown, how could that child then trust a complete stranger to do anything more?

Before she could say anything, he pulled her against him. "I want us to be together, Marina." His hand stroked her hair, and his breath warmed her scalp. "I know what your dreams mean to you, though, and I'd never ask you to give up any of them."

"But—"

"Shh… hear me out." He stepped back and gave her a fierce look of total possession, as though he had to convince her. "I transferred here, so you won't have to move. And I learned to swim. You won't have to give up anything."

"You learned to swim? For me?"

"Yeah, well, I figured you and your damned boats..."

She laughed and flew into his arms. "I've fallen for you already, Brent Logan. And I assure you, I'm not giving up any dreams." She looked up at him, wondering how she'd gotten so lucky. "Because you *are* my dream."

His mouth came down on hers in a hungry, soul-shattering kiss. His lips were hot, silky, and made her want to weep they felt so good. It had been too long since she had him like this, and she thrust her tongue against his, stroked his mouth, his teeth, everything she could touch. He tasted like sin and desire, and as he moved against her, pressed her to the door of the medic hut, she felt his hunger in the hard ridge behind the fly of his jeans.

"Oh, God, Brent," she moaned, "I've missed you." She wrapped a leg around his hip, wanting him much closer than their clothes would allow.

He nibbled her bottom lip, and then kissed a hot path along her jaw, and down her neck. "I've missed everything about you, baby," he said, and swirled his tongue over the pulse point in her throat. "I've even missed boat sex."

"Well then, you're in luck, because two slips away..."

He lifted his head, impaled her with lust-darkened eyes. "What? What's two slips away?"

"Wet Dreams."

"How appropriate." Wicked thoughts and sensations speared her as his hot palm stroked her hip. "Because that's what I've been having about you for months."

"Months, huh?" She trailed a finger down his chest, over his rippling stomach, to where his hard cock strained against the seam of his jeans, and she experienced a stab of feminine pride when his breath hissed between clenched teeth. "Sounds like you owe me a lot of orgasms."

"Then we'd best get started."

Taking his hand, she led him toward her baby, the boat her father would have loved but that she'd bought for herself. Before she got there, she pulled up and turned to Brent.

The cool ocean breeze stirred his hair, and the waves rocked the dock, but he stood steady, his eyes dark and dangerously aroused, his earring glinting in the marina lights. She ached, throbbed with something much more powerful than lust. This was her man. Her very own pirate. One she didn't want to lose.

She glanced at Wet Dreams' stern, and then back at him. "Are you sure?"

He inhaled a long, deep breath, and threw back his head to stare at the cloudless sky. Just as her nerves began to flutter, he brought his gaze back down to her, a gaze so full of passion her breath caught.

"I've never been so sure of anything. I want the Marina who loves the ocean and boats. The Marina who speaks her mind and isn't afraid to cuss like the big boys. The Marina who is just a little bold and crazy."

"Wow," she breathed. "I sound like a great catch."

He laughed at her sarcasm, and pulled her close once more. "Don't ever change. I want you the way you are. Wet Dreams and all."

Marina melted against him, happier than she ever thought she could be. She'd been so terribly wrong. Love didn't force people to give up dreams. It let people live them.

About the Author:

Larissa Ione, an Air Force veteran and former EMT, is the author of spicy paranormal romance and sexy contemporary romance with a medical flair. She currently resides in Virginia with her Coast Guard husband, nine year old son, and two mice. She loves to hear from readers, so please stop by her website at www.Larissaione.com.

Good Vibrations

by Kate St. James

To My Reader:

When I sat down to write my first erotic novella, I decided to have some fun and let my muse run wild with a title inspired by a scene from another of my stories and only a hazy idea of my hero and heroine in mind. What a thrill it was to experience Lexi and Gage taking over, surprising me with the depth of their feelings for one another, which turned out to have been present all along but required the sizzling abandon of one intense weekend to unearth. Lexi has no idea what she's getting into when she sets her sights on seducing Gage before sentencing herself to two years of celibacy while she attends grad school. And he has no intention of letting her go now that he's got her where he's wanted her for months—in his bed and in his heart.

My thanks to Wenda Dottridge and Sue Chiswell for offering vivid descriptions of the Calgary Zoo, and my gratitude to my good friend Mary J. Forbes and her husband, RCMP Assistant Commissioner (ret.) Gary Forbes, for answering my endless questions about law enforcement. All errors are mine.

I dedicate this story to Steve, whose wild weekend visits *improved* my GPA.

Chapter One

"Hey, stop that! This isn't a playground." Lexi O'Brien whipped out from behind the cash counter of Grin & Bare It. Only five minutes to closing on a Friday night and she had to be saddled with a couple of college-aged gorillas playing Toss the Condoms dangerously close to the massage oil display.

The taller kid leered at her. "Sure, it is, hot thing. Want to play with us?" He lobbed the giant box of Mint to Please You condoms at his guffawing friend. They both reeked of beer.

Lexi jammed a hand on her hip. "No, I do not want to play with you. I want you to stop. Now. Before I call the cops."

No other customers lingered in the small adult novelty shop, but Lexi wasn't afraid of these drunk kids. The short one swayed, and the blond guy's eyes crossed whenever he caught the condoms. A well-placed kick to Shorty's crotch and a blast of pepper spray at Blondie would send them both crying home to their mamas.

"Aw, I could make it worth it your while." Blondie winked.

"That I sincerely doubt." Shooting them a pointed look, Lexi grabbed the phone off the counter and tugged her spray from a front jeans pocket. "I said *now*."

Blondie flung up his hands. "Okay, okay."

The short goon flipped him the condoms. The carton whacked Blondie's chest and careened to the floor. The huge box split, dozens of mint green packets scattering.

Blondie stared down at them. "Whoops."

Lexi rolled her eyes. "Now get out of here."

The kid's gaze rose—then he grinned. "You asked for it, sweet stuff." He snatched a bottle of massage oil from the display and hurled it at her. "Catch!"

"Shit!" Lexi slammed down the phone and lunged for the flying bottle. Her hand gripping the pepper spray collided with a display shelf, and pain shot through her wrist as the safety glass crashed to the floor. Several vibrators bounced on the linoleum. Two or three began humming.

"You assholes!" Lexi shook her aching fist at the kids.

They raced to the exit, hooting and hollering.

"Come back here and clean this up!"

"Can't! Gotta go get pizza!"

Agh. Lexi plunked the pepper spray on the counter, then pushed her hair out of her facc and surveyed the damage. The bottle of massage oil had landed on a stack of rude and funny T-shirts, but the shattered display case would take ages to tidy.

She blew out a breath. Damn her deviant Aunt Beth for escaping the sub-zero Calgary winter weather by fleeing to Mexico at the last minute and asking Lexi to watch over Grin & Bare It. Managing her outrageous aunt's store was *not* her idea of a good time, but the city was enjoying an unprecedented boom, rendering it almost impossible to retain employees continually on the lookout for something better. Besides, Beth had been a friend to her for years, so she'd wanted to repay her.

Gingerly, she lowered to one knee and brushed aside the safety glass chunks clustered around three buzzing vibrators: one a light flesh tone, another vibrant purple, and a massage wand of white plastic.

She fished out the flesh-colored unit and turned it off, then reached for the purple Hum-Ding-Her. *Two more weeks.* In two weeks, Aunt Beth would return and Lexi would be outta this den of debauchery. She didn't mind selling the joke stuff or sensual massage and aromatherapy items, but talking up the sex toys to a certain element of customer always made her feel smarmy.

As she switched off the purple Hum-Ding-Her, the shop door tinkled. Damn it, she should have locked up first.

"Sorry about the mess." She remained focused on her task, placing the purple vibrator beside the flesh-colored dick-stick before cautiously extracting the massage wand from the safety glass debris. "Feel free to browse, and I'll be with you in a minute."

"Thanks, but it looks like you could use some help."

That voice. Lexi froze with the massage wand vibrating in her hand. Warmth suffused her panties, and her nipples perked to attention. There was no mistaking the deep, husky timbre and sensual, naughty undertones that had supercharged her fantasies throughout the long winter.

It's him. Her favorite customer—and drop-dead gorgeous dream lay.

The one downside to leaving her aunt's employ was the thought of never seeing him again. *Gage*. Even his name inspired erotic images in her sex-starved mind. Gage… cage… shackles… handcuffs.

Fuzzy leopard-print ones.

Yup, it worked for her.

Nerves fluttering, she glanced up as he crouched beside her. His gray trousers stretched at the knees… and groin, outlining an impressive bulge.

Blushing, she flicked her gaze to his smiling midnight blue eyes with sooty lashes thick and long enough to leave a girl crying in envy—especially a mascara-dependant redhead like Lexi. Whisker stubble emphasized his sensual lips and strong jaw. And his ebony hair, worn neatly trimmed but luxuriously textured, hinted at natural curl if he grew it any longer.

High school biology might be a distant memory, but Lexi figured there was no way in hell their kids would have straight hair. Not with her corkscrews contributing to the gene pool.

Her throat tightened. *Their kids? Right.* Next stop: business school.

But if she *were* ready for the picket fence and a couple of rug rats, a guy as attractive and nice as Gage Templeton would top her candidate list.

She returned his friendly smile. "Thanks, but I don't need any help. I'm nearly done."

His deep, rich chuckle tunneled from her chest to her toes. "You've barely started."

He didn't stand, so neither did Lexi. She liked having him a scant whisper away, their knees nearly bumping and his musky aftershave teasing her nostrils. His large hand covered hers, and the vibrations from the massage wand spread up her arm, soothing her sore wrist.

"Let me help you. What happened here, anyway?"

"Uh…" Heat pooled between her legs. Lordy, for nearly five months now she'd dreamed of Gage Templeton touching her, fondling her… fucking her. However, aside from a few accidental hand-grazes when they'd visited the bistro around the corner for one of her rare coffee breaks, he hadn't come close.

But then, why would he? A sales rep for a Toronto telecommunications firm, he visited Alberta maybe once a month, staying overnight in Calgary and then Edmonton further north. Considering the vast quantities of condoms and massage oils he bought whenever he dropped into the store, the man possessed one wild sex life and no doubt a woman or two or twenty in every port. With such an extensive harem at his disposal, why would he want an everyday Jane like Lexi in his bed?

"College kids broke the display case," she said. "They were fooling around and got carried away."

He glanced around the disheveled store. "You should report them to the cops. This is nuts."

"I will." No, she wouldn't. Not anymore. In a strange way, she owed the two buffoons. If not for their antics, she would have closed shop before Gage arrived.

And missed her last chance to see him.

His blue gaze drifted to her hand, his big thumb grazing her scraped wrist. "You're hurt," he murmured, concern deepening his tone.

The massage wand continued buzzing. She shrugged, oh-so-nonchalantly. Hopefully harem-like. "A little."

"Do you have ice? It would help prevent swelling."

She shook her head. "There's a mini-fridge in back, but no ice trays."

He smiled. "We should turn this off."

Good luck. Her nipples might never retract again. But of course he meant the massage wand.

"Okay." She didn't move.

Another low chuckle issued from him. "I'll buy some ice around the corner. In the meantime, find a chair and relax. I'll deal with the mess while you tend to your hand."

She'd rather *he* doctored her, and she'd tidy the place later. "Thanks, Gage, but you don't have to go to all that trouble."

His thumb brushed her wrist. "I want to."

Her pulse skittered like a hummingbird's on speed. "Um, but you dropped in to… buy something, right?" Like another three dozen condoms. "There must be somewhere you need to go." *And someone you plan to pleasure all night. Sadly, not me.*

"No place." One corner of his mouth crept up. "I came to see you."

"You did?"

Nodding, he slipped the jiggling massage wand from her hand. "I'm in town until Tuesday. It's not often I stay more than one night, as you know." He turned off the unit and set it aside with the others. "I was hoping you'd show me the sights… unless you're seeing someone."

She grinned. "Are you kidding? With the double shifts I've been working this winter, the only guy I'm dating these days is Juan Valdez." And that was how it would remain. Thirty months of planned celibacy while she took her MBA loomed before her. Maintaining her grades would demand all her attention.

However, with Aunt Beth coming home and Gage unlikely to return for a month, the opportunity to grab some harmless bone-jumping time presented itself. She could harem it up with Gage Templeton this weekend and then never see him again.

Her heart tweaked at the finality of that last thought, but she bumped the sadness away.

"I'm on tomorrow until five. But I don't work Sunday or Monday."

"Great. We'll start with dinner tomorrow night. My treat."

She sucked in a breath. *Courage. Tell him what you want.*

"All right," she murmured. "But dessert is me."

He laughed. "You mean dessert's *on* you."

Pulse hammering, she tried a coy smile. "Is me… on me… your choice. However, if *on* me is how you want to go, might I suggest raspberries and thick, rich cream?"

His gaze widened in surprise… and pleasure. The emotions warred on his face before disbelief all too quickly arrived and walloped them both.

Grinning, he shook his head. "You're quite something, Lexi. A jokester, like your aunt. You had me going for a second there." He patted her knee.

A blush singed her neck. She declared her desire to increase his Calgary harem, and he gave her a freaking *knee-pat?*

She forced a laugh. "I did good, huh?"

He studied her. "You sure did." He rose and adjusted the collar of his black leather jacket. "Now rest that hand, and I'll find some ice."

Lexi focused on his perfect butt as he left the store. Then she dropped her head into her hands and groaned. Her *one* chance in months to indulge her hidden wild side—and she'd blown it.

Damn it, she needed a sex fix, and the only guy who could satisfy her craving was Gage.

Gage Templeton strode briskly back toward Grin & Bare It, his jacket collar high against the frigid March breeze and the cups of ice chilling his hands. Christ, the Calgary weather was as unpredictable as Lexi O'Brien. One day delivered balmy sunshine while the next dumped four-foot-high snowdrifts. Oddly, he actually looked forward to experiencing the wild fluctuations on a regular basis when he moved home. *If* the relocation occurred. Tuesday's interview would determine that. However, much more than reacquainting himself with the city of his childhood, he anticipated pursuing the woman who'd occupied his thoughts since November.

He'd never before met a woman who intrigued him on first sight the way Lexi had. He'd dropped into the store to visit her aunt, only to discover Beth's absence. The unexpected pleasure of drinking in Lexi's dark auburn curls and moss green eyes had wiped every coherent thought from his brain, and he'd wound up buying ten bottles of massage oil he'd yet to use.

Reaching the store with its yellow-painted window and funky lettering, he shouldered open the door and stepped inside. As the bell tinkled, Lexi glanced up from sweeping the shattered safety glass. The condoms still covered the floor, but the sample and packaged vibrators lined the cash counter like the perverted emperor Caligula's soldiers.

He raised his eyebrows. "Ignoring my instructions?" He'd told her to relax.

She smiled. "Sorry. I'm not the type to sit around when there's work to be done. And... it's been twenty minutes. I thought maybe you weren't coming back."

"Not on your life." He elbowed two soldiers to the back row and set the ice cups on the counter. "I always do what I say I'm going to, Lexi."

"I hope that's not the only reason you returned."

He grinned. "It isn't." Her upbeat sense of humor and cheerful disposition attracted him as much as the sexy curves and uncommon beauty she didn't seem aware she possessed. His palms itched to cup the large breasts her creamy sweater showcased. The turtleneck collar draped in front, drawing his attention to her slim neck and delicate chin... and that mouth.

Damn, that mouth.

Full and alluring, Lexi's mouth looked tailor-made for giving and receiving all sorts of sensual delights. Gage had imagined it on every inch of his body, her tongue thrusting and mating with his, her lips wrapped around his rigid cock.

"Could you lock the door?" she asked. "I closed the register while you were gone. I don't want more customers tonight."

"No problem." He returned to the door. After her comment about being tomorrow night's dessert, the simple action of snapping the dead bolt flooded his mind with abduction scenarios, and he cursed himself for his jackass response to her earlier teasing. A primary disadvantage of growing up a geek was that even though the physical changes evident since late adolescence enabled him to enter a room and have his choice of available women, if a woman expressed interest first, he never quite believed her.

Careful not to scatter the glass chunks Lexi had swept into neat piles, he strode over and halted the broom's rapid motion with his hand. His pinky and ring fingers covered her thumb, which jumped against his palm as if scorched. At six-two, he stood ten inches over her, and when she gazed at him, she blushed.

"Your wrist, remember? Let me finish."

Her green gaze captured his, and her tongue darted out to wet her lips. Leaving them slick and shiny. And ripe for kissing. *Fuck.*

His attraction to Lexi's body and spirit was so intense that he hadn't slept with a woman since he'd met her, and the effects of depriving himself were rapidly making themselves known. If he still felt as connected after spending three days getting to know her, moving back to Calgary promised a new beginning on personal *and* professional levels.

"Okay," she murmured. "There's a garbage can and dustpan behind the counter. I'll gather the condoms while you sweep up."

He shook his head. "You're not doing anything until I check that wrist. Do you have a chair in back?"

She nodded.

"Go, sit and rest. I'll be there as soon as I can."

She opened her mouth as if to object. One hand firmly gripping the broom, Gage pointed to the door at the rear of the store. "Show me how well you follow orders, Lexi. Go."

A sexy smile quirked her mouth. Her head tipped, her auburn curls rolling on her shoulders. "Oh, I can follow orders, Gage. Especially if you deliver them… just so."

Leaning closer, he brushed a curl off her face. "And how would you like me to deliver them?"

Her gaze didn't waver. "Forcefully," she whispered.

His cock twitched. "Lexi…"

"I'm asking for it."

That she was. Former geek or not, he wasn't a moron. He'd give her what she wanted.

"Go," he growled with a light swat to her ass.

She grinned and preened her shoulders. Her breasts jiggled beneath her sweater, the pointed nipples begging for his touch. He settled for stroking her with a heated gaze.

"I knew you had it in you," she teased. "You just needed coaxing."

"You'll coax me into a spanking if you're not careful."

"Ooh-la-la." She winked. "Only if you're good."

Gage laughed. She was sexy, cute, *and* interested. He'd hit the jackpot.

She released the broom, and it clattered to the floor. Shit, when had he let go of the thing?

Her laughter filling the air, she turned and sashayed to the back room. Her long curls bounced against her spine, and the belt cinching her waist lured his gaze to her firm ass. He'd barely grazed her jeans as he'd played her game, but the brief touch had left him needing more.

The door closed behind her, and he shook his head. *Unfriggingbelievable*. Another dreary night in an anonymous hotel room had transformed into what could be the most erotic experience of his life.

But not if he didn't a move-on.

He picked up the broom and started sweeping like a mad man.

Chapter 2

Lexi's entire body hummed with anticipation... and she couldn't blame the incredible sensation on the after-effects of handling the vibrating massage wand. No, all her senses, thoughts, and desires were heightened and focused on one thing. One man. Gage. The waiting—and she hadn't even waited for him for five minutes yet—stoked her arousal higher.

Heart beating crazily, she paced the small stockroom. She'd boldly stated her desire for Gage not once, but twice. If he'd laughed at her the second time after he'd returned with the ice cups, she would have died of humiliation.

But he hadn't laughed.

Her skin tingled as she recalled how his midnight blue eyes had darkened with raw, sensual need. Just how she'd always imagined him... how she'd always wanted him.

And now she would have him—or kill herself trying. This weekend with Gage held the potential to fuel her fantasies for the next two and a half years while she dedicated herself to her MBA. Relationships were too distracting while she attended school, and her grade point average suffered. Not this time... because she'd have Gage *before* starting her program, not during.

His footsteps echoed on the other side of the door, and her pulse kicked up.

"Lexi? Could you open the door? I have the ice."

"Coming." With any luck, *very* soon.

She wiped her hands on her jeans and let him in. His smile crinkled his eyes as he gazed at her, mouth tipped with sensual appreciation for what he saw. For *her*. His very presence seemed to reach out, consume her, and her body hummed with awareness and excitement all over again.

Her breath trapped in her lungs. *Have mercy.* Months of celibacy had turned her into a human tuning fork. She'd be lucky if she lasted beyond their first kiss.

An odd feeling pinched her chest. *Their first.* It sounded so… important. Meaningful in a way she didn't want it to be.

One wild weekend, she reminded herself, and then she and Gage would part ways. He'd return to his harem, she to her trusty Hum-Ding-Her. It couldn't happen any other way.

Trying to ignore her fluttering insides, she asked, "You cleaned already? That was fast."

"I had great motivation." He glanced around the stockroom that doubled as a staff break room. "Let's sit at the table. Your wrist still sore?"

"A bit." She sank onto an old wooden chair. She didn't care about her wrist. She wanted Gage to touch her, and if she had to endure the charade of doctoring her hand to make it happen, she would.

Aware of Lexi watching him, Gage found a clean washcloth in a drawer near the sink, then sat at the small table where he'd placed the ice cups. His foot bumped hers, and her teeth sunk into her lower lip as if she savored even that most casual of physical connections.

Lust drove through him. He'd had no idea Lexi O'Brien was so receptive and responsive. Moments ago, as she'd closed the door, the warmth and cramped interior of the stockroom had cloaked them in immediate intimacy. However, no matter how much she tempted him, he vowed he wouldn't sleep with her tonight. Having sex too soon could set the tone for the whole weekend—screw, sleep, screw, sleep, then screw some more—could leave Lexi thinking sex was all he wanted. Yet, at this early juncture, telling her he *thought* he needed more but was reserving judgment could make him look like an indecisive asshole. Or, worse, scare her off.

He looked into her beautiful green eyes. "Where would you like to eat tomorrow? I thought maybe the bistro."

She rested her sore arm on the table. "Sounds good."

"I could meet you here after work, and we'll walk if it's not too cold. My hotel's nearby—nice lounge, live piano music. Perfect for a nightcap afterward."

She smiled. "How would I… get home?" Her hushed tone implied she wouldn't mind staying over.

"I have a rental car. I'll drive you." He placed the washcloth on the table.

A sigh of disappointment drifted from her mouth, and he suppressed a chuckle. Gently, he cradled her forearm with her palm facing up and pushed back her sweater sleeve. The red scrape from the display case tainted the soft flesh of her wrist.

"Ouch," he said. "This might bruise."

She shrugged. "It's not so bad."

He brushed the tender-looking skin, and she winced. "Sorry. It'll feel better soon."

Carefully, he placed her hand on the table then retrieved three ice cubes from a plastic cup. He wrapped the cubes in the washcloth, twisting the corners to form a miniature ice pack. Cupping her hand again, he positioned the pack to her scraped wrist.

"Ooooohhhh," she moaned.

"That sting?"

Lips pressing together, she nodded. "More than it did a couple of minutes ago, actually."

"Well, don't give up on my first aid skills yet."

The ice cubes shifted beneath the washcloth. Gripping the corners tighter, Gage skated the ice pack over her scrape. Her eyes shut, her lashes creating feathery crescents against her ivory skin. Her full lips parted, her slackening jaw both serene and sensual. "Aaaaahhhh."

Fuck me sideways. Gage shifted on his chair to accommodate his twitching penis. Lexi's oohing and ahhing could corrupt a monk.

"This pressure okay?"

"Oh, more than okay." Her eyes remained closed. "It's heaven."

"Good." He glided the ice pack again, and goose bumps dotted her forearm. Her breasts rose and fell beneath her creamy sweater, her nipples jutting from the contact of the cool cloth and—unless he'd lost all ability to read the signs of an aroused woman—also from pleasure.

"Gage..." she whispered, her mellow voice prompting him to glance up.

Her eyes were open, light color dusting her cheeks. Evidently, she'd caught him visually devouring her breasts, and she wasn't as blasé about it as she wanted him to believe, if her brazen comments in the store were any comparison.

Good, let her squirm. He might not intend to bed her tonight, but he wasn't above some intense flirtation, and God knew she deserved the torture. In fact, as she'd pointed out, she'd asked for it.

He slid his gaze down her rack and zeroed in on her nipples. As if in response, they peaked further.

"Nice." He lifted his gaze to hers. "Cold?"

"Actually, I'm quite warm."

His cock hardened. "I'll bet."

Still cradling her hand, he removed the ice pack. "Oh, please don't take it away," she murmured. "It feels so good."

"Then this will feel even better." Setting aside the washcloth, he selected a fresh ice cube. The melting chunk chilled his fingers. "It's wet," he murmured, never stripping his gaze—or his hand—from Lexi's. "I like it wet."

Her breath hitched.

He lifted the dripping cube to his mouth and slowly sucked.

Lexi's gaze tracked his movements.

"Want some?" he asked, voice rough.

She nodded.

"Where?"

The briefest pause. "In my mouth."

Anticipation drilled him, but he stayed his course. "Tough." He smiled. "Because I'm not giving it to you."

Placing the cube to his lips, he sucked. Swirled his tongue around the slick coolness when he'd rather mate with Lexi's mouth. Slowly, he pulled the cube away and touched it to her scraped wrist.

Her eyes snapped shut, and a breath of pure pleasure skidded from her. Gage slid the chip over her wrist again before trailing it up her inner arm. Lowering his head, he licked the icy dew left behind, smoothing his tongue over her flesh with long, slow strokes. She smelled faintly of vanilla, and he wondered if she used scented soap. He loved it.

He licked again, and her arm trembled. From the corner of his eye, he saw her shudder, her dainty lashes still closed, her expression approaching bliss.

Unexpected tenderness tightened his chest. He barely knew her, yet he couldn't shake the feeling that she could grow to mean a great deal to him… if he let her.

And right now he wanted to let her as much as he wanted to fuck her until she screamed.

Lifting his head, he skimmed the dwindling cube to her wrist. Her fingers curled as if to catch the ice, but she didn't move fast enough and was operating blind. He skipped the chip along her arm until it bumped her sweater sleeve. He pushed up the sleeve another two inches, revealing the vulnerable crook of her elbow. However, this time, instead of teasing her with the ice, he deposited the chip on the washcloth and traipsed his fingers over her soft skin. A sultry moan drifted from her.

"Your wrist still sore?"

"No." Her eyes fluttered open, the pupils dilated and hazy. "It's numb."

"Hmm. I hope all of you isn't numb."

She smiled. "Hardly. The rest of me is so horny, I'm on fire, Gage. For you."

His dick strained his briefs and trousers. A guy could only take so much.

Tugging her hand, he stood. "Come here."

She rose from her chair with the dignity of a nineteenth century noblewoman accepting an invitation to dance. But that was where the illusion ended. In the next moment, she was in his arms, and Gage wasn't sure if he'd dragged her there or she'd leapt. All he knew, all he felt, was the springy texture of her curls as he slid his hands up her neck to cup her jaw, the heat and plush velvet of her mouth beneath his, her breasts cushioning his chest through his jacket.

She reached between them and scooted the jacket zipper downward. A sharp yank parted the bottom mechanism, and her hands roamed his dress shirt, curving to his back and holding him close before pushing at the bulky leather encasing his shoulders.

She pulled away. "Your coat."

He tore off the jacket and tossed it at a chair. The coat collided with the cups, and melting ice cubes clattered across the table and linoleum. "Shit. Sorry."

She laughed. Then blew him away completely by retrieving a tiny cube from the table and popping it between her lips.

Green eyes sparkling, she crooked a finger and beckoned him to her. They kissed, Lexi thrusting her tongue to meet his, sharing the slippery ice with him as the frigid temperature chilled his mouth.

Her laughter reverberated against his lips, coaxing a low chuckle from him. He'd never enjoyed kissing a woman more, had never laughed while kissing. She tongued the rapidly disappearing ice back into his mouth. Breaking the kiss, he chewed and swallowed the chip while she grinned and said, "There's a lot more where that came from."

"Please don't, my mouth is a deep freeze."

"I know how to warm you." Without hesitation, she dragged off her sweater, her blazing curls flouncing.

Speechless, he drank in the sight of her voluptuous breasts spilling over the cups of her practical beige bra. She tossed the sweater onto the counter and flipped him a sexy-as-hell glance. "How's that?"

Desire pumped through him. "You're beautiful."

"Gee, thanks. You're not so bad yourself." A mischievous glint lit her eyes as she glanced at the bulge tenting his trousers. "Yes, I think you'll do nicely."

He grinned. "What am I, a stud horse?"

"From what I can tell, oh, yeah." A playful yet lustful edge roughened her tone.

Surprising him for the second time in as many minutes, she pushed herself into a sitting position on the table. A puddle of melted ice from the remaining cup trickled to her hip and dampened her jeans, but she didn't seem to notice. She opened her thighs and, leaning forward, ground her pelvis intimately against the scarred wood.

He sucked in a breath. "Can two play?"

"That's the idea."

Grabbing his belt, she hauled him between her thighs. His wool trousers knocked her casual denim, jostling the cup, which rolled toward them. Gage shoved it with the remaining cubes onto the floor, then fitted his palms to her ass and pulled her against him so she could feel his stiff penis. Her legs wrapped around his hips, increasing contact, creating friction. Their mouths fused, and she rocked against his aching cock until he groaned.

God, she was amazing. Giving and beautiful and so fucking impulsive his blood burned to take her any way he could.

Her breasts crushed to his chest, the hard nipples poking through her bra. Pushing one hand between them, he slipped it into her bra cup and palmed her breast. He rubbed her beaded nipple with the base of his thumb and plied her breast with his fingers.

Her heart pounded against his hand, and a soft whimper rose in her throat. Legs cinching him, she explored the front of his trousers and grasped his erection through the wool.

Gage groaned, riding the firm grip of her hand while gently pinching and rolling her nipple. Their tongues twined in ever deepening kisses before she withdrew a fraction.

"If you don't take off this damn bra, I will," she murmured against his ear.

Man, he would love nothing better than to oblige her. He inhaled roughly. "Lexi… this wasn't what I planned."

"So? Go for the moment. I want to."

She continued stroking, and he gritted his teeth against the rushing sensations. Sweet heaven, his cock was on fire. Sinking into Lexi the only balm.

"Gage..." Her soft voice tickled his ear. "If you touched me, even through my jeans, I swear, I would come."

Well, all right. He could do that.

As her grip slipped off his trousers, he swept his fingers between her thighs. Her legs loosened around his hips as he located her clit beneath the thin denim and rubbed.

She gasped against the side of his face. "N-no."

He removed his fingers. "I thought you said—"

"I *will* come if you keep this up. But I don't want to come yet. Not this way."

"How then?"

She brought her face around to look at him, her profile so close their noses almost touched. For the first time, he noticed a tiny brown freckle high on her left cheekbone, just beneath her eye.

His freckle. His Lexi.

His woman.

God help him, he hadn't expected this onslaught of emotion. It was crazy.

Her warm breath hovered over his mouth, stoking his drive to possess her.

"I want to come with you," she murmured. "With you inside me. I want you to fuck me like I've never been fucked before."

Chapter 3

Nerves hammering, Lexi barely breathed as she regarded Gage, her legs locked around his hips, her clit throbbing beneath her jeans. The damp imprint of his hand branded her left butt cheek, and the melted ice water from the toppled cups seeped through the denim, chilling her thigh. In arousing contrast, her panties felt so hot where his erection pressed against her, she feared the scrap of sensible white cotton might spontaneously combust.

"Damn it, Lexi, you're killing me," he muttered.

The carnal agony threading his voice sounded much more promising than his apparent refusal to get the lead out. She, Lexi O'Brien, who never slept with a guy on the first date, had just asked Gage Templeton to screw her senseless before they'd dated once.

It would be nice if he displayed some signs of cooperation. Example: despite her asking, he'd yet to take off her bra.

Did a girl have to do everything herself?

Don't rush, Lexi. He's special. Let it happen when it's meant to.

She blinked. Where had *that* thought come from? Obviously, she'd rented too many tearjerker movies over the long winter. Developing a romantic attachment to Gage would just muck up her plans.

She gazed at him from beneath lowered lashes. "You don't feel dead to me, Gage." She squeezed his stiff penis through his trousers. "Nope, you feel very much alive." Sensual power filling her, she stroked him.

Eyelids lowering to half-mast, he groaned. "Lexi… that feels so good."

She allowed herself a satisfied grin. "You helped me with my aching wrist. Let me help with your aching—"

"Lexi." His hand clamped hers, immobilizing her in mid-stroke. "I can't believe I'm saying this, but I need you to stop."

"You're close, huh?"

"That's not what I mean." He lifted her hand away from his trousers.

She gawked at him. Gage Templeton of the eight dozen bottles of massage oil was turning her down? "Oh, come on." Legs trapping his hips, she squirmed against him. "You know you want to."

He gave a strained laugh. "I'm not denying I *want* to. But I'd like to get to know you better first."

"We know each other well enough." A huge deviation from her standard M.O., but necessary to keep her traitorous "he's special" thoughts at bay.

"Not enough for me." He unhooked her legs from around his hips and stepped back from the table.

Lexi gasped. Lock her in a cellar and call her root rot, he was serious! He could use the multitude of condoms he bought on a monthly basis with other women, but not with her?

She could only watch in mute shock as he strode to the counter and retrieved her sweater. Returning to the table, he draped the top delicately on her lap—as if he were wooing her with flowers or chocolates rather than slamming her with a rejection.

"I think you should put this on." Restrained need roughened his tone. Desire still tightened his face and body, so what was the problem?

"Do you now?"

His hooded gaze drifted to her breasts, and she wished she'd worn one of her sexy satin bras today instead of this ugly, full-support boob-cage. Who knew, maybe Gage was allergic to functional beige cotton? Or—horrors—maybe he thought she'd sag to her waist without the hideous contraption.

Damn laundry day.

His gaze found hers, a pained look contorting his handsome features. "We have the whole weekend, Lexi. Let's not get ahead of ourselves."

"Oh, I'm too fast for your liking?" Clenching her sweater in one hand, she hopped off the table. Her boobs bounced. "Let's get one thing clear, Gage. You'll have sex with me *after* we see the sights, but not before?"

He pushed his hands into his trouser pockets. "Something like that."

"That's bullshit. I'm not some 'ho who jumps every guy with an impressive bulge, you know. I never make the first move with a man." And she doubted she ever would again. His rejection stung.

He grasped her arm. "Whoa, Lexi. I don't want to hurt you. I *like* you."

"I like you, too." The honesty of her statement burned her. Gage Templeton was more than her dream lay, more than a handsome face and hot bod destined to ratchet up her fantasies throughout grad school. On the basis of their few meetings since November, she genuinely cared about him. How insane was that?

"But I… couldn't help myself with you," she admitted. "Normally. I'm not this aggressive. But, damn it, Gage, I want you, and I'm not ashamed to tell you. *Or* show you. If you weren't prepared to make love with me tonight, then what was the deal with the ice cubes? 'I like it hot'?" she quoted him. "*Please.*"

"Extended foreplay?"

His earnest expression caught her off-guard, and she laughed. It wasn't lost on her that she'd progressed from the F word to "having sex" and now "making love" with Gage. Some wild woman she was. Kool-Aid probably ran in her veins.

Her anger evaporating, she shook her head. "You—" she poked his chest "—need to learn that you can't torment a girl with those magical hands and amazing kisses, then leave her high and dry." Well, not quite dry. Lust-juice still dampened her panties. "You want to wait? We'll wait. I did say I'd be *tomorrow* night's dessert. But if you're not willing to satisfy me tonight, I'll find a… a… an approximation of a man who will!" Sweater in hand, she strode to the stockroom door and flung it open.

"An approximation? What does that mean?"

His footfalls thudding on the scuffed floor, he followed her into the store. As she negotiated a display case, she noticed the chrome legs from the ruined vibrator shelf lined up against the pegs of fuzzy handcuffs and velvet eye masks. Clearly, Gage could accomplish a lot in five minutes. Too bad he wouldn't dare accomplish it with her.

"The vibrators," she answered breezily. "I'm sure one of them qualifies as damaged goods. If I can't sell it, I might as well use it." She'd extended-foreplay *him.*

She tossed her sweater on the joke T-shirts and snatched up the purple Hum-Ding-Her, switched it on. The cool plastic rumbled pleasurably against her palm. She cocked her eyebrows. "Ten inches of pure pulsing pleasure. Mmm."

His gaze narrowed. "Over my dead body."

Laughing, she aimed the humming vibrator toward her jeans zipper, but restrained from making contact. Her nipples puckered inside her bra. The vibrations weren't responsible for her burgeoning excitement, however. Witnessing the effect of her actions on Gage could easily get her rocks off. His complexion grew ruddy, his eyes registering fascination and arousal.

She touched the vibrator to the denim seam between her legs… where she most craved his touch. Her pulse leapt as the Hum-Ding-Her tingled and warmed her through the layers of fabric.

Milking the moment, she closed her eyes and leaned back her head. Her hair cascaded on her shoulders, and she licked her lips and moaned.

Gage's vibrant curse reached her ears. Her eyes popped open as he grabbed the Hum-Ding-Her and thumped it onto the counter so hard that it turned off. He pulled her to him.

"You want it, baby? You got it." His commanding tone swooped erotic sensations through her.

His mouth covered hers, tongue delving. His palms raising tingling paths on her skin, he caressed her waist, her back, then deftly unclasped her bra. With a nudge of his fingers, the straps slipped off her shoulders. Stepping out of his arms, Lexi let the bra fall to the floor and reached for his belt.

"No." Another hand-clamp. A damn sight better than a knee-pat. "On my terms."

He sounded like a pirate intent on ravishing her against her will.

Except she was so very willing.

"I want you inside me," she murmured, and he slanted an immoral grin.

"Didn't your mother ever tell you that you can't get everything you want?"

Lexi didn't want to think about her mother! Or the next logical mind-leap, her aunt—and whether Beth would disapprove of what was about to happen in her store. *Gee, thanks, Gage.*

He cupped one breast, molded and massaged it. "You're amazing, Lexi. So much to offer, yet incredibly firm."

A few pregnancies would likely eliminate the firmness, but there was no point in disillusioning the man.

"I have big glands," she whispered, and he chuckled.

His thumb grazed her nipple, arcing sensation southward. Concern for what her mother or aunt might think vacated her mind.

Closing her eyes, she relished his touch as he rolled and teased first one nipple and then both. Her labia swelled with wanting, and dizziness washed through her. "Oh, God."

"No need to deify me," he murmured.

A soft laugh slipping from her mouth, she opened her eyes. "Your belt."

"Nope. My terms. If you break them, I'm gone."

"Bastard."

"How quickly I've fallen." He unzipped her jeans then shoved them down her legs with her panties. When the garments reached her shins, he dropped to his knees and dragged them down until they bunched at her ankles. She began shaking off a shoe, but he wrapped his hands around her calves, trapping her.

She got the message: he wanted total control.

What a quandary.

She sighed, and he glanced up, a sexy half-smile on his lips. Never releasing her gaze, he hunched his big body and pressed his chin to her knees. His five o'clock shadow scraped her kneecaps, and his nose hovered at mid-thigh. Her overly sensitized flesh jumped as warm breath filtered from his nostrils and mouth.

He caressed the backs of her legs, creating more trails of sensation. Then he dipped his nose to her thighs… and *sniffed.*

"Ohhh." She planted her hands on his shoulders. "Wh-what are you doing?"

"Vanilla," he murmured huskily. "You smell like Christmas cookies. Is this perfume?"

She shook her head. "Body cream. It comes in five flavors—uh, scents. Chocolate Mousse, Strawberry Sundae, Vanilla Bean. I can't recall the other scents, but we sell it."

He smiled. "Well, I'm going to make you come. In vanilla. The flavor."

He inched his face upward, pausing now and then to sniff and inhale. Her heart burst into her throat. She measured his progress from the view between her breasts. Moisture pooled between her legs, and the sensitive outer lips of her vagina thickened with need.

Lordy, she might come *before* he reached his destination.

His dark head tickled her mound. His eyes level with her curls, he flicked his gaze up. Midnight blue ensnared her. "Auburn." His voice rumbled. "I'd wondered."

Grip steady on the backs of her thighs, he tucked his nose into her curls and sniffed. "*Ahhh.*"

The primal sound coursed through her. His nose delved again, and she felt like he might inhale her whole.

"Vanilla and honey-musk," he murmured. "And all mine."

Her head swam as waves of affection washed over her. Her knees buckled slightly, but he supported her, holding her tight.

"I love the scent of your arousal, Lexi," he whispered roughly. "And your wetness…" He stroked a finger between her slick inner and outer lips. "You're so wet."

Lexi moaned. She tried to inhale deeply, but barely managed a shallow panting. Wet? Hah. She was a freaking rainstorm.

He gazed up again. "I'm about to break a rule for you."

"Wh-what rule?"

"This one." His tongue lapped her sensitive nub, and her body contracted, desire spiking. "I promised myself I wouldn't taste you tonight. But right now an army storming through the door couldn't stop me."

An army couldn't stop *her* from responding to him, either. She clung to the very last vestiges of her control. But her legs threatened to give way beneath her.

Sweeping her palms over his shoulders, she whispered, "I can't stand and do this."

"Do what? Come?"

She nodded.

"Sure you can." He lapped her clit again, and she bit her lip. Gage nibbled, tugged, sucked. Desire tightened her breasts, her nipples more sensitive than ever before… and he wasn't even touching them.

Lordy, could nipples come?

He continued licking, pressure swirling in her clit… and deeper… deep inside her. Where she wanted, craved him.

Pulling his mouth a whisper away, he slid in one then two fingers. Slowly, he started pumping. His mouth found her nub while his fingers plunged, and she cried out.

Grunting as if the movement cost him effort, he stood. His fingers still stroked, and he breathed heavily. The scent of her desire saturated his lips.

"*Gage…*"

His fingers kept thrusting. "That's it…" Sensuality rode the taut lines of his features.

She closed her eyes, but he whispered, "Look at me."

Yes, master.

"Now come."

The base of his thumb ground her clit, and her body clenched in rapturous spasms. Her orgasm exploded in a roiling, sensation-drenched flood. Helpless, she cried her release.

He brought his mouth down on hers, his tongue mimicking the former movements of his fingers, now held motionless but still settled deep inside her. Claiming her. Owning her.

Loving her.

"You're incredible," he whispered, then kissed her temple.

Lexi's heart squeezed. What a dweeb she was, thinking about love. People didn't fall in love over one heavy make-out session. And even if some people did, *she* didn't need this. She had plans, damn it!

Relieved he couldn't read her mind, she dragged in a breath. He wasn't falling in love with her, and she didn't love him, either. He'd finger-fucked her, that was all.

She struggled to find her voice. "Your turn."

He smiled. "I think you have another one in you. Or two."

She shook her head. "I wish. I've never come that strongly before, Gage. I'd die if it happened again."

"We'll see." He pumped his fingers, and her tender flesh contracted.

"Gage! Give a girl a break. At least a downtime of two minutes!"

A decadent grin quirked his mouth.

Whump!

"Shit! What was that?" With her ankles restrained by her jeans, her spine whacked the counter edge. Vibrator boxes tumbled like bowling pins, one toppling to the floor.

Whump! Whump-whump-whump!

Gage's fingers slipped from her body. He glanced to the front of the store. "The door." He grabbed her bra and sweater.

"The door? Who the hell—?"

"Calgary Police Service!" a muffled voice broadcast. "Open up!"

Chapter 4

"The cops?" Lexi clapped a hand to her chest, and her nude breasts wobbled. If she didn't look so freaked out, Gage would have found the picture arousing. "Omigod, I'm half-naked!" She jerked up her panties and jeans.

Her hands shook on her zipper. Gage passed her the bra and sweater. "Don't worry, baby, I'll see what they want. You run in back and finish dressing."

She hugged the sweater to her chest, covering herself. "Thanks. But what about you? I'm still… on you." Her gaze fixed on his mouth.

"I know you are. And I love it." He inhaled her subtle musk, and his cock throbbed.

Her eyes widened. "But what if one of them… smells it?"

"Then he'll probably race home tonight and screw his wife's or girlfriend's brains out."

Lexi's look of shocked horror intensified, and he winked. "I'll try not to breathe their way."

Face crimson, she dashed to the stockroom. Gage visualized butcher knives and a woman named Bobbitt. Dutifully, his erection subsided.

Wiping his mouth on his shirt cuff, he strode to the door. When he opened it, frigid night air wafted in around a lone Calgary police officer. The guy stood shorter than Gage, but the breadth of his shoulders and hands suggested he could easily wrestle a brick wall and win. A streetlamp cast a glow over a parked police cruiser, and Gage glimpsed a second officer behind the wheel. The profiles of two occupants bobbed in the caged back seat. Were they the ignorant assholes who'd trashed Grin & Bare It?

His grip on the doorknob tightened. "What can I do for you, officer?"

"Good evening," the cop returned in a deep baritone. "I'm Constable Harkness with Calgary Police Service. I understand there might have been some trouble here about an hour ago. Are you the proprietor?"

"No, I'm a friend. Gage Templeton. The manager's in back, but she'll be here in a minute."

The constable nodded. "May I come in?"

"Sure. It's freezing tonight." Opening the door wider, Gage gestured to the police cruiser. "How'd you know those idiots were here earlier?" Lexi had yet to identify the young men, so Gage shouldn't assume they *were* the same idiots. He knew what it was like to get caught on the wrong side of the law as a kid. Except he'd been even younger—fourteen—and categorically guilty. A geek juvenile delinquent.

Thank God for Lexi's aunt. Beth's unrelenting optimism and commitment to counseling troubled teenagers had helped turn him around.

"We'll wait for the manager before taking the matter further." Constable Harkness stepped inside.

"Fair enough."

Before Gage could shut the door, a balding, middle-aged man huffed-and-puffed up the sidewalk, his hands crammed into the armpits of his red ski jacket. "Wait up!"

"Sorry, we're closed."

"I'm with the cops!"

Gage looked at Harkness, and the big cop rolled his eyes. When the man reached the doorway, Harkness addressed him, "Mr. Fabbrizzi, we already have your statement. You can return to your place of business."

"I want to make sure they get what's coming to them." The man said to Gage, "Damn kids trashed my place. Massage oil all over my washroom mirrors. And you should see what they did to the paper towel dispensers!"

The cruiser door opened, and the second cop's head poked over the roof, her sleek black hair pulled neatly under her police cap. "Need help?" she asked Constable Harkness.

He motioned her to stay with the kids. "I've got it." The cruiser door closed, and the burly officer turned to Fabbrizzi. "Sir, I recommend you leave. You don't want to say or do anything to interfere with the investigation."

"I haven't said a word that isn't true. I caught those apes red-handed!"

The constable frowned. "Mr. Fabbrizzi, it's for your own good. If you step out of line, you could be held accountable for obstruction of justice."

Fabbrizzi grunted. "*I'm* the victim."

"I understand that. But laws are laws."

"Hunh." Fabbrizzi's jaw thrust forward. "All right, all right, I'll go. *After* I see the owner." He extended a hand to Gage. "Carl Fabbrizzi. I own the pizza place around the corner. You've heard of it? Fabbrizzi's?"

Gage shook his cold, bare hand. "Yeah, I think I ate there once. Great food."

"Thanks." Tucking his fingers back into his armpits, Fabbrizzi ambled inside. "I know Beth. She okay?"

"She's not here." Gage closed the door, and the chill from the sidewalk receded.

Confusion creased Fabbrizzi's face. Then, "Oh, yeah, she went south for the winter. Her niece is in charge. Nice girl. Damn vandals got me so riled, I forgot."

The constable shot Fabbrizzi a stern look, and the man clammed up. For a moment, everyone stood silent. Finally, the stockroom door opened, and Lexi threaded her way through the merchandise displays, her long auburn curls tidied and her sweater in place. Nervously, she scratched one shoulder, and she wouldn't quite meet Gage's gaze.

When she reached the group, she asked Harkness, "You caught the kids? But I didn't even call it in." She looked at Fabbrizzi. "Carl? Why are you here?"

"Yours wasn't the only place they visited," Fabbrizzi grumbled with a wary glance to the cop. "I wanted to make sure Beth—uh, you were okay."

Lexi smiled. "I'm fine."

Constable Harkness advised Fabbrizzi, "Now might be a good time to consider leaving."

The man waved a hand. "Yeah, yeah. I'll call you tomorrow, Lexi. We'll talk about this then."

"Thanks, Carl."

Gage cupped Lexi's elbow as the police officer escorted Fabbrizzi to the door. "He like your aunt?" he murmured.

She nodded, her soft curls brushing his hand. "She tolerates him," she whispered. "He probably only showed up tonight so I'll tell her the next time she calls."

"As long as he doesn't pester *you,*" Gage whispered back.

Lexi smiled. "He doesn't."

"Good." Gage felt very possessive of her at the moment—and he liked it.

The cop closed the door behind Fabbrizzi. "Sorry about that," he said, striding back.

"Carl means well," Lexi assured him as Gage let his hand fall off her elbow.

"I'm certain he does." The big man's features smoothed. "But it was in his best interests that he leave." Harkness shook Lexi's hand. "I'm Constable Harkness."

"Lexi O'Brien. My aunt, Beth Chandler, owns the store. Currently, I'm the manager and generally here Tuesday through Saturday."

He nodded, retrieving a hardcover notepad and black pen from a jacket pocket. "You had some trouble here earlier tonight?" He flipped open the pad.

"Yes. With two college-aged boys."

Harkness's gaze turned to Gage. "Was your friend here at the time?"

"No." She rubbed her arms. "Gage showed up maybe two minutes after they left, though. And I… I'd like him to stay while we talk, if you don't mind."

Harkness's assessing gaze swept over Gage again.

"I cleaned up a lot of the damage," he explained. "Maybe I can fill in some details." He hoped corroborating Lexi's damage report wasn't the reason she'd requested he stay. He wanted to support her because he cared about her—more than he'd thought possible in such a short time. With her chutzpah and compassion, she was nothing like the uptight corporate woman he usually encountered. Learning she returned his feelings would be the proverbial icing on his cake.

"Fine by me if you stay then." The cop turned to Lexi. "What time did the suspects enter the establishment?"

Lexi pushed her hair behind one ear. "Around eighty-fifty. I was serving another customer, so at first I thought they were browsing."

"Could you describe the suspects for me?"

She supplied the information while the constable scribbled on his notepad. He extracted a plastic evidence bag from his jacket pocket. A nearly empty bottle of red liquid sat in the bag.

"We found this bottle on one of the suspects." He handed Lexi the bag. "The name of the store is on the sticker, and allegedly the suspects bragged about lifting it from here. Do you recognize the item?"

Lexi examined the bottle through the plastic. "Yes, it's scented massage oil, one of our best sellers." She returned the bag to Harkness. "They threw another bottle at me, but it didn't hit me. It landed on the T-shirts."

"And leaked all over them," Gage informed her.

She glanced at him. "Really?" Sighing, she addressed the constable again, "I didn't realize they'd shoplifted this bottle."

Pride bloomed within Gage as he watched her interact with the officer, outlining the kids' shenanigans. Harkness took notes while she showed him the broken condom box and destroyed display case. The constable's features remained composed as he surveyed Caligula's fallen soldiers on the counter, and neither the cop nor Lexi blinked when Gage retrieved the vibrator that had crashed to the floor. However, when Harkness noticed the pepper spray, he sent Lexi a questioning look.

"I didn't use it," she said. "I just aimed it at them. They were getting so rowdy."

Harkness flipped shut his notepad. "Could you drop by the station in a couple of hours? Or I could come back here…"

"Um, why?"

"It'll give you a chance to estimate damages, remember details that might be missing from your statement. We'll also need you to I.D. the suspects before we can charge or release them. If it's easier for you, I could bring by the photo lineup when it's ready."

Lexi glanced at Gage. "I wasn't planning on pressing charges. I was thinking more along the lines of having them make reparations."

"Reimbursing you for the damages?" the cop clarified, and she nodded.

Gage rubbed her shoulder. "Why wouldn't you press charges, Lexi? They could—and *should*—still compensate you."

She ventured a weak smile. "Because… if not for the mess they made, I would have closed up before you arrived. We might have… missed each other."

The constable's gaze passed between them, and he cleared his throat. "I'll be outside. Give you a moment to talk."

"Thanks." Lexi chewed her lip until he left.

A wide grin split Gage's face. Again, he rubbed her shoulder. "Baby, what you said was very flattering, but I still think you should press charges. You're not doing them any favors if you don't. Believe me, I know." God, he loved touching her, and it didn't have to be sexual. He craved any and all physical connection between them.

"You know, huh? You're not a reformed convict, are you?"

He chuckled. She was too damn perceptive. "That's a story for another time."

"You *are* a reformed convict?" she whispered, eyes wide.

He laughed. Since meeting her, he'd yet to mention his past association with her aunt. However, he hadn't told her that he'd grown up in Calgary, either. Usually, they didn't have much time together and his history had never come up.

Now, after asking her to show him the sights only an hour ago, he couldn't confess he was already well acquainted with the city… although not through *her* eyes, which was how he wanted to enjoy it. Tomorrow night, over dinner, he'd tell her. She had enough to deal with tonight.

And, shit, he hadn't expected their relationship to progress so quickly. He didn't regret one second of tonight, but he needed time to wrap his mind around the powerful emotions crowding his heart.

"Let's say I pulled a few stunts in high school that got me in deep water. Getting caught was one of the best things that ever happened to me. I didn't think so at the time, but I quickly learned otherwise." Thanks to Lexi's aunt. "Now, these kids aren't juveniles, and maybe they've pulled crap like this before, and maybe they haven't. Either way, if they don't take responsibility for their actions, if you don't *help* them to—"

"By pressing charges?"

He nodded. "They'll think they can do what they want with no consequences. Next time, the vandalism could be worse. Someone might get hurt." He squeezed her hand. "Let the police handle this. Whether these idiots wind up doing community service or get hit with a rap sheet, they brought the outcome upon themselves, *you* didn't."

"Hmm." She pursed her lips, and the sexy gesture drove the need to kiss her again—very soon—through him. "You talk a good game, Templeton… but can you play one?"

He grinned. "What do you mean?"

"Well… it occurs to me that I have you at a disadvantage."

"Because I want you to do the right thing and press charges?"

"Yep. I have the upper hand, and I do believe I'll play it."

Gage crossed his arms, leaning forward. "Fire away, sweetheart."

An impish smile curved her lips. "I'll press charges and save those two boys from a life of heinous crime *if* you agree to one condition."

"Hmm. Such as?"

"Well, that's the trick of it, Gage. You have to agree without knowing what the condition is."

Lexi allowed herself a wicked grin as she entered the lobby of Gage's upscale hotel, the yellow shopping bag she'd stuffed with erotic delights before leaving work today swinging at her side. The capricious Calgary sun had come out in full force around noon, pulverizing last night's deep freeze. Good thing, because the skimpy dress she wore beneath her coat barely covered her thigh-high nylons. Add on that she'd neglected to wear panties and yesterday's temperatures might have produced icicles on her muff.

Of course, then Gage's hot tongue could have thawed her...

Heat buzzed between her legs as memories of last night in the store swarmed her: Gage's dark head moving as his nose nudged her intimate curls, his velvet tongue stroking her folds while his expert lips nipped and sucked. *Oh, yes.*

They'd parted ways well after midnight, following a trip to the cop shop where Lexi had identified the vandals. Apparently, Blondie and Shorty didn't have any priors. After a night in the drunk tank, they'd likely face community service and restitution of damages. The outcome suited her—as long as the nimrods never again entered Grin & Bare It.

Her high heels snapping on the faux-marble floor, she approached the reception desk and lined up. While she waited, Gage's handsome face filled her mind. Only not in the context of their visit to the police station, but their stop at the bistro beforehand. They'd needed to kill time while the constable prepared the photo lineup. And, oooh, what a way to do it.

Over decaf lattes and cheesecake, she'd specified where and when she wanted to meet him tonight... and what she wanted him doing when she arrived. She chuckled, remembering the excitement glinting in his dark blue eyes at the promise of a "treat" before dinner. Now, after racing home to shower and change, she just needed to collect his room key and she'd be with him in five minutes... and have him at her mercy in ten.

Another hotel clerk advanced to the reception desk, and Lexi moved to his station. "I'm a friend of Mr. Templeton's in room 1402. He said a key card would be left here for me."

"Very well, miss. May I have your name?"

"Lexi O'Brien."

The clerk accessed the computer, his fingers tapping the keys. "I.D., please."

Lexi produced her driver's license. Moments later, the clerk slid an electronic key card across the counter.

"Thank you."

Lexi proceeded to the elevators, excitement drilling her. Tonight was about wild, uninhibited sex. The more, the merrier, the hornier, the happier. In fact, if she had it her way, she and Gage would never make it to dinner. If the damn man became hungry, he could just... eat her.

Warm hotel air fluttered up her skirt as she entered an empty elevator and inserted the key card in the slot. She punched the button for the fourteenth floor then stepped back and clenched the cord handle of the Grin & Bare It bag. The small bruise on her wrist pinched, and she slackened her death grip.

The elevator zoomed upward, momentarily dizzying her. The mirrored elevator walls reflected her flushed face and glittering eyes, and nerves crept in beneath her bravado. The elevator halted so quickly her tummy swooped. The doors swished open.

A man and woman in the hall moved out of the way so she could exit. Lexi returned their smiles, then studied the room number wall plaques. Turn left. No, right. Room 1402. The very end of the hall.

Good, nice and private. But for some reason the room number bugged her.

By the time she reached the door, her palms had sprouted sprinklers. She stared at the room number for a full five seconds: 1402. A perfectly presentable number. So what the hell was her problem?

Then it hit her. Day, month. February 14th. *Valentine's Day.*

Gage was staying in a room with a number that symbolized love and commitment and everything else she did not flipping need in her life? Of all the coincidences in a world chock full of them, did she have to encounter this one?

Breathe, Lexi, damn it. Cupid isn't out to get you. You're paranoid.

With an effort, she forced herself not to turn and flee, stop this craziness with Gage Templeton before she dove headlong into the Sea of Complication. Unless she came up with a mother of an excuse, if she left now she *would* never see him again. Because he—because any man, anyone—would turf her out on her naked tush for acting so silly.

She set the bag on the carpet and pressed her hand over her galloping heart. Logically, she realized the source of her panic. Despite her impulsive streak—or maybe because of it—she liked picturing her life in precise stages, a habit that had served her well her twenty-six years. A fling here and there provided the salsa in her otherwise sour cream existence. Which was fine and dandy except…

Gage Templeton didn't *feel* like a fling. That he felt more like the type of man she'd always envisioned meeting in her mid-thirties didn't bode well for her screw-him-and-lose-him plan. Gage was MBA, work, work, fall in love, marry, have kids, work, travel, then fall in love some more—with the same guy.

Gage Templeton was her forever man.

Her tummy tightened. Not *her* forever man. *A* forever man. Shit, there was a difference!

She drew in a long, slow breath. *Relax, Lex. It's just sex.* Screw him and lose him. Fuck him and shuck him. She could do it.

Her hand fluttering over her heart, she paced the hall until her panic subsided and images of her straddling Gage, riding him, took their rightful place. Desire simmered, that brazen wench. Heat gathered, and her heart raced. But not because she loved Gage. Nope. Because she wanted him, plain and simple.

Relieved, she strode to his door, unlocked it, then poked her head into the room. A radio played beyond the short entrance, and faint remnants of Gage's musky cologne scented the air.

To her right, the bathroom door stood closed, the heavy sounds of the whirring fan and thrumming shower letting her know he'd followed her instructions. *Good sex slave.* She smiled.

She slipped inside the room and let the heavy door fall shut in short increments. Just before the lock clicked, Gage's deep voice reached her. He sang that old song about being too sexy for his shirt.

She tiptoed to the king-sized bed and set down the bag against one wall. Her coat came off next. Where to put it?

She eyed the armchair on the far side of the room. Her original plan had been to undress and surprise Gage in the shower with one of the sexy items in her bag. However, after spazzing out in the hallway, she wasn't quite ready to jump him. She needed a warm-up.

Not wanting to risk making noise crossing the room, she folded the coat and placed it on top of the bag. High heels removed, she sat on the bed's edge and inhaled deeply.

Hump him and dump him. Boff him and boot him. Piece of cake.

She lifted the covers and crawled into the bed, breathing in Gage's sexy scent on the plush pillows. Closing her eyes, she inhaled again.

Mmm. More Gage. This must be the side he'd slept on.

The intimacy of lying where *he'd* lain hugged her heart, and she tensed. She visualized him sleeping, and soon the image segued to fantasies of what he might do in the bed if he *weren't* sleeping.

Had he touched himself, thinking of her? His head thrown back, his hand pumping as he imagined her there with him, her mouth on his cock, her eager lips sucking.

Desire curled through her, and the warmth of a full-body flush swept her limbs. *Oh, Gage.* The familiar throbbing pulsed between her thighs. Eyes shut, she parted her legs beneath the heavy bedcovers. *Too heavy.*

She tossed them off, and cool air teased her naked mound. Moaning, she plied her breasts through her silky dress and lace bra. Her nipples beaded, and she circled them slowly with her thumbs. Temptation sped between her legs.

Heart pounding, she skated her dress up her thighs, and, with tentative fingers, touched herself. Within seconds, her fingers became his, her caress his heated touch. Not as tentative now. Then not tentative at all. But bold, fast. Slick, hot.

"Gage…" She moaned.

Her fingers moved rapidly, her climax seizing her in a rush. But it wasn't enough, she realized as the throbbing eased and her pulse calmed. She wanted Gage heart, soul, and body. In her, with her, beside her, cradling her. She wanted what she'd never dared want before.

But was she brave enough to name it?

She bit her lip hard. Unequivocally, without question, *no.*

With a cry, she pushed down her dress and opened her eyes. Then gasped. Gage stood there nude, within touching distance, a towel hanging from one hand. His thick cock fully erect, his skin dewy from the heat of his shower.

Swearing, she struggled to sit. "Gage! You scared me."

"I see you've come," he murmured. And then he smiled.

Chapter 5

"Y-you watched me." Lexi scrambled into a half-sitting position on the bed, her emerald green dress hitching up to reveal the lacy tops of her stockings… and exposing a tantalizing glimpse of damp auburn curls. Her indignation was so complete she didn't appear to realize she was continuing her sexy peepshow. "How long have you been standing there?"

Gage arched his eyebrows. With her hands planted behind her and her arms bent, her large breasts announced themselves in all their glory, luring his gaze to the cleavage scarcely contained by her low-cut dress. His cock hardened to the point of pain. He could look at her all night.

He tossed the wet towel onto the foot of the bed. "Long enough," he murmured, voice low and taut with the desire threading his body.

"Gage! Masturbation is… is private stuff!"

"You don't say?" He wrapped his hand around his straining cock and pumped once. "Then why were you doing it in my hotel room?" Heat flared in his balls. Tightening his grip on his iron-hard dick, he stroked again.

The annoyance on her face ebbed as she monitored his slow thrusts. "You were supposed to stay in the shower."

"Hot water ran out." Which was partly true. He'd also heard her enter the room, and he'd started singing the most ridiculous song he could think of to help cover her noise and give her confidence.

Last night, when she'd ordered him to remain in the shower until she knocked on the bathroom door, he'd figured she meant to surprise him by joining him under the hot spray. However, as the minutes passed and the water chilled, he'd decided to investigate. Lexi had been so absorbed in her pleasure that she hadn't even heard him turn off the water. The erotic sight of her rubbing and touching herself had jolted his dick into action.

Her gaze played over his swollen cock, and she looked at him coyly. "The cold water doesn't seem to have affected you."

"The shrinkage factor? Nope." Not with thoughts of Lexi keeping him primed and ready.

Her tongue flicked out and touched her lips. "Why are you doing that?" she asked softly.

He pumped twice. "Catching up. Watching you was so incredible, Lexi. I had to."

Peachy color warmed her features. "You liked watching me?"

"Oh, yeah."

A sensuous smile flirted at the corners of her mouth. "Well, I'm not as great a fan of… watching. If anyone's going to catch you up, Gage, it's gonna be me."

Repositioning herself onto her hands and knees, she crawled toward him. The slippery fabric of her dress shifted to settle in the small of her back, unveiling her firm, round ass.

Her pale, flawless skin reminded him of pearls.

"Keep holding it steady, but don't stroke," she whispered. "And keep in mind, I haven't done this a lot. It might take me a while to catch on."

She must be joking. Just the sight of her moving toward him tightened his balls and stoked the raging fever in his cock. "I have a feeling you're a natural."

"I have a feeling you're right." Her gaze sought his. "But if I'm a natural, it's only because I'm with you, Gage. This is for you."

Her fingers splayed on the striped bed sheets. On all fours, she lowered her head to flit her mouth over the tip of his cock. Her corkscrew curls draped forward like an exotic, beaded curtain… but softer, so much softer.

"Should I get a condom?" he asked.

A tiny shake of her head. "Not for this. I'm safe…"

He heard her unspoken question. "Me, too. Clean bill of health last month. Since then, there's been no one."

She glanced up. "No one?"

"Not for several months. I've been saving myself for you." He winked, eliciting her quiet chuckle.

"Pretty confident this would happen, huh?"

He shook his head. "Just hopeful."

"Well, hope no more, Mr. Templeton. Because I'm about to taste you."

She returned her attention to his cock, her long hair brushing his hand. He groaned, closing his eyes and sailing to bliss when the perfect mouth he'd fantasized about for months closed around his rigid dick and her tongue swirled and licked. Except months ago her lush mouth had represented little more than a convenient body part. Now, after one short day of knowing her on a deeper level, he already envisioned this amazing woman in his future.

Tomorrow, the next day, and way, way down the line.

Hell, until they needed rocking chairs.

As the nightstand radio played a slow, sultry love song, her mouth and tongue moved up and down his shaft. Her wet lips bumped his hand, then glided back. Again, again, again. Increasing the mind-bending suction.

A drop of pre-come released from the engorged head, and she lapped it up.

"*Aaaah.*" His balls constricted like they were trying to climb a cliff. He opened his eyes. "*Fuck.*"

Her lips slipped off him. "Soon."

He chuckled. "Now."

"'Fraid not. I'm quite happy here."

"Let me lie with you on the bed, Lexi. I want to hold you."

"Remember last night?" she murmured. "I could barely stay on my feet, but you wouldn't stop until I came. Now it's your turn, Gage. Can *you* come standing?"

Wench. "Time for payback?"

"You bet." She stared at his dick. "You can let go now," she murmured.

He did. She rocked back on her haunches—causing her dress to slip down over her bare ass, damn it—and pulled herself to the very edge of the mattress. She grasped his dick and squeezed. Desire shot through him, and he moaned.

"Lexi, baby, careful there, sweetheart."

"I'm hurting you?"

"Just the opposite, baby. I might come."

"Ah, my evil plan is working."

Desire rumbled through him, releasing in another moan. Giving himself up to whatever she wanted, he caressed her face with one hand. Shutting his eyes and sucking in air when her warm, moist lips closed around him, he traced patterns of memory with his fingertips, sweeping her jaw, neck, and ear before settling into the cushiony curls at her temple.

His hips moved with the sensual rhythm of her mouth. Clenching his jaw, he held back as long as he could, wanting to plunge deeper, aware he could hurt her.

He never wanted to hurt her.

The pressure built inside his balls. Without warning, she released his throbbing dick. Her fingers whisked down to cup and fondle his sac. The pleasure was so intense, his mind swirled.

"Lexi." He swore. "If you don't watch it, I *will* come."

Her hot mouth popped off him. "So come."

"Get ready to pull away."

"No. Come in my mouth."

Fierce need gripped him. "You're sure you want to—?"

"Swallow you?" she asked huskily. "Yes. This is a definite first for me, Gage. I want to share it with you."

His blood burned. All he could do was nod. She took him deep within her mouth, his cock riding the back of her tongue as she licked and sucked. With a jolt, his orgasm exploded. Her hand slid rapidly up and down, her throat contracting with strong swallows as she drained him.

When finally she pulled her mouth and hand away, his penis remained engorged and proud, three-quarters erect. Pursing her lips, she studied it.

"Huh. Not the result I anticipated."

"After that wild ride? It still thinks it's in heaven. But eventually it'll calm down."

Her gaze lifted shyly. "For the night?"

"Not by a long shot. Prepare yourself for round two."

Placing his hands beneath her elbows, he coaxed her onto her knees, then wrapped her in his arms and kissed her. The salty spark of his seed danced on her tongue as she swept her hands around his neck and pulled him close.

He unzipped her dress and pushed down the sleeves. Her lacy bra tickled his chest. Impatient, he tugged at the clasp. Finding it combative, he stepped back.

"Get out of those clothes for me," he whispered hoarsely. Then, pausing, he reconsidered. "Just your bra and dress, down to your stockings." He wanted to remove those himself.

Smiling, she stood on the bed and shucked off her dress and bra. Her mound hovered inches from his mouth, the creamy scent of her growing arousal driving him wild. Her auburn curls flowed over her shoulders to veil her breasts. Her skin was pure alabaster, milky and perfect. As she gazed down at him, her eyes reflected keen desire.

"You're so beautiful," he murmured.

"You think?" She looked absurdly pleased. "I've always thought of myself as average. My breasts are too big. They don't match my hips."

"Women. Always searching for imperfections where they don't exist. You're gorgeous, Lexi. Like a redheaded Lady Godiva without a horse."

Her delighted gaze drifted to his penis, already thickening with renewed vigor.

"You can be my horse," she whispered, and the excitable beast jerked.

"I'll consider that a compliment."

"You should." Clad only in her thigh-high nylons, she planted her feet apart on the sheets and set her hands on her bare hips. "What next, my steed?"

Gage visualized her in an English hunting cap and low-heeled black boots, smartly flicking a riding crop. The horse fantasy would have to wait for another time, though. He wanted to pleasure her gently and thoroughly, until she understood what he already knew—that she belonged to him. They belonged together. He realized that now as surely as he knew he'd do whatever necessary to keep this relationship going. The results of Tuesday's interview didn't factor into his decision any longer. He wanted Lexi in his life no matter what. He wanted to feel her incredible love filling his heart.

And he would. They would.

Together. He was sure of it.

"Sit down and wait," he said. "I'll find the condoms."

He started for the bathroom, but she called his name, and he turned to see her reclining on her elbows, smiling prettily. "I brought some." She pointed to the wall by the night table. "In the bag under my coat."

He gestured toward the bathroom. "Mine are just in there."

"I don't want to let you out of my sight," she whispered.

Contentment filled him. He knew exactly how she felt.

He strolled to the large paper bag. As he moved her coat to the carpet, he glimpsed the bag's logo. "A Grin & Bare It bag?" He crouched. "Looks interesting."

"Um, there's some stuff in there I don't want you to see yet, so just... get the condoms."

Gage pulled back the first layer of tissue. "Like what?"

"Just get the condoms, Templeton."

Chuckling, he retrieved the box. A tiny bottle of liquid peeped through the next layer of tissue. Also some sort of bronze candleholder... a glimpse of fuzzy leopard-print—

"Gage!"

He glanced up.

"I said don't look," Lexi chastised.

"You brought sex toys?"

She huffed out a breath. "Sexy... surprises."

Box of condoms in hand, he stood. "We don't need sex toys to have great sex, Lexi. Just each other."

A naughty smile tipped her mouth. "Did I ask you to bring me the sex toys, as you insist on calling my surprises?"

"So then why did you haul them over here?"

"You'll see, lover. But only if you're patient. Now come here."

Lifting one stocking-sheathed leg, she pointed her toes toward him. The angle exposed the plump seam of her vulva.

"Okie-dokie," Gage said, appreciating when he was beat.

Returning to the bed, he tugged several condom packets from the box and scattered them on the nightstand. The clock radio continued playing soft rock and romantic ballads. With the nightstand lamp off and the curtains drawn, the hotel room was dim without being too dark.

He cupped the heel of her raised foot and stroked her arch through the nylon. Her rosy nipples puckered. His cock heavy with mounting arousal, he pressed her foot against his abdomen. Securing it there, he leaned forward, and her knee bent slightly. He hitched his fingertips into the top of her nylon and peeled the sheer sheath down her thigh.

She fondled his balls with her free foot. The glide of nylon and her flexing toes ventured to the base of his shaft. Her toes probed, capturing the rapt attention of his cock. He hardened.

"You were right," she murmured appreciatively. "That wasn't hard at all. Well, you *are* hard. But getting you that way again wasn't tough." She placed her heel on the mattress.

Gage smiled, rolling the stocking down her right shin until it bunched at her toes. She lifted her foot. He whisked off the stocking and tossed it over his shoulder, feeling inexplicably like Tarzan.

"That's one," he whispered.

He repeated the process with her left leg. This time when her free foot kneaded his sac and penis, the pressure of her warm, bare flesh was more erotic than the slipperiest nylon.

He sucked in air through his teeth.

A pleased look brightened her features, and she closed her eyes. Tilting her face up as if inviting sunbeams, she shook her hair back: Eve, not giving two figs about finding a fig leaf.

The second nylon joined the first on the floor. Lexi's eyes remained closed as her right foot slipped off his penis and settled on the mattress. He held her bare left foot, admiring her manicured toenails with frosty pink polish. Her graceful feet begged a man to develop a fetish. Mesmerized, he slid a finger between her big and second toes… and she sighed.

He massaged each toe with his thumb and forefinger, working from the base up to the pink-frosted nail. When he reached her baby toe, he rubbed it gently, whispering, "This little sex fiend loves ice cubes..."

A soft chuckle floated from her lips, making her breasts jiggle. He transferred his fingers to her fourth toe. "This little sex fiend loves to come... by the counter."

"Standing up," she added in a husky whisper.

Middle toe. "This little sex fiend makes threats with handy vibrators..."

Lexi laughed, and her eyes opened. "Sorry."

"No need." He'd screwed up the order of events, but she wasn't complaining. Second toe. Her eyes drifted shut again. "This little sex fiend touches herself... on my bed. And I nearly come just from watching her."

Remembering her ardent fingers, he let his gaze fall to her sex. The wet flesh of her opening glistened, and he knew without asking that her clit had started thumping.

The thought hammered his veins, and he groaned.

Finally, her big toe. His thirst for her strung his voice tight. "And this little sex fiend is gonna sigh 'ooh, ooh, ah' as I make love to her until dawn."

Lexi's mouth dropped open. "Ooohhh..."

"Quick learner." He skimmed his lips over the tips of her toes before drawing her big toe into his mouth. She giggled. However, as he sucked, her amusement gave way to another sexy sigh. Plying the ball of her foot with both thumbs, he sucked and licked. He swept one hand up her calf... and felt the toned muscle tremble.

Her eyes slipped open. "Gage..."

He coaxed his mouth from its pleasurable task.

"A condom, honey," she whispered. "Please. Now."

He retrieved a packet and ripped it open. She pulled herself into a cross-legged position on the mussed sheets, and he sat beside her. Feet planted on the carpet, he rolled on the condom.

Finished, he rested a hand on her thigh and gazed at her. "Just so you know, I'm crazy about you." Crazy didn't cut it. She was so free and giving, he felt like he was falling in love.

Uneasiness shone in her eyes. "I feel... the same. I never expected this, Gage." She pressed a hand over her left breast, as if coveting her heart. "You make me feel incredible. I've never felt like this before, and it scares me."

"Don't let it scare you, baby. Cherish it." He caressed her thigh. "Like I cherish you."

"Oh, Gage." She reached for his face, her fingers splaying on his shaven jaw as they kissed. With gentle movements, he encouraged her to fall back onto the flung-open bedspread. Their mouths released, and her head landed on the foot of the bed, nowhere near a pillow.

She opened her legs beneath him. Gage pulled himself up on his elbows and looked deep into her eyes. He fought the urge to plunge into her. Instead, he kissed the faint bruise on her wrist from last night, then made love to her mouth and breasts. Her hands swept his back, chest, and nipples. She thumbed the flat discs, and his cock swelled.

"Now," she whispered in his ear. "I'm so wet, I want you all at once. One thrust."

His heart pounded. "You're sure?" He was no pencil-dick. What if he hurt her? "If it's been awhile for you—"

"All at once, Gage, damn it."

He gritted his teeth. Then plunged. One long, forceful stroke, and he sunk to the hilt. Her heat enveloped him, squeezing him, her hips arching up, a gasp tearing from her throat, evolving into a cry, then a scream of pleasure.

"Oh, shoot! Oh, Gage, I'm—"

Her slick sheathe clenched and pulsed, milking him as her orgasm raged. Her cries driving him, he pumped once before coming in a blinding white light of passion. "*Aaaagh.*" The tendons in his neck nearly snapped.

Too late, he recalled his wish to make love to her gently and thoroughly. Fuck, he was no better than a horny goat, ejaculating at the slightest provocation. With some control, he could have held off, revved her up again…

He brushed her hair off her temples. "Shit. I'm sorry, Lexi."

A laugh tumbled out of her. "For what?"

"For coming after two thrusts."

"You planned to be a gentleman?"

"And feel you come again? Hell, yes."

Her eyes danced. "Gage, I can't believe you're apologizing for the best sex I've ever had. I didn't exactly make *not* coming an option for you."

He grinned. "I lost control."

"I'm glad. Because we lost it together." Her eyes widened. "Wow. That's never happened to me before. Last night, at the shop, I thought you were amazing. But tonight… Gage, *wow.*"

"Thanks, but it wasn't just me."

"Shut up and kiss me, Templeton."

He claimed her mouth, and love crashed over him.

Yeah, he thought. *Wow.*

Chapter 6

"An MBA? You?"

Lexi zapped Gage the hairy eyeball. He sat across from her at the round table lit by votive candles she'd retrieved from her goodie bag and placed around the hotel room. The tiny flames cast an amber glow illuminating the bed, Gage's blue eyes and ebony hair, the bed, the window with the drapes now open and overlooking city lights, the bed, the bed, the bed. If the man who'd inspired her to such romantic measures didn't look so studly in his hotel bathrobe, she'd be insulted.

At it was, she was only faking. "Yes, me." She lifted a forkful of tender cordon bleu to her mouth. "Why? You don't think I can do it?"

"Not at all. You're just so spontaneous, you don't seem the MBA type." He forked in a mouthful of the herbed rice they'd ordered to accompany their chicken, salads, and white wine.

"Ah, so now there's a type?" Lexi reached for her wineglass, the sleeve of her robe swaying. After making love, they'd shared a hot bath, which had led to more incredible lovemaking... and another bath. The cycle might have repeated indefinitely if Gage's stomach hadn't begun rumbling. Lexi could live on sex, no problem, but apparently he needed to eat.

As she sipped her wine, husky saxophones seduced Sade's rich voice from the portable CD player she'd dug out of the goodie bag and hooked up to a miniature speaker.

"Once your aunt returns and you leave the store, I pictured you doing something more artsy," Gage said.

Lexi set down her wineglass. Had revealing that her employment at Grin & Bare It would soon end been wise? Her enthusiasm for her bop-him-and-drop-him scheme was rapidly waning—hence the confession. Why would she want to drop the best bop she'd had in months, *well, let's face it, Lexi, in years?* She scrunched up her nose. Okay, in *ever.*

With Gage in town only once a month, her grades wouldn't suffer. Upon starting her program at the University of Calgary's Haskayne School of

Business, she could study her little brains out between his visits and then bop-bop-bop until she dropped when he was here.

"Artsy?" She feigned shock. "I am *not* artsy. Although many business students are. Creativity isn't limited to the fine arts, you know. Numbers can be very creative… and sexy."

He grinned. "I can't win here, can I?"

"Nope." Her banter was a defense mechanism, she realized. The emotions he roused within her were stronger than she'd ever experienced. She needed to deflect them somehow. "I admit I have a wild streak, but you wouldn't believe how rarely it emerges. Aside from this weekend with you, I'm usually not this spontaneous… or simultaneous." Winking, she popped a cherry tomato into her mouth.

"You're trying to convince me you're boring? Sorry, baby, I don't buy it."

His heated gaze caressed her, and her heart swelled with rampant emotion. Lordy, *what* had she gotten herself into?

"What did you major in?" He cut into his cordon bleu.

"Economics."

He pretended to gag. "You're right, you *are* boring."

"Hey!" She whacked his hand with her fork… gently. "You work in telecommunications. Wires and cables and fiber optics. *That's* exciting?"

"Well, I *am* in sales. Lots of personal communication there." He paused. "As long as we're sharing secrets, I have one for you. When I asked you to see the sights—"

"The zoo and the view from the Calgary Tower are must-sees."

"—I neglected to mention I've seen them before."

She put down her fork.

"I grew up here, Lexi. Calgary was my home… and it might be again."

She blinked. "So when you said you wanted me to show you the sights—that was a line?"

"No." He wiped his mouth with a napkin. "Exploring a city as an adult and with someone you care about is totally different from plodding through foggy childhood memories alone. I want to create new memories of Calgary, Lexi. With you."

"Oh." Elation soared through her. She was so screwed. "Do your parents still live here?"

He shook his head. "My brother and sister-in-law live an hour outside the city, but my parents moved to Vancouver for Dad's promotion two years ago. I think you'd like Russ and Angie—my brother and his wife.

I definitely know they'd like you. So would my parents." He sipped his wine, his gaze intent, fixed on her. "There's more."

Heart tripping, she pushed back her chair. "Later, lover. We're finished talking. Now I want action."

"Oh?" Pleasure washed the strong angles of his face bathed in the flickering candlelight.

"Mm-hm." As she rose, she parted the lapels of her bathrobe, revealing her cleavage and instantly capturing his attention. The terry cloth grazed her nipples, and helixes of desire whirred.

She retrieved the goodie bag from the armchair, where it had sat since she'd lit the candles. As she approached Gage, he shoved back his chair and reached out an arm. Clasping the bag in one hand, she lowered herself onto his lap and adjusted her robe at the knees while he adjusted his burgeoning erection snug and warm against her bottom. He hugged her close, his nose dipping into her cleavage. Kisses hopscotched on her tub-and-desire-warmed skin: breast bone, above each breast, the pulse at the base of her neck, beneath each corner of her jaw as she lifted her neck to the light, skipping touch. Then, finally, her mouth.

The pressure was weightless, too gentle. She parted her lips, twining his tongue with hers. The sharp tang of Swiss cheese played a seductive medley with residual notes of the herbed rice, dry wine, and heavenly Gage.

The goodie bag knocked her legs. Afraid she might drop it, uncertain why it mattered, she grasped the cord with both hands, relying on Gage to support her. He did, one hand pressing the small of her back through the robe, the other slipping between the lapels to cup her breast. He rolled her nipple, and she moaned into his mouth.

Still tweaking her nipple, he drew away. "Whatcha got in the bag?"

"Let me show you."

His hand moved away from her breast. She pouted, and he chuckled. "I'm waiting."

She shoved her hair out of her face and rummaged through the tissue for a tiny vial, which she set on the table. "Sensual essential oil."

"I saw that when I was looking for the condoms. I thought it was your love potion."

"Close. It's a blend of jasmine, myrrh, and patchouli. Guaranteed to rev your engines."

"Mine doesn't need revving."

His cock stiffened against her bottom, and she giggled. "No insult intended," she said.

He caressed her back. "None taken."

Smiling, she pulled out the brass essential oil warmer. "I pour a few drops in here..." His arms slipped around her waist as she opened the vial and sprinkled essential oil into the tiny basin at the top of the warmer "...and put a lit candle here." Careful not to burn her fingers, she picked up the nearest votive candle and inserted it into the cup at the base of the warmer. "As the oil heats, it creates scent and a wonderful atmosphere."

"Mmm. Done this a lot, have you?"

She looked at him. "No. I've used essential oils myself at home, but never this blend. And not for this purpose. Not with any other guy, either, Gage. Just you." She'd never use the warmer again without remembering him and this night.

His blue gaze stroked her, and tender emotion bloomed in her chest. With gentle movements, he brushed her hair over her shoulder then urged her forward for a soft kiss. This time she didn't deepen the contact, just savored the compelling warmth and strong affection building between them.

The exotic scents lifted from the essential oil warmer, teasing her senses while Gage teased her mouth. All too quickly, he pulled away.

"What else do you have in there?" Desire roughened his voice.

She reached in, rustling tissue. "Massage oil. A special blend that warms to the touch." She placed the bottle of wheat-colored oil on the table. "It has a light scent. Very relaxing. I didn't want a strong scent interfering with the essential oil."

"You *are* a planner."

"Yep." She withdrew the last item from the bag: fuzzy leopard-print handcuffs.

Sexual interest flared in his eyes. "You want me to use those on you?"

Shyness enveloped her, but she pressed on, "I'm using them on you."

He grinned. "Have you checked the headboard, baby? Unless you're clamping me to this chair..."

She glanced at the solid wood headboard. Shit. "We'll have to pretend you're handcuffed then. We can use these tomorrow night at my place. I have a brass bed with the perfect headboard." She wiggled her eyebrows.

He grunted as if he disapproved, but his cock twitched against her rear, assuring her otherwise.

He slipped the handcuffs off her finger and dropped them into the bag, then moved it onto the floor. Scooping her up, he lifted her as he rose from the chair. Lexi squealed and grabbed the massage oil before he whisked her to the rumpled bed and dropped her. She bounced on the mattress, and her robe flew open to her waist.

Gage pressed one knee to the mattress, and his own robe parted, cock jutting. He grabbed the belt of her robe and untied it, then flipped the garment fully open.

His gaze scanned her face, breasts, belly. Settled on her mound, where she grew moist and swollen. Looking pleased, he pushed the terry cloth off her shoulders. Lexi took over, dropping the bottle of massage oil onto the sheets and dispensing of her robe while Gage flung his to the floor.

"Lie face down on the bed," she murmured, retrieving the oil.

He lay with his face turned on a pillow, arms at right angles, hands grazing the headboard. Need pulsing, she straddled his muscular ass. Her knees dug into the striped sheets, toes flexing on either side of his hair-sprinkled thighs. A moan issued from his mouth. As his eyes closed, she pressed herself against his taut butt, and he moaned again.

Sitting up slightly, she parted her labia. Slickness drenched her fingers, and sensation spiraled. She put down the oil and parted herself once more. Open like petals, she pressed herself onto his warm buttocks. The heat of her need for him coupled with his firm flesh.

He lifted his ass and ground it against her clit. For a moment, she lost herself in her tightening arousal. But she wanted to touch *him,* love him, pleasure *him.* Give him everything he'd already given her—and more.

"Lie still," she whispered.

A moan of protest slid from him, but he obeyed.

As Sade's sultry voice floated from the CD player, Lexi opened the bottle of oil and warmed a dab between her palms. She placed the bottle near a low candle on the nightstand, then straddled the backs of Gage's thighs and glided oil-heated palms over his candle-shadowed ass and lower back.

More oil, and she moved higher, massaging his deltoids and shoulders as he murmured his enjoyment. She worked her way downward. Repositioning herself on the backs of his knees, she dropped her mouth to his tempting butt… and bit gently.

A sound of exquisite torment tore from his mouth. Her excitement pulled tight as the warmth of his oil-warmed skin filled her nostrils. Slipping lubed fingers between his legs, she massaged the base of his balls, and he gratified her with a low groan.

"Ah, Lexi. I'm harder than a fucking baseball bat. Put me out of my misery, please."

Satisfaction rushed through her, and she smiled. "Turn over," she whispered, moving off his legs and reaching for a condom. He rolled, his cock huge and straining. Heart pounding, she quickly sheathed him. He supported her hips with his palms while she grasped his massive erection and guided it between her legs. Her labia ached, but she refused herself, rubbing the thick head of his cock against her slickness, extending the delicious torture.

At last the head slipped in, and she released her hold. Splaying her hands on her upper thighs, she held his gaze in the amber candlelight and slowly inched herself onto his shaft.

Pleasure swarmed. She gasped and urged him deeper. Finally, she couldn't take him any further, not sitting up like this with the deepest access and him so big.

Closing her eyes, she rocked down onto his chest, sought his mouth. He pumped up into her, and she clamped her legs around his hips, staking her rhythm. Her pussy heated, expanded to grip more of him, *all* of him.

Encouraged, she released his mouth and sat up again, her hands spreading on his abdomen as she slid half-off his stiff penis. Steeling herself for his size but wanting him as deep as she could, she inched down. And down. Until she felt only hot, bursting pleasure.

Dragging in a deep breath, she rode him. Sometimes taking him all the way, other times rocking shorter, faster.

Craving his mouth, she eased herself onto his chest again. He cradled her spine with one hand while the other cupped the back of her head.

He kissed her deeply. Without warning, he flipped her onto her back. Lexi squeaked once as his cock withdrew then plunged, over and over. The angle was too much, her pleasure too great. The tension flew apart, and she cried out as her orgasm shook her.

Seconds later, he uttered a short, harsh cry and stiffened deep within her. Her pulse scattered and her soul brimmed with wonder that she'd lost her heart to this wonderful man who'd possessed her mind for months.

Chapter 7

Gage woke to sun streaming through the window and Lexi's hair tickling his nose. Throughout the night, they'd made love several times, each coupling more intimate than the last. Finally, around three, they'd fallen asleep spooning, his arms wrapped beneath her breasts, her pert rear tucked against his penis and her knees raised. They'd slept so soundly, their positions had barely changed. Now, slowly, so he wouldn't wake her, he extricated his arm from beneath her and flexed his fingers. Spiky tingles radiated up his arm, but he didn't give a shit. Holding Lexi in the pre-dawn hours was worth sacrificing all the blood in his body.

He parted her hair at the back of her neck and placed a light kiss on her skin. She stirred, murmuring drowsily, and his dick stiffened.

Christ, no woman had ever made him this randy. He couldn't get enough of her. Would go insane with missing her and wanting her once he returned to Toronto. His only saving grace was knowing he would come back to Calgary soon. No matter what happened Tuesday, his life was about to change. He needed to tell her, learn if she'd welcome exploring the deep connection they'd uncovered this weekend as much as he did.

But right now his morning erection took precedence. With her knees raised, her warm pussy beckoned, stoking his arousal. He palmed her rear lightly, then slid a finger partway inside her. She moaned in her sleep, snuggling into her pillow as he stroked in and out, never sinking in fully, just enough to tease and test her.

Within seconds, she was wet. He eased out his finger and waited. A soft sigh lifted from her mouth, and she burrowed her face deeper into the pillow.

He smiled and reached for the last condom on the nightstand, along with the hotel mints he'd found on a pillow. Surprising Lexi with a morning fuck was one thing—he drew the line at blasting her with morning breath.

He lay on his back and rolled on the condom, then opened both mints and popped them into his mouth.

Lexi stretched on the sheets and rubbed her face. "Gage?" she whispered, voice dreamy. "You awake?"

"Good morning," he murmured, scooping his arms around her and sliding in from behind.

"Oh…" She moaned. Laughing and turning her face up so their gazes linked, she swatted his hand. "You could have asked."

He pumped. "Do you mind?" he asked as her eyes drifted shut and she moved with him.

Her beautiful smile blossomed. "Mmm… no." Her eyes fluttered open again, and she glanced back at his mouth. "What are you sucking?"

"You… in a minute." He winked. "Hotel mints. Instant toothbrush. See how thoughtful I am?"

"May I have one?"

"Be my guest," he mumbled around the mints before stilling his thrusts and extending his tongue for sharing.

"Greedy. You took the only two?"

He nodded.

Her fingernail grazed his tongue as she plucked off a mint and slipped it into her mouth. She sucked and crunched the small candy. "Mmm. Good idea."

Sighing, she closed her eyes. Turning her face onto her pillow, she clasped his hands beneath her breasts. Then lifted her rear, angling it toward his body, inviting him to thrust again.

He dipped his nose to her neck and kissed her soft skin. As his desire heightened, he tugged his hands free of hers. Her heavy breast filled one palm. He skimmed the other down her tummy to probe her curls.

Her tiny cries, moans, and movements let him know she was on the edge. Rubbing her nub, he took her over. Her warmth clenched around him, spurring his own release, and he groaned his pleasure into her neck.

For long seconds, as their heart rates decelerated, they didn't move. Then Lexi turned in his arms, and his penis inched from her body. As she snuggled against his chest, rich contentment filled him.

Moments passed before her quiet voice drifted upward. "Gage… do you believe in love at first sight?"

His throat tightened. He caressed her back beneath the sheets. "I do now."

Curls shifting, she gazed up. Happiness glimmered in her moss green eyes, but also a sliver of doubt. "I need to use the can," she whispered.

A smile tugged his lips. He'd expected more talk of love, not bathroom needs. "Same here. But ladies first."

"Thanks."

She scooted off the bed. After locating a robe and donning it, she padded to the bathroom. Gage flipped back his bedcovers and strode to the hotel desk for a tissue. As he rid himself of the condom, his gaze swept around the messy room—plates and candle drippings everywhere. The maid would blow a gasket.

Lexi emerged from the bathroom. The spearmint scent of his toothpaste materialized with her. Hands buried in her robe pockets, she smiled. "Bathroom's all yours."

He dropped a kiss to her lips as he passed. He entered the can and took care of business. When he came out, Lexi wore her sexy emerald green dress and was pushing her bare feet into her high heels. Her stockings sat balled on the carpet.

"We don't have to get out of here yet," he said. "If the maid service is anything like yesterday, she won't show up until afternoon."

Lexi gestured to the clock radio: nine a.m. "I didn't realize it was so late. If we're playing tourist today, I need to go home and change."

He turned to the closet. "I'll come with you."

"No, that's okay. You have your shower and breakfast. I'll meet you later at the zoo."

He faced her. "I can come with you, Lexi. We'll shower together and have breakfast at your place." The domesticity of the scene intrigued him. He yearned to share hundreds—no, thousands—of lazy Sundays with her.

She shook her head. "I'm expecting a phone call, and… I need to feed my fish."

"Fish?"

"Yes." She shrugged into her coat and grabbed her purse. Retrieving the Grin & Bare It bag, she began dumping in items. "I have this huge salt water aquarium. It requires a ton of care. It was my father's, but I've always admired it, so he gave it to me last summer. I have this beautiful blue angelfish—I know it sounds like it should be blue, but it's mainly yellow with blue edging and a blue stripe over its eyes. I also have these funny-looking spotted clown triggers…" She waved a hand. "I'm babbling."

"I'm not complaining." He wanted to know everything about her.

The Grin & Bare It bag full, she returned to his side of the room. Lifting on tiptoe, she kissed him gently. "Mmm. Thanks for lending me your toothbrush—"

He chuckled.

"—and for using it for me, too." She rubbed his arm through his robe. "Maybe you should go back to bed, lover… grab some extra shut-eye. You'll need energy later." She grinned. "I haven't forgotten those handcuffs."

Gage kissed her. "Lexi, let me come with you."

"Tut-tut." She pressed a finger to his lips. "A girl needs to maintain a certain aura of mystery, you know. How long has it been since you visited the zoo?"

He rubbed his jaw. "Fifteen, sixteen years?"

"You'll be amazed how much it's changed." She glanced back at the nightstand clock. "Meet me at the underwater hippo viewing area around twelve-thirty. It's in the African Savannah building, and there's only one hippo pool, so you can't miss it."

Wiggling her fingers goodbye, she left. Gage stared at the closed hotel room door.

"Do I *stink?*" he asked the empty room.

He'd just experienced the most amazing night of his life, and she needed to feed her damn fish.

"Ariel, I think I'm in love. What should I do?"

The brightly hued angelfish darted in and out the vaulted windows of the aquarium's massive pink castle.

"No, thanks," Lexi muttered, her hands lowered onto her denim-covered thighs as she stooped to watch her fish—an activity which usually calmed her, but not today. "I'm rather fond of my legs. Any more ideas?" Ariel zipped to the opposite side of the tank. "Well, *sorry,*" Lexi said. "But I am."

Arguing with a fish about her love life. She *was* insane.

Sighing, she glanced at the antique wooden clock on the fireplace mantel of her cozy four-plex apartment. One hour until she left for the hippo tank. Would Gage even come? She wouldn't blame him if he didn't. Her behavior this morning had been bizarre.

She hadn't wanted to run out on him, but she'd desperately needed space… especially on the heels of their tender morning lovemaking. Getting fingered while pretending to sleep—*that* she could deal with. But when he'd entered her from behind and started thrusting in slow, sensual strokes, the soul-deep connection had felt as intimate as if they'd been face to face and he was gazing into her eyes.

Afterward, curled in his arms, her mind had filled with images of curly-haired toddlers racing into a bedroom she and Gage might share someday, jumping on the bed and happily yelling for Mommy and Daddy. *Urk.*

Worse, the images had skipped from that disturbing enough vision to another of them working side by side in a garden she didn't have, in a house she didn't recognize, at an age she wouldn't see for decades.

In other words, a lifetime.

Her love-him-and-shove-him-off scheme had halted quite unexpectedly at *love.* As a wild woman hell-bent on a weekend fling, she was an abject failure.

Her stomach growling, she entered the kitchen and whisked two eggs in a small plastic bowl. Zapping a pan with non-stick spray, she continued obsessing.

How was it that she'd fallen in love in a span of thirty measly hours? Had she loved Gage since first meeting him, but had perfected the art of denial? Or had she simply overdosed on post-orgasmic endorphins?

Sighing, she turned on an element and placed the pan on the stove. The cordless phone beckoned from the countertop. Heart teetering, she picked it up. She could call Gage, give him directions to her place... maybe try out the handcuffs before leaving together for the zoo.

She punched the Talk button. Then turned it off again. On, off, on, off. Like a hyperactive channel-surfer. *Make up your mind!*

She plunked the phone onto the counter. Verdict: chickenshit.

She poured the eggs into the hot pan. A ribbon of fragrant steam lifted into the air, and the wooden spoon clunked and whirled. As she slid the cooked eggs onto a plate, the phone rang. Mouth dry, she set down the pan and answered. "Gage?"

Her aunt's husky laugh transmitted over the receiver. "Gage? Is there something you're not telling me, honey?"

"Hi, Aunt Beth." The call she'd been expecting. "How are you?"

"Wonderful. I'm relaxed as a sun-roasted lizard, but it'll be nice to get back. I've missed the place—and you, and your mom. How are things at the store?"

Leaving the plate on the stove, Lexi crossed to her kitchen table and scraped out a chair. Sitting, she told her aunt about Friday night's vandalism.

"Shit, damn kids," Beth said.

Lexi didn't flinch at her aunt's earthy language. Beth was in her mid-forties—eight years younger than Lexi's mom. As long as Lexi could remember, Beth had related to her more like an older cousin than an aunt. They shared secrets and supported one another.

"Well, you reported them to the cops, the right thing to do," Beth added in her usual optimistic manner. "Hopefully, they'll learn a valuable lesson. And it could have been much worse. I'm just glad you weren't badly hurt, honey." She paused. "You said Carl came by?"

"Yes." Lexi squinted in the split-second before an invisible light bulb beamed. "Why, auntie, don't tell me you miss Carl?"

Beth's laugh skittered nervously. "That horny old pest? Of course not." A weighty pause. "Well… some."

"You miss him *some?*" Lexi teased.

A not-thrilled-with-myself-but-there-it-is-anyway breath puffed over the line. "I know, I know. Pathetic, huh? I can't believe it, but I do miss the bastard. The men here are nice, but… wrinkled. And they sleep a lot. Carl might be a pain in the ass, but at least he's entertaining."

Lexi laughed. Her aunt and Carl Fabbrizzi—how obscene and perfect. Lexi's mom would have a fit at the odd pairing, but if Beth liked Carl, good for her.

"Lexi, please, it's not like I'm happy about this development," her aunt muttered. "Besides, what about this Gage you mentioned? You don't mean Gage Templeton, do you?"

Lexi's heart clomped. "How'd you know?"

"Well, for one thing, Gage is an unusual name. Gage Templeton is a friend of mine from way back. He comes to see me whenever he's in town."

An eerie sensation slithered up her spine. "Gage is a regular, as in customer. He's never mentioned a friendship."

Beth laughed. "I know this kid like the back of my hand. Let's see if we can piece this together. He came by the store, oh, let's say, November. Asked for me, and you told him I went south for the winter. He might have looked surprised at that."

"Um, yeah." Her aunt's trip had been sudden—Beth's attempt to deflect her growing attraction to Carl? "He bought a huge pack of condoms and left. Then in December he came back. Bought about five bottles of massage oil and another three packs of condoms. I thought, this guy must get laid more often than James Bond."

"Not Gage. Don't get me wrong. He could have hundreds of women if he wanted. But he's not the type. More a one-woman guy. A real sweetheart." Affection warmed Beth's tone. "He must have been quite taken with you, Lexi, buying stock so he'd have an excuse to return. And he's stopped in every month since?"

Lexi's mouth twisted. "Yes." What was wrong with this equation? She'd been fantasizing about Gage all winter. That he'd thought of her too should thrill her… and it did. But that she hadn't picked up on his vibes set butterflies loose in her stomach. If she couldn't trust her own insight up to this point, could she trust what she felt for him now?

"How much stock has he bought?" Beth asked.

Lexi quoted a figure, and her aunt chortled. "Oh, honey, it must have been love at first sight for poor Gage. He's never bought anything sexy from me. He just drops in to talk. Well, that first time, he was in a rush, looking for a funny birthday card for his father. He came into the store by mistake, did a double-take when he saw the vibrators—" she broke off, laughing. "But then he saw me, and he stayed an hour. We picked up where we'd left off."

"You knew him from when he lived here?" What, had Beth babysat him? Gage was at least twelve years younger than her aunt.

A serious note entered Beth's tone. "I guess he hasn't told you… it probably embarrasses him. Honey, he was one of my kids. I counseled him. I shouldn't say any more. It's his story to tell. Don't hold his past against him, though, Lexi. And enough with your crazy idea that you can't mix a love life with your studies. The right man would support your efforts, not plead neglect or distract you. If you like Gage, go for it. He's one great guy."

Lexi frowned. What else hadn't Gage told her? Did she know him at all?

Lordy, she must be off her rocker, dreaming of building a future with the man on such a short history. The timing wasn't right, she didn't know him well enough, he didn't fit into her plans…

Wait, what had her aunt said about Gage and falling in love at first sight?

Chapter 8

She spotted him behind a throng of kids gathered at the underwater viewing area of the hippo pool and suddenly wished she'd asked him to meet her at a less popular area of the zoo. One hippo rose to the surface of the specially filtrated water while the other lumbered on the tank's bottom amidst silvery tilapia fish, eliciting the children's noisy squeals of delight. In such crowded surroundings, Lexi's chance to grab a private moment with Gage sat squarely at nil.

Maybe, subconsciously, that had been her intention. What better way to avoid the feelings he aroused within her than guaranteeing they wouldn't be alone? She was one capital-C Coward. Or she *had* been. No more.

As if he sensed her homing in on him, his gaze turned from the hippos to collide with hers, and her heart bumped. *I love him.* Now. Forever.

And she was quite happy that she did.

He moved out of the path of children and parents, his expression awkward. And put there by her. *Sorry, lover.* This was the first time she'd seen him in jeans—comfy-fitting and faded with wear. A cranberry red Henley shirt winked from his unzipped jacket. The casual attire suited him, although, in her admittedly biased opinion, he looked just as devastatingly sexy in the trousers and dress shirt he'd worn Friday night.

Gage, her man for all reasons. And, if she had anything to say about it, for all the seasons of her life.

"Hi," she said. "Have you been waiting long?"

He shook his head. "I wasn't sure you'd come."

"I know." She clasped his hand. "I'm sorry. This weekend happened so quickly…" Mindful of innocent ears and eyes clustered nearby, she whispered, "I expected the… hot and heavy, but there was no way I could have prepared myself for the way you make me feel."

He smiled. "That good, huh?"

She squeezed his hand. "Yes," she whispered. "But not just the… s-e-x. Although that *is* amazing." She pressed her free hand over her heart.

"How you make me feel in here."

The sensual humor in his eyes bloomed into passionate affection. His gaze slipped to a little girl watching them while sucking her thumb. He looked at Lexi. "Can we get out of here? I want to see the zoo with you, baby, but there's so much I need to tell you first."

"I know the perfect spot. Still in the Destination Africa complex, but more private." Their hands shifted so his large one covered hers. She led him past the hippo tank with the view of giraffes behind it. Families and couples mingled around them, but not so close now that they needed to hush their voices.

As they exited the Savannah building, she asked, "Why didn't you tell me you knew my aunt as more than the owner of the store?"

"Whoops. Am I dead now?"

The brisk mid-day breeze fluttered her hair. Lexi shivered in her Gore-Tex jacket and curled her hand more cozily within his. "No. Well, initial knee-jerk reaction? Yes, I was a little unsettled when Aunt Beth called and I found out..."

"The mystery phone call," he murmured.

"Your name... slipped out. But I wasn't angry with you, Gage. Just confused, and maybe ticked at myself for misreading you so badly. I thought you were some womanizing stud with an endless need for condoms—"

He laughed.

"—so I planned to have my way with you this weekend and then toss you aside."

Amusement lit his gaze. "Considering how many condoms I bought this winter, I guess I can't blame you for getting the wrong impression."

As he maneuvered them around a huddle of baby-laden strollers and parental units, he placed his palm on her back. The gentlemanly gesture spoke of caring and protection, and contentment burrowed through her.

"Talking to my aunt helped me realize that, deep down, I think I've always known you and I could share something special, and... it scared me. The timing is seriously screwed, Gage, what with me starting two jobs in a few weeks and then grad school in September."

She pointed him toward the TransAlta Rainforest building. His thumb brushed her hand. "I love your dedication to your studies, Lexi. I wouldn't stand in your way."

"I know."

"So are you still scared?"

"No." She smiled. "I'm excited. I've never known anyone like you, and I'm not giving you up. Toronto is too far away, but with you coming here once a month—it's not perfect, but it's a start."

A disquieting look masked his features, and her nerves slapped. If Gage didn't want what she did…

The double automatic doors of the Rainforest building whisked open, distracting her. A wall of heat and the heavy scent of earthy foliage swamped them.

"Wow." Gage glanced ahead of them. "The Savannah building was great, but this place feels like we're entering a jungle."

"It gets better." With the piped-in mist and displays of exotic fish, lizards, beetles, and innumerable tropical plants, trees, and flowers, the Rainforest exhibit teemed with vigor and life. Not to mention curl-frizzing humidity. Oh, the cruelties she suffered for love.

"The spot I mentioned is this way." She guided them past the snakes, fruit bats, and tiny turtles. They strolled through a layer of mist and across a wooden bridge along a manmade mountain. A steep staircase detoured from the main path and extended up the faux mountain. "This leads to the top of the gorilla enclosure. It's stifling hot, but also very private."

"Then let's go."

He released her hand as they climbed the stairs. When they reached the top, only a man and young boy overlooked the enclosure of western lowland gorillas. The area lacked the usual… aromatic monkey-house scents. To Lexi, the tiny space with the simulated-mountainside view of primates was enchanting and romantic.

"Incredible." Gage scanned the enclosure while they held back from the pair at the Plexiglas railing. The cramped area offered standing room only—four adults would stretch its limits.

The father glanced over his shoulder, and Lexi smiled at the kind-looking man. "Take your time," she said.

However, the boy mumbled that he wanted a closer look at the gorillas, so the man steered the child to the exiting staircase. A cooler viewing area with benches and deep pocket windows awaited them below.

Gage and Lexi stepped to the barrier. Lexi unzipped her jacket to seek relief from the heat. Gage watched the gorillas then looked at her. "How much did your aunt tell you?"

"That you were one of the kids she counseled years ago. She didn't explain why you started seeing her, though. I figured it had something to do with those stunts you said you pulled in high school."

"What a fourteen-year-old geek will do to get the attention of the cool chicks…"

Lexi swept her gaze up and down His Exquisiteness. "You were *not* a geek."

"Yes, I was. A skinny techno-whiz with too much time on his hands and hormones going bananas." Grinning and nodding to the gorilla enclosure, he added, "Little pun."

Lexi laughed.

Gage turned up a hand. "I could tell you how I cut pictures from Russ's girlie magazines—"

"Oh, *Russ's* magazines—"

"—and taped them all over my Social Studies teacher's current events collage. This thing was massive, Lexi, and he didn't discover the pictures for days."

A giggle bubbled out of her. "You didn't!"

"Yes, I did. Or I could tell you how, when that prank earned me a few interested looks from the hot chicks—"

"I thought they were cool chicks."

"They were warming up to me. I could tell you about breaking into the girls' locker room during a volleyball tournament and stealing the bras of the ones who wore those stretchy—" he gestured over his pectorals "—you know…"

"Sports bras?"

"Yes, under their uniforms for their games. Or I could skip over the small stuff and tell you about hot-wiring the principal's vintage muscle car and joyriding around the neighborhood until I crashed it into an outside table at the Dairy Queen."

"Oh, Gage." Lexi pressed a hand to her mouth. She tried to imagine a skinny adolescent Gage acting out to such disastrous results, but couldn't. With his genes, forget her earlier obsession with curly-haired babies—God help their kids.

"My parents were great, so it's not like I had major problems at home. Just the usual crap. But to an unpopular fourteen-year-old, 'the usual crap' feels momentous."

"Awwww." She kissed him. "What did your parents do?"

"Ensured I suffered the consequences of my actions, like they should have. After the wreck, agreeing to counseling was one of the conditions that saved me from appearing before the judge. I was assigned to your aunt. She was maybe twenty-seven and quickly became an important part of my life."

Thick heat layered on them, making Lexi glad she'd worn a T-shirt beneath her heavy jacket. The smothering humidity felt like she was inhaling porridge, but she'd suffocate in their intimate hidey-hole before she stopped Gage from finishing his story.

"Beth helped me through a rough time. My parents couldn't afford a computer, and we didn't have a lab at the high school then. Beth introduced me to a Rotary computer club for dorky tech kids. Through her, I learned to direct my energy into something positive. Developing self-confidence came next. After that, everything fell into place. Hitting a growth spurt helped."

Lexi's heart squeezed for the troubled adolescent, and she brushed Gage's hand atop the barrier. Learning her aunt had befriended them both as teens stirred something deep inside her. Call it kismet, fate, destiny—her life and Gage's had been linked for years, although neither of them had known it.

And now their lives and hearts would be entwined for all time.

"I regretted losing touch with Beth as I grew older," Gage said. "So when I ran into her at the store last summer, I kept coming back. Then I met you, and I went ape on the condoms and massage oil so you'd remember me whenever I returned."

"My favorite customer. I couldn't have forgotten you if a laser beam had zapped my memory. And now I understand why you were so adamant about me reporting those kids Friday night."

His thickly lashed eyes engulfed her until she swam in midnight blue. "I was hoping you'd feel that way… about everything. Because I want to stay in your life, Lexi. I'm falling in love with you, baby. I think I have been for months."

Happy tears pricked her eyes. "I'm falling in love with you, too. Except I'm not certain 'falling' is the right word. I'm already there."

"Oh, baby, I'm there, too." He curled his arms around her waist beneath the open jacket. With excruciating tenderness, he kissed her. "Lexi, I love you," he murmured against her mouth.

She touched his jaw. "And I love you. I'm so glad we have tomorrow. What time do you leave Tuesday?"

His mouth hooked up. "Um, yeah, about that… there's one more thing I need to tell you."

He could surprise her from now until she slept on the wrong side of the grass, and she'd still want him. "What?"

"When I said I'm in town until Tuesday… I'm not seeing customers, Lexi. I have an interview with CyberVerge Systems."

"CyberVerge?" Only the most innovative telecommunications firm in the province. And an up-and-coming competitor to his current employer.

He nodded. "In sales management, meaning less travel, but still interacting with people—my forte. I've waited ages for an opportunity like this. I like Toronto, but Calgary is my home. After you left the hotel this morning, I scouted newspapers for apartments for rent. I'd love to view some tomorrow—with you, if you want to."

Panic blipped in her chest. Her once-a-month man was telling her he could be her whenever-she-wanted? "What if you don't get the job?"

He stroked her back beneath her jacket. His hands drifted to her rear. He tugged her close, his pelvis fitting snugly against her tummy. Welcome desire coiled.

"I want to move back regardless of what happens with CyberVerge. With the way this town is booming, I can find another job, hell, maybe even break out on my own. A partner with an MBA would come in handy." He smiled. "I don't have to stay in telecommunications, Lexi."

Sweet emotion soared on strong, stable wings. He was incredible. And she was so lucky. Bye-bye Juan Valdez.

"What we have, baby… it's once in a lifetime," he murmured. "With your say-so, I want to give my notice as soon as I get back to Toronto. This time next month, I want to be living here. Who knows, maybe in a few months we can move in together."

"You can move in right away. We don't have to wait." *Blip-blip.* Precise Planners Anonymous, had *she* changed. But only for the better.

Gage grinned. "Thanks, but I don't want to rush you. This is right between us—I know it. We can take our time."

"But no long-distance romance." Relief coursed through her. Until now, she hadn't realized how torturous leaving half the country between them would have been.

"Hell, no." He kissed her. A sound of primal need rumbled deep in his throat… rushed up, vibrated through her… oh, so good. His palms swept her ribs to graze the sensitive undersides of her breasts. Drawing back, he looked at her nipples pointing beneath her thin cotton T-shirt. Potent male admiration softened his features. "Ah, Lexi, the things you do to me."

Tucking her close so she could feel his arousal, he kissed her. "This could be the start of something big," he murmured.

Smiling, she gazed downward. "Well, look at that," she whispered. "It already is."

About the Author:

Kate St. James lives in Canada with her husband and two sons. When she's not trying to whip her disobedient muse into submission, you can find her chasing her dog in the hills above an azure lake, ignoring the smoke alarms blaring from the kitchen, or endlessly renovating her house. Kate also writes romantic comedies under another name, but if she told you what it was, there'd be no mystery to solve, would there?

You can visit Kate on the web at www.katestjames.com.

Virgin of the Amazon

by Mia Varano

To My Reader:

Do you remember your first time? You can bet Anna Winter will never forget hers with a mysterious British adventurer amid the hot, steamy jungle of the Amazon.

Chapter 1

Anna swatted at the blue and gold dragonfly zipping around her head. At least it resembled a dragonfly. If only she'd paid attention, she might know if the thing shot poisonous venom into its unsuspecting victims or not.

Undeterred and unrelenting, the insect attempted another landing on Anna's shoulder. She ducked, and its wings brushed her face. That touch of gossamer unleashed a fresh jolt of terror, and Anna scrambled over the rocks, howling like a wounded dog.

The scream never even made it past the canopy of trees that hung overhead, housing untold numbers of creepy crawlies. She slapped at her bare legs, squishing mosquitoes into the mud caking there. Why bother? She had enough mosquito spray on to repel an army of the little critters—the twenty-four hour stuff.

She checked her watch. Surely the tour guides would notice her absence from both groups before her twenty-four hours were up. Wouldn't they?

She couldn't believe she allowed this to happen. Had she morphed into the dumb, busty blonde she'd held at bay for over ten years now? Morphed into her mother? Her sister?

She clenched her jaw and did serious injury to the bug beneath her hiking boot. Her sister. She blamed Jenny for all of it.

She peered up river, into the darkness. The sun blazed up there somewhere, but it waged a losing battle against the heavy foliage of the rainforest. Had she made a mistake trying to follow the four-wheel drive Jeeps up river, rather than following the boats back to the base camp?

A smooth rock beckoned, and she perched on its edge. Didn't want to relax too much. Never knew what lurked out there ready to grab you. She eyed the murky water tumbling over the rocks and shifted her feet away from the banks of the river. She had listened enough to catch the warning about crocodiles lurking in there. Plenty of them. Hungry ones.

Don't think about hungry. She shrugged out of her backpack and swung it into her lap. Mission accomplished. She pulled a granola bar out and unwrapped it.

Its sweet scent replaced the damp, earthy smell that permeated her nostrils. That primitive smell cloaked something mysterious and frightening. Granola represented safety.

Anna prized safety. At least she did before her sister wormed back into her life and stole her fiancé. That act unleashed an unexpected torrent of emotions in Anna.

Especially when she walked in on Vincent and Jenny.

She experienced rage at finding her fiancé and sister together, but the manner in which she found them triggered a disturbing response.

A whisper of a breeze lifted the leaves, and Anna crumpled the wrapper in her hand. Don't think about it. She bent over and stuffed the wrapper in her backpack.

She straightened up, and a twig snapped behind her. She spun around.

At least ten men, a few with long spears, formed a semi-circle behind her. Her eyes darted from one to the other, looking for a familiar face. Her tour guides dressed in modern khaki clothing, but these men wore some sort of tribal dress–loincloths, headdresses, piercings, and painted faces.

She raised her eyebrows. Did they work for the tour group? Maybe they were members of some dance troop sent to look for her.

"Do you speak English? I'm Anna Winter, the missing tourist." She tried on her best smile, the one she reserved for cooperative students in the university library.

The men mumbled among themselves. Progress. She jumped up from the rock and secured her backpack. "Lead the way."

One of the men pointed to her head. "Hat."

She ran her fingers along the edge of her soft-brimmed safari hat. "Yes, hat."

Another man gestured for her to pull it off.

What did they want? Was there some grotesque creature clinging to her hat? She whipped the hat off her head and flung it to the ground.

The men all began talking at once as they stared at her hair. What the heck? She ran her hands over the top of her head and down her braid.

They laughed. She laughed. She'd laugh at anything as long as they led her out of this God-forsaken jungle. She gestured up the river. "The Jeeps?"

They all nodded. A few of them repeated, "Jeeps."

Now they were getting somewhere. She picked up her hat, brushed it off, and squashed it back on her head.

The men formed a loose circle around her, as they slogged along the river bank. She knew a little Spanish and tried it out on them. Not much response. She figured her fluent French and German would be useless out here.

If she had to chuck it all when she walked out on Vincent, at least she could've chucked it for Paris or Rome. No, too much in character for her. She needed a huge change, a clean break for her summer vacation. Well, she got it. Nobody knew she'd headed down here to the Amazon. Not her mother. Not Jenny. Certainly not Vincent. Not even her best friend, Nicole.

Her escorts cut away from the river, and began plowing through the thick undergrowth. The smell of the dank earth overwhelmed her, stirring the uneasiness in her gut. The men followed no path or trail, but they seemed to know where they were going. Now this is what she called an up-close-and–personal tour of the rainforest. Much better than the Jeeps.

But not faster. She checked her watch and gasped. They'd been walking for almost two hours. She stopped. They stopped. "Where's the rest of the tour group?"

A few of the men murmured, "Group."

Her belly clenched around the vestiges of that granola bar she downed two hours ago. Where were they? "You are with the tour group, aren't you? Rainforest Rendezvous?"

They laughed, the sound not so friendly now. "Where are you taking me? I'm with Rainforest Rendezvous. Where are the Jeeps?"

One of the men took her arm. "Jeeps."

She shook him off and dug her heels into the mush beneath her hiking boots. Did they know with whom they were dealing? She could silence the entire Northern Connecticut University Library with a raised finger. She could reduce a pre-law student to a blushing, stammering schoolboy.

She put a chill in her voice. "Which one of you can speak English?"

They all shrugged, and a few of them said, "Jeeps."

She drew in a deep breath, and then someone said, "Almost there."

Swiveling her head from side to side, she choked out, "Who said that? Sounds like pretty good English to me."

Grins met her darting gaze, as the men continued along the path that only they seemed to see.

The tour company couldn't send out a better rescue squad than this? Even the Donner party got better service. She'd be making a few phone calls when she got home.

Not that she looked forward to going home. How could she face them all? Having done her dirty deed, Jenny left Connecticut, dumping Vincent in the process. Vincent came crawling back to Anna with contrition etched on his red face, but she told him to take a hike.

She believed all his crap about saving themselves for marriage. Well she saved all right while he spent like a drunken sailor.

The trees began to thin out, and she smelled smoke. Thank God. Civilization. Or maybe not.

They edged into a clearing, busy with women hauling bowls of water and sticks for the fire. Tents flapped around the border of the clearing and animal carcasses hung on lines between the trees.

Her rescuers nudged her into the clearing, and the activity ceased. All eyes, wide with surprise, rested on Anna. Had they given her up for dead already?

Then whoops and cheers rose from the little tent village, and people gathered around her, touching her braid, nodding, and smiling. What a wonderful greeting. Perhaps she didn't realize how much danger lurked in the rainforest. They sure seemed happy to see her.

She smiled and murmured words of thanks, even if they didn't understand her.

A hush descended as a man's low voice called out something in an unfamiliar language. Portuguese? The group parted until a clear path opened up between her and the newcomer.

Her mouth dropped open. The man towering above of her sported a loincloth that drooped low on his hips and hung half-way down his powerful thighs. His flat belly flared up to an impressive chest. Although his magnificent body could make Calvin Klein drool, or at least Calvin Klein's advertising department, his chiseled face mesmerized her. This was no Amazon native.

He spread his hands, bowed his head to the assembled group, and said something in that strange language.

The people began chanting, "Coop, coop, coop."

One of the women shoved Anna forward, and she stumbled toward the man. He gripped her wrist and yanked her into the tent behind him.

Once inside, he pulled her toward him until his loincloth brushed against the front of her khaki walking shorts. His blue eyes glinted dangerously. "What the bloody 'ell are you doing here?"

Mad dogs and Englishmen. Anna shook off his hand. He looked ridiculous. Her eyes tracked down from his broad shoulders to his flimsy loincloth. Okay, maybe ridiculous wasn't the appropriate word. "I'm a tourist."

His brows shot up. "A tourist? Way out here?"

She flung her arm back. "They brought me here. I'm with the Rainforest Rendezvous tour group. I messed up. I meant to take the Jeeps in for another hike, but I wandered too far down a path and when I returned, both the boats and the Jeeps were gone. Each probably thought I went with the other group."

He shook his head, his dark, tangled hair brushing his shoulders. "Bloody 'ell."

She wrinkled her nose. "Will you stop cursing?"

He didn't resemble any Englishman she'd ever met before. The few visiting scholars from England they had at the university were refined, intellectual… skinny, pale. She dragged her eyes away from his bronzed chest. His masculinity overpowered the small tent, and his small loincloth overpowered her senses.

She took a step back. "So what are you doing here? Looks like you're playing dress-up."

His grin just about sucked out any air she had left in her lungs. Definitely too close in here.

"I am."

"Excuse me?"

He took a turn around the tent, his loincloth flapping dangerously around his muscled buttocks. He stopped in front of her and leaned in close. His lips brushed her ear, sending a river of sweet honey through her veins. "I stumbled on the tribe several months ago. They have little contact with the modern world and found the gadgets I carried miraculous. They think I'm a god-king called forth by their shaman."

She snorted. "Right and I'm Marilyn Monroe."

His gaze raked her, leaving a path of fire in its wake. "Really? Well you are blond and err… amply endowed."

The heat scorched her cheeks, as she folded her arms over her chest. She thought this blouse did a good job of hiding her embarrassment of riches. She gave him her best withering smile, designed to strike fear into the hearts of college freshman. "Don't change the subject. Tell me the truth."

A smile curled his lip as he shrugged. "I am."

No college freshman here. "You can't be serious. This is the twenty-first century, not the seventeenth."

The smirk deepened. "You sound just like one of the schoolmistresses back home, and I know what century it is. Nevertheless, that's the truth. Didn't you see how they reacted to me out there?"

She drew her lip between her teeth. Could it be? He definitely had an odd setup here. "What does 'coop' mean?"

"It's my name."

"What were you doing out here in the first place?"

"I'm an adventurer." He winked. "Sort of like you."

Was he making fun of her? She'd never been accused of being adventurous in her life. Tilting her chin, she asked, "How long do you intend to stay here?"

He lifted a powerful shoulder. "Until I get tired of playing king, which may be never."

A charlatan. She pursed her lips to show her complete and utter disapproval of his charade. Well, she didn't want any part of it. When the tribe found out, they'd probably eat him, and what a tasty dish he'd make. She wiped her brow with the back of her hand. Way too hot in this tent. "What about me? What do they want with me?"

He laughed. "I don't think you have to worry. How old are you?"

What did that have to do with the price of bananas? "Twenty-six."

"Much too old. You're safe."

She clenched her jaw so hard it hurt. Twenty-six hardly qualified her for the early-bird special. "Safe from what?"

His blue eyes glinted with humor. "Their shaman had a vision that if he mated with a woman with pale skin and golden hair, the tribe would be safe from outsiders."

Her stomach flip-flopped. "Mated?"

"There'd be a marriage ceremony first, but even though you have the right coloring, you won't do at all."

She didn't want to be some shaman's wife, but he didn't have to be so insulting. Narrowing her eyes, she ground out, "Why is that?"

Coop winked again. "The shaman needs a virgin."

Chapter 2

The schoolmarm's creamy white skin turned a shade whiter. Bloody 'ell, she couldn't hear the word "virgin" without fainting? He thought these American birds were made of stronger stuff.

She even resembled one of the women made famous in the Amazon with her tall stature and lush figure. Those knee-length khaki walking shorts had to go though, along with that white blouse buttoned up to her chin and that vest. A vest! Did she realize how hot it could get out here? Only the sweat soaking her blouse revealed she had a body under all those clothes. From the little he saw, the shaman would be only too pleased to explore that body. He wouldn't be the only one.

Lucky for her a twenty-six year old American wouldn't fit the bill. Coop had a mutually beneficial deal going on with the shaman, but if the shaman wanted to deflower a pale-skinned virgin, Coop couldn't do much to stop him. At least not too much.

"Here, sit down." He offered her a gourd of water from his bowl. "There's no need to worry."

Her hand trembled as she took the gourd from his. That martial light died out of her bottle-green eyes, and her lower lip quivered, making her seem more vulnerable than the stiff, blond icicle who ushered a chill into his tent.

He rubbed her arm, his fingers lingering on her smooth skin. "We'll have you back on the trail to your camp in no time, but I'd appreciate it if you kept quiet about your encounter here."

She gulped the water, dipped her fingertips in the remaining drops, and dabbed her temples. A smile curved her mouth. She'd been so busy pursing her lips in disapproval he hadn't noticed how ripe they were before.

"What do you hope to accomplish here, Mr. Coop?"

Mr. Coop? He sat here naked, except for his loincloth, and he'd only pulled that on when he heard the commotion outside, and she acted like they were taking tea at bloody Buckingham Palace. "Just call me Coop."

"That still doesn't answer my question."

The ice age returned and the lips thinned out again. Maybe her husband wouldn't be too thrilled at her return after all. "It's not every day a man can be king. I'm enjoying the ride while it lasts."

Frowning, she shook her head. "I think it's silly, and it could be dangerous."

He snatched the gourd from her. "I'm not the one who wandered away from my tour group in the middle of the rainforest. Won't your husband be sending out a search party?"

She grew still and clasped her hands between her knees. "I don't have a husband."

"Boyfriend?"

Her face softened again, and her long lashes swept down. "No."

"You're not with one of those lesbian tour groups, are you?"

She jumped up, knocking the gourd out of his hands. "I'm traveling by myself. Nobody knows I'm here. I doubt the tour group even realizes I'm missing because I joined the group for this tour only. I'm all alone."

He held up his hands to defend against her rapid-fire words. Must be a sore point, but relief swept through him that this tasty package didn't do women. "All right. What's your name anyway?"

"Anna Winter."

That figured. Placing his hands on her shoulders, he guided her back to her seat, and then retrieved the gourd and filled it again. "Have some more water, Anna Winter."

She sipped slowly, the color stealing back into her cheeks. English women were supposed to have the peaches and cream skin, but Anna's could rival the complexion of all the Englishwomen on the whole bloody island.

Her tongue darted out to catch a drop of water glistening at the corner of her mouth. "I'm sorry. This whole situation is unreal. I just want to get back to the camp."

Getting ready for the hard part, he took a deep breath. "We'll get you back to your camp. Just as soon as the inspection is over."

The tongue stopped, and he relaxed because if he had to watch it sweeping across her full bottom lip one more time, his loincloth would resemble this tent he called home.

Her golden brows shot up. "Inspection?"

He pushed up from the floor and busied himself with the tent flaps. The other ones. "Remember, I told you the shaman needs a virgin?"

"Yes."

Her voice sounded very far away, so he peered over his shoulder. She clasped her hands between her knees again. She did a lot of clasping.

"It's a small matter, really. He just needs to make sure." He felt such a coward, so he swung around to stand in front of her.

Bad move.

Her eyes were slits, resembling some creature out here in the jungle. "Sure of what?"

He crouched in front of her, his loincloth swinging to the floor. "He needs to make sure you're a virgin. Or not, in this case."

She swayed toward him, and he caught her in his arms inhaling her floral scent. Despite her austere appearance, she smelled and felt like pure woman. "It's not as bad as it sounds, Anna. He doesn't perform the inspection himself. The women do."

He began to enjoy the feel of her soft body against his when her head shot up from his shoulder. "The women?"

"His other wives."

A wail started somewhere deep in her throat, and he clamped his hand over her mouth before it could explode in the tent. "Shhh. It won't be so bad. Think of it as a gynecological exam. Once they determine you're, ummm, not intact, you'll be on your merry way."

Her eyes formed two huge circles above his hand, and he dragged his thumb across her lips before caressing her cheek. "There won't be any men present, and I'm sure they'll allow you to leave the rest of your clothes on."

She knocked his hand away. "You're insane. I'm not submitting to any exam. This is the twenty-first century."

Why did she keep bringing up the bloody century? He shook his head. "Not here."

She rose from the stool and thrust her shoulders back. Did she realize one of the buttons on her blouse had popped off, revealing the lacy edge of her bra? He didn't need to point that out.

"Aren't you King Coop? Tell them I'm not a virgin and have them take me back to the camp. I won't tell a soul about this crazy place. I'd rather forget it."

Anna obviously knew how to order people around. Maybe a few weeks in this Amazon hideaway would do her some good, bring her down from her high horse. Unlike the men in her world, the men in this community possessed all the power. And he was the cock of the walk.

"It's not that easy, Anna."

"Yes it is. Tell them."

"The shaman won't be satisfied until he gets an official report from his wives. Relax. Once that report comes back stamped 'impure', you're history."

All her bravado seemed to seep from her body as she sank to the stool and bowed her head. "There's only one problem."

He crossed his arms to keep from stroking her golden hair. He'd like to see it loosened from that restrictive braid. In fact, everything about her screamed hands-off. Why did she hide under all those clothes and that superior attitude?

"Your modesty? I told you; think of it as a gynecological exam. Surely even you've had one of those."

She snapped, "Of course, I have."

Yeah, probably in a darkened room wearing a burlap sack. "Then what's the problem?"

Her gaze met his for a fleeting moment before she dropped it. "I am a virgin."

Chapter 3

She stared at the dirt floor. In the silence, flies buzzed around the tent flap. She dared not look at him. When she confessed her hymenally-challenged status to the boyfriend before Vincent, he tagged her as a freak. Then promptly dumped her.

Vincent had been pleased and wanted to keep her that way. When she discovered him with her sister, she understood why.

Seems Vincent eschewed actual sex in favor of getting punished for the bad boy he wanted to be. Jenny had called her earlier that day inviting her to Vincent's to discuss the wedding plans. When Anna arrived, she heard noises from Vincent's library. Unusual, since he rarely let anyone enter his sanctum.

For some reason, she tiptoed toward the half-open door of his library. Not that they would've heard her if she'd come charging in on an elephant.

Jenny had Vincent, stark naked, bent over his mahogany desk, hands tied behind him with his Yale tie, his backside bright red. Jenny prowled behind him brandishing a paddle, chastising him.

When she drew her arm back and smacked his bare ass, Anna cried out as if she'd been struck. Two pairs of eyes turned in her direction, Jenny's mocking, Vincent's glazed over with a look Anna had never seen from him before… lust.

In the days following, Vincent tried to explain it all away as an experiment. Insisted he never had actual sex with Jenny. No, and he probably didn't want to have sex with her either.

Vincent's little fetish didn't bother her as much as the realization that he chose her specifically because he saw her as the domineering type. Just the kind of woman to fulfill all his fantasies.

She didn't want to fulfill those fantasies for him or anyone else.

Coop crouched in front of her again, his loincloth swinging between his legs. Did the man have no decency? He placed his finger beneath her chin and tilted her head up. "You're telling the truth, aren't you?"

She blinked her eyes furiously against the tears threatening to spill down her cheeks. "Yes."

Holding her breath, she waited for the laughter, the derision, the pity.

"Bloody 'ell." He pinched her chin.

She dashed her hand across her eyes. The man possessed an unexpected gentleness. Maybe twenty-six year old virgins weren't so unusual in England. "What are we going to do? Won't the shaman just take my word for it? Can't you just explain that twenty-six year old virgins don't exist in my world?"

He caught an errant tear on the edge of his thumb and sucked it into his mouth, his blue eyes burning into hers. "Apparently they do."

Her nipples crinkled beneath her bra, her blouse, and her vest. She felt grateful for all three of them. "The shaman doesn't need to know that."

Spreading his hands before him, he lifted his shoulders. "He neither understands nor cares about the social expectations of the outside world. He just wants his virgin."

What does King Coop want? She stuffed the thought back into her shorts. "You're the god-king. Surely, you can prevent this."

He jumped up and strode to the far side of the tent but not far enough. The swinging loincloth revealed the hard curve of his buttocks before settling back into place. Anna clamped her legs together. If she had to stay in this tent any longer with him, her virginity would seriously be threatened. Not from the shaman.

Turning back toward her, Coop said, "I'm here because the shaman conjured me. He dubbed me the god-king to replace his rival, the real king. Now he holds all the cards. I can't interfere with his vision now, but I have a plan."

If his plan involved ravishing her right here on the dirt floor, she'd take it. "A plan?"

He raked his hands through his long, dark hair. "Yes, but I'm sorry Anna, you're going to have to follow through with the inspection to avoid suspicion."

Hugging herself, she rose from the stool. "Then he'll find out I'm a virgin."

"True, but I can delay his shagging you to give us some time."

She peeled her tongue from the roof of her suddenly dry mouth. "Sh-shagging? Is that some kind of ritual?"

He grinned and slapped his forehead. "You Yanks. Sorry, it's a rather crude term for screwing, which I guess is still a crude term."

He must think she's completely naïve. Worse, a prude. What did she expect? That's the image she cultivated all these years… and for good reason.

She'd never forget the lascivious stares of the men and the nasty comments from the women in the small town in Hilbock County, Indiana, where she grew up, when her skinny little girl's body began blossoming and then blooming and then exploding into womanhood. "Just like her mother." "Just like her sister." "Hide your sons and husbands." "There's another Winter woman of Hilbock County on the prowl."

She gulped back her tears. "How are you going to delay it?"

"Leave it to me. I'm King Coop."

The low thumping of a drum resounded outside, along with high-pitched shrieking. Anna grabbed Coop's hand.

He brought her hand to his lips, and her heart thumped along with the beat of the drum. "It's the shaman. Let's get this over with."

Coop led her out of the tent where a crowd now formed. A huge man, both in height and girth, surged into the circle. His long hair, styled with feathers and leaves, hung down his back. Fantastic tattoos decorated his body, with a bright blue snake curling down his large belly and disappearing into his loincloth. She didn't want to think about where it led.

Anna trembled, and Coop squeezed her hand and whispered, "The shaman."

Oh God. She couldn't give up her virginity to this man. King Coop better have a full-proof plan.

The large shaman stepped in front of her and Coop. He frowned and shook his massive head from side-to-side.

Maybe he didn't like her. Maybe he didn't want her. Dressing like a prude had its advantages.

Coop spoke rapidly, and then bent his head to hers. "The shaman says you have too much covering. He wants to see more of your body."

Anna shrank against Coop. "I'm not taking my clothes off in front of all these people."

He patted her shoulder. "Not all your clothes. Start with the vest and the blouse."

Coop folded his arms across his chest. This he had to see. The shaman didn't specifically request that she disrobe, although he did want to make sure her body matched her pale face. Coop's the one who suggested she remove a little of her clothing, but Anna didn't have to know that. Luckily she didn't speak Portuguese, especially this distinct dialect of the language.

What were the chances of the last virgin in the States stumbling down here into his little kingdom? When she uttered those four words, a hot thrust of lust zapped him right under the loincloth.

He wanted to suggest that he dispense with her virginity right then and there to save her, but he didn't figure this tight-ass schoolmarm would go for that. The thought of her tight ass sent another zinger under the loincloth.

Anna shrugged out of the vest and dropped it to the ground. Her unsteady fingers unfastened the buttons on her blouse, skimming over the missing one, until it hung open.

The shaman drew closer to peer at her flat, white belly, and Coop whispered, "Take the blouse off."

She peeled the blouse from her shoulders and stood clenching it in her hand. Obviously she never performed a striptease before.

The shaman smiled and nodded, and Coop's mouth watered at the swell of Anna's breasts rising from her lacy white bra. Marilyn Monroe got nothing on you, luv.

The shaman pointed to Anna's hiking boots and thick white socks. She glanced at Coop before bending over to remove her shoes and socks. Then the shaman reached forward and tugged at the leg of her baggy shorts.

In answer to Anna's wide-eyed appeal, Coop said, "That's all, I swear."

His groin tightened as she unzipped the shorts, let them fall down her legs, and then stepped out of them. Her pink flowered bikini panties hugged her hips. Guess a thong was too much to hope for from a schoolmarm.

The shaman made a circling motion, and Anna turned for him slowly. Her delicious, rounded derriere jiggled beneath her knickers, and this time Coop's loincloth did turn into a tent.

Folding his hands in front of him, he asked the shaman if she matched his vision.

He replied that her skin color pleased him, but he wanted to see her hair loose.

He wasn't the only one. Coop said to Anna, "Take your braid out. He wants to see your hair."

She pulled the band from the end of her braid and loosened it. Her silky blond hair spilled over her shoulder, caressing her ample bosom. That had to be natural blond, just like every other part of her. How had this ripe peach remained a virgin? Were all the blokes in the States gay?

The shaman clapped his hands twice. Three women scurried forward into the circle and bowed before the shaman, touching their foreheads to the dirt.

Coop glanced at Anna. She'd never be able to achieve that level of subservience, but Coop would have a helluva good time trying to train her.

He marveled at the beauty of his plan. He'd save Anna from the shaman's bed, but in the process he'd teach her a little humility. Maybe he'd even help her unleash that fire he saw burning in her green eyes. The fire she kept encased in a block of ice.

The three wives, heads still bowed, spun on their knees and touched their foreheads to the ground in front of Coop. One of the wives hunched forward and brushed the dirt from his feet.

One glance at Anna's tight face told him everything he needed to know. His eyes met hers. That's right, my proud virgin, women don't give the orders around here. They take them. You'll learn to love it in no time.

The shaman commanded his wives to their feet and told them to take his proposed bride to his tent and inspect her hymen.

If Anna Winter, virgin schoolmistress, ever used a particularly large dildo to pleasure herself, all bets were off. That would certainly solve her problem, but a mean little voice in his head, one he'd been trying to curb for years, hoped her prudishness prevented her from indulging in sex toys.

Two of the wives took Anna's arms, while the other led the way. Anna sent a beseeching look back at him. Ever the gallant, he asked, "Do you want me to be there?"

Roses bloomed in her cheeks as she shook her head. Then the wives led Anna, voluptuous in her underwear, into the shaman's tent for her inspection.

Chapter 4

Why hadn't she ever used the giant pink dildo Nicole made her buy at that party? Why hadn't she ever taken up horseback riding?

Why did she just strip down to her bra and panties in front of Coop? He enjoyed it. A man couldn't hide much beneath a loincloth. Especially a man like that. He must wear an XXL in loincloths. Did they make an XXL?

Her stomach heaved. The shaman had to have at least an XXL and that didn't represent what he had under the loincloth, at least she hoped not, but rather what he had hanging over it. Coop's mysterious plan better work.

The wives had her stretch out on a cot, remove her panties, and bend her legs at the knees. Anna took several deep breaths. Just like Dr. Amari's office.

She peered between her knees. The wives were chanting, as they washed their hands in a bowl of water. Okay, not quite like Dr. Amari's office.

Anna closed her eyes. She blamed Jenny for all of this. If Jenny hadn't discovered Vincent's deepest, darkest fantasies, and then played them out for him, Anna and Vincent would be married now. They'd be living in that little house among other university employees, and riding their bikes to work each day. When Vincent had a break from teaching a class, he'd come to the library and have lunch with her.

At night… at night? What then? Would he have expected her to bend him over his desk and give him a good paddling? Maybe that's why he never pressured her into sex. Maybe that's why their engagement lasted for two years. He must've been afraid to tell her what he wanted. She wouldn't have minded a little role playing, but would he have reciprocated?

Shame curled her toes. More than her anger at seeing her sister swatting her fiancé's bare bottom, she felt turned on. Not that she wanted to take her sister's place in punishing Vincent. No, she wanted to be in Vincent's place. There. She finally admitted it to herself.

The chanting stopped. She felt something cold and wet between her legs. She jerked up in time to see one of the wives wielding a long blade. Oh my God. She'd read about these practices taking place in Africa.

One of the wives giggled and pinched her thigh, while the one holding the blade began to shave her pubic hair. Taking a deep breath, Anna flopped back onto the cot. Made sense. Didn't the Brazilian bikini wax originate here?

Once they rinsed her off, Anna felt cool fingers prod her lips. She tensed up. Even though she had a female gynecologist, this woman's small delicate fingers on her most private area made her uncomfortable.

Especially after being cooped up with the half-naked Coop in that little tent. Pure lust speared her more times than she could count during that exchange, and the panties she just peeled off were as damp as that rainforest out there. One thing she knew. Vincent never had that effect on her. He seemed almost effeminate compared to King Coop.

The small finger made its progress, and Anna gasped, her bottom rising up from the cot. The wife doing the primary examination smiled and nodded.

She must've passed inspection. Hymen intact.

Closing her legs, they dropped her panties in her lap. They motioned for her to stay in the tent, while they rushed outside. Probably to tell the shaman he had another wife.

She yanked her panties on. Her clothes were still outside, but she'd be pickled if she'd walk out there in her underwear.

The flap of the tent rustled, and the shaman walked in followed by Coop and the three wives. Coop grinned from ear to ear. Why did he look so happy? Wouldn't it have been better news if they reported her impure?

The shaman addressed Coop, who then turned to Anna and said, "The holy shaman is pleased that the pale-skinned woman is pure. It satisfies his vision. The pale-skinned woman will be honored to learn that the shaman will take her to wife."

She swallowed hard. What happened to the plan? She opened her mouth, but Coop shook his head slightly.

He continued. "After consulting with his god-king Coop, the shaman understands his vision further. The god-king Coop shall train the pale-skinned woman, and she shall serve the god-king to prove her worthiness to service the shaman for life, thereby protecting our tribe from the outsiders forever."

Anna's brows shot up. "Serve?"

The shaman shouted and thrust his spear into the ground.

Her eyes flew to Coop's face, and he lifted his finger to his lips. What did he mean by serve? At least it sounded like she had a reprieve before she had to become the shaman's wife. Coop said they needed to buy time. Looks like they just did.

The shaman spoke to Coop, gesturing toward Anna's underwear.

Coop smirked. Anna could swear she spotted a smirk. He said, "The shaman orders his pale-skinned bride-to-be to dress appropriately."

She eyed the wives' attire. They wore short skirts slit up the sides, but at least a garment hung from their shoulders, covering their chests. Pursing her lips, she nodded.

The shaman and Coop left the tent, and the wives scrambled to find her clothing.

Once again her panties came off, and the women fastened a strand of beads around her waist, from which hung two strips of cloth. She towered above the native women, so the loincloth hit above mid-thigh, but at least the lacing at the sides of the hips kept it from swinging too freely.

Anna grabbed for the top, but the women gestured for her to remove her bra first. Anna never went braless. She had too much to support. The women were adamant. They chattered angrily, and Anna caught the words "shaman" and "Coop" quite frequently. They definitely feared those two men.

Anna stood her ground until the women reached up and ripped the bra from her chest. They giggled as her breasts, unbounded, spilled forward.

The old shame at the size of her breasts burned in her chest. They caused quite a sensation before she realized the existence of minimizing bras and the concealing effects of tailored blouses. Her mother and sister pronounced her nuts, since they flaunted their over-abundance of riches with frequent abandon.

The wives pulled the top over Anna's head. It hung to her midriff, exposing a band of belly. She felt naked without her bra.

The women whipped the tent flap aside and nudged Anna outside. To her horror, the entire village awaited her emergence from the tent with big smiles claiming their faces.

Humiliation burned in her chest. They all knew she just underwent an inspection and passed the purity test. Now she stood completely exposed in these two tiny strips of cloth with King Coop looming in the center of the circle wearing the biggest smile of all.

His smile alone transformed her humiliation into a conflagration of desire so hot it threatened to incinerate her protective shell.

Anna looked like an Amazon goddess. Her long, shapely legs moved gracefully beneath the loincloth. Her magnificent, unfettered breasts jostled beneath the skimpy top, and her gleaming hair streamed about her shoulders. All this and a virgin too.

Smiles wreathed the shaman's face, and he didn't even try to hide his erection. Coop had more class than that. Just.

Anna strode into the center of the circle, and the shaman turned to Coop and expressed disappointment that the woman didn't know her place. No, Anna didn't know her place yet, and she'd be royally tweaked when she realized it.

Let the lessons begin. He stepped forward. "The shaman orders that you show proper reverence to his holiness and his god-king."

What the heck did that mean? "Proper reverence?"

Coop gazed past her face. "The wives will show you."

He ordered the three wives to show the pale-skinned woman the proper form of greeting. Once again, they dropped to the ground and placed their foreheads in the dirt before the shaman, and then scurried to Coop and repeated the motion.

Coop's gaze rested on Anna's face. Her green eyes threw sparks. He swallowed his grin and tilted his chin up. "Pale-skinned woman will show proper reverence."

Anna shuffled to the shaman, kneeled in the dirt, and touched her forehead to the ground. Then she crawled on her knees to Coop and lowered her head to the dirt. She began to rise, but he pushed her head back down. "My feet. Dust them off."

An angry red flush marched across Anna's face, but she glanced at the shaman's spear and swiped her hand across Coop's feet.

She stood up and joined the wives, hands folded in front of her, head down. The crowd began dispersing to get ready for the evening meal, and Coop took Anna's arm. He said, "Time to start your training."

The shaman nodded, and Coop guided Anna back to his tent.

Once inside, Anna turned on him, eyes blazing. "What is going on? How am I to serve you?"

He clicked his tongue. "I just saved your arse, and a nice one it is, I might add, and this is the thanks I get?"

"Saved it for what?"

"What does it matter? You're not shag… umm screw… umm sleeping with the big fat shaman any time soon, are you?" Talking to a prude had its challenges.

The disapproving lips narrowed again, but the effect fell flat with those little strips of cloth covering her essentials. They were doing a poor job of it at that. When she moved quickly, the bottom swell of her breasts appeared beneath her insignificant clothing. Bet she didn't realize that. She'd had those puppies bound and tamed into submission for so long they were now enjoying their freedom. So was he.

She crossed her arms over her bounteous mounds. "What did you mean before, that I would serve you?"

"No big deal. Serve my food. Sweep out my tent. Wash my dishes." Her face relaxed, and he continued the list in his head. Wash my hair. Bathe me. Give me a massage. Suck my…

Her forehead creased. Must be reading something in his face. He cleared his throat. "You must greet us properly. You can handle that, can't you?"

"Kneeling in front of a man and brushing the dirt off his feet? What's next? Kissing them?"

He raised his eyes to the ceiling. "That would be brilliant."

She chucked a wooden spoon at him. "When can I leave?"

Time for the hard sell. Gripping her shoulders, he said, "Listen, Anna, although this situation has its amusing side, the shaman is a dangerous man. His rival for power, the previous king, disappeared from the village. My guess is he's dead. Don't think you're not being watched here. You'll never be allowed to walk away freely."

Her eyes widened and she jerked beneath his touch. "Then how am I supposed to get back to the camp?"

He slid his hands around her narrow waist. Her body, shaped like an hourglass, had all the sand at the top. "Once the shaman believes you've accepted your place as his bride-to-be, the watchdogs will relax. I have a few young lads who are loyal to me. We'll be able to count on them when the time comes."

According to his well-laid plan, the time wasn't going to come any time soon until he had a little fun with his uptight virgin. "That's why it's important to do as I say. Do you understand?"

She nodded. "Why aren't there any children in this camp?"

She better not start asking a load of questions. He wanted to conceal his identity just like he always did on these jaunts. "It's a betrothal camp. Unattached men and women come here to mingle and find a spouse. At the end of the season, the shaman performs a mass wedding ceremony, and the new couples return to the village to start their families."

The sticks tapped out time for the evening meal, and Anna twisted in his grasp. "What's that?"

"Time for supper. Now go out there and show how obedient you can be."

Anna studied his face for signs of the smirk, but his face creased along serious lines. Deadly serious. She didn't want to anger this shaman.

The meat cooking over the open fire smelled delicious, and her stomach rumbled in response. She hadn't eaten since that granola bar this afternoon, so she joined the line of women and held out her plate for the savory meat.

She carried her food to one of the logs circling the fire and sank down to enjoy her meal. Whispers flew around the circle, and she glanced up. All of the women were still standing. Only the men sat on the logs.

One of the women grabbed her arm and pulled her up. A man took her place on the log. The shaman, with a scowl on his heavy face, settled into a carved-out seat at the top of the circle. The woman pushed Anna toward him.

She watched as the other women carried plates of food to the men seated on the logs, bowing before them before they withdrew to provide them with water and more food.

Dragging in a breath, she approached the shaman and presented him with the plate of food. He settled it on his ample lap, and she bowed before him.

Coop sat at the bottom of the circle, and Anna knew what he expected of her. She returned to the line of women, piled another plate high with meat and steamed vegetables, and made her way to King Coop.

She offered him the food, and then bowed at his feet. At least they weren't dirty.

He patted her head. "Good girl."

Was he serious? She threw him her fiercest scowl, but he didn't even notice—too busy eating. For the next half hour, she trotted from the food-ladened tables to the logs, fetching food and water for Coop and the shaman. They didn't even thank her. They barely looked at her. Once she even had to brush Coop's feet off… and they looked fine to her.

Her stomach grumbled along with her until at last the men ate their fill. They passed a pipe between them as the women stood by the tables eating. Someone shoved a gourd into Anna's hands, and she gulped the liquid which singed a path down her throat. She coughed and sputtered as she eyed the alcohol. Maybe she could endure this better if she were a little intoxicated. She squeezed her eyes shut, and tossed back another shot of the fire water.

The way the women stuffed food into their mouths amazed her. Until she figured out why. Ten minutes later, the women returned to the men to wash their faces, hands, and feet. Did these guys have foot fetishes or something?

Sighing, Anna followed them on unsteady legs. She soaked a cloth in the pot of water heating over the fire and kneeled in front of the shaman to wipe his face, his hands, and his feet.

While she worked over him, he chatted with the man sitting next to him. She rose to tend to Coop, but the shaman grabbed her wrist and yanked her back to her knees. Now what?

He continued his conversation and gestured to Anna's chest, his white teeth gleaming against his brown skin. He grunted and motioned for Anna to raise her top. Didn't Coop assure her she wouldn't have to strip? So much for Coop's assurances.

The shaman grunted again and prodded her thigh with the end of his spear. Okay, as long as he asked nicely. She flipped up her top and exposed her breasts to the shaman and his buddy. Maybe nobody else would notice.

The shaman reached forward and pinched both of her nipples between his fingers. He shouted something to the other men in the circle, and they all nodded and laughed. Anna winced. So much for anonymity.

He pushed her back and waved her away. She stumbled to her feet, her cheeks blazing. Her worst nightmare just came true. If Coop witnessed the spectacle she'd die right here of embarrassment. Scurrying back to the water, she glanced his way. Yep, he saw it all.

If this was her worst nightmare come true, why did she feel that thumping heat between her legs? Had to be the humidity. Or the alcohol. She soaked another cloth and crouched in front of Coop.

Swiping the cloth across his high cheekbones, she asked, "What just happened?"

He emerged from the cloth with a grin tugging at the corners of his mouth. "Don't know if I should tell you."

She swirled the cloth down his chest, lingering over the hard slabs of muscle. "That bad?"

"Not from my perspective."

Since no humiliation she suffered seemed bad from his perspective, his response didn't alleviate her uneasiness. She propped his foot up on her knee and scrubbed. "Since it concerns me, I'd like to hear it."

He flexed his toes. "You missed a spot."

She slapped his foot with the cloth. "Tell me."

"The shaman wants to see your nipples... pierced."

The cloth fell to the dirt. "How is that not bad?"

He shrugged. "Lots of women have that done in the States, don't they? It's not that uncommon."

Oh really? As if she needed to draw more attention to her breasts. "W-would he really do that?"

He lifted the cloth with his toe. "You'll be long gone before that happens. Looks like you'll have to start all over on my feet."

He watched her huff away, the skimpy skirt swinging around her shapely derriere. When the shaman pinched her nipples and shouted out to the circle that he wanted to see the pearls atop the giant globes pierced with gold rings, Coop nearly choked on a berry. He wouldn't mind seeing the same thing, but the shaman's attraction to Anna troubled him.

Anna returned with a fresh warm cloth and bathed his feet again. Her subservience to him kept him hard all night. He didn't know how much longer he could stand to have her here. If she had the same effect on the shaman, he'd have to cut her visit short. Or make another deal with the shaman.

Despite what Coop told Anna, the shaman was a reasonable bloke. As long as Coop pretended the shaman conjured him to replace the previous chief, he pretty much let Coop do as he pleased.

"Is that to your satisfaction, King Coop?" She glanced up at him through her golden lashes, and he just got harder.

"That'll do. Join the others, woman."

She rose, and the shaman called out to Coop. Anna turned a questioning look his way, and he waved her back down. "Sorry for this, Anna, but I'm going to have to ask you to lift your top again. Come on, it's nothing women don't do every year during Mardi Gras."

Before she dragged the skimpy garment up to her neck, she murmured, "I don't live in New Orleans."

Her hard nipples, rosy in the firelight, poked out from her breasts. He rolled her nipples between his thumb and forefinger, and her breath hissed through her teeth. With her lids half-closed and her lips parted, she looked like a woman ready to succumb to anything. Why disappoint her?

He pinched her nipples, and then ducked his head to draw the left one between his lips. She let out a soft moan. Not wanting the right one to feel lonely, he swirled his tongue over it before taking the hard nub into his mouth. Anna arched her back, and he suckled her briefly before pulling away.

He called to the shaman that yes, indeed, the pale-skinned woman's nipples were ripe for piercing.

Anna still kneeled before him, clutching the material of her top to her throat, her eyes closed. Her breasts looked even larger than before, swollen with need. He envied the first man to ignite that fire. But he didn't want the job. Didn't deserve it.

His voice turned hard. "I'm done with you, woman."

Pulling her top down, she staggered to her feet and took her place behind the logs with the other women.

An unfamiliar pinprick of guilt needled his gut. He exaggerated the shaman's ferocity to Anna. Once he persuaded the shaman Anna didn't fit his vision, it would be a simple matter for Coop to escort her back to her camp. Hell, he even knew the guides at Rainforest Rendezvous.

Despite that fact, he couldn't resist the challenge to bring this uptight woman to her knees, literally, ready to fulfill his every command. She possessed a know-it-all attitude, but she had a lot to learn about herself.

He had a powerful urge to teach her.

Anna stood with the other women behind the circle of logs, clasping her hands in front of her. What had she just done? Must be the alcohol. She allowed Coop to pinch her nipples and caress them into his mouth. She should have slapped his face. Instead, she offered him more, and he took it. He would take what he wanted, offered or not.

When Vincent told her they should wait until marriage before having sex, she agreed. It's not like she didn't have needs. She satisfied those on her own, but until now, she'd never experienced this hot, aching desire that throbbed in her veins, and her subservience to King Coop made it easy to forget her hang-ups about sex, about her body.

With the food cleared away, a few of the men gathered at one edge of the circle, and the pure notes from a wooden flute pierced the sultry night air. A steady drumbeat followed. Into the flickering light from the dying fire, a young woman tiptoed into the circle of logs. She raised her arms above her head and began a sinuous dance.

The rhythm of the drums echoed in Anna's belly, thumped between her thighs. A few of the men in the circle rubbed themselves under their loincloths as they watched the woman sway and bend before them in a seductive dance.

The beat got faster, and more women tripped into the circle to join the dance. The lithe figures mesmerized Anna. A hand grasped her wrist and pulled her into the circle. Oh no. She couldn't do this.

Still foggy from the fire water, she stumbled after the women. Her limbs began to feel light, just like her head. The drumbeat pulsed in her chest, and she swayed her hips to its insistent rhythm. Bending from the waist, she swept her hair to the ground, and then tipped her head back and raised her arms. She pulled her shoulders back in a shimmy, feeling her unrestrained breasts roll beneath her flimsy covering.

The beat of the drums possessed her. She whipped her hair through the air and her body undulated like a flow of hot lava. She had the circle to herself. The other women retreated, giving her center stage.

The heat from the flames licked her body, and sweat rolled between her breasts. She pulled her top over her head and tossed it to the ground. Most of the men were now pumping their shafts in time to her thrusting hips, or their women worked them with their hands or mouths.

Peering into the darkness, Anna saw one of the shaman's wives between Coop's legs, her head bobbing in time to the rhythm. His glittering eyes tracked Anna's every movement.

The flutes and the drums reached a crescendo, and the men moaned with their release. When the last note died out, Anna flung herself at King Coop's feet, touching her forehead to the ground in supplication.

The men staggered up from the logs, taking their women with them. Two women supported the shaman on either side, as they retreated to his tent.

Anna remained in the dirt, awaiting King Coop's command. The woman, who serviced him during Anna's dance, crouched at his side, stroking him beneath his loincloth. He said something to her, and she jumped up and scurried to the shaman's tent.

His voice husky, he said, "You danced like a woman possessed. You keep that up, and the shaman won't want to wait until you're properly trained."

He pushed up from the log, retrieved her top, and tossed it to her. "Put this back on before you inspire another orgy."

Would he take her now? She'd never been more ready in her life. She struggled into her top and followed him to his tent where she waited while he washed his face and brushed his teeth.

"Since you're my responsibility for the time being, you're sleeping in here."

Her heart thrummed in anticipation as she glanced at his cot. He laughed. "You still don't get it, do you? You're my slave. You're sleeping there."

He gestured to a mat on the floor at the foot of the cot. A chill stole over her body. He didn't want her.

Slipping out of his loincloth and into his cot, he said, "Goodnight, Anna."

Before she curled up on the mat, she washed up, but left her clothes on. She didn't even get a good look at what lurked under that loincloth.

She sighed. Anna Winter was going to bed, alone, again, still a virgin.

Chapter 5

Anna's eyelids fluttered, and she rolled over to snuggle into the pillows. Just five more minutes before she got up for work. The pillow scratched her nose, and she rubbed it, smelling… straw. She remembered everything now.

She buried her head in her arms. The humiliating inspection. The disgraceful clothing. The embarrassing display of her breasts. Her uninhibited dancing. Coop's rejection.

Something tickled the bottom of her foot, so she crossed it over her ankle. It tickled again. She didn't trust anything in the Amazon, so she drew up her legs and crunched forward, peering toward the edge of the mat.

Anna screamed and scrambled to her feet. Grinning, Coop loomed over her dangling a big, hairy spider.

"Get that away from me!" She wrapped her arms around her midsection and jumped.

Coop's grin got wider. "Just one of the alarm clocks we use around here."

That creature crawled on her foot? Coop delighted in torturing her, and his dismissal of her last night ranked right up there as the most excruciating torture yet. "Take it out. I'm going to be sick."

He opened the tent flaps and shooed the tarantula on its way. "You have to admit, it's effective."

Anna dropped her arms and rolled the kinks out of her shoulders. If the bugs didn't kill her, that hard mat would. "Where do we get breakfast around here, or do we have to hunt and gather first?"

His blue eyes alight, Coop chuckled. "I never took you for a slow learner, Anna."

Her SAT scores were a perfect 1600. She got a full academic scholarship to Northern Conn U. She graduated with a perfect 4.0. In addition to English, she spoke two languages fluently. Too bad they didn't include Portuguese. "I am not a slow learner."

"Then you should realize by now, you don't get breakfast until I get breakfast. In fact, you slept in. It's your job to wake up before me to get everything ready."

If he didn't want her, then she'd be pickled if she'd make this easy for him. She yawned and stretched her arms above her head. "What does that entail?"

He held up his large hand and ticked off his fingers. "A trip outside to the larder table to get my breakfast. Breakfast in bed. Sponge bath in bed. Shave. Blow job."

Her gaze halted its path from his bare chest, to his low-slung loincloth, and she swallowed… hard. Maybe he did want her.

His lips quirked into a smile. "We'll skip that last item."

Disappointment lanced her belly, but she shrugged. "Fine by me."

His eyes held hers. "I mean, since you are a virgin and all."

Breaking away from his gaze, she bent down to fold her mat. "I never said I was a virgin everywhere."

His brows shot up, as he studied her lips. "Oh, so you're skilled in the fine art of fellatio?"

Not exactly. She'd given her previous boyfriend a few blowjobs before he found out about her virginity. Then she got a lesson at Nicole's sex toys party… with a cucumber. That hardly made her an expert. Probably couldn't compete with that petite little hottie nestled between his thighs last night. But oh, she wouldn't mind giving it a try.

She licked her lips. "Yes."

His turn to swallow… hard. She spun around. She didn't beg. "Should I get your breakfast now?"

He growled, "Yes, and about bloody time too."

She slipped outside and hurried to the food laid out on the larder table, as it had been for last night's feast. The women were already clearing the food away, so she ran forward and gathered as much of the leftovers as she could into Coop's bowl.

The women muttered under their breaths, shooting her sideways glances. Had she offended? Smiling, she backed away from the table with her spoils. Did Coop have fresh water? He could get that himself.

Coop reclined on his cot, propped up by fluffy pillows. She pointed. "Where'd you get those?"

He plumped up the pillows. "The tribe raids houseboats occasionally."

Laying out his food, she said, "You couldn't spare one of those for me last night?"

"What if someone saw you? You're here to serve, not get preferential treatment."

Her stomach growled as she placed a tray of breads and fruits on his lap. His brows drew together. "Where's my fresh water?"

Once again, Anna ventured outside, this time carrying Coop's water bowl. The women of the village were now balancing bundles of clothing on their heads, following a trail away from the village. Must be washing day.

Anna filled the water bowl and returned to the tent where Coop finished off the last of the fruit. He snapped his fingers for the water.

She scowled. "You don't have to keep up this pretence in the privacy of your own tent."

His eyes widened. "Look at that tent flap. Do you see a lock on it?"

"Noooo."

"There's no privacy here, Anna. Anyone could walk into my tent at any time."

She glanced over her shoulder and shivered, and then filled his gourd from the water bowl and brought it to the cot. "When do I get to eat?"

He shoved the tray toward her. "You finish my leftovers. So you see it's in your best interest to fill up my food bowl and do it early before everything's gone."

Her stomach rumbled again as she eyed the lone hunk of bread on the tray. She reached for the bread, but he grabbed her wrist. "When you finish your other duties."

He took this master thing seriously. Best to keep up appearances in case one of the shaman's men had his ear to the tent flap. She lugged the bowl of fresh water to the cot, along with a clean cloth. He even had a bar of soap, which she held up. "Courtesy of the houseboats?"

"That and the razor."

He settled back against the pillows, as she dipped the cloth into the water and began washing his face, pushing his tangled locks from his brow. Didn't bother stealing combs from the houseboats, did they? "So how did you wind up here?"

He closed his eyes. "I thought I told you. I'm a world traveler and adventurer."

"Where do you get your money?"

"Here and there."

"What's your real name?"

He opened one eye. "Coop."

Just great. This man held her life in his hands, and he wouldn't even tell her his name. She squeezed out the cloth, dipped it in the water again, and soaped it up. She dragged it across his shoulders and along his neck, her fingers brushing his beautifully made body, hard and smooth like a sculpture. "You don't get tired of this life?"

He tightened his abs as she swirled the cloth down his chest and belly. "Beats life in an English country village."

Working the cloth underneath his arms, she sighed. "If it's anything like life in a small Midwestern town, I agree."

He tilted his head. "That explains a lot. Are all the girls from small Midwestern towns prudes?"

Is that what he thought? She squeezed the cloth in her fist. "I'm not a prude."

"You may have had a momentary lapse last night when you were shaking your stuff in the fire circle, but you're a prude."

At one time she preferred the prude label to its opposite, but she regretted it now. Maybe that's why he shunned her last night. "I may be conservative, but I'm no prude."

"Bloody 'ell, you're a twenty-six year old virgin, and you dress like an eighty-two year old schoolmistress. *Are* you a schoolmistress?"

Anna clenched her jaw. "I'm the head librarian at the Northern Connecticut University Library, and just because I don't flaunt my body..."

"That's an understatement. You hide it under three layers of clothing. Why? Don't forget, I've seen your breasts. Women pay thousands of dollars to get a pair like that."

She twisted the cloth over the bowl, watching the drops splash in the water. "I-I never wanted attention that way. Just for my body."

He took the cloth from her and scrubbed his arms. "I can understand that, but you've gone over the top."

How had this conversation changed direction? She set out to discover something about Coop, his full name would be nice, and all she got out of him is that he grew up in a small English village.

She blew out a long breath. "You don't understand."

"You got that right. Why would a beautiful, feminine woman, with a body like a porn star hide it?"

She grabbed the cloth from him. "You said it yourself. I don't want people thinking I'm a porn star, or a slut, or the town pincushion."

He pinched her chin. "Like?"

Oh God, who was he, Dr. Phil with an English accent and abs of steel? She started scrubbing his feet. "Like my mother, okay?"

"Your mother was the town pincushion?"

"Yeah, and because we lived in a small town, there weren't that many pins. Everyone knew it. My dad left after she cheated on him one too many times. Then it just got worse. My older sister followed in her cheap stilettos, and when I reached maturity, everyone expected the same from me."

He traced his finger along her jaw line. "You were determined to prove them wrong?"

Why did he have to be gentle? She almost preferred his mocking arrogance. "Yes, and I did."

"At what price, Anna?"

She scrubbed his other foot. "Price? Why, none at all."

"Yeah, right."

Running the cloth up his legs, she stopped at his thighs. "Do you…?"

He crossed his arms behind his head and nodded. Where'd Dr. Phil go? She pushed up the hem of the soft material and dabbed the cloth between his legs. Her fingers collided with his semi-hard penis. How'd it get way down there?

She brushed over his shaft, and it sprang to life. She wanted to sneak a peek last night, and now she had her chance. She nonchalantly pushed up the loincloth and drank him in, or rather gulped. Definitely an XXL.

His slightly bobbing penis seemed to be pointing at her accusingly. Well, she could put a stop to that. She grasped him in her soapy hand, her fingers failing to meet around his girth. His hips jerked upward, and his blunt head plowed into her palm. She held him aloft, tracing the fingertips of her other hand across the veins that pulsed along the length of him.

He drew in a sharp breath as she ran her fingernails down to his base, teasing them across his heavy balls. His sac tightened, and her finger played beneath it, strumming him, tuning him.

She caressed his balls before working her hand back up his shaft. He grew to full attention, and he pumped his hips again.

Dropping her head, she swept her hair across his belly, and planted her lips on the inside of his thigh. It worked like a magic key, as he bent his legs and dropped his knees to the sides, opening up to her, displaying all his masculine charms.

Her lips trailed up one solid thigh and down the other, her nose colliding with his sac, now drawn up tightly beneath his stiff cock. She hadn't washed here yet, and his musky scent, so similar to the verdant rainforest, fueled her desire.

She lapped at his balls with her tongue, sucking each one into her mouth, bathing it in her wet caress. He groaned and pushed into her face. She must be doing something right.

Her tongue zigzagged up his considerable length, zeroing in on the bead of creamy moisture crowning his tip. She licked it off, and another took its place. Rolling her thumb over the fresh drop, she spread it around his head. Again, he lunged into her palm.

Her fingers tripped through the springy, dark hair clustered around his proud cock. Thrashing his head, he speared her wrist and plowed into the air, desperate to make contact.

Show time. Licking her lips, she grasped his base, and then placed his head against her closed, moist lips. She parted her lips just enough to ease him into the warm, wet darkness of her mouth, closing around every inch of him. More drops of his salty fluid dribbled onto her tongue.

She drew him in until the tip of his cock bumped the back of her throat, and still more than half of him remained outside her greedy mouth. She swallowed, taking as much of him down her throat as she could.

When he filled her mouth, she slowly eased him out again. With her lips encircling him, she drew him in, until he pumped into her, his hips bucking wildly. Each time he thrust into her, she relaxed her throat. Just like that cucumber at Nicole's party.

His cock seemed to grow with each thrust. Not exactly like that cucumber. He laced his fingers through her hair, digging into her scalp. A shudder wracked his body and then another, as he brought his knees together, imprisoning her head between his muscled thighs as he spilled his hot seed down her throat.

She gulped every drop until he lay spent. His legs loosened their grip on her head, and she rolled to the side, resting her head on his thigh. Technically, she could still call herself a virgin, but she sure didn't feel like one.

His fingers teased her hair, and then fluttered to her aching lips, tracing their edges. "You didn't have to do that."

She must've been a disappointment even though he hadn't exactly been complaining. She yanked his loincloth down over his thing of beauty before she got any more bright ideas and sat up. "I thought you told me to."

He swung his legs over her head and the side of the cot. "Actually, I just meant for you to wash me."

The heat crawled across her cheeks. Obviously he didn't appreciate her amateur attempts.

He tossed his washcloth and a few loincloths at her. "Now if you're so anxious to please, do my washing."

With a grin plastered on his face, Coop watched Anna stalk out of his tent, her arms full of dirty laundry. When he saw the last of her rounded buttocks, he collapsed on his cot, raking his hands through his hair.

The virgin gave the best blow job he'd ever had in his life. He knew those lips would be good for something other than pursing in disapproval. He should've never allowed her to continue.

When her washcloth swirled up close to the edge of his loincloth and she asked if she should go further, he said she should as a joke. He never imagined she'd actually touch his cock, let alone go for the full Monty. The librarian had the body of a top dollar call girl and a soul to match.

Or maybe she'd been so busy stuffing down her natural sexuality all these years, it came out in gangbusters. With an emphasis on busters.

He couldn't exploit that. Wouldn't. Being in a subservient position allowed Anna to release her inhibitions. After all, if someone coerced her into performing these acts, she wouldn't have to take responsibility for her actions. Wouldn't be acting like her mother, the pincushion.

Maybe he could just break through that dam for her, and she could hightail it back to that university in Connecticut and find some nice professor to practice on. Lucky S.O.B.

Chapter 6

The small, neon blue bug moseyed across Anna's hand. The fact that she didn't flip him off or squash him into oblivion demonstrated just how far she'd progressed in one week of living in the wilds. She missed the tour guide's learned discourse on the flora and fauna of the rainforest, even though she daydreamed through most of it. Coop knew a lot, but his knowledge encompassed mostly the bugs and plants the natives used in their everyday lives.

Her study of the little critter relieved her boredom while Coop read and jotted down notes in a book he called his travel journal. When she tried to snatch one of his books, he slapped her hand away, admonishing her that women weren't allowed to read in the camp. Women weren't allowed to do much of anything in this camp, except serve the men.

Then why wouldn't Coop make love to her? Since that morning when she gave him her all, he'd been avoiding physical contact with her. He waved her away when she tried to bathe him in the mornings, although he still allowed her to shave him and fetch and carry.

She tipped out of the hammock and wandered down the path to the small tributary the women used for washing. Coop told her about a clear pool with a waterfall that he used for bathing and promised they'd sneak away together to bathe. Because apparently, women weren't allowed to bathe either. He hadn't mentioned it lately though.

The women crouched by the river's edge, pounding the clothing against rocks, stopping only to wipe the sweat from their brows.

Anna approached them with a smile hovering on her lips. Since that first day, the women of the camp hadn't been very friendly.

She nodded and said, "*Oi*!" Languages came easily to her, and she already picked up a smattering of Portuguese.

The women turned up their noses and turned their backs on her. An insular people. How had Coop fit in so quickly? Speaking their language must've helped. How did he learn this particular dialect? The man revealed very little of himself, except for his body. Revealed a whole lot of that.

Anna shrugged and picked her way along the river bank, stooping to pluck flowers.

The women, all chattering at once, tossed their washing aside and followed her. Must be quitting time. They pressed in on her until she felt the heat rise from their bodies. A small hand pressed against her back, and Anna spun around.

Dark eyes flashed. Hands clenched. The chatter hitched up another notch.

Anna picked up her pace, but still they followed close on her heels, screeching into her ear. She thought she learned a little of the language? She didn't understand one word they said.

She stumbled over a root, and one of the women grabbed her arm and yanked her to her feet. Another woman pinched Anna's other arm in vice-like fingers, and both women propelled her forward, as she tripped between them.

Why were they angry with her? She thought only the men were allowed to get miffed around here.

She wriggled in their grasp, but they tightened their grip. She kicked her legs out. Big mistake. Two other women grabbed her ankles, sweeping her legs out from under her, until she hung between the four women just like that hammock in front of Coop's tent.

Hard work made these women strong. Anna twisted in their grasp, trying to find some decency as her skirt hung down from her body, exposing her bare backside to the scuttling creatures below her. She hoped none of those creatures got any ideas.

Her body bounced as the women carried her, their high voices rivaling the squawking birds calling from the canopy. They staggered into the camp clearing, punctuating the silent, heavy air with their sharp cries.

The men roused themselves, stumbling out of their tents, rubbing their eyes at the unusual sight. One of the shaman's wives hurried to his tent, while the other women called out, "Coop, Coop, Coop."

The man himself sauntered out of his tent, adjusting his loincloth, his eyes widening at the spectacle.

Anna stopped squirming. It made things worse. She hung between the four women like a sloth, while they spoke rapidly first to the shaman and then to Coop.

Coop's face formed along serious lines, although his blue eyes sparkled, indicating danger.

The shaman, rolling his eyes and pointing at the angry women, spoke to Coop.

Coop gestured toward the women, and they placed Anna on her feet, where she smoothed her clothing over her curves.

His eyes tracking her movements, Coop swallowed. "It seems you've been shirking your responsibilities."

"What responsibilities?" She'd done everything Coop told her to do—served him his food, bathed him, shaved him, washed his clothes and dishes, even gave him that blow job. That had to be worth something, even though he never requested a repeat performance.

His arm swept across the camp, and his chin tilted up in his King Coop mode. "You haven't been helping with the general washing or the food gathering and preparation. You sleep too late. You swing in my hammock."

She sputtered. "Y-you told me I could, and you never mentioned those other duties."

He lifted his broad shoulders, which made him look even more powerful. "The other women believe you put yourself above them because of your golden hair and big breasts."

Did they really say that? She choked out, "But you..." She swiveled her head back toward the women, their arms crossed and lips pursed. Hey, they just co-opted her look reserved especially for disobedient students.

Her gaze darted around the gathering crowd, looking for a sympathetic face. The wide grins plastered on the men's faces made her belly roll. No sympathy there.

Coop stood with his legs astride and placed his hands on his hips. "The women demand your punishment."

Anna gulped a bitter pill of fear. "What kind of punishment? Will they hurt me?"

"I'm your master, and your punishment falls to me."

That was supposed to make her feel better? Her tongue cleaved to the roof of her mouth, and her feet felt rooted to the ground.

Coop pulled her toward him and whispered in her ear, "I won't hurt you, but you have to play along. If you fight this, there's no telling what the rest of the tribe will do."

His hands landed on her shoulders and pressed her down. "Show proper reverence."

Okay, she could do that. She dropped to her knees and touched her forehead to the ground, even brushing off his feet for good measure.

He gave her a shove with his foot. "Now to the women you offended."

She crawled toward the fuming group of women as a rumble swept through the cluster of men. This must be new. Coop must be making this stuff up as he went along. She placed her forehead in front of the women and stayed put as Coop strode toward the shaman's tent.

"Come to me." He settled on a massive tree trunk outside the tent. She rose, but he cut in, "On your hands and knees."

She crawled toward him wondering how much skin that piece of cloth covered in the back. The smirk on his face answered her question.

When she reached him, he said, "Over my lap."

She jerked her head up, trying to catch his eye, but his gaze tracked over the crowd of people, who were clustering around the tree trunk.

Biting her lip, Anna draped herself over his knees. He reached behind the tree trunk and withdrew a round wooden paddle. The crowd murmured its approval, while Anna's jaw dropped. This matched her fantasy exactly, except for the hordes of Amazon natives drinking in the sight.

Despite her humiliation at being over a man's lap in full view of others, tendrils of pleasure crept up between her thighs.

Coop held the paddle in front of her face. "Kiss it."

Oh no. She had to draw the line somewhere. She started to roll from his lap, but an iron grip around her waist scuttled that idea.

She pressed her lips against the smooth, cool wood. Then she squeezed her eyes shut and clenched her teeth… along with everything else.

Expecting the smack of the paddle, instead she felt warm, moist air caressing her bottom as Coop whipped up the back of her skirt.

The blood thundered in her head, and then between her legs, plumping up her sex. To maintain what little dignity she had left, Anna willed her body to stay still. Then the paddle smacked the underside of her bare bottom. She kicked her legs and lunged forward, her breasts swinging freely. Not exactly the dignity she had in mind.

Clenching her butt cheeks, she prepared for the next one. Given his strength, Coop held back. That hardly hurt at all. She could handle this.

The paddle returned in front of her face. Coop's voice boomed for all to hear. "Kiss the paddle and thank your master." He repeated the phrase in their language.

She clawed his leg, but she didn't want him to stop now. So she kissed the instrument of her punishment and said, "Thank you, King Coop."

The paddle swept behind her, delivering another stinging snap, more sound than fury. After each smack, Coop brought the paddle to her lips for her kiss and thank you.

Three paddles later, her bottom felt swollen and heated, and that fire burned right through to her lips, trailing its heat between each moist fold.

Anna pushed her hips against Coop's lap, relishing the answering fire in his hard cock. With each blow, her thighs opened a little more as she ground into Coop's long shaft.

She needed relief, but instead Coop stopped after ten smacks. She humped her buttocks up in the air, craving the pressure of the smooth wood against her flaming bottom cheeks.

One of the village men growled out a comment, and the women giggled. Anna pressed and squirmed against Coop's lap, and then he placed the palms of his large hands against her red, hot derriere and shouted something to the crowd.

One long finger traced down her cleft, and Anna froze. The finger continued its path toward Anna's swollen lips and caressed her wet petals. No hope of pretence now. Coop knew exactly how much that spanking aroused her.

His finger dipped inside her and withdrew her thick cream, spreading it back up toward her tight bottom hole. He teased the hole with his wet fingertip, and she clamped around his finger, urging his exploration.

He smacked her bottom with his hand, and she released him. Now two fingers probed her engorged lips, sampled her juice again, and inched toward her throbbing clit.

Sobbing, she pushed against his fingers, and he pinched her hard nub between his fingertips. That's all it took. She exploded, rocking on his lap, the waves of her orgasm cresting over the length of her body from the tips of her toes to her breasts, almost brushing the ground.

While her climax engulfed her, Coop curled two fingers inside her, pressing his thumb against her shaved mound, extending her pleasure, riding it with her. She lay limp and spent over his lap. He brought his fingers, sticky with her cream, to her face.

Without even waiting to be asked, Anna opened her mouth, and he slid his fingers inside where she greedily sucked them, tasting her own sweet juice for the first time.

The act signaled the end of the public punishment. Couples drifted away, the men sporting erections and the women peeling out of their skimpy garments, as they followed their men to their tents.

Breathing hard, Coop stood up, lifting her in his strong arms. She wrapped her arms around his corded neck, her head falling to the hollow of his shoulder. Now. He'd take her now. He carried her to two bamboo posts drilled into the ground and set her on her feet.

His rod stood straight out from his body, and she longed to draw him into her wet, feminine core, still clenching from her climax.

He tied her wrists to the posts. The haze of her passion cleared, and Anna jerked against her restraints.

Coop's half-lidded eyes glinted, as he tucked the hem of her skirt into her waistband, exposing her flaming bottom. He patted her burning cheeks. "The rest of your punishment."

He turned and retreated to his tent, grabbing one of the native women on his way.

A guttural cry rose to Anna's throat as she thrashed her head from side to side and bucked against the ropes that bound her.

He just dealt her the greatest punishment of all.

An hour later, Coop emerged from his tent, sated and yet strangely restless. He squirted into the young woman's mouth over and over again, his eyes clamped shut, picturing Anna's creamy arse with his hand imprinted in red on both cheeks.

Her punishment started as a joke. He thought it would do her some good to get a bare-bottomed paddling in front of the rest of the camp. Maybe she'd lose that librarian air once and for all before he sent her back to Connecticut.

But her response shocked the hell out of him. He expected anger. He expected her to scratch his eyes out, but she submitted and began grinding into his cock until he'd been ready to explode.

When he fingered her wet, swollen sex, he knew just how much he turned her on. It took every grain of willpower he possessed not to plunge into her in front of everyone. He couldn't deny her need any longer, and one little tweak sent her over the edge. What a long drop.

He could've taken her then. Sure the shaman would be angered for a day or too, but Coop could talk him out of that. After all, Coop helped him get rid of his rival for power, the previous chief. Not that he believed for a minute the shaman killed Chief Aminah. Coop scammed Anna on that one too.

He'd be damned if he'd use this ruse to steal her virginity.

She still dangled between the two bamboo posts, her red bottom on display. Everyone else in the tent village got satisfaction after her erotic spanking… everyone but her.

Coop stepped in front of her, and she lifted her head from her shoulder, her eyes red-rimmed. His gut clenched, and he traced her jaw with the pad of his thumb. "Did the paddling hurt that much?"

She shook her head and then nodded.

Coop snapped his fingers at one of the passing women and asked her to bring balm. Then he smoothed his hands over Anna's face, brushing her hair back from her brow. "I'm sorry. I didn't mean to hurt you."

Closing her eyes, she bit her lip. Why wouldn't she say something? Damn, he only meant to smack her a few times on the fleshy underside of her bottom cheeks, but she seemed so into it, he continued.

The native woman hurried back with a pot of balm and knelt behind Anna. She scooped some of the cream out with her fingers and dropped two dollops on Anna's derriere. Anna jolted forward, her breasts bouncing in front of her.

Coop shooed the woman away and took her place behind Anna. He smoothed the dabs of cream over the red blush on Anna's rounded backside, and the breath hissed between her teeth. Must be sore.

The palms of his hands swirled over her, feeling her heat. She swayed as he rubbed the cream into her skin, and she parted her legs. Coop stopped and glanced up at her. A little moan escaped her lips, as she arched her back, thrusting her bottom toward his face.

She whispered, "Don't stop."

He scooped out more cream and caressed her flesh, now glistening with the cool balm. "Does this feel good?"

She murmured, "Mmmm," and spread her legs apart even more.

He circled down, cupping her bottom globes, his fingertips brushing her outer lips. They pulsed at his touch, and he reached in further between her legs. Her sex swelled with desire again, her musky scent signaling her readiness.

She wiggled her ass, opened her legs even wider, and thrust toward him. "Please, Coop. Please, King Coop."

Her pink flesh, plump and engorged, visible between her spread legs beckoned to him. He slipped a finger into her slick, silky passage, and she ate him up. A second finger followed. Her tight muscle closed around his fingers, and his thumb nudged her hard clit.

Lunging forward, she gasped. "Oh yes. Please, all of you. I want all of you, King Coop."

He glanced over his shoulder. A few of the villagers smiled and nodded at the spectacle of him fingering Anna, his hard prick jutting out of his loincloth.

Bloody 'ell. He'd be damned if he would take this woman's virginity in front of a passel of grinning men. He slid his fingers out, and Anna clenched her buttocks.

"Sorry luv. This isn't going to happen."

She whimpered and bucked against her restraints.

He pulled her skirt down and walked around to face her to untie the ropes that bound her wrists.

Her lush lips parted, and her glassy eyes widened while she sucked in a shaky breath. "Why don't you want me, Coop?"

He lifted his brows. "I'm supposed to be preparing you for the shaman, not shagging you myself."

A tear trembled on her long lashes. "H-he doesn't seem to mind that I sleep in your tent or that you touch me."

Coop continued working the knot. "That's not the same as intercourse. You're still a virgin, and a virgin you'll stay if we both want to get out of here alive.

The tear rolled down her cheek. "Would he really hurt you if you took my virginity?"

Did she care? He lied. "I'm here at the whim of the shaman. I don't want to anger him, and neither do you. Besides, you've waited this long, you don't want to give it up to some charlatan in the middle of the Amazon, do you? Save it for the man you love."

He rubbed her chaffed wrists, and then stalked back to his tent, his erection dying.

With her brows drawn together, Anna stared after him. She didn't understand him. He wanted her. A man couldn't hide much behind a loincloth, especially a man of his size. Did he really fear the shaman? Coop didn't seem to fear anything or anyone. Maybe he held back to protect her from the shaman's wrath. Or to protect himself.

One of the village women took her wrist and pulled her toward the larder. She pointed to Anna, and then pointed to the larder. Anna followed. They passed Coop's tent, and the woman pointed to it and then, grinning, patted Anna's backside.

A fire burned in Anna's face. Oh, she understood that, all right. Get to work or King Coop will give you another bare bottom, public paddling.

She should be so lucky.

Chapter 7

For the next few days, Anna worked hard in the camp alongside the women. She picked and washed fruits and vegetables, helped cooked the food, and traipsed through the camp for endless buckets of water.

She rose early to snag Coop the best fruits for breakfast. She heated his water so he could have a warm sponge bath. She swept out his tent throughout the day, keeping it immaculate. She served his dinner, lit his pipe, and cleaned his feet. She was the best darned slave in the camp.

Coop praised her efforts, telling her that the shaman dropped his guard and it wouldn't be long before he could sneak her out of the village and back to the Rainforest Rendezvous base camp.

The thought of leaving Coop gouged a hole in her heart. The tight grip she'd kept on her emotions and her body all these years seemed to be unfurling like so many petals in a rain shower. She felt unencumbered by expectations and criticisms. She enjoyed this simple life. Coop demanded her subservience, and she gave it willingly.

At first she gave it because she feared what the shaman would do to her. A small element of that motivation still existed, but somewhere along the line it changed. She wasn't sure if the public humiliation of that spanking and her reaction to it broke her down or just the day-to-day servicing of Coop, but now she reveled in her subservience to him. It liberated her.

The teasing between them continued, although it didn't go much further than tantalizing brushes of hands or probing fingers. She washed his cock daily, but he wouldn't allow her to suck him. He took that pleasure elsewhere, even though she pleaded with her eyes.

When he touched her, he always managed to brush against her breasts, her nipples tightening in response. When it got too much for her, she begged Coop to make love to her, telling him the shaman would never have to find out.

She underestimated the shaman. When Anna had been there for two weeks, Coop summoned her before the shaman. The shaman's beady eyes, glistening from the folds of his fat face, traveled over her body.

He spoke, and Coop translated. "Pale-skin woman ripe. Almost ready for shaman."

Anna's jaw dropped. Coop was right. The shaman still planned to take her as a wife. She tried to catch Coop's eye, but he kept his gaze trained on the shaman.

The shaman turned to Coop and spoke as he gestured to Anna. Coop answered him, shaking his head.

Coop said, "The shaman wishes to confirm your virginity."

Anna took a step backward. "He already did that, or rather his wives did."

Coop shrugged. "The shaman says you're no longer the hard, tight seed you were when you arrived. You're now lush, ripe, and ready to be picked. He's afraid someone may have beaten him to the harvest."

Anna gritted her teeth. "I am not a piece of fruit."

"Anna!" Coop spoke sharply, nodding toward the gathering storm on the shaman's face. "Go with his wives to his tent. Don't worry. It'll be just like last time."

The three women appeared at the shaman's side, and Anna followed them to the shaman's tent. Coop knew the shaman better than she did. What if she and Coop had given into their passion? What if the shaman discovered she lost her virginity? She shivered as she stepped into the shaman's tent.

Once again, she stretched out on the cot, bent her knees, and let them fall to the sides. If only it were Coop between her legs now instead of these three women, the youngest of whom she knew serviced Coop with her mouth.

They repeated the ritual chanting and shaving of her mound and lips. Anna closed her eyes. Smooth just for Coop. Small fingers prodded her folds, and Anna imagined Coop's tongue following the same path. The fingertips circled her opening, and they became Coop's broad head demanding entry into her passage.

The liquid fire singed her nipples and burned a path from her belly to her sex. A soft moan escaped her lips, as the fingers pushed back her swollen layers, exposing her sensitive tip.

Anna arched her back, her hips pumping in the air. The fingertips clamped around her clit, rolling it between their delicate touch. Anna gasped, her eyelids flying open.

The three women positioned between her open thighs smiled at her. Anna tried to squirm away from them, but one of the women had her clit firmly pinched between her fingers. She couldn't do this, but she succumbed to the pleasure. Anna felt herself pulse and throb under the woman's touch.

She fell back on the cot and gave herself up to the searing heat blazing through her veins. Cupping her own breasts, Anna pushed them together, running her thumbs over her elongated nipples. She lifted her pelvis in wanton invitation, and the woman continued to play with her, burrowing her fingers into her plump lips.

The woman spread Anna's juices down her thighs and between the cleft of her pumping buttocks, circling her tight hole. She then flicked Anna's hard, desperate nub, and Anna cried out as her orgasm claimed her.

She writhed in passion and longing for Coop as a narrow finger wiggled inside her wet passage, prodding and poking, as the spasms of Anna's climax gripped it.

The shaman's laugh filled the tent, and Anna jerked up, her chest still heaving from her climax. Between her open thighs and beyond the three smiling women, the shaman and Coop stood at the tent opening, both sporting huge erections.

One of the shaman's wives held up her finger and nodded. Passed inspection again. The two men left, the tent flap closing behind them.

Anna collapsed back against the cot, covering her face. They'd both been standing there while she allowed another woman to masturbate her to orgasm.

The women giggled and one woman held her hands out about a foot apart. "Coop."

Anna whipped back the tent flap and stormed through, looking like the goddess of fire. "How dare you."

His subservient woman just vanished. He liked this one even better. He lifted his hands. "Anna, it wasn't my idea. The shaman wanted to check on the examination. I didn't want to let him go in there alone."

She took a turn around the room, her little skirt flying up in the back. "Why would you want to miss all the fun?"

She's right. He's glad he didn't miss any of that fun. He and the shaman waited outside the tent for the results, but Anna's moans prompted the shaman to peel back the tent flap. They couldn't look away. Anna spread open like a buffet of sweets, caressing her milky white mounds, and the shaman's wife playing with Anna's pussy. His head almost exploded. Both of them.

"How did I know you'd be in there letting the shaman's wife masturbate you?"

Her lips peeled back in a snarl. "I didn't let her."

"She forced you?"

"Sh-she just did it."

"You loved it. The shaman knows women. You are a fruit ready to be plucked." His gaze wandered to her heaving bosom, her nipples poking through the thin fabric of her top. "Melons, I'd say."

She screamed and pounced on him, fists flying, legs kicking. He pinned her wrists with one hand, but her long legs continued their assault, her aim clear.

He pushed her back onto the cot and fell on top of her, drawing her arms over her head, and pinning her squirming body with his. Her top rose in the struggle, exposing one breast with its taut, rosy nipple.

He couldn't resist. His tongue lapped at the pearl, and Anna lurched beneath him. He pulled her nipple between his teeth, scraping it gently. The nipple puckered in his mouth, and he latched onto her breast, suckling her. Her hips pressed against his crotch, and he knew he had her again. Her body quivered, a mass of tight strings waiting to be played, her full melody not yet realized.

If she wanted him this badly, was it wrong to satisfy her needs? Even if she offered under false pretences. He'd been manipulating the situation from the beginning, pretending the shaman required the examinations, required her to dress like a native, required her punishment by paddling. When all along those were his own ideas. Until he had her primed and ready for the taking. His taking.

All he had to do was spread her open and dive right in. Instead, he pushed aside the rest of her top, and his tongue trailed to her other breast, circling lazily toward her peaking nipple. Her dark pink areola began to crinkle, and he ran his tongue over the little bumps, stopping to nip at her hardening nipple with his teeth.

She jerked beneath him and drew in her breath. He whispered, "The shaman had the right idea. These should be pierced."

Anna groaned and pushed her breasts forward. He licked between them, up her throat, and along her jaw line. A pink blush bloomed on her creamy cheeks, and he pressed his lips to their warmth.

Her body cleaved to him, until all her soft curves filled in the dents and hollows of his body. He devoured her mouth, feasting on her bottom lip. When he released her wrists, her hands settled on his ass, pressing him against her opening thighs.

She swept his loincloth aside and dug her fingernails into his buttocks. Moving against her, he explored her mouth with his probing tongue. She trailed her fingers up his cleft, and his balls tightened.

He never wanted a woman more in his life. He never deserved one less.

The shaman already offered his virgin to Coop. He secured the tribe's contentment and solidified his power. Thanks, in part, to Coop.

Then there was the shaman's oldest wife. She threatened to kick the shaman out of her bed if he claimed Anna as another wife. Even in this isolated, male-dominated community, the delicate balance of power between the sexes shifted daily.

Coop had to get Anna out of here before she did something she'd regret.

He disentangled himself from the warm clasp of her arms, denying himself every kind of dessert in the pastry shop window. With his balls aching, he pushed himself up from the cot and the sweet promise it offered.

Anna reached for him, and his gut clenched. Her desire for him wasn't real. He fueled it with lies. Trapping her fluttering hands in his, he brought them to his lips. "I'm going to take my bath, luv. Why don't you take a nap?"

He escaped the tent before he could change his mind and stalked toward a group of women gossiping as they prepared the evening meal. His few favorites smiled in anticipation when they saw him charging their way, leading with this erection.

Grinding his teeth together, he veered off onto the path toward the pool. Even that didn't help anymore. It had to be Anna.

She was a freak. Seems she couldn't even give it away. If Coop wouldn't allow the shaman to ever get to the point of actually bedding her, why did it matter if Coop beat him to it?

They could make love, and then she could leave. The shaman would never know. Coop worried too much. Maybe he just didn't want her.

No. She may be a virgin, but she knew when a man wanted her. Even if he could have the pick of all the women at the camp. The ladies stood in awe of his legendary size, and Anna's heart thumped hard in her chest when she imagined taking all of him inside.

Size really didn't matter. Nope. Anna did something stupid on her summer vacation. She fell in love with an Englishman. Not just with your garden-variety Englishman—with a charlatan, an adventurer, an out-and-out rogue. She didn't even know his full name. Didn't know where he went to school. Didn't know where he grew up. Didn't even know if he had a wife stashed away somewhere.

She did know his smile made her heart sing. His tales of his adventures stimulated her curiosity and fueled late-night conversations in his tent. His touch and a warm look from his blue eyes encouraged her to tell him about all her life's disappointments and fears. She even told him about Vincent.

She couldn't even begin to catalogue what Coop did to her body.

Before she pulled the thin sheet over his cot, she buried her face in it, reveling in Coop's masculine scent. How could she ever leave this man?

"Anna?"

Still clutching the sheet in her hands, she twirled around at the sound of Coop's voice.

His brows collided over the bridge of his nose. "Are you all right?"

She glanced down at the rumpled sheet, and then smoothed it across the cot. "Yes"

He took two steps into the tent and crossed his arms. Anna's heart fluttered, but he still frowned.

His chest rose and fell. "Anna, you've played your part too well. The shaman believes you're ready to become his wife. After the wives perform one more examination, there will be a ceremony and the shaman will take you before the whole tribe."

Anna searched Coop's face, set in hard lines. She swallowed the sour knot of fear clawing its way up from her belly. This was really happening. That grotesquely huge man expected her to have sex with him—in front of the entire village. No way. She wanted just one man to take her virginity, and he stood an arm's length in front of her. She extended her hand to him. "What are we going to do?"

His warm fingers closed around her hand. "We're going to get you out of here. The shaman is convinced you've settled down in the village and are ready to accept its way of life. His watchdogs have become lax, and I have two men in my confidence who can take you back tomorrow morning."

"So soon?" She needed more time. More time with Coop.

He raised one brow. "Soon? Do you want to be the shaman's fourth wife?"

No, your first. She jerked her hand away from his and covered her face so he couldn't read the longing stamped on her every feature. "I'm just afraid he'll stop us."

"He won't. The feast and dancing occur tonight. He'll probably be going at it with all three of his wives all night long, especially if you put on another sexy show for him. He'll be knackered tomorrow morning, as will most of his men."

She dropped her hands, tears choking her voice. "Will he suspect you? Will this be the end of your sweet deal?"

He turned away from her, hiding his own worry. If anything happened to him because of her, she'd never forgive herself. She'd never know. She'd never see him again.

Wrapping her arms around his waist, she laid her cheek against his muscled back. "I-if he's going to suspect you and punish you in some way, I think I can do what he asks."

"No!" Coop broke away from her, and she stumbled back. He spun around, clenching his fists, his chiseled features twisted with pain. "You're getting out of here tomorrow morning. This is no place for you. Go back to the safety of your library and your buttoned-up blouses."

Anna blinked back hot tears. Was he angry at her? It almost sounded as if he wanted to get rid of her for reasons that had nothing to do with the shaman. She whispered, "Just tell me what to do. I'll be ready."

He cupped her face in his large hands, running his thumb across her lips. "I'll have your clothes in my tent. While everyone's sleeping off the previous night's bacchanal, my two men will spirit you out of the camp."

She resisted an urge to draw his thumb into her mouth. "What about you?"

Before dropping his hands, he pinched her chin. "Don't worry about me, luv. I always land on my feet. I'll convince the shaman your disappearance is a good omen."

A good omen for the shaman maybe, but not for her. How could she go back to her old life? She belonged with Coop. Maybe she should just tell him that. Despite the way he treated her at times, she knew he wanted her. He couldn't hide it. She gathered in a deep breath and dropped her lashes. "Coop, maybe I could stay with you. Away from this place and the shaman."

Guilt punched him in the gut. Why should he be surprised at her request? Isn't this what he groomed her for? He formulated his plan the minute he learned of her virginity. His manipulation of women always worked for him, but this was the first time it flogged his conscience.

Anna's pride took a hit due to a mingling of fear and desire—emotions he'd encouraged. If he rejected her outright, that old pride might just kick in and steer her in the right direction—on a fast boat out of this jungle.

Coop curled his lip and tipped up her chin. "That would never work, Anna. I'm an adventurer, and you're a… librarian. A virgin at that. I prefer my women a little more experienced. Go back to your university and your professor where you belong."

Gritting his teeth so hard he felt as if his jaw would lock, he patted her cheek and somehow made it out of the tent. He didn't want to stick around for the tears, for the hurt, or even for the anger. He had enough of that pumping through his own veins.

Through narrowed eyes, Anna watched the prime specimen of male masculinity stumble out of the tent. He played his part impeccably well. Throughout his tough-talking speech, he got the words right, and the careless curl to his lips, and even the stern jaw, but he couldn't even meet her eyes. Did he feel guilty? Did he even possess that emotion?

He had nothing to feel guilty about. Sure, he took a few… uh, liberties with her body, but she couldn't blame him for the shaman and the tribe's rules and requirements for women. He'd done his best with the situation. He punished her himself instead of turning her over to the shaman, who might have hurt her. He also protected her from the shaman's lust for as long as he could.

Anna watched the tent flap quiver for a moment. Then she straightened her shoulders, a smile curling her lips. She wasn't a Winter woman from Hilbock County for nothing.

A few hours later after helping prepare the meats and vegetables for the evening feast, Anna ducked behind a large tangle of roots to watch Coop's tent. Late afternoon when much of the tribe took naps, Coop headed out for his bath. This time, Anna planned to go with him. It would be her last chance.

Coop stepped out of his tent carrying a leather satchel, which Anna knew contained a bar of soap and a small towel. He took the path that led to the washing stream, and Anna tiptoed behind him.

He passed the stream and cut further into the jungle while Anna crouched behind the thick foliage and padded in his wake. The trees parted to reveal a clear watering hole fed by a sparkling waterfall.

Anna flattened herself behind a tree as Coop drew to the water's edge. He stepped out of his loincloth and stretched, raising his arms above his head. Anna drank in the sight of his lean, powerful body, the hard muscles of his buttocks tensing as he balanced on a narrow rock ledge jutting out over the water. His huge cock added to the impression of pure masculinity that radiated from every inch of his body.

He placed the soap and towel on the rock next to his loincloth and dove in, his perfect form slicing the glassy surface of the water. He surfaced beneath the waterfall, its droplets bouncing off the pool like diamonds, and sluiced his long dark hair back from his face.

When he ducked beneath the water again, Anna crept up to the rock. Trembling, she pulled her clothes from her body and dropped them next to Coop's. Now or never. She curled her toes over the edge of the rock and shook her hair loose from its braid. Pulling back her shoulders, she arched her back and waited.

Coop rose from the water and took a few strokes toward the rock. His head jerked back, and his eyes widened. "Anna!"

She crouched down, letting her hair cascade over one shoulder. Picking up the bar of soap, she asked, "Looking for this?"

"What are you doing here?"

Straightening up, she pouted, licking her full lower lip. "You promised I could take a bath here and since I'm leaving tomorrow, I thought you should make good on that promise."

His eyes darting beyond her, he swallowed. "Do you think this is a good idea?"

Using a little trick from Jenny, she rolled her shoulders back and let them drop, causing her breasts to jiggle. Coop's eyes followed every bounce.

She said, "I'm tired of sponge baths. If I'm going to get back into my clothes tomorrow, I need a bath. A real one."

"Uh, you might want to be careful. There could be animals in this water. Even snakes."

She glanced down where the clear water lapped about his waist and let her gaze wander up his sculpted torso until it locked onto his blue eyes. "Oh, I'll watch out for those snakes. Especially the big ones."

Coop blinked and a red tinge touched his cheeks. She made him blush? She caught on quickly. Must be those Winter genes.

"Suit yourself." He dipped back under the water and popped up further away from her.

Clutching the bar of soap in her hand, Anna jumped into the rippling water, which enveloped her in its cool embrace. She rose near Coop and said, "Don't worry, King Coop. I'll wash you first."

He backpedaled toward the waterfall. "That's not necessary."

She held up the soap. "Sure it is. One last act of servitude before you send me on my way."

Was he afraid of her? Suddenly she possessed all the power. She paddled toward him and lathered up the soap as she treaded water. Running her hands over his neck and shoulders, she drew closer. His skin glistened under the suds, and she spread her hands across his chest, following the hard, familiar planes.

His heart thundered beneath her palms as she gently swirled her fingertips around the nipples of his heaving chest. She floated around to his back and worked the lather into his shoulders. She skimmed the soap down his back beneath the water, and then cupped his buttocks. He clenched as she trailed her fingers along his cleft.

She ducked beneath the water, nudging her head between his legs. He spread them open, and she swam between his thighs, rising up in front of him again. His eyes burned with a blue flame, and his nostrils flared like a bull ready to charge.

Holding up her hands, she said, "Oops. I lost the soap. May I borrow some of yours?"

Without waiting for an answer, she wrapped her arms around his neck and pressed her breasts against his soapy chest. She swayed in the water, dragging her peaked, aching nipples across his hard slabs of muscle.

His erect cock poked between her thighs, but she edged away from it, her legs floating out behind her. He grunted and cinched an arm around her waist, drawing her back toward him and his pulsing spear.

He devoured her lips with his mouth, and she curled her legs around his narrow waist. His tongue plunged into her, mimicking the rocking of his hips. Then he drew away and pulled her to the waterfall until the spray caressed them both. Cupping her face in his hands, he kissed her eyelids, her nose, her jaw. He licked the curve of her earlobe and drew it into his mouth. She wanted to feel him everywhere.

Anna raised her legs higher and rubbed against Coop. The cool water swirling around them did nothing to temper the hot desire racing through her veins.

He guided her through the waterfall and, spanning her waist with his hands, hoisted her on top of the flat rock behind it. He pulled himself up next to her, and she lowered her head to his cock now jutting out from his body.

"Time to service my king."

Taking her shoulders, he laid her on the smooth rock. "No, it's my turn."

He took her right nipple between his lips and sucked on it until pinpricks of pleasure needled her entire breast. Then he gathered both breasts at the sides, pushed them together, and buried his face in their abundance, his tongue darting between the two.

Raking his tongue down her cleavage, he left a trail of fire that pooled in her navel as he flicked his tongue there. Keeping her legs clamped shut, she lifted her pelvis off the rock.

He brushed his fingertips between her thighs, sending shivers of anticipation to her belly. Her legs fell open in invitation, and he pushed them apart, opening her to his gaze.

Her sex pulsed under his scrutiny. With two fingers, he spread her outer lips open. She'd never felt so completely exposed before. The intensity of his gaze scorched her, and she felt her clit growing larger, protruding from her folds, quivering under his stare.

She whimpered and pumped her hips again. A frown furrowed his brow. "Am I hurting you?"

"Oh God, no."

The frown disappeared, replaced by his smile. Then slowly, deliberately, maddeningly, he took her clit between his fingertips and rolled it. She twitched beneath his touch. When he released her, she groaned, feeling abandoned.

But not for long. He burrowed his head between her legs, his hair tickling her thighs. She held her breath, as she watched in fascination his dark head between her legs. His warm tongue traced around the swollen folds of her sex.

This exceeded her wildest imaginings. Much better than her own touch. Better than a vibrator. Oh… better than chocolate.

He drew her clit between his lips, and she gasped and clutched at his hair. He sucked once, and a tingling wave crested through her body over and over until it gathered in her very core, turning into spasms of sweet pleasure that seemed to go on forever.

When she opened her eyes, Coop knelt between her thighs, his cock high and hard, a dollop of cream on its tip. She reached forward and dabbed at the drop, catching it on her fingertip. Looking deep into his eyes, Anna sucked his salty fluid from her finger. A flush rose on his chest, as he swallowed hard.

Was the man made of steel? He couldn't refuse her now. She wrapped her legs around his thighs and tilted her hips forward.

His voice hoarse, he asked, "Anna, are you sure?"

She really didn't want to discuss the merits of her virginity right now. She gripped his thick cock at the base and pulled him forward. Could she be any clearer?

Apparently not. Coop let out a long breath as he prodded her opening with his blunt tip. He dipped into her, as if testing the waters, and then eased in slowly, watching her face with a crease on his brow.

She smoothed her thumb across his forehead. "I'm fine. Go on."

Balancing his palms on either side of her, he moved his hips forward, sliding into her wet sheath, his eyes never leaving hers. She closed around him as he filled her up, and she entwined her legs around his waist, urging him on.

A sharp pain pierced her as Coop thrust home up to the hilt, but she bit her lip and received all of him. She raised her head to see their bodies connect, his springy hair tickling her smooth mound. They joined as one.

Coop slid out and back in again, and Anna moved to the sensuous rhythm he set. Each time he pulled away from her, she felt empty until he filled her again.

His gentleness soon gave way to a fierce thrusting, as he pounded into her. He cried out, his body stiffening, his seed shooting deep into her womb. She sucked out every drop until he had nothing left.

Still inside her, Coop covered her body with his, memorizing every curve, the softness of her skin, her fresh scent, now enriched by the primal smell of sex. He'd remember each aching detail long after she returned to Connecticut.

She mewed and stirred beneath him. He shifted to her side, slipping out of her wet core and wanting to stuff himself right back in again.

She closed her thighs and, pointing her toes, stretched her legs straight out in front of her. Her golden lashes swept down over her eyes, and a smile illuminated her face. Coop caught his breath. Anna rivaled the most beautiful creatures in the rainforest.

Her fingers trailed along his hip, and his cock twitched in response. Her smile deepened, and she asked, "When can we do it again?"

If Mr. Happy down there had his way, he'd be prepared for lift-off in about five minutes, but Coop had two heads, and the one on his shoulders told him he just tricked a perfectly respectable woman out of her virginity.

Anna rolled to her side and inched down his body, searing him with her smooth skin. She plumped her breasts together and gathered his awakening cock into her warm cleavage. Well, this was perfectly respectable too.

He massaged her scalp as she licked him like a lollipop. He had only one head again, and it craved her warm, wet embrace.

She sucked him almost to the point of no return until he pulled out of her mouth and said, "Now that you're initiated, you may as well learn all the tricks."

Her green eyes widened. "Tricks?"

He raised one brow. "Don't forget who's still in charge around here."

Her delicious giggle sent vibrations down to his toes. Anna Winter giggled? He pursed his lips in his best imitation of… Anna Winter. "On your hands and knees."

She crouched beside him, wiggling her derriere. Really, the woman had no shame. He smacked her round bottom. "Prepare to receive your king."

Chapter 8

The drums thumped out a rhythm that reminded Anna of the afternoon she just spent with Coop. Standing outside the circle of logs, Anna rolled her shoulders and swayed her hips to the beat. The sensuous music found an answering chord along her nerve endings.

Coop insisted she leave tomorrow morning. At the bathing pool, they alternated between tender and passionate lovemaking, and then Coop sent her back to the camp alone. He spent the rest of the afternoon hunched over his notebooks while Anna spun fantastic plans.

When she got back home, she'd see him again. She had to, even though Coop hadn't exactly mentioned any future plans that included her. What did she know about him anyway? He still refused to tell her his full name. How would she ever find him again?

Perhaps she wasn't meant to. Maybe she dreamed this entire vacation. But oh, what a dream.

The other women beckoned to her to join them in the circle. This time she didn't hesitate, and she didn't need the potent punch. With her eyes half-closed, she shook her hips and shimmied her shoulders, all the while feeling the drumbeat pulse between her legs, heating her blood.

Whatever happened with Coop after this point, he freed her, allowing her to become a woman in tune with her body, not afraid of it. For that she'd have to thank him.

Coop watched Anna give herself over to the music, the firelight dancing off her shining hair. Once he released the floodgates this afternoon, Anna had been insatiable. He'd been insatiable too. He wanted to explore every inch of her body, and he did so—with his fingers, his lips, his tongue, and his cock. She opened herself completely to him until he felt as if he'd never been with another woman before. As if he lost his virginity along with hers. She truly belonged to him now, just as surely as he belonged to her.

He had to send her away.

The last few notes of the flute dissipated in the night air, leaving a melancholy emptiness. Couples wandered away together, hand-in-hand, and Anna knelt at Coop's feet, leaning her head against his thigh.

Their last night together. He stroked her hair, and she sighed and nestled closer. Maybe he'd make love to her one last time. Selfishly, he wanted to keep her here with him, but she didn't belong here. Hell, he didn't belong here. He had work to do.

The shaman had afforded him a brilliant opportunity to live among his people and to record their lifestyle and rituals, especially the betrothal village, but his presence altered the very culture he observed. Time to go home. Once Anna left, he didn't want to stay anyway.

He shifted his legs, and Anna swayed to the side. He caught her and brushed the hair from her face. She slept soundly. Probably just saved him from making a big mistake.

He swept her up against his chest. Murmuring his name, her arms came up around his neck. He kicked open the tent flap and settled her on the mat, tucking a pillow under her head.

"Good night, my love," he whispered.

Anna bolted upright and flailed at her legs where something tickled up her calf. So much for the rainforest's natural insect repellant Coop recommended. She peered into the darkness at his cot. After what they experienced this afternoon, he couldn't share his cot with her? Even on their last night together? She stifled the sob rising from her throat. She had to see him again. When he ended his charade down here, he'd come to her.

Then what?

She couldn't picture Coop in the stuffy confines of the Northern Connecticut University Research Library. Heck, she couldn't picture Coop clothed. Didn't want to.

She'd taken Nicole's advice about a summer romance to the extreme. Now it was over, like all summer romances, and she had to somehow pick up the pieces of her former life, shuffle them into some recognizable pattern, and carry on.

Although this journey changed her, she could be this woman in Connecticut. Couldn't she? She could lose the tight bun. Lose the severe clothing. Find a man.

Hunching over, she folded her arms across her belly. She didn't want another man. She wanted Coop.

Then go get him. She eased up on her toes and crept toward Coop's cot. If she slipped in next to him, he couldn't refuse her. Once her bare skin met his, all of his reservations seemed to fly right out the window or the tent flap, anyway.

She knelt next to his cot and reached out, her fingers eager to make contact with his warm skin, but finding emptiness. Biting her lip, she rocked back on her heels. Where could he be at this time of night? Everyone had to in a dead sleep after the night's revelry.

Anna tiptoed outside, scanning the circle of other tents. A soft glow emanated from the shaman's tent. Was Coop enjoying some orgy with the shaman and his wives? If so, why should she torture herself with the image? Her feet tripped over the ground anyway, carrying her to the light like one of the Amazon's giant bugs to the flame.

Low voices, punctuated by the occasional laugh, rumbled from the tent. At least there were no moans and groans. Anna crouched down and scurried toward the back of the tent, where the light reflected the shadows of two men.

She heard a familiar male voice, and Coop answered. Anna scooted in closer to the tent, brushing her ear against its side.

The voice belonged to the shaman, and he spoke perfect English. Anna's fingers curled in the dirt as she leaned forward to listen.

The shaman said, "How much longer do you plan to stay, Coop?"

"How much longer do you need me?"

The shaman laughed. "Now that I've sent Chief Aminah back to the village with his tail between his legs, I have supreme power here. The people are no longer fearful, and everything is running smoothly. You can leave when you please."

Anna expelled a breath. So the shaman didn't murder the former chief, and he seemed to accept Coop as a mere mortal.

Coop said, "As much as I've been enjoying my own stint as the god-king, I'll be heading out soon."

The shaman sputtered and gulped down some liquid. "Have you fucked that sumptuous blonde yet?"

Anna covered her mouth to hold in her gasp and fell back on her bottom.

"No."

"Well, if you didn't, someone else got to her first. A woman doesn't move her body like that unless she's been thoroughly shagged." The shaman laughed and slapped something. His thigh? Coop's back?

Coop's face?

The leaner shadow rose and stretched. Coop said, "I'm sending her back tomorrow morning while the rest of the camp sleeps. What are you going to tell your people about her disappearance?"

The shaman snorted. "I'll tell them my god-king decided to take her for himself and since he claimed her virginity, I sent her away. I can have my wives do another examination before she leaves just to confirm the fact. You enjoyed that, didn't you?"

Coop's voice sliced through the air. "That's not necessary."

Anna's fists bunched at her sides. She'd show him what was necessary. A good, hard kick in the groin. This had all been a game to him. The shaman didn't want her for a wife. He posed no danger to her. But Coop posed plenty of danger.

Anna lunged to her feet and scrambled to the tent's entrance. She threw the tent flap back and stood with her hands clenched at her sides. Both men jerked their heads up.

Anna loomed at the entrance, legs apart, eyes blazing in the soft light of the kerosene lamp. Even now, Coop's blood heated at the sight of her magnificent body quivering with rage. "Anna!"

Her nostrils flared. "Don't Anna me, you pig. All this time you've been using me, playing me for a fool." She mimicked his English accent. "Oh, Ahhnna, the shaman is a dangerous man. Oh, Ahhnna, the shaman insists you be punished. Oh, Ahhnna, the shaman requires weekly examinations of your hymen."

The shaman held his big belly, as it shook with laughter. "I did require that first one."

She rounded on him and yelled, "Shut up!"

His cheeks creased, and he wiped tears from his eyes.

Coop reached out to Anna, but she slapped his hand away. Bloody 'ell. He never wanted her to find out this way. If he could've told her himself, he could've put a better spin on it. Maybe she'd even see the humor. Her green eyes narrowed to slits until she resembled a jungle cat.

Maybe not.

She couldn't deny she got off on it all. She practically raped him at the bathing site today. She should be thanking him instead of eyeing his crotch with evil intent.

"Anna, it was all on the level… at first. The tribe had enough of Chief

Aminah's cruelty. People are supposed to enjoy themselves here, find a mate, marry, and go back to the village to start families, but Chief Aminah split couples up just because he could. The shaman wanted him out, and when I stumbled on the scene, he got the perfect opportunity."

Didn't look like his philanthropy impressed her. She wedged her hands on her hips. "So you just lied to everyone and told them the shaman summoned you. Where's Chief Aminah's body buried?"

The shaman choked. "You told her I killed him?"

Anna's lips got thin again. Bad sign. She spit out, "You had to be the big, bad shaman, so I would run to Coop for protection. Ha!"

If he could just get her alone and explain everything to her, tell her how much he cared about her. He reached for her again, but she turned her back on him. "Anna, the shaman did come up with that vision of the virgin, but he never expected to make good on it. When the men discovered you, they thought they were fulfilling the shaman's vision."

She spun around. "How long?"

Coop blinked. "How long?"

"How long since the two of you agreed you didn't need me for the vision?"

The shaman struggled to his feet. "If the two of you don't mind, I have three impatient wives waiting for me." He poked his head out of the tent and called to his wives, and then escaped outside to round them up.

Anna's lip trembled. "How long, Coop?"

He couldn't lie anymore. "About a week after you got here."

A Kaleidoscope of emotions traveled across her face, settling on his least favorite—the disapproving schoolmistress.

She said, "It must have been a big joke to you. How long before you could make the prude beg for your sexual favors?"

Bloody 'ell. He knew she'd see it that way. Anna still had no idea of her allure, how completely she captivated him. "No, Anna, what we shared earlier wasn't a joke. I held off before because I didn't want to take advantage of you, but I couldn't resist you any longer. You made that impossible."

"Now that you've had your fun, it's time to send the prude back home? Well, I can't wait to get out of here. Back to civilization. Back to civilized men."

She just pushed it too far. "Yeah, it's so civilized to cheat on your fiancé. I'd never cheat on you, Anna."

Her eyes shimmered, and she swallowed hard. "Good night, Coop.

Don't you dare try to come into that tent or see me tomorrow morning. I'll be sleeping in your cot tonight… alone."

Coop didn't try to come into the tent, and it's a good thing. The man could make her believe anything. If he didn't want to use her, he should've just told her the truth. Then what? She would've returned to the Rainforest Rendezvous base camp, her adventure over.

He wanted to have his fun first. What about hers? He never made her do anything she didn't want to do, but she did it under false pretences. Would she have gone along with all his outrageous demands if she didn't feel the shaman's threat hanging over her?

The thoughts and questions tumbling around her head all night disturbed her sleep, and she woke up with a headache and an even worse ache in her heart.

Someone placed her folded clothes on top of the stool, and set out fresh water and a bowl of fruit on the table by the cot. Keeping an eye on the tent flap, she washed and dressed, feeling suffocated under all her clothing, minus the damaged bra.

Two young men waited for her outside the tent, and her gaze darted around the sleeping village, looking for signs of life. Looking for signs of Coop. Why would he see her off? She warned him against it.

One of the young men handed her a walking stick, and she traipsed after them, shooting one last glance at the little tent village—the scene of her awakening.

They hiked back to the main river and stopped to eat. Anna kicked off her heavy hiking boots and dangled her feet in the cool water of the river.

The two men stripped off their loincloths and waded into the river, beckoning her to join them. Smiling, she shook her head. Nothing shocked her anymore.

Refreshed, they returned to the trail, and after another hour of walking, one of the men stopped and lifted his nose to the air. Anna sniffed and smelled bacon cooking. When they rounded a bend in the river, Anna saw two boats docked with "Rainforest Rendezvous" painted on their sides.

Her two guides pushed her in the direction of the smoke rising above the trees, and she stumbled over a tangle of roots and fell. When she rose from her knees, the men disappeared, sucked back into the lush foliage, back to Coop.

She brushed off her legs and marched toward the smells and sounds of civilization, a world where women were treated with respect.

A few tourists curiously glanced up at her approach, and then returned to the business of packing their backpacks. Sheesh, she got a better reception from the folks at the tent village. Of course, they thought the virgin who'd save them from the encroaching outside world just stumbled in. Instead that virgin no longer existed. A sob hitched in her throat, and she gulped it down.

A small, wiry man dressed in the Rainforest Rendezvous khakis and hat burst out of a tent and clapped his hands. The head tour guide, Raoul, said. "Okay, people, last day-hike of the tour. Get your backpacks ready and don't forget the mosquito repellant."

He jerked his head toward Anna's bedraggled figure, a wide smile spreading across his face. "Welcome back, Anna."

Her jaw dropped. That's it? The rainforest swallowed her whole for over two weeks, and that's the greeting she got? Anger fizzed in her veins, and she spit out, "Why didn't you send out a search party? I could've been killed out there, mutilated by wild animals, died of starvation." *Ravished by a wild jungle man in a loincloth.*

Hunching his shoulders, Raoul spread his hands. "I knew you were safe with Coop."

Her blood percolated. She could almost feel steam shooting from her ears. "You know Coop?"

Raoul tossed a bottle of bug spray to one of the tourists and turned back toward Anna. "Sure I know Coop. He's a regular in this part of the world, although I don't think he's ever stayed with that particular tribe before."

Anna ground her teeth together. She never understood the concept of gnashing teeth. Until now. "How did you know Coop had me?"

He looked her up and down, a smile tugging at his lips. Oh God. Was it that obvious? Did Coop make a habit of seducing lost tourists?

Raoul answered, "He sent word."

Anna sank to the nearest camp chair. If it hadn't been there, she would've just collapsed.

Raoul tilted his head. "You are okay, aren't you? He indicated he'd send you back with a couple of the tribesmen when you'd had enough of roughing it."

When *she'd* had enough? When Coop had had enough of toying with her. "I-I'm fine."

"Actually, you're very lucky. Not many tourists get to experience the rainforest like that." Raoul wandered off to take care of his group.

Lucky? Coop tricked her into believing the shaman would do her harm if she didn't stay and agree to become his wife. Tricked her into wearing those clothes, serving him, opening up to him.

Or did he?

Coop never forced her to dance, or give him blowjobs, or have sex. Coop never forced her body to respond like it did. She did it all on her own. In the end, he would've sent her away still a virgin if she hadn't seduced him at the pool.

A tear balanced on the end of her lashes. Maybe he achieved the ultimate goal of his game. Make her beg for it.

Well, he won.

Raoul asked, "Anna, are you coming with us? It's our last hike before we leave tomorrow. If you prefer to stay, another guide will be here packing up."

She shook her head. "I'll stay. Is my stuff still here?"

He pointed to one of the tents, much sturdier and more comfortable than the one she'd inhabited for the past few weeks. Much lonelier.

The rest of the tourists headed for the trail, and Anna shuffled to the tent. She dug through her duffel bag, pulling out a clean pair of walking shorts and a wrinkled blouse, along with some soap and toothpaste.

She washed up, and she peeled off her dirty clothes and dropped them in a pile. She grabbed a bra and hooked it in the back, and then slipped into her blouse, buttoned it to the top, and stuffed it into the waistband of her shorts. Then she brushed out her tangled hair and braided it.

There. She was safe again. She didn't have to bow down to any man. Didn't have to worry about getting paddled. Didn't have to submit to humiliating inspections. Didn't have to worry about getting pulled into an orgy of abandoned dancing.

Didn't have to see Coop again.

For the first time ever, her safety made her cry.

Chapter 9

Anna crumpled the flyer in her fist. She could tell this stuffy Brit, the Earl of Covington, a thing or two about the lost tribes of the Amazon. Ensconced in his ivory tower, did he really think he understood the people of that verdant jungle?

Her phone rang, but she let the machine pick it up. She couldn't take another teary session with Vincent. His tears, not hers.

Instead, Nicole's voice scolded over the machine. "Anna, pick up. This is not Vincent. Pick up."

Anna grabbed the phone. "Hi, Nicole."

"Is that two-timing little wussy still bugging you?"

Nicole never did like Vincent, even before she knew he was a two-timing little wussy. "Yeah, but I think he's starting to get the hint."

Nicole giggled. "Just tell him you're not a virgin anymore. That'll stop him in his tracks."

The status of her virginity was not up for grabs... anymore. She confessed to Nicole, but even Nicole didn't know everything.

Anna gripped the phone. "I'm not telling him a thing, and neither are you."

Nicole took a quick breath. "My lips are sealed. You are going to Lord Covington's talk on the lost tribes of the Amazon, aren't you? Even I'm going. I heard the man is quite eccentric. He already left a Canadian university in an uproar after one of his lectures."

What did he do, raise his voice above a monotone? The thought of listening to another boring lecture depressed her, but Anna had to go. The University Research Library sponsored the talk. "I suppose."

Nicole's voice bubbled over the phone. "Listen, Anna, maybe this Lord Covington knows something about your King Coop. They're both English, right? Maybe Covington ran into Coop down there. Maybe he knows where he is now."

Tears scalded Anna's eyes, just like they did every time she thought about Coop and the fact that she'd never see him again. One of the tears escaped and dripped down the side of her nose. She cleared her throat. "I think that's pretty unlikely, Nicole. I doubt Coop and the Earl of Covington run in the same circles."

Nicole sighed. "Are you crying again? Anna, I know your first time is always special. Even though my first time occurred at sixteen, I still remember the song that played on the radio, the type of car we were in, and the fact that it took the guy two minutes to come."

The tears kept up a steady stream. Anna remembered so much more than that. The taste of Coop's skin, his musky scent, the hard planes of his body, and the way his eyes burned into hers when he entered her for the first time.

"Thanks for sharing, Nicole."

"Well, I think you should give it a shot with this Covington. Tell him about your experience down there, not all of it, mind you. Ask him if he knows about King Coop."

Coop wanted to keep his little charade under wraps, which is about the only thing he kept under wraps, and Anna refused to betray him. Even if he did betray her.

"Maybe I will. Now I have to finish getting dressed. I'll meet you over there."

Nicole rang off with a warning. "Now remember, lose the suit of armor."

Since returning from her trip, Anna made a few adjustments to her wardrobe. Nothing drastic, no mini skirts and tube tops, but she no longer wore her blouses buttoned up to her chin, and she cut back on a few layers, exposing a little more skin. Just testing the waters.

Her subtle alterations raised a few eyebrows, but so far nobody mistook her for the University good-time girl, although Vincent pronounced her attempts to mimic her sister degrading and unnecessary. Yeah, he'd really win her back with those compliments.

She buttoned the jacket of her dark green pantsuit over a beige camisole, its edge of lace just visible above the jacket's lapel. Turning in front of the full-length mirror, Anna frowned. The suit jacket cinched in at the waist, emphasizing her shape, and she ran her hands over her hips. That's a good thing, Anna. You're a woman. You can be feminine and professional at the same time.

The crisp fall air needled her face as she strolled from her apartment across the campus. She crunched the leaves beneath her boots and inhaled the sweet scent of the maple trees. Ahh, safety.

As the distance and the season took her farther and farther away from that hot, steamy jungle with its cartoon-like colorful foliage and deep, earthy smells, she felt more herself. More in control. More serious. More unhappy.

She strode into the library, completing the transformation. Despite the camisole and the high-heeled boots, Miss Anna Winter, virgin librarian, took control.

A group of female students, talking and giggling, created a disturbance in the corner of the reference area, and Anna's old instincts clicked into gear. She marched up to the table, her jaw hardening, her lips thinning. "You know the rules. If you want to talk, study someplace else. The library is not the proper venue for socializing."

A young woman wearing a pair of jeans, hanging so low they looked ready to succumb to gravity, smirked. "We're waiting for Lord Covington's talk on the Amazon, Miss Winter."

This was a first. She'd never seen this particular group of girls at the library's lectures before. "Very well. The talk starts in five minutes. Keep it down until then."

The students all said in unison, "Yes, Miss Winter."

Were they mocking her? Maybe it was the camisole. Anna spun around and climbed the stairs to the lecture hall. She spotted Nicole in the front row, saving her a seat.

Nicole eyed her as she sat down. "Nice suit. Are you going to keep that jacket buttoned all night?"

"Maybe." She didn't want to admit it to Nicole, but it was just easier to embrace her image, what she strived to be all her life–the untouchable Miss Winter, above reproach, above scandal. Nobody's pincushion.

The side door swung open, and Dr. Crespi, the chairman of the social sciences department walked in, followed by a tall man in a navy blue suit.

Anna's heart skittered in her chest. Her head felt like a balloon ready to pop. The tall man with the long, stylishly cut, dark hair smiled, his eyes raking the audience. As Dr. Crespi introduced the Earl of Covington, the Earl's blue eyes flicked across the front row.

Oh God. King Coop didn't even recognize her.

Dr. Crespi droned on about how Lord Covington, Cooper Daventry, the ninth Earl of Covington, spent the last year living among a native tribe in the Amazon.

The familiar fire raced from Anna's cheeks down to her toes, with a few detours along the way. The man who taught her how to embrace her sensuality, taught her how to relinquish control, taught her how to revel in her femininity, the man who claimed her as his own now stood in front of her wearing a Savile Row suit and an expensive haircut, and he didn't even know her.

Nicole leaned over and whispered, "This guy is hot. Not your typical academic dweeb."

All the women in the packed audience sat at attention in their seats. They laughed at his witticisms. Ooohed and ahhed over his pronouncements. Asked insipid questions.

Lord Covington smiled, nodded, and joked. He lightly teased the girl in the low-cut jeans. He bantered with another. He completely ignored Anna in her dark green suit, sitting in the front row.

The liquid fire of desire and longing morphed into a burning ball of rage in Anna's gut. He belonged to her. Or rather, she belonged to him. A drop of sweat ran down the side of her face, and she fanned herself with the program.

She tried to focus on his words. Was he fessing up to the lie he perpetrated on that Amazon tribe? He talked of living among the tribes of the Amazon but no mention of King Coop or setting himself up as some god-king to fool the people. No mention of perpetrating more lies on unsuspecting tourists to get them to submit to humiliating, completely unnecessary, practices.

He started his slide show, and pictures of the people in the tribe she knew so well flashed on the screen. He pointed out the shaman and his practice of keeping multiple wives. A picture of the fire circle appeared, and Covington explained how the women served the men and washed them after the meal before they could eat. How they greeted the men they served by touching their foreheads to the ground in front of them and dusting off their feet.

One woman in the audience stood up. "Lord Covington, how did you feel about living among a people who treat women as second class citizens? Didn't it disturb you?"

Anna held her breath.

He answered, "Please, call me Coop. Yes, it did disturb me, but one thing you must learn as a cultural anthropologist is that you're there to study and observe a different culture. It's not your place to apply your cultural standards to them."

Anna snorted, and Nicole glanced at her with raised brows. If Coop heard, he ignored her.

An attractive brunette stood up. "Did you have women serving you as well? Is it a case of when in Rome, or do you try to hold onto your own cultural values?"

Coop held up his hands. "I simply observed."

Anna choked, and Nicole whispered, "Anna, what's wrong with you?"

Anna's suit jacket felt like a straightjacket. She undid the top button, and rubbed the back of her neck. Coop laughed at another question. Anna hit the breaking point. She jumped from her chair and shouted out, "Do you mean to tell us that you offended your hosts by hanging onto your own cultural practices, rejecting their hospitality?"

Finally, he turned to her, his gaze tracking from the top of her head to the tip of her brown boots. His eyes gleamed in the old way that signaled danger. Danger for her.

Did he recognize her now?

He lifted one shoulder, and the exquisitely tailored suit did nothing to hide the power and muscle of that shoulder. "You got me there, Miss, err… Miss. "One woman did insist on serving me."

The room of mostly women gave a collective sigh.

Anna set her jaw. "She insisted?"

He shook his head. "It's as you said, Miss, err… Miss. I didn't wish to offend."

Her eyes narrowing, Anna said through clenched teeth, "You would have offended this woman had you refused her… ministrations?"

His blue eyes burned into hers. "Absolutely. You see, she had an innate desire to please me. To serve me. It was in her nature."

Oh God. He knew her. Anna sat down, crossed her legs and squeezed. His power over her was not limited to the jungles of the Amazon. Miss Anna Winter, virgin librarian, sat here in her own library, her own domain, her own seat of power… quivering in her wet panties.

A serious-minded woman in the back asked, "Do you really believe that, Lord Covington? Don't you think that particular woman, and the others, served the men because to assert their independence would result in punishment?"

Coop dragged his gaze away from Anna. "Definitely some of the women, including my own, tried to exert their independence more than others with covert acts of defiance, but the instances were few and far between, and they were dealt with summarily."

Nicole's hand shot up. "How were they dealt with? How did you deal with your disobedient woman?"

Strolling back to the podium, Coop said over his shoulder, "Oh, I'm not sure we need to go into that."

The entire room erupted in protest, and Dr. Crespi said, "Lord Covington, we're a free-thinking American university with a thirst for knowledge. There's no need to sugarcoat."

Coop spun around, his blue eyes sweeping the room. "I'm so glad to hear that, Dr. Crespi. In fact, a little demonstration would do much to highlight my points."

Arms waved all over the room, including Nicole's, and Coop tapped his chin. "Not a student, I think."

The women groaned, and Coop sauntered across the room and stood in front of Anna. "Perhaps?"

Dr. Crespi bustled forward. "Perfect. This is Anna Winter, our head librarian here at the University Research Library. A worthy subject, I believe."

Heat burned in Anna's cheeks but she rose as if in a trance. How many times had she dreamed of this over the past few months?

Coop inspected her with a frown, and then reached behind the podium to grab a large bag. He withdrew two pieces of clothing and held them up. Everyone in the room gasped, and Anna swayed. Those belonged to her.

Coop waved the skimpy top and loincloth in the air. "This is what the women of the tribe wore. We won't ask Miss Winter to change into them, a little small I think."

The audience laughed, and Anna scowled at Coop. Cheap shot.

He dropped the clothing. "You should leave your jacket at your seat, however, Miss Winter."

Anna unfastened the remainder of her buttons and hung her jacket on the back of her chair and returned to stand before Coop.

"Now, Miss Winter, may I call you Anna and you can call me Coop?"

Someone piped up from the back. "Would your slave girl really call you by your first name?"

"No, never. For our exercise, you may call me King Coop, Anna."

The heat washed into her face again. What kind of game was he playing? How far would she go?

He folded his arms and looked down at her. She could almost imagine him wearing his loincloth again, his hard muscles gleaming in the firelight. "Down on your knees, Anna."

Anna knelt before him, as nervous giggles scattered behind her.

Coop said, "Remember I told you about the common way women greeted the men they served?" His voice, very soft now, caressed the back of her neck. "Anna, do you remember?"

His voice took her back, kneeling in the dirt before King Coop, her body naked under her flimsy clothing, the sound of the drums reverberating in her chest, the smell of the moist earth all around her.

"Yes, King Coop." She bowed, dipping her forehead, and touching it to the floor before her master.

Coop breathed out, "Perfect form."

One of the students asked, "How long would she stay like that?"

"Until I told her she could move." To prove his point, he walked away from Anna, leaving her bowed over on the floor. More questions followed, but Anna stayed in her subservient position. She couldn't move now even if she wanted to. The old desire washed through her, weakening her knees, stealing her breath.

Coop sauntered back in front of Anna and said, "I believe my feet are dirty, Anna."

Some of the students gasped as Anna reached forward and wiped his expensive loafers with the edge of her camisole.

"I think Anna would make a very good slave girl in the wilds of the Amazon, don't you?"

The audience laughed and applauded. Nicole hissed behind her, "Anna, Anna."

But Miss Winter, the virgin librarian, had dissolved into the Amazon jungle. She belonged to King Coop and would do whatever he commanded.

A male student asked, "What about the punishment?"

Coop heaved a sigh. "I knew we'd have to get to that. Not that we could ever envision Anna doing something she shouldn't, since I'm sure she always follows the rules, but let's just imagine for a moment that Anna shirked her duties."

Dr. Crespi coughed. "You're not going to hurt Miss Winter?"

Coop touched the top of her head. "I'd never hurt my slave."

Coop returned to the bag, and whatever he drew out, made the audience gasp. Anna kept her eyes trained on the floor. The chair in front of the room squeaked as Coop sat down. He snapped his fingers. "Come here, Anna, and take your punishment."

Through the silence of the room, Anna crawled to Coop. He patted his lap, and she draped herself over his knees. She could now see he held a wooden paddle in his hand, almost identical to the one he used at the village.

"Ah, I can see by your faces, you know what's coming, and you're correct. Disobedient women receive a public paddling. Naturally, I won't paddle Anna, unless...?"

The blood roared in her ears, all her nerve endings alive with a thudding need. Squeezing her eyes shut, she nodded her head and said, "Yes, King Coop."

"You're right, Dr. Crespi. Anna is a perfect subject, absolutely gets into the spirit, such a thirst for knowledge. Of course, I won't hurt Anna. The lightest of taps, just to show you how it's done. Oh, and the subject always had to pay homage to the instrument of her punishment."

Coop's voice rendered her powerless. Powerless in the face of her own sexual desires. He held the paddle in front of her face, and before Dr. Crespi, before Nicole, and before a roomful of students and faculty, Anna kissed the paddle.

Everyone in the room let out a breath before Coop brought the paddle down on her derriere. True to his word, she felt the merest of taps. "That's how it's done. It would sting a little more than that because the subject always had a bare bottom. Of course, I won't paddle Anna's bare bottom, unless..."

Anna craved his touch, craved his dominance over her. She wanted to submit to him before this room full of people, to claim him as her own. The pressure between her legs threatened to explode. She squirmed against his muscled thighs. She nodded and said, "Yes, King Coop. Please, King Coop."

The room sucked in its breath, as Coop reached beneath her and unfastened her trousers. He unzipped them and yanked them down along with her panties.

Miss Anna Winter, virgin librarian, dangled over King Coop's knee, pressed slacks around her ankles, and derriere propped over his lap. He brought the paddle back around to her face. She kissed it once again, and King Coop smacked her bare bottom.

Epilogue

Anna caught the blue and gold dragonfly on her fingertip. Its gossamer wings tickled her cheek before it flew away. The entire rainforest welcomed her back.

After the uproar she and Coop created at his lecture, she resigned before she could be fired. She'd been wearing a smile, and little else, ever since.

A pair of strong arms wrapped around her waist, and she turned to face her captor. Coop covered her face with light kisses before settling on her mouth, exploring its depths with his tongue.

She placed her hands against his smooth, broad chest and disentangled her mouth. "Are you going to eat breakfast before you indulge in dessert?"

He cupped her breasts, on display in a flowered bikini top, in his hands and buried his face in her cleavage. He said in a muffled voice, "A man doesn't need breakfast on his honeymoon."

Her fingers raked through his hair. "I'll serve it to you in bed. Then I'll shave you and wash you."

"And the blowjob?" He quirked a dark eyebrow at her.

She groped the fast growing bulge beneath his cargo shorts. "And the blowjob."

"I have to warn you. I've had the best, right here in this very jungle."

"I'll try my hardest."

"First I want you to feel my hardest." He dropped his shorts on the deck of the boat, and his erection lanced forward, fully at attention.

She kneeled before him and took him in her mouth, but her husband demanded more.

Lowering himself next to her, he said, "Now it's time for me to serve you, my queen."

He served her again and again on the deck of the boat in full view of the Amazon, but Anna Winter was no librarian.

And she was no virgin.

About the Author:

Mia Varano has hordes of virile men and strong but luscious women in her head, all clamoring to escape and realize their destinies. It makes for some interesting headaches until she sets them free to fulfill their fantasies and those of her readers. In addition to highly sensual, and somewhat kinky, erotic romance, Mia writes nail-biting romantic suspense as Carol Ericson. If you just can't get enough, please visit Mia's website at www.carolericson.com *"where romance flirts with danger."*

Secrets, Volume 1

Listen to what reviewers say:

"These stories take you beyond romance into the realm of erotica. I found ***Secrets*** absolutely delicious."

—Virginia Henley,
New York Times Best Selling Author

"***Secrets*** is a collection of novellas for the daring, adventurous woman who's not afraid to give her fantasies free reign."

—Kathe Robin, *Romantic Times* Magazine

"...In fact, the men featured in all the stories are terrific, they all want to please and pleasure their women. If you like erotic romance you will love ***Secrets***."

—*Romantic Readers* Review

In ***Secrets, Volume 1*** you'll find:

A Lady's Quest by Bonnie Hamre

Widowed Lady Antonia Blair-Sutworth searches for a lover to save her from the handsome Duke of Sutherland. The "auditions" may be shocking but utterly tantalizing.

The Spinner's Dream by Alice Gaines

A seductive fantasy that leaves every woman wishing for her own private love slave, desperate and running for his life.

The Proposal by Ivy Landon

This tale is a walk on the wild side of love. *The Proposal* will taunt you, tease you, and shock you. A contemporary erotica for the adventurous woman.

The Gift by Jeanie LeGendre

Immerse yourself in this historic tale of exotic seduction, bondage and a concubine's surrender to the Sultan's desire. Can Alessandra live the life and give the gift the Sultan demands of her?

Secrets, Volume 2

Listen to what reviewers say:

"***Secrets*** offers four novellas of sensual delight; each beautifully written with intense feeling and dedication to character development. For those seeking stories with heightened intimacy, look no further."

—Kathee Card, *Romancing the Web*

"Such a welcome diversity in styles and genres. Rich characterization in sensual tales. An exciting read that's sure to titillate the senses."

—Cheryl Ann Porter

"***Secrets 2*** left me breathless. Sensual satisfaction guaranteed… times four!"

—Virginia Henley, *New York Times* Best Selling Author

In ***Secrets, Volume 2*** you'll find:

Surrogate Lover by Doreen DeSalvo
Adrian Ross is a surrogate sex therapist who has all the answers and control. He thought he'd seen and done it all, but he'd never met Sarah.

Snowbound by Bonnie Hamre
A delicious, sensuous regency tale. The marriage-shy Earl of Howden is teased and tortured by his own desires and finds there is a woman who can equal his overpowering sensuality.

Roarke's Prisoner by Angela Knight
Elise, a starship captain, remembers the eager animal submission she'd known before at her captor's hands and refuses to become his toy again. However, she has no idea of the delights he's planned for her this time.

Savage Garden by Susan Paul
Raine's been captured by a mysterious and dangerous revolutionary leader in Mexico. At first her only concern is survival, but she quickly finds lush erotic nights in her captor's arms.

Winner of the Fallot Literary Award for Fiction!

Secrets, Volume 3

Listen to what reviewers say:

"***Secrets, Volume 3***, leaves the reader breathless. A delicious confection of sensuous treats awaits the reader on each turn of the page!"

—Kathee Card, *Romancing the Web*

"From the FBI to Police Detective to Vampires to a Medieval Warlord home from the Crusade—***Secrets 3*** is simply the best!"

—Susan Paul, award winning author

"An unabashed celebration of sex. Highly arousing! Highly recommended!"

—Virginia Henley, *New York Times* Best Selling Author

In ***Secrets, Volume 3*** you'll find:

The Spy Who Loved Me by Jeanie Cesarini

Undercover FBI agent Paige Ellison's sexual appetites rise to new levels when she works with leading man Christopher Sharp, the cunning agent who uses all his training to capture her body and heart.

The Barbarian by Ann Jacobs

Lady Brianna vows not to surrender to the barbaric Giles, Earl of Harrow. He must use sexual arts learned in the infidels' harem to conquer his bride. A word of caution—this is not for the faint of heart.

Blood and Kisses by Angela Knight

A vampire assassin is after Beryl St. Cloud. Her only hope lies with Decker, another vampire and ex-mercenary. Broke, she offers herself as payment for his services. Will his seductive powers take her very soul?

Love Undercover by B.J. McCall

Amanda Forbes is the bait in a strip joint sting operation. While she performs, fellow detective "Cowboy" Cooper gets to watch. Though he excites her, she must fight the temptation to surrender to the passion.

Winner of the 1997 Under the Covers Readers Favorite Award

Secrets, Volume 4

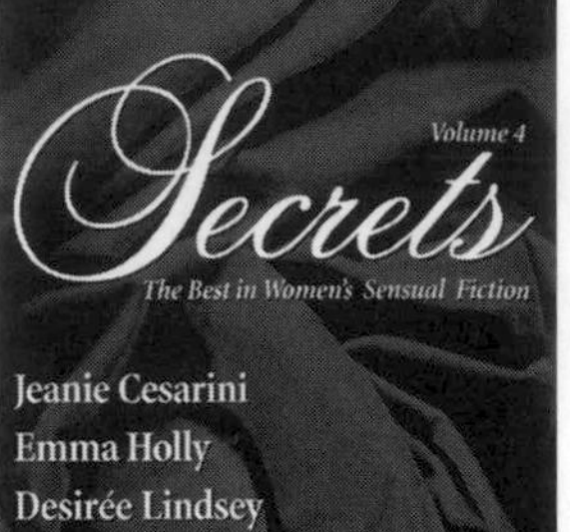

Listen to what reviewers say:

"Provocative… seductive… a must read!"

—*Romantic Times* Magazine

"These are the kind of stories that romance readers that 'want a little more' have been looking for all their lives…."

—*Affaire de Coeur* Magazine

"***Secrets, Volume 4***, has something to satisfy every erotic fantasy… simply sexational!"

—Virginia Henley, *New York Times* Best Selling Author

In ***Secrets, Volume 4*** you'll find:

An Act of Love by Jeanie Cesarini

Shelby Moran's past left her terrified of sex. International film star Jason Gage must gently coach the young starlet in the ways of love. He wants more than an act—he wants Shelby to feel true passion in his arms.

Enslaved by Desirée Lindsey

Lord Nicholas Summer's air of danger, dark passions, and irresistible charm have brought Lady Crystal's long-hidden desires to the surface. Will he be able to give her the one thing she desires before it's too late?

The Bodyguard by Betsy Morgan and Susan Paul

Kaki York is a bodyguard, but watching the wild, erotic romps of her client's sexual conquests on the security cameras is getting to her—and her partner, the ruggedly handsome James Kulick. Can she resist his insistent desire to have her?

The Love Slave by Emma Holly

A woman's ultimate fantasy. For one year, Princess Lily will be attended to by three delicious men of her choice. While she delights in playing with the first two, it's the reluctant Grae, with his powerful chest, black eyes and hair, that stirs her desires.

Secrets, Volume 5

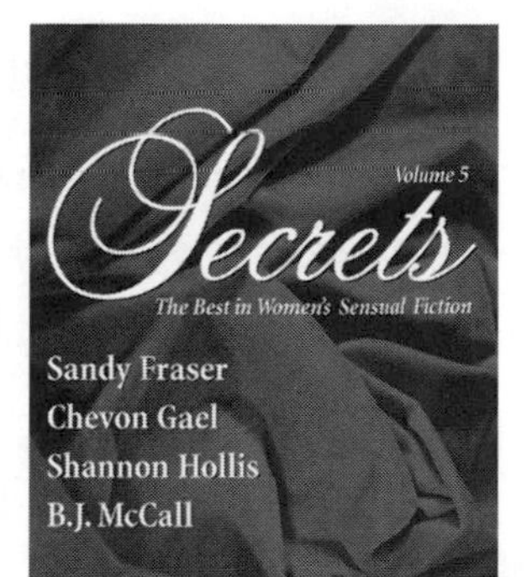

Listen to what reviewers say:

"Hot, hot, hot! Not for the faint-hearted!"

—*Romantic Times* Magazine

"As you make your way through the stories, you will find yourself becoming hotter and hotter. ***Secrets*** just keeps getting better and better."

—*Affaire de Coeur* Magazine

"***Secrets 5*** is a collage of luscious sensuality. Any woman who reads ***Secrets*** is in for an awakening!"

—Virginia Henley, *New York Times* Best Selling Author

In *Secrets, Volume 5* you'll find:

Beneath Two Moons by Sandy Fraser

Ready for a very wild romp? Step into the future and find Conor, rough and masculine like frontiermen of old, on the prowl for a new conquest. In his sights, Dr. Eva Kelsey. She got away once before, but this time Conor makes sure she begs for more.

Insatiable by Chevon Gael

Marcus Remington photographs beautiful models for a living, but it's Ashlyn Fraser, a young corporate exec having some glamour shots done, who has stolen his heart. It's up to Marcus to help her discover her inner sexual self.

Strictly Business by Shannon Hollis

Elizabeth Forrester knows it's tough enough for a woman to make it to the top in the corporate world. Garrett Hill, the most beautiful man in Silicon Valley, has to come along to stir up her wildest fantasies. Dare she give in to both their desires?

Alias Smith and Jones by B.J. McCall

Meredith Collins finds herself stranded overnight at the airport. A handsome stranger by the name of Smith offers her sanctuary for the evening and she finds those mesmerizing, green-flecked eyes hard to resist. Are they to be just two ships passing in the night?

Secrets, Volume 6

Listen to what reviewers say:

"Red Sage was the first and remains the leader of Women's Erotic Romance Fiction Collections!"

—*Romantic Times* Magazine

"***Secrets*, *Volume 6***, is the best of ***Secrets*** yet. ...four of the most erotic stories in one volume than this reader has yet to see anywhere else. ...These stories are full of erotica at its best and you'll definitely want to keep it handy for lots of re-reading!"

—*Affaire de Coeur* Magazine

"***Secrets 6*** satisfies every female fantasy: the Bodyguard, the Tutor, the Werewolf, and the Vampire. I give it Six Stars!"

—Virginia Henley, *New York Times* Best Selling Author

In ***Secrets, Volume 6*** you'll find:

Flint's Fuse by Sandy Fraser

Dana Madison's father has her "kidnapped" for her own safety. Flint, the tall, dark and dangerous mercenary, is hired for the job. But just which one is the prisoner—Dana will try *anything* to get away.

Love's Prisoner by MaryJanice Davidson

Trapped in an elevator, Jeannie Lawrence experienced unwilling rapture at Michael Windham's hands. She never expected the devilishly handsome man to show back up in her life—or turn out to be a werewolf!

The Education of Miss Felicity Wells by Alice Gaines

Felicity Wells wants to be sure she'll satisfy her soon-to-be husband but she needs a teacher. Dr. Marcus Slade, an experienced lover, agrees to take her on as a student, but can he stop short of taking her completely?

A Candidate for the Kiss by Angela Knight

Working on a story, reporter Dana Ivory stumbles onto a more amazing one—a sexy, secret agent who happens to be a vampire. She wants her story but Gabriel Archer wants more from her than just sex and blood.

Secrets, Volume 7

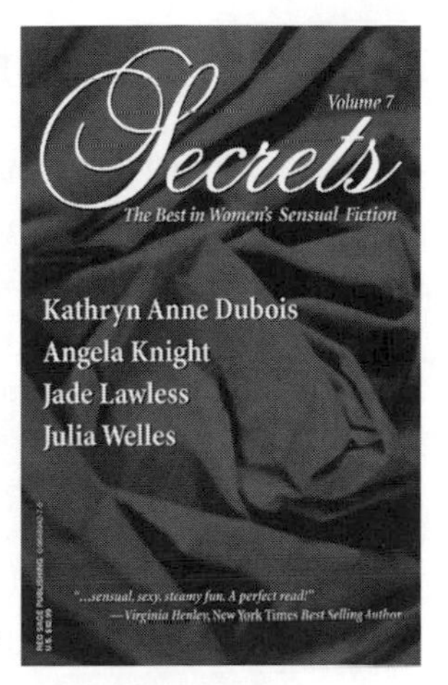

Listen to what reviewers say:

"Get out your asbestos gloves—***Secrets Volume 7*** is... extremely hot, true erotic romance... passionate and titillating. There's nothing quite like baring your secrets!"

—*Romantic Times* Magazine

"...sensual, sexy, steamy fun. A perfect read!"

—Virginia Henley,
New York Times Best Selling Author

"Intensely provocative and disarmingly romantic, ***Secrets, Volume 7,*** is a romance reader's paradise that will take you beyond your wildest dreams!"

—Ballston Book House Review

In ***Secrets, Volume 7*** you'll find:

Amelia's Innocence by Julia Welles

Amelia didn't know her father bet her in a card game with Captain Quentin Hawke, so honor demands a compromise—three days of erotic foreplay, leaving her virginity and future intact.

The Woman of His Dreams by Jade Lawless

From the day artist Gray Avonaco moves in next door, Joanna Morgan is plagued by provocative dreams. But what she believes is unrequited lust, Gray sees as another chance to be with the woman he loves. He must persuade her that even death can't stop true love.

Surrender by Kathryn Anne Dubois

Free-spirited Lady Johanna wants no part of the binding strictures society imposes with her marriage to the powerful Duke. She doesn't know the dark Duke wants sensual adventure, and sexual satisfaction.

Kissing the Hunter by Angela Knight

Navy Seal Logan McLean hunts the vampires who murdered his wife. Virginia Hart is a sexy vampire searching for her lost soul-mate only to find him in a man determined to kill her. She must convince him all vampires aren't created equally.

Winner of the Venus Book Club Best Book of the Year

Secrets, Volume 8

Listen to what reviewers say:

"***Secrets**, **Volume 8***, is an amazing compilation of sexy stories covering a wide range of subjects, all designed to titillate the senses. …you'll find something for everybody in this latest version of ***Secrets***."

—*Affaire de Coeur* Magazine

"***Secrets Volume 8***, is simply sensational!"

—Virginia Henley, *New York Times* Best Selling Author

"These delectable stories will have you turning the pages long into the night. Passionate, provocative and perfect for setting the mood…."

—*Escape to Romance* Reviews

In ***Secrets, Volume 8*** you'll find:

Taming Kate by Jeanie Cesarini

Kathryn Roman inherits a legal brothel. Little does this city girl know the town of Love, Nevada wants her to be their new madam so they've charged Trey Holliday, one very dominant cowboy, with taming her.

Jared's Wolf by MaryJanice Davidson

Jared Rocke will do anything to avenge his sister's death, but ends up attracted to Moira Wolfbauer, the she-wolf sworn to protect her pack. Joining forces to stop a killer, they learn love defies all boundaries.

My Champion, My Lover by Alice Gaines

Celeste Broder is a woman committed for having a sexy appetite. Mayor Robert Albright may be her champion—if she can convince him her freedom will mean a chance to indulge their appetites together.

Kiss or Kill by Liz Maverick

In this post-apocalyptic world, Camille Kazinsky's military career rides on her ability to make a choice—whether the robo called Meat should live or die. Meat's future depends on proving he's human enough to live, man enough… to makes her feel like a woman.

Winner of the Venus Book Club Best Book of the Year

Secrets, Volume 9

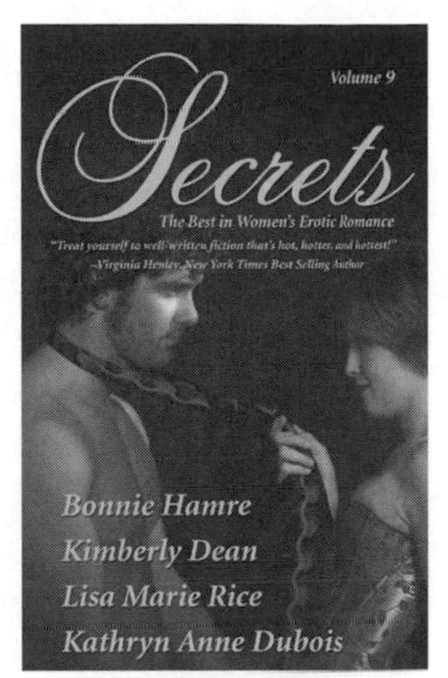

Listen to what reviewers say:

"Everyone should expect only the most erotic stories in a ***Secrets*** book. ...if you like your stories full of hot sexual scenes, then this is for you!"

—Donna Doyle Romance Reviews

"***SECRETS 9***... is sinfully delicious, highly arousing, and hotter than hot as the pages practically burn up as you turn them."

—Suzanne Coleburn, Reader To Reader Reviews/Belles & Beaux of Romance

"Treat yourself to well-written fiction that's hot, hotter, and hottest!"

—Virginia Henley, *New York Times* Best Selling Author

In ***Secrets, Volume 9*** you'll find:

Wild For You by Kathryn Anne Dubois

When college intern, Georgie, gets captured by a Congo wildman, she discovers this specimen of male virility has never seen a woman. The research possibilities are endless!

Wanted by Kimberly Dean

FBI Special Agent Jeff Reno wants Danielle Carver. There's her body, brains—and that charge of treason on her head. Dani goes on the run, but the sexy Fed is hot on her trail.

Secluded by Lisa Marie Rice

Nicholas Lee's wealth and power came with a price—his enemies will kill anyone he loves. When Isabelle steals his heart, Nicholas secludes her in his palace for a lifetime of desire in only a few days.

Flights of Fantasy by Bonnie Hamre

Chloe taught others to see the realities of life but she's never shared the intimate world of her sensual yearnings. Given the chance, will she be woman enough to fulfill her most secret erotic fantasy?

Secrets, Volume 10

Listen to what reviewers say:

"***Secrets Volume 10***, an erotic dance through medieval castles, sultan's palaces, the English countryside and expensive hotel suites, explodes with passion-filled pages."

—*Romantic Times BOOKclub*

"Having read the previous nine volumes, this one fulfills the expectations of what is expected in a ***Secrets*** book: romance and eroticism at its best!!"

—*Fallen Angel Reviews*

"All are hot steamy romances so if you enjoy erotica romance, you are sure to enjoy ***Secrets, Volume 10***. All this reviewer can say is WOW!!"

—*The Best Reviews*

In ***Secrets, Volume 10*** you'll find:

Private Eyes by Dominique Sinclair

When a mystery man captivates P.I. Nicolla Black during a stakeout, she discovers her no-seduction rule bending under the pressure of long denied passion. She agrees to the seduction, but he demands her total surrender.

The Ruination of Lady Jane by Bonnie Hamre

To avoid her upcoming marriage, Lady Jane Ponsonby-Maitland flees into the arms of Havyn Attercliffe. She begs him to ruin her rather than turn her over to her odious fiancé.

Code Name: Kiss by Jeanie Cesarini

Agent Lily Justiss is on a mission to defend her country against terrorists that requires giving up her virginity as a sex slave. As her master takes her body, desire for her commanding officer Seth Blackthorn fuels her mind.

The Sacrifice by Kathryn Anne Dubois

Lady Anastasia Bedovier is days from taking her vows as a Nun. Before she denies her sensuality forever, she wants to experience pleasure. Count Maxwell is the perfect man to initiate her into erotic delight.

Secrets, Volume 11

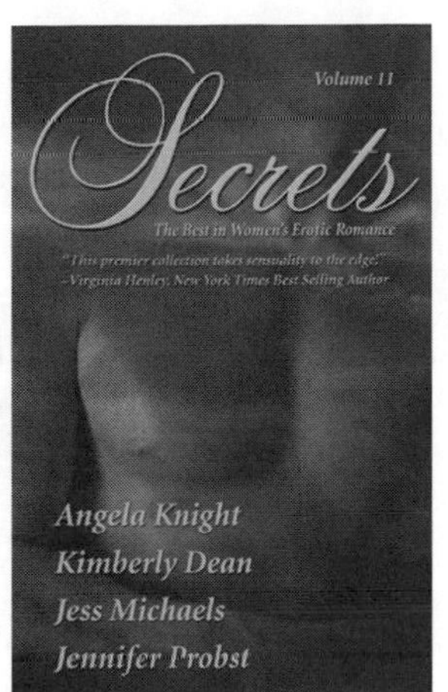

Listen to what reviewers say:

"***Secrets Volume 11*** delivers once again with storylines that include erotic masquerades, ancient curses, modern-day betrayal and a prince charming looking for a kiss." **4 Stars**

—*Romantic Times BOOKclub*

"Indulge yourself with this erotic treat and join the thousands of readers who just can't get enough. Be forewarned that ***Secrets 11*** will whet your appetite for more, but will offer you the ultimate in pleasurable erotic literature."

—*Ballston Book House Review*

"***Secrets 11*** quite honestly is my favorite anthology from Red Sage so far."

—*The Best Reviews*

In ***Secrets, Volume 11*** you'll find:

Masquerade by Jennifer Probst

Hailey Ashton is determined to free herself from her sexual restrictions. Four nights of erotic pleasures without revealing her identity. A chance to explore her secret desires without the fear of unmasking.

Ancient Pleasures by Jess Michaels

Isabella Winslow is obsessed with finding out what caused her late husband's death, but trapped in an Egyptian concubine's tomb with a sexy American raider, succumbing to the mummy's sensual curse takes over.

Manhunt by Kimberly Dean

Framed for murder, Michael Tucker takes Taryn Swanson hostage—the one woman who can clear him. Despite the evidence against him, the attraction between them is strong. Tucker resorts to unconventional, yet effective methods of persuasion to change the sexy ADA's mind.

Wake Me by Angela Knight

Chloe Hart received a sexy painting of a sleeping knight. Radolf of Varik has been trapped for centuries in the painting since, cursed by a witch. His only hope is to visit the dreams of women and make one of them fall in love with him so she can free him with a kiss.

Secrets, Volume 12

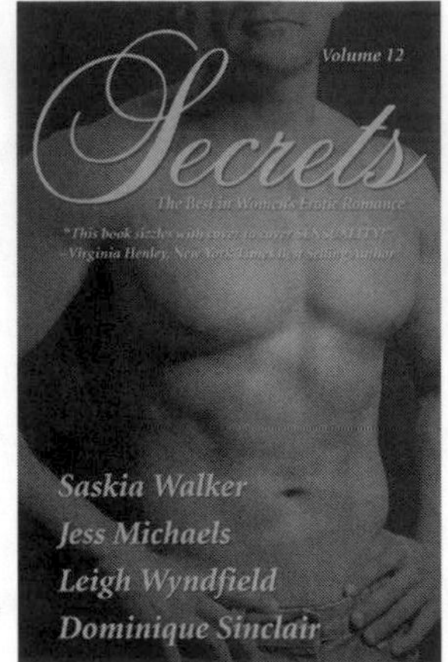

Listen to what reviewers say:

"***Secrets Volume 12***, turns on the heat with a seductive encounter inside a bookstore, a temple of naughty and sensual delight, a galactic inferno that thaws ice, and a lightening storm that lights up the English shoreline. Tales of looking for love in all the right places with a heat rating out the charts." **4½ Stars**

—*Romantic Times BOOKclub*

"I really liked these stories. You want great escapism? Read ***Secrets, Volume 12***."

—*Romance Reviews*

In ***Secrets, Volume 12*** you'll find:

Good Girl Gone Bad by Dominique Sinclair

Reagan's dreams are finally within reach. Setting out to do research for an article, nothing could have prepared her for Luke, or his offer to teach her everything she needs to know about sex. Licentious pleasures, forbidden desires… inspiring the best writing she's ever done.

Aphrodite's Passion by Jess Michaels

When Selena flees Victorian London before her evil stepchildren can institutionalize her for hysteria, Gavin is asked to bring her back home. But when he finds her living on the island of Cyprus, his need to have her begins to block out every other impulse.

White Heat by Leigh Wyndfield

Raine is hiding in an icehouse in the middle of nowhere from one of the scariest men in the universes. Walker escaped from a burning prison. Imagine their surprise when they find out they have the same man to blame for their miseries. Passion, revenge and love are in their future.

Summer Lightning by Saskia Walker

Sculptress Sally is enjoying an idyllic getaway on a secluded cove when she spots a gorgeous man walking naked on the beach. When Julian finds an attractive woman shacked up in his cove, he has to check her out. But what will he do when he finds she's secretly been using him as a model?

Secrets, Volume 13

Listen to what reviewers say:

"In ***Secrets Volume 13***, the temperature gets turned up a few notches with a mistaken personal ad, shape-shifters destined to love, a hot Regency lord and his lady, as well as a bodyguard protecting his woman. Emotions and flames blaze high in Red Sage's latest foray into the sensual and delightful art of love." **4½ Stars**

—*Romantic Times BOOKclub*

"The sex is still so hot the pages nearly ignite! Read ***Secrets, Volume 13***!"

—*Romance Reviews*

In ***Secrets, Volume 13*** you'll find:

Out of Control by Rachelle Chase

Astrid's world revolves around her business and she's hoping to pick up wealthy Erik Santos as a client. Only he's hoping to pick up something entirely different. Will she give in to the seductive pull of his proposition?

Hawkmoor by Amber Green

Shape-shifters answer to Darien as he acts in the name of the long-missing Lady Hawkmoor, their hereditary ruler. When she unexpectedly surfaces, Darien must deal with a scrappy individual whose wary eyes hold the other half of his soul, but who has the power to destroy his world.

Lessons in Pleasure by Charlotte Featherstone

A wicked bargain has Lily vowing never to yield to the demands of the rake she once loved and lost. Unfortunately, Damian, the Earl of St. Croix, or Saint as he is infamously known, will not take 'no' for an answer.

In the Heat of the Night by Calista Fox

Haunted by a century-old curse, Molina fears she won't live to see her thirtieth birthday. Nick, her former bodyguard, is hired back into service to protect her from the fatal accidents that plague her family. But *In the Heat of the Night*, will his passion and love for her be enough to convince Molina they have a future together?

Secrets, Volume 14

Listen to what reviewers say:

"*Secrets Volume 14* will excite readers with its diverse selection of delectable sexy tales ranging from a fourteenth century love story to a sci-fi rebel who falls for a irresistible research scientist to a trio of determined vampires who battle for the same woman to a virgin sacrifice who falls in love with a beast. A cornucopia of pure delight!"
4½ Stars

—*Romantic Times BOOKclub*

"This book contains four erotic tales sure to keep readers up long into the night."

—*Romance Junkies*

In ***Secrets, Volume 14*** you'll find:

Soul Kisses by Angela Knight

Beth's been kidnapped by Joaquin Ramirez, a sadistic vampire. Handsome vampire cousins, Morgan and Garret Axton, come to her rescue. Can she find happiness with two vampires?

Temptation in Time by Alexa Aames

Ariana escaped the Middle Ages after stealing a kiss of magic from sexy sorcerer, Marcus de Grey. When he brings her back, they begin a battle of wills and a sexual odyssey that could spell disaster for them both.

Ailis and the Beast by Jennifer Barlowe

When Ailis agreed to be her village's sacrifice to the mysterious Beast she was prepared to sacrifice her virtue, and possibly her life. But some things aren't what they seem. Ailis and the Beast are about to discover the greatest sacrifice may be the human heart.

Night Heat by Leigh Wynfield

When Rip Bowhite leads a revolt on the prison planet, he ends up struggling to survive against monsters that rule the night. Jemma, the prison's Healer, won't allow herself to be distracted by the instant attraction she feels for Rip. As the stakes are raised and death draws near, love seems doomed in the heat of the night.

Secrets, Volume 15

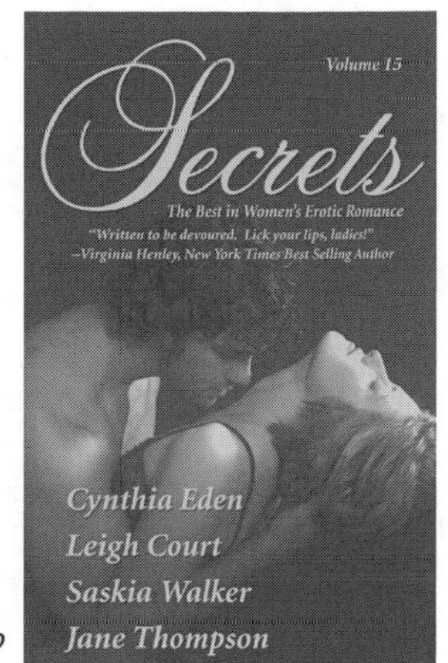

Listen to what reviewers say:

"***Secrets Volume 15*** blends humor, tension and steamy romance in its newest collection that sizzles with passion between unlikely pairs—a male chauvinist columnist and a librarian turned erotica author; a handsome werewolf and his resisting mate; an unfulfilled woman and a sexy police officer and a Victorian wife who learns discipline can be fun. Readers will revel in this delicious assortment of thrilling tales." **4 Stars**

—*Romantic Times BOOKclub*

"This book contains four tales by some of today's hottest authors that will tease your senses and intrigue your mind."

—*Romance Junkies*

In ***Secrets, Volume 15*** you'll find:

Simon Says by Jane Thompson

Simon Campbell is a newspaper columnist who panders to male fantasies. Georgina Kennedy is a respectable librarian. On the surface, these two have nothing in common… but don't judge a book by its cover.

Bite of the Wolf by Cynthia Eden

Gareth Morlet, alpha werewolf, has finally found his mate. All he has to do is convince Trinity to join with him, to give in to the pleasure of a werewolf's mating, and then she will be his… forever.

Falling for Trouble by Saskia Walker

With 48 hours to clear her brother's name, Sonia Harmond finds help from irresistible bad boy, Oliver Eaglestone. When the erotic tension between them hits fever pitch, securing evidence to thwart an international arms dealer isn't the only danger they face.

The Disciplinarian by Leigh Court

Headstrong Clarissa Babcock is sent to the shadowy legend known as The Disciplinarian for instruction in proper wifely obedience. Jared Ashworth uses the tools of seduction to show her how to control a demanding husband, but her beauty, spirit, and uninhibited passion make Jared hunger to keep her—and their darkly erotic nights—all for himself!

Secrets, Volume 16

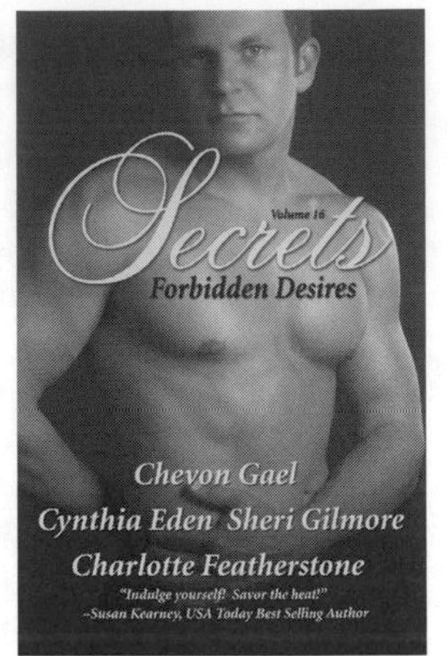

Listen to what reviewers say:

"Blackmail, games of chance, nude beaches and masquerades pave a path to heart-tugging emotions and fiery love scenes in Red Sage's latest collection." **4.5 Stars**

—*Romantic Times BOOKclub*

"Red Sage Publishing has brought to the readers an erotic profusion of highly skilled storytellers in their Secrets Vol. 16. … This is the best Secrets novel to date and this reviewer's favorite."

—*LoveRomances.com*

In *Secrets, Volume 16* you'll find:

Never Enough by Cynthia Eden

For the last three weeks, Abby McGill has been playing with fire. Bad-boy Jake has taught her the true meaning of desire, but she knows she has to end her relationship with him. But Jake isn't about to let the woman he wants walk away from him.

Bunko by Sheri Gilmoore

Tu Tran is forced to decide between Jack, a man, who promises to share every aspect of his life with her, or Dev, the man, who hides behind a mask and only offers night after night of erotic sex. Will she take the gamble of the dice and choose the man, who can see behind her own mask and expose her true desires?

Hide and Seek by Chevon Gael

Kyle DeLaurier ditches his trophy-fiance in favor of a tropical paradise full of tall, tanned, topless females. Private eye, Darcy McLeod, is on the trail of this runaway groom. Together they sizzle while playing Hide and Seek with their true identities.

Seduction of the Muse by Charlotte Featherstone

He's the Dark Lord, the mysterious author who pens the erotic tales of an innocent woman's seduction. She is his muse, the woman he watches from the dark shadows, the woman whose dreams he invades at night.

Secrets, Volume 17

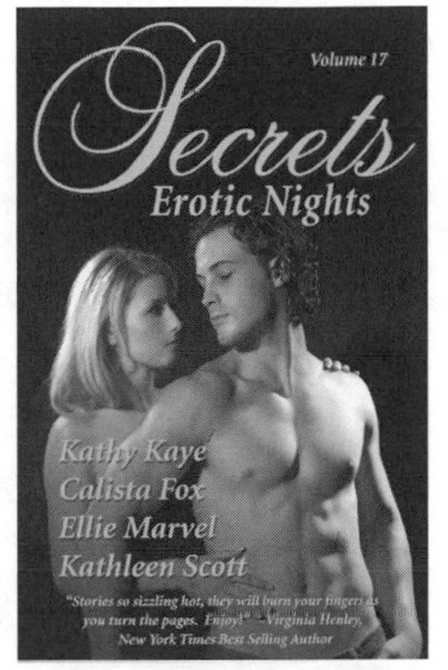

Listen to what reviewers say:

"Readers who have clamored for more ***Secrets*** will love the mix of alpha and beta males as well as kick-butt heroines who always get their men."
4 Stars

—Romantic Times BOOKclub

"Stories so sizzling hot, they will burn your fingers as you turn the pages. Enjoy!"

—Virginia Henley, *New York Times* Best Selling Author

"Red Sage is bringing us another thrilling anthology of passion and desire that will keep you up long into the night."

—Romance Junkies

In ***Secrets, Volume 17*** you'll find:

Rock Hard Candy by Kathy Kaye

Jessica Hennessy, the great, great granddaughter of a Voodoo priestess, decides she's waited long enough for the man of her dreams. A dose of her ancestor's aphrodisiac slipped into the gooey center of her homemade bon bons ought to do the trick.

Fatal Error by Kathleen Scott

Jesse Storm must make amends to humanity by destroying the computer program he helped design that has taken the government hostage. But he must also protect the woman he's loved in secret for nearly a decade.

Birthday by Ellie Marvel

Jasmine Templeton decides she's been celibate long enough. Will a wild night at a hot new club with her two best friends ease the ache inside her or just make it worse? Well, considering one of those best friends is Charlie and she's been having strange notions about their relationship of late… It's definitely a birthday neither she nor Charlie will ever forget.

Intimate Rendezvous by Calista Fox

A thief causes trouble at Cassandra Kensington's nightclub, Rendezvous, and sexy P.I. Dean Hewitt arrives on the scene to help. One look at the siren who owns the club has his blood boiling, despite the fact that his keen instincts have him questioning the legitimacy of her business.

Secrets, Volume 18

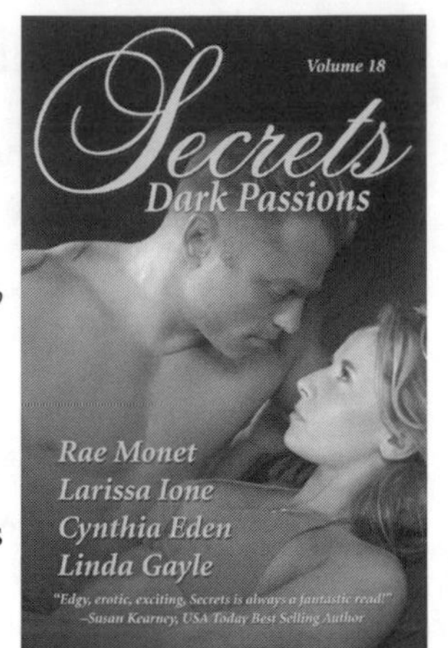

Listen to what reviewers say:

"Fantastic love scenes make this a book to be enjoyed more than once." **4.5 Stars**

—*Romantic Times BOOKclub*

"*Secrets Volume 18* continues [its] tradition of high quality sensual stories that both excite the senses while stimulating the mind."

—CK^{2}S Kwips and Kritiques

"Edgy, erotic, exciting, *Secrets* is always a fantastic read!"

—Susan Kearney, *USA Today* Best Selling Author

In *Secrets, Volume 18* you'll find:

Lone Wolf Three by Rae Monet

Planetary politics and squabbling over wolf occupied territory drain former rebel leader Taban Zias. But his anger quickly turns to desire when he meets, Lakota Blackson. Focused, calm and honorable, the female Wolf Warrior is Taban's perfect mate—now if he can just convince her.

Flesh to Fantasy by Larissa Ione

Kelsa Bradshaw is an intense loner whose job keeps her happily immersed in a fanciful world of virtual reality. Trent Jordan is a laid-back paramedic who experiences the harsh realities of life up close and personal. But when their worlds collide in an erotic eruption can Trent convince Kelsa to turn the fantasy into something real?

Heart Full of Stars by Linda Gayle

Singer Fanta Rae finds herself stranded on a lonely Mars outpost with the first human male she's seen in years. Ex-Marine Alex Decker lost his family and guilt drove him into isolation, but when alien assassins come to enslave Fanta, she and Decker come together to fight for their lives.

The Wolf's Mate by Cynthia Eden

When Michael Morlet finds Katherine "Kat" Hardy fighting for her life in a dark alley, he instantly recognizes her as the mate he's been seeking all of his life, but someone's trying to kill her. With danger stalking them at every turn, will Kat trust him enough to become The Wolf's Mate?

Secrets, Volume 19
Released July 2007

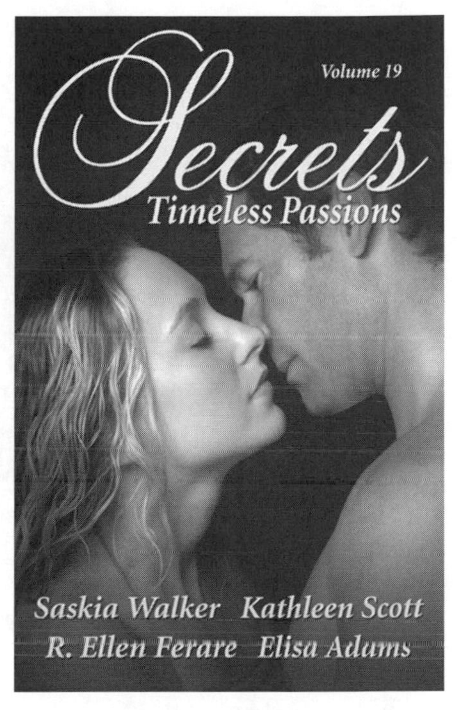

Volume 19
Secrets
Timeless Passions
Saskia Walker Kathleen Scott
R. Ellen Ferare Elisa Adams

Affliction
by Elisa Adams

Holly Aronson finally believes she's safe and whole in the orbit of sweet Andrew. But when Andrew's life long friend, Shane, arrives, events begin to spiral out of control again. Worse, she's inexplicably drawn to Shane. As she runs for her life, which one will protect her? And whom does she truly love?

Falling Stars
by Kathleen Scott

Daria is both a Primon fighter pilot and a Primon princess. As a deadly new enemy faces appears, she must choose between her duty to the fleet and the desperate need to forge an alliance through her marriage to the enemy's General Raven.

Toy in the Attic
by R. Ellen Ferare

When Gabrielle checks into the top floor of an old hotel, she discovers a life-sized statue of a nude man. Her unexpected roommate reveals himself to be a talented lover caught by a witch's curse. Can she help him break free of the spell that holds him, without losing her heart along the way?

What You Wish For
by Saskia Walker

Lucy Chambers is renovating her newly purchased historic house. As her dreams about a stranger become more intense, she wishes he were with her now. Two hundred years in the past, the man wishes for companionship and suddenly they find themselves together—in his time.

Secrets, Volume 20
Released July 2007

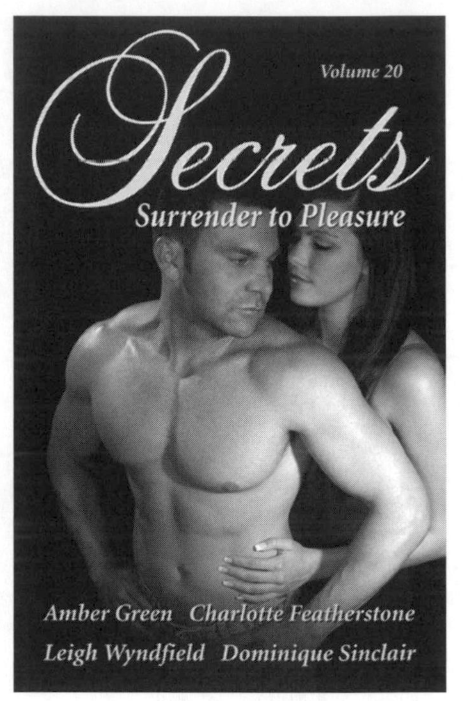

The Subject
by Amber Green

One week Tyler is a hot game designer, signing the deal of her life. The next, she's on the run for her life. Who can she trust? Certainly not sexy, mysterious Esau, who keeps showing up after the hoo-hah hits the fan!

Surrender
by Dominique Sinclair

Agent Madeline Carter is in too deep. She's slipped into Sebastian Maiocco's life to investigate his Sicilian mafia family. He unearths desires Madeline's unable to deny, conflicting the duty that honors her. Madeline must surrender to Sebastian or risk being exposed, leaving her target for a ruthless clan.

Stasis
by Leigh Wyndfield

Morgann Right has a problem. Her Commanding Officer has been drugged with Stasis, turning him into a living, breathing statue she's forced to take care of for ten long days. As her hands tend to him, she suddenly sees her CO in a totally different light. She wants him and, while she can tell he wants her, touching him intimately might come back to haunt them both.

A Woman's Pleasure
by Charlotte Featherstone

Widowed Isabella, Lady Langdon is tired of denying her needs and desires. Yearning to discover all the pleasures denied her in her marriage, she finds herself falling hard for the magnetic charms of the mysterious and exotic Julian Gresham—a man skilled in pleasures of the flesh. A man eight years her junior. A man more than eager to show her *A Woman's Pleasure.*

Secrets, Volume 21
Released December 2007

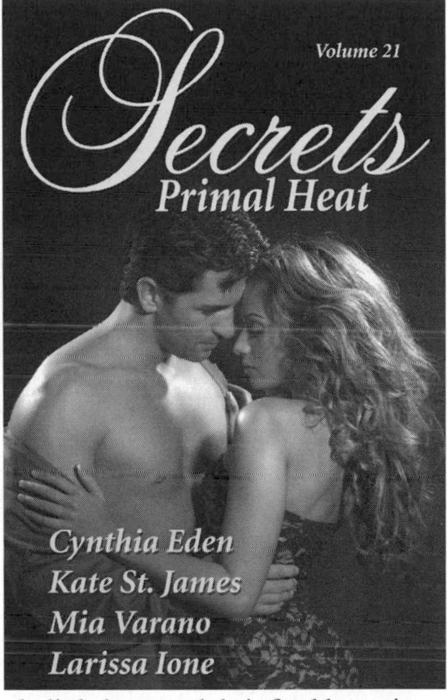

Caged Wolf
by Cynthia Eden

Alerac La Morte has been drugged and kidnapped. He realizes his captor, Madison Langley, is actually his destined mate, but she hates his kind. She blames Weres for the death of her father, but when captor turns captive, will Alerac convince her he's not the monster she thinks?

Wet Dreams
by Larissa Ione

Injured and on the run, DHS agent Brent Logan needs a miracle. What he gets is a sport-fishing boat owned by Marina Summers. Pursued by killers, ravaged by a fierce storm, and plagued by engine troubles, they can do little but spend their final hours immersed in sensual pleasure.

Good Vibrations
by Kate St. James

Lexi O'Brien vows to swear off sex while she attends grad school, so when her favorite out-of-town customer asks her out, she decides to indulge in an erotic fling guaranteed to super-charge her fantasies throughout academia. Little does she realize Gage Templeton is moving home, to her city, and has no intention of settling for a short-term affair..

Virgin of the Amazon
by Mia Varano

Virgin librarian Anna Winter gets lost on her Amazon vacation and stumbles upon a tribe whose shaman is looking for a pale-skinned virgin to deflower. Coop Daventry, a British adventurer and the tribe's self-styled chief, wants to save her, but which man poses a greater threat to Anna's virginity?

The Forever Kiss
by Angela Knight

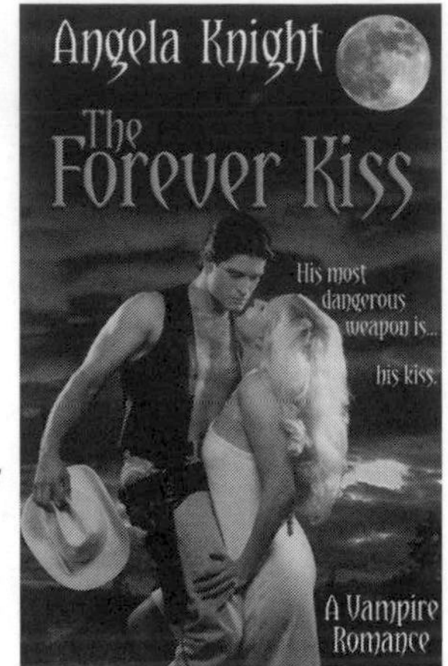

Listen to what reviewers say:

"***The Forever Kiss*** flows well with good characters and an interesting plot. … If you enjoy vampires and a lot of hot sex, you are sure to enjoy ***The Forever Kiss***."

—*The Best Reviews*

"Battling vampires, a protective ghost and the ever present battle of good and evil keep excellent pace with the erotic delights in Angela Knight's ***The Forever Kiss***—a book that absolutely bites with refreshing paranormal humor." **4½ Stars, Top Pick**

—*Romantic Times BOOKclub*

"I found ***The Forever Kiss*** to be an exceptionally written, refreshing book. … I really enjoyed this book by Angela Knight. … 5 angels!"

—*Fallen Angel Reviews*

"***The Forever Kiss*** is the first single title released from Red Sage and if this is any indication of what we can expect, it won't be the last. … The love scenes are hot enough to give a vampire a sunburn and the fight scenes will have you cheering for the good guys."

—*Really Bad Barb Reviews*

In ***The Forever Kiss***:

For years, Valerie Chase has been haunted by dreams of a Texas Ranger she knows only as "Cowboy." As a child, he rescued her from the nightmare vampires who murdered her parents. As an adult, she still dreams of him—but now he's her seductive lover in nights of erotic pleasure.

Yet "Cowboy" is more than a dream—he's the real Cade McKinnon—and a vampire! For years, he's protected Valerie from Edward Ridgemont, the sadistic vampire who turned him. Now, Ridgmont wants Valerie for his own and Cade is the only one who can protect her.

When Val finds herself abducted by her handsome dream man, she's appalled to discover he's one of the vampires she fears. Now, caught in a web of fear and passion, she and Cade must learn to trust each other, even as an immortal monster stalks their every move.

Their only hope of survival is… ***The Forever Kiss***.

Romantic Times Best Erotic Novel of the Year

It's not just reviewers raving about *Secrets*. See what readers have to say:

"When are you coming out with a new Volume? I want a new one next month!" via email from a reader.

"I loved the hot, wet sex without vulgar words being used to make it exciting." after ***Volume 1***

"I loved the blend of sensuality and sexual intensity—HOT!" after ***Volume 2***

"The best thing about ***Secrets*** is they're hot and brief! The least thing is you do not have enough of them!" after ***Volume 3***

"I have been extremely satisfied with ***Secrets***, keep up the good writing." after ***Volume 4***

"Stories have plot and characters to support the erotica. They would be good strong stories without the heat." after ***Volume 5***

"***Secrets*** really knows how to push the envelop better than anyone else." after ***Volume 6***

"These are the best sensual stories I have ever read!" after ***Volume 7***

"I love, love, love the ***Secrets*** stories. I now have all of them, please have more books come out each year." after ***Volume 8***

"These are the perfect sensual romance stories!" after ***Volume 9***

"What I love about ***Secrets Volume 10*** is how I couldn't put it down!" after ***Volume 10***

"All of the ***Secrets*** volumes are terrific! I have read all of them up to ***Secrets Volume 11***. Please keep them coming! I will read every one you make!" after ***Volume 11***

Finally, the men you've been dreaming about!
Give the Gift of Spicy Romantic Fiction

Don't want to wait? You can place a retail price ($12.99) order for any of the *Secrets* volumes from the following:

① **Waldenbooks and Borders Stores**

② **Amazon.com** or **BarnesandNoble.com**

③ **Book Clearinghouse (800-431-1579)**

④ **Romantic Times Magazine** Books by Mail (718-237-1097)

⑤ Special order at other bookstores.

Bookstores: Please contact Baker & Taylor Distributors, Ingram Book Distributor, or Red Sage Publishing for bookstore sales.

Order by title or ISBN #:

Vol. 1: 0-9648942-0-3
ISBN #13 978-0-9648942-0-4

Vol. 2: 0-9648942-1-1
ISBN #13 978-0-9648942-1-1

Vol. 3: 0-9648942-2-X
ISBN #13 978-0-9648942-2-8

Vol. 4: 0-9648942-4-6
ISBN #13 978-0-9648942-4-2

Vol. 5: 0-9648942-5-4
ISBN #13 978-0-9648942-5-9

Vol. 6: 0-9648942-6-2
ISBN #13 978-0-9648942-6-6

Vol. 7: 0-9648942-7-0
ISBN #13 978-0-9648942-7-3

Vol. 8: 0-9648942-8-9
ISBN #13 978-0-9648942-9-7

Vol. 9: 0-9648942-9-7
ISBN #13 978-0-9648942-9-7

Vol. 10: 0-9754516-0-X
ISBN #13 978-0-9754516-0-1

Vol. 11: 0-9754516-1-8
ISBN #13 978-0-9754516-1-8

Vol. 12: 0-9754516-2-6
ISBN #13 978-0-9754516-2-5

Vol. 13: 0-9754516-3-4
ISBN #13 978-0-9754516-3-2

Vol. 14: 0-9754516-4-2
ISBN #13 978-0-9754516-4-9

Vol. 15: 0-9754516-5-0
ISBN #13 978-0-9754516-5-6

Vol. 16: 0-9754516-6-9
ISBN #13 978-0-9754516-6-3

Vol. 17: 0-9754516-7-7
ISBN #13 978-0-9754516-7-0

Vol. 18: 0-9754516-8-5
ISBN #13 978-0-9754516-8-7

Vol. 19: 0-9754516-9-3
ISBN #13 978-0-9754516-9-4

Vol. 20: 1-60310-000-8
ISBN #13 978-1-60310-000-7

Vol. 21: 1-60310-001-6
ISBN #13 978-1-60310-001-4

Vol. 22: 1-60310-002-4
ISBN #13 978-1-60310-002-1

The Forever Kiss:
0-9648942-3-8
ISBN #13
978-0-9648942-3-5 ($14.00)